Obsession

by

Jann Rowland

One Good Sonnet Publishing

This is a work of fiction based on the works of Jane Austen. All of the characters and events portrayed in this novel are products of Jane Austen's original novel or the authors' imaginations.

OBSESSION

Published by One Good Sonnet Publishing

ISBN: 198792939X
ISBN-13: 978-1987929393

To my family who have, as always, shown
their unconditional love and encouragement.

ACKNOWLEDGEMENTS

Pleased to release another novel,
Eager to share my work with the world.
Acknowledgements go to family, friends, partners, all who help me
Receive inspiration, pushing me always to
Create and write. Final acknowledgements go to my
Editor, Betty, who helped polish this work.

Chapter I

It is generally understood that when a woman of limited means receives an offer of marriage from an eligible gentleman, she had best accept it. Most young women, however, are not named Elizabeth Bennet.

It should be understood that Elizabeth was indeed the daughter of a gentleman, and as such, she was a member of a privileged class. Her father, Mr. Henry Bennet, had been the proprietor of his estate for more than a quarter of a century, having inherited it as a young man upon his father's untimely death. Mr. Bennet had lived as a bachelor for some years before chance had brought him to the acquaintance of one Frances Gardiner. After a swift courtship, they had married and settled down to raise their family.

But though Mr. Bennet was indeed a landowner and his estate was prosperous, it was small and did not propel the family into the upper sphere of society. He was a simple country squire with a sufficient income to support his family's needs in comfort, but with a wife whose extravagance in clothing her daughters in the finest fashions was almost legendary, he was able to put little away to provide for his daughters' future.

Unfortunately for Mr. Bennet, Frances was not the woman he thought he was marrying. She was good-humored and pretty, laughing with all, gossiping, and flirtatious. All these things seemed to recommend her as a companion. What she was not, however, was intelligent. She possessed little knowledge of literature, current events, or any other subject which a gentleman would find to be of interest. Indeed, though she was a good and doting mother to the daughters who soon arrived, she was not in any way a companion for the much worldlier and intellectual Mr. Bennet.

Furthermore, in the years after their marriage, Mrs. Bennet developed a tendency for histrionics and complaints about her nerves, which could only grate on Mr. Bennet's patience. These complaints worsened with each girl-child Mrs. Bennet delivered, until, on the birth of her fifth daughter, all hope for an heir who could guarantee her security in her old age seemed lost. By this time, all affection for his wife was similarly lost, and though Mr. Bennet attempted to provide for his family as well as he could, his penchant for more scholarly pursuits and disinclination for his wife's company resulted in his secreting himself in his study, where the walls and thick, sturdy door at least blunted the force of his wife's shrill shrieking.

Of more import to the matter at hand, however, is the fact that the lack of an heir resulted in Mrs. Bennet turning her attention upon her daughters with the intention of seeing them all married off and in good situations. For in Mrs. Bennet's mind, true security for a young woman could only be purchased by making a good match with a man of means. And if her daughters were married to men who could support *them,* then they would possess the ability to support *her* too.

Now, it must be said that though Mrs. Bennet was a silly and vapid woman, she was not a malicious one. Her foremost thought in promoting marriages for her daughters was, at heart, their own welfare, though it is true that her own support was never far from her mind. But she could not comprehend that her daughters might not agree with her with respect to what exactly would provide them happiness. To Mrs. Bennet, marriage was everything, as long as a man could provide a good home and support a wife.

In particular, her eldest two daughters had seen the results of a marriage without respect and had determined they required something more than mere security from their future husbands. Having been influenced to a great degree by their aunt and uncle in London—Mr. Gardiner being Mrs. Bennet's younger brother and an intelligent, industrious sort of man—both Jane and Elizabeth knew what they wanted in a marriage. And while security was one of their requirements, it was by no means at the top of the list.

When Jane had gone to London to stay with the Gardiners at the tender age of fifteen, she had happened to meet a man acquainted with her aunt and uncle. The man, taking a liking to the pretty, reticent young woman, had taken to calling on her, showering her with compliments and some rather poorly written verses. Jane did not welcome the man's attentions, and he had soon ceased, seemingly realizing that she was as of yet too young to be wooed.

But Mrs. Bennet had lamented the matter loud and long, not only for Jane's inability to attach herself to the man, who was reputed to be quite well off, but also because she likely sensed that attaching her daughters to men of means when they possessed little in the way of dowry and connection to tempt him might be more difficult than she had anticipated. Thus, her efforts were redoubled, and soon even sweet, patient Jane found herself wishing her mother would desist.

For Elizabeth, her coming out was accomplished at the age of fifteen, much as her sister's before her, and though Elizabeth felt herself unready for the event, she approached it with good humor and a sense of adventure. In the environs of Meryton, the market town close to which Longbourn was situated, she found that she could face society cheerfully without needing to worry about how she would be received or if she would make mistakes which would make her the object of ridicule.

Meryton was not known for its high society, and there was a dearth of available young men in possession of an estate and a need for a wife. Elizabeth and Jane were happy for this circumstance, as it allowed them the ability to enjoy society without the pressure of their mother continually throwing them at this man or that.

And so it continued until the year 1808. Elizabeth had turned seventeen early that summer, and Jane was eighteen, and would be turning nineteen early the following year, which was a source of constant worry for Mrs. Bennet; her eldest daughter, after all, remained unmarried at such an age, even though she was the acknowledged beauty of the neighborhood. Mrs. Bennet was particularly exasperated with Elizabeth, as her second daughter was fond of reading with her father, lively—and in Mrs. Bennet's opinion, impertinent—conversation, and traipsing all over the countryside without a care as to the state of her petticoats. Indeed, Mrs. Bennet found her second daughter almost incomprehensible, and she feared the girl was unmarriageable, which led her to be more critical toward Elizabeth than she was toward any of her other daughters.

But Elizabeth deflected her mother with good humor, consoling herself in the knowledge that Mrs. Bennet truly did love her, regardless of how her fear made her act. Moreover, Elizabeth knew her father would never force her to accept the attentions of a man whom she did not like and could not respect. And so Elizabeth was content.

That summer, everything changed with a new arrival to their neighborhood. In truth, Mr. Winston Pearce was not unknown in Meryton. He was the owner of an estate situated to the north of Meryton within an easy distance, though it was nearer to Stevenage than Meryton, which meant the Pearces had for generations been members of *that* town's society. He was a tall and austere man, well-favored, and possessing, if not happy manners, at least those which allowed him to move with ease in society.

Of more immediate relevance to the circumstance was his situation. Mr. Pearce's estate was small, though somewhat larger than Mr. Bennet's estate Longbourn, and was rumored to produce an income in excess of two thousand five hundred pounds per annum. By happy circumstance, the neighboring estate was owned by the man's elderly relation, and it was to devolve to Mr. Pearce by way of entailment upon the current proprietor's death. As that estate produced an income of more than three thousand per year, Mr. Pearce's future income and his position in life were fortunate indeed.

However the man was also possessed of an unsavory reputation. There were rumors rampant of his conquests and his unhealthy appetites, and it was said that there were few young women who would take positions in his employment, as he would often demand other . . . services in addition to those for which he paid. He was a known philanderer and libertine and had fathered several children with those unfortunate enough to have come to his attention. Of course, he was also known to pay the women off with a small stipend and send them away with very little other support.

Why Mr. Pearce suddenly appeared in Meryton society was something of which Elizabeth was never certain—surely there were other eligible women who could offer him more in the society he normally inhabited. Regardless of the reason, soon he was appearing at many social events, be they dinners, parties, or assemblies. And to the tall and handsome Mr. Pearce many a matchmaking mother's eyes were turned with a covetous glint for their daughters' sake.

The first time the man asked Elizabeth to dance was at the assembly in July, not long after her birthday. And though Elizabeth was initially surprised that he should single her out, subsequent observation suggested that he was pleasing to all and sundry and asked many young women for the same honor.

"I can see you dance competently, Miss Bennet," said Mr. Pearce after they had been dancing for several minutes.

"I practice with my sisters," said Elizabeth. "You must expect country misses to know the steps. An assembly is always an anticipated event, and my youngest sisters, Kitty and Lydia, cannot wait for their own coming out so they may also partake in the amusement, though Lydia is naught but twelve years of age."

Mr. Pearce nodded sagely. "I can see how that might be. To a sheltered young woman, unaware of the pleasures of life, dancing might seem to be the pinnacle of achievement."

That was not what Elizabeth had said, but she allowed the comment to pass without challenging him on the matter. "Only to some young women, sir. There are those of us who are equally content with conversation, literature, theater, and all the benefits of an enlightened society."

An elegant eyebrow rose in response to her statement. "You enjoy the arts, do you?"

"I confess I do, when I have the chance to partake of them. My aunt and uncle are good to Jane and me when we visit London and often can be persuaded to escort us to such delights. I confess I enjoy Shakespeare very much, and the theater is my favorite of all such amusements."

"Ah, what young lady does not?" asked Mr. Pearce. "'Shall I compare thee to a summer's day?' I dare say any young woman would wish to be flattered with the words of the immortal bard."

Whereas Elizabeth's comments had been playful and sincere, Mr. Pearce's tone conveyed nothing more than condescension, and Elizabeth was immediately offended by them. The knowledge that she was dancing with a much older man did nothing to assuage her insult, but she endeavored to control her response, mindful that her mother was looking on with a great deal of interest and would no doubt berate her if she slighted him.

"Perhaps a woman might feel flattered, sir. But I should think that she would be so only if the words were sincere. Furthermore, though poetry has often been said to be the food of love, I think a woman would find heart-felt statements in the man's own words to be superior to hearing a man regurgitating words penned by another."

Mr. Pearce smiled at her, the condescension now flowing from him in waves. "You might think so, Miss Elizabeth. I believe you should wait for your own experience before you judge further."

Having had enough of the man's patronizing manner, Elizabeth gathered herself to deliver a stinging retort when he changed the subject.

"I understand you have been in society now for several years. Have you had no suitors yet?"

Studying the man gave no indication of what he was thinking, and though she was not disposed to continue their discussion, she replied, though in a clipped manner: "I have not. I do not feel myself ready for marriage, so it is of little matter."

"Not ready? You are now seventeen years of age and fully marriageable."

"On the contrary, sir," said Elizabeth, now quite annoyed, "I believe I require a little more maturity before I can fully understand what such a step entails and can pledge myself to another."

"I think, Miss Bennet, that you will find your opinion quite changed on the subject ere long."

Then they parted due to the steps of the dance, and when they came together again, Mr. Pearce said nothing further. This suited Elizabeth well, as she was not of mind to continue the conversation and determined that she would give the man no notice in the future.

When the dance came to an end, Mr. Pearce escorted her to her sister Jane, and after bowing over her hand, he departed without saying another word. Though Jane made some comment concerning her dance with the man, Elizabeth answered in a distant manner, ending the conversation, not wishing to discuss her disagreeable partner. The next dance started and her next partner—a more agreeable man—came to collect her, and all thoughts of Mr. Pearce were forgotten.

Until, that is, the next event Elizabeth attended. It was a soiree at the home of one of her neighbors, and once again Mr. Pearce attended and, after paying her some notice, complimenting and flattering her in equal measure, went away yet again. Elizabeth was vexed with his behavior, as his attentions appeared designed to confound her. He certainly did not play the part of the suitor—even her mother did not see that much in his attentions—but still he would speak to her, all in his superior and knowing manner.

This continued on for some weeks, and eventually Elizabeth began dreading the next event, as she knew invariably he would appear and act in the same manner. Mrs. Bennet, seeing enough in his manners to suggest that he at least held a hint of interest, often berated Elizabeth, telling her that if she put herself forward, she might be able to capture him. It went without saying that Elizabeth did not tell her mother that she wanted nothing more than for the man to cease his inconsistent attentions, sparing her the vexation of his presence.

On a morning in early August, Elizabeth left the house in the morning as was her wont, intent upon walking the environs of her father's estate and losing herself in the delightful vistas of Hertfordshire. It was a hot day, typical of early August, and there was little to hold her at home and every reason to escape her bickering younger sisters and a mother who could not be induced to stay silent. As a result, Elizabeth stayed away from her home longer than she perhaps should have, and it was almost time for luncheon by the time she once again entered Longbourn's driveway and walked toward the house.

She had no sooner entered the vestibule than the door to the sitting-room opened, and her mother came bustling out, clucking over Elizabeth's habit to stay away for hours.

"I do not know what I shall do with you, child," said she, as she grasped hold of Elizabeth's arm and began to lead her back from whence she came. "But should matters proceed in the manner I expect, I will be happy to cede that responsibility to another."

Perplexed at her mother's words, Elizabeth's response was on the tip of her tongue when the door opened in front of her, and she caught a glimpse of the occupant of the room. There, leering at her in all his glory, stood Winston Pearce.

"Come, Lizzy," said Mrs. Bennet, ushering her into the room, "Mr. Pearce has come to visit you. Such a fine, tall, well-favored man, indeed.

"Here she is, Mr. Pearce!" exclaimed Mrs. Bennet to the man who was now grinning at them, reminding Elizabeth of a fat cat who had once lived at Longbourn when she was much younger. It had, on occasion, managed to get into the cream, and when it had sated itself, it appeared to smile, much the same as Mr. Pearce was doing now.

"I believe that I was summoned by cook for some matter concerning dinner," said Mrs. Bennet, as she sat Elizabeth down on a sofa close to where Mr. Pearce stood by the mantle. "I shall return directly. Until then, Lizzy can entertain you, sir."

With that, Mrs. Bennet exited the sitting-room with nary a by-your-leave, or, indeed, any notion that leaving her young, maiden daughter with a man more than twice her age was not only improper, but unwise. When Elizabeth looked up at the man with some bewilderment, she noted that he was looking at the door through which her mother had just departed.

"I must own that I am excessively fond of your mother," said he, in a tone which suggested that he might not even be aware he had spoken aloud. "She is perhaps not the most intelligent specimen, but she is quite talented at creating situations most advantageous for others."

"I am not certain exactly what you consider advantageous, Mr. Pearce," said Elizabeth. She rose to her feet to cross the room and open the door—not only was the situation improper, but Elizabeth did not care to listen to anything Mr. Pearce had to say.

Before Elizabeth could leave the room, the sound of his voice arrested her. "I believe your mother wishes you to stay with me, Miss Bennet."

Elizabeth jumped, for he had, unnoticed, moved so that he stood right behind her. Before she could take another step or do anything further, Mr. Pearce gently took her elbow and moved her to the side, and he pushed the door to the doorframe, leaving it open slightly.

He turned to her with a grin, saying: "There, Miss Bennet. That should be enough to guarantee our privacy while still respecting the rules of propriety. Now, shall we sit for a moment?"

"I had not—"

"Please, Miss Elizabeth," interrupted he. "I dare say once you have heard what I have to say to you, that you will not be displeased."

Though bewildered, Elizabeth's protests died on her lips, and she found herself being led back to the sofa, even though she had every intention of leaving the man by himself in the sitting-room. Through pursed lips she watched him as he stepped away once she was seated, remembering that good manners were paramount, and that she could surely withstand a few moments in the man's company.

To Elizabeth's surprise, Mr. Pearce did not sit and make small talk with her. Instead, he wandered about the sitting-room, inspecting the various items scattered about, inspecting this, and wiping some hint of imaginary dust off that. He appeared to be in no hurry to come to the point, or even to speak to her.

"Your father's estate is a prosperous one, Miss Elizabeth."

Cocking her head to the side and wondering why he would choose to speak on such a matter, Elizabeth could only respond: "I believe it is. He is prodigiously proud of Longbourn. It has been in the family for many generations."

"And yet it is destined to pass from the Bennets' hands to that of a distant cousin."

"Again, I am sure you must be correct, sir. The entailment was instituted in my great-grandfather's time, and is set to expire after papa's cousin inherits."

"Ah, yes, entailments. They are an unfortunate necessity, as they prevent estates from being broken up when no direct heir is available. I myself shall benefit from an entailment."

"I have heard such a thing."

"You know," said Mr. Pearce, his tone conversational, "when I inherit my second estate, I plan to rebuild the manor and expand it extensively. I have spoken with several architects about the plans, and they all agree it shall be a sight to see. After that, I believe I shall purchase a house in town. It will be easier to attend the events of the season with a London residence, you understand."

More confused than ever, Elizabeth nodded, saying: "I imagine that would be agreeable indeed, Mr. Pearce. I wish you well in it."

Mr. Pearce turned at last, smiling faintly. He was condescending, but as it was his usual behavior, Elizabeth did not think anything of it. He appeared to have some expectation of her, though what it could possibly be, Elizabeth could not fathom.

"This coquettishness is charming indeed, Miss Bennet, but I believe that we may dispense with it in light of the current situation."

"Coquettishness, sir?" asked Elizabeth, beginning to feel cross at his presumption. "I am sure I do not know to what you refer."

"I am speaking, of course, of our attachment and our future felicity."

"Attachment?"

The word came out as a squeak, and had Elizabeth not been looking at the man with horror, she might have berated herself for losing her composure in such a manner.

"Yes, attachment. You must understand, Miss Bennet, that I have come here today with the express purpose of making an offer to you. Your father's estate is a pleasant enough little property, I suppose, but I know you have little other than your charms—which are considerable, of course—to recommend you. This suits me well indeed as I am interested in a wife to warm my bed and obey my edicts, and a worldly woman of society would be such a bother. You shall do nicely."

"I *shall not* do nicely!" cried Elizabeth, rising to her feet, poised to flee. "You cannot make me an offer I would be tempted to accept, sir, so I beg that you do not do so."

That infuriating eyebrow rose once again, and Elizabeth found herself wishing she could slap it from his face.

"You would not be tempted by my offer? I find that difficult to believe."

"Why should you not believe me? I am a rational creature."

"Because you cannot be such a simpleton as to misunderstand the benefits of a match with me. Why, you could not otherwise expect an offer from any man of half my consequence, your portion is so small and your situation so distasteful."

"*If* my situation is objectionable, why would you deign to ask for my hand, sir? Should you not, even now, be fleeing as fast as your feet can carry you?"

A slight smile came across his face. "I have already explained why I find you to be acceptable. I will own that you do show a distressing amount of intelligence, but that might be remedied when your efforts are directed to more ladylike pursuits. Your pert opinions concerning Shakespeare and other literature are amusing, of course, but as a woman you can have no true understanding. Once I get a few children from you, you will be far too busy to waste your time on activities which shall not make you a better wife."

Now Elizabeth was truly offended. Mr. Pearce had received an education at one of the lesser universities, the name of which Elizabeth could not even remember, but his own understanding of the matters they had at times discussed was as lacking as his manners. For him to suggest that she did not understand, when in fact *he* was the one deficient, was highly insulting.

"Then let me respond to your proposal, sir, though you have not, in fact, made one. I thank you for the *honor* of your offer. I understand what mortification it must have cost you to make it to one as inferior as I. But you may now go away with the freedom to choose some other woman who will meet your needs in a wife, for I refuse your offer. I will not marry you."

"Some might consider such words to be the height of foolishness."

"And some might consider your *proposal* to be the height of rudeness. You did not actually make any such offer. You merely belittled my intelligence with arrogance and condescension, informed me that I would not be allowed to pursue those activities which bring me pleasure, and crowed about how fortunate I am to be the recipient of your attentions. I can tell you, sir, that I cannot consider myself to be fortunate at all with such a proposal."

Through all of Elizabeth's diatribe, Mr. Pearce's demeanor did not alter a jot. In fact, he appeared even more amused the more steam her rant gathered, and he watched her with arrogance exuding from every pore.

"So you would prefer that I propose from bended knee, shower you with gifts and flattering words designed to induce the romantic sensibilities of a young maiden to take flight? Typical of young women of a disposition such as yourself. The world is a serious place, Miss Bennet, and I am a serious man. You would do well to remember that."

"Indeed, I wish for no such thing," said Elizabeth, clenching her teeth together in frustration. "I only wish to be left alone. As I doubt such words from you would be sincere, and I would not receive them with any pleasure, my answer would still be the same. You cannot offer for me in any possible manner which would tempt me to accept you. Can I be any plainer than this?"

At these words, Mr. Pearce actually threw his head back and laughed, and Elizabeth, feeling the insult, decided it was time to depart. She would not stay in a room with this odious man for another minute!

"I shall give you time to think the matter through," floated Pearce's voice behind her. "I am assured you will come to the right conclusion."

But Elizabeth no longer cared. She climbed the stairs to her room and closed the door behind her with excessive force. What an insufferable man!

It was not long before shrieks of outrage alerted Elizabeth to the fact that her mother had heard the news of her refusal of Mr. Pearce's proposal. The sound of hurried footsteps with their accompanying wails approached Elizabeth's door soon after, and the door was flung open with enough force to crash against the wall behind it.

"Elizabeth! What do you mean by refusing Mr. Pearce's proposal?"

"I thought my purpose was clear, Mother," said Elizabeth, maintaining her calm in the face of her mother's near hysteria. "I will not have Mr. Pearce."

"But why? The man is eminently suitable. Do you not understand that he will have more than five thousand a year?"

"I do not care if he has fifty thousand a year!" cried Elizabeth. "I will not be married to such a man."

Her mother gasped. "Do you wish to be destitute upon your father's death? You can have a good home, be mistress of your own estate. What more could you want?"

"I would not be Mr. Pearce's only *mistress*," said Elizabeth, sneering her disdain for the man. "Mother, you know his reputation. How could any woman be happy married to such a man?"

"It does not signify if he keeps a mistress. If he does, then he shall not trouble you overmuch once you give him an heir. You must tell him you have changed your mind!"

"I shall not! To live in such a condition would be demeaning. I will not have it!"

Her mother actually growled, her displeasure was so severe. "Then we shall speak to your father. *He* shall make you see sense!"

Though Elizabeth knew her father would do no such thing, she allowed herself to be cajoled down the stairs and into her father's bookroom. Mr. Bennet appeared annoyed at the intrusion, though he clearly understood what had prompted it. But he feigned ignorance, demanding his wife inform him as to the problem or leave him in peace. Mrs. Bennet lost no time in complying.

"Mr. Bennet, we are all in uproar."

"On the contrary, Mrs. Bennet," said her husband, "it appears to me that *you* are the only one in such a heightened state. Lizzy appears to be quite calm."

"And well she might," spat Mrs. Bennet. "Do you know what this foolish girl has done?"

"Something to displease you, I dare say," said Mr. Bennet. His tone was dismissive and curt, and Elizabeth was certain he was even more annoyed with his wife than normal. Elizabeth was not happy with his behavior—this kind of interaction was exactly what she wished to avoid in her own marriage—but in this instance, she was thankful that he would almost certainly support her.

"She has refused Mr. Pearce's proposal!" cried Mrs. Bennet. "A proposal which would see her protected for the rest of her life and see the family's fortunes rise in response. And the foolish girl has rejected him!"

"As I do not have the highest opinion of Mr. Pearce myself, I commend Elizabeth's sagacity. Would you have me go against her character and make her marry a man she does not like?"

"Yes! For as you well know, Mr. Bennet, there is no security for her unless she marries. Would you have her live in poverty when you are gone? Would you condemn the entire family to such a fate?"

Mr. Bennet rolled his eyes. "I am certain you overstate the situation, Mrs. Bennet, as is your wont."

"You do not have to concern yourself on the matter, as you will be dead!"

"A man might wish for death when faced with *this*," muttered Mr. Bennet. But though Elizabeth heard him clearly, Mrs. Bennet, still clearly overwrought, had turned away and continued her pacing. It was clear she had not heard, or she had chosen not to hear.

To a certain extent Elizabeth pitied her mother. She did not have the respect of her husband, and though she was not the cleverest of women, she did not deserve such derision as Mr. Bennet heaped on her daily. The true tragedy was that she did not even understand most of it, though she was certainly aware that he was making sport with her. It was a sad way to live one's life, and Elizabeth was determined to have no part of it.

"Oh, very well," said Mr. Bennet, when his wife had carried on for some minutes. Though Elizabeth felt a spike of fear that her beloved father actually meant to force her to marry Pearce, his wink told her a different story.

"Your mother has informed me at great length and noise that you have refused an offer of marriage to Mr. Pearce."

"I have," said Elizabeth.

"And might I ask why?"

Elizabeth released an exasperated huff. "You even have to ask? The man is a philanderer of the worst sort, he is condescending, unpleasant, and he is more than twice my age. I would rather marry Mr. Charles, than marry Mr. Pearce."

Though Mrs. Bennet looked on Elizabeth with horror at her reference to Longbourn's aged gardener, Mr. Bennet only chuckled. "But what of your security? Your mother is quite insistent that you will be destitute should you not marry Mr. Pearce. In fact, I believe I might even now hear the sound of the hedgerows, beckoning you into their embrace."

"It would be better to suffer through poverty than live with a man I cannot respect and actively detest, father."

"I believe you have made an intelligent decision."

Turning to his wife, Mr. Bennet said: "I believe you have your answer, Mrs. Bennet. Lizzy refuses to have Mr. Pearce, and I dare say her choice is one she arrived at with due consideration."

"She must!" shrieked Mrs. Bennet.

"Mrs. Bennet," said Mr. Bennet, his tone hard and unfriendly, "I will thank you to remember that it is a *father's* prerogative to either approve or disapprove of these matters. I am convinced Lizzy will be miserable with the man, so I will not force her."

"She will marry him, or I will never see her again!"

"You should take care lest *you* are the one who is never seen again. Now, be gone!"

Her lip trembling with suppressed tears, Mrs. Bennet wailed once more before she fled. The sounds of her lamentations followed her up the stairs to her chamber, where they were abruptly muted with the crash of her door slamming behind her.

Elizabeth breathed a sigh of relief and turned her attention to her father. Mr. Bennet was regarding the open door with exasperation mixed with distaste. A particularly loud cry from his wife caused him to wince, and he shook his head, contempt evident in his manner.

"I hope you appreciate what I have done for you, Elizabeth," said Mr. Bennet. "I doubt we have heard the last of her diatribes."

"Perhaps not," said Elizabeth. She rose from her chair and approached him, pressing a kiss on his head. "But I shall remain firm. I have no doubt Mr. Pearce will lose interest and eventually turn his attentions to some other unfortunate young lady."

"No doubt he shall. But that is a matter for another time."

Knowing a dismissal when she heard one, Elizabeth thanked him again and left the room. Tonight she would ask Hill to bring her a tray for her supper. She could not imagine dining in the company of her mother when the woman's hackles were raised in such a manner.

Chapter II

Unfortunately, the matter did not end there. For the rest of that week and into the next, Elizabeth was not allowed to rest. Whether it was dire predictions of what would happen to her should she not accept the proposal before her or threats of what her mother would do should Elizabeth not follow her mother's instructions, Mrs. Bennet rarely allowed more than ten minutes to pass without making her opinion known. It was amusing to Elizabeth that despite such warnings, her mother never made the actual consequences of disobedience clear.

Everyone within the range of Mrs. Bennet's high-pitched and loud voice soon became tired of her constant diatribes and wished for a return to the boisterous, but contented, household. Even Mr. Bennet's demands that his wife cease her caterwauling had little effect, for Mrs. Bennet would subside with a sulk, only to once again raise her voice when he had left the room.

That week Elizabeth found herself walking even more than normal. The only rest she could find from her mother's harangues was in sleep—which her mother often interrupted early in the morning and did not allow until late at night—or when she was absent from the house. And as the weather remained fine, Elizabeth took advantage of that retreat at every opportunity.

While she walked, her mind constantly turned back to the situation, and she was continually angry, a fact which made itself known in the vigorous swinging of her arms or the way she would often pick up twigs and use them to behead unassuming and innocent flowers she saw along the way. Surely her mother could not be so selfish and senseless as to expect her daughters to live the life she lived. What mother did not wish the best for her children?

But the fact of the matter was that in Mrs. Bennet's eyes, marriage, no matter what form, *was* the best for her children. Her fear of being homeless had been steeped for so long in the depths of her mind that no other consideration mattered.

Elizabeth often wondered what kind of girl her mother had been. Surely she had dreamed of a good match with a handsome man who held her heart. Surely she had wished for something more from her marriage than what she could currently boast. For what girl did not? At times Elizabeth almost wondered if this was some sort of vindictive form of revenge her mother wished to visit on her own daughters. Was it nothing more than wishing someone else to be as miserable as she was herself? But Elizabeth could not believe that of her. She was improper at times and more than a little self-centered, but malicious behavior was not part of her character.

Of course, the whole situation might be made better, would her father only exert himself to take his wife in hand and insist she obey him. But her father's approach was to laugh at her and tease her, demand her silence when he was in the room, and do nothing when he left. Her constant cries disturbed and annoyed him, but he would much prefer to attempt to not hear her than to actually do something about it. Elizabeth loved her father. But at times she was also disappointed in him. Now was one of those times.

Early the next week, the Bennet family was invited to the Lucas estate for an evening in company, and Elizabeth was more than happy to be able to remove herself from her home and spend time in the company of her friends. Charlotte Lucas, though several years older than Elizabeth, was a good and true friend, and one who was always willing to lend a sympathetic ear and a helping hand. Elizabeth had not seen her since Mr. Pearce's proposal and was quite happy to once again commiserate with her friend.

Once they arrived at the Lucas estate, Elizabeth put herself out of the sphere of her mother's influence as soon as she could. What she could not escape was the sound of her mother's voice carrying on about her daughter's lack of understanding or her willful disobedience. As

Elizabeth stood speaking with some of her friends, snatches of her mother's conversation invaded her consciousness, assaulting her like hundreds of stinging bees.

". . . more than five thousand a year, perhaps as much as six!"

". . . do not know how I shall keep her . . ."

". . . must be made to change her mind . . ."

"Oh, how that girl vexes me!"

Through it all, Elizabeth did her best to ignore her mother. It was not an easy thing to accomplish, for her friends could obviously hear what Mrs. Bennet was saying, and the looks they cast Elizabeth's way were full of questions. But Elizabeth was determined not to answer. In her mind, the matter was decided, and she would not recant.

Late that evening, Elizabeth found herself in close conference with Charlotte and Jane, and though her mother's proclamations had died down to a certain extent, Charlotte chose that moment to canvass the matter further with Elizabeth.

"What of this matter of Mr. Pearce, Eliza?" asked Charlotte.

Elizabeth did not wish to discuss the subject, and she said so in a manner which could not be mistaken.

Charlotte only shook her head. "I understand your aversion, but perhaps you have not considered all the ramifications of your decision?"

"I have considered it all, Charlotte," replied Elizabeth, a trifle primly. "I comprehend Mr. Pearce's situation in life, his income, his personality, and even how he treats his dogs. No amount of security is worth living in misery for the rest of my life with such a husband. I will not live like my mother."

A compassionate nod was Charlotte's response, and Jane, though she was obviously ill at ease to hear Elizabeth speak of her mother in such a fashion, could only echo Charlotte's gesture.

"Perhaps Mr. Pearce is not the best of men—"

"If there was a scale, I am certain he would be nearer the bottom than the top of the ledger," snapped Elizabeth.

"You may be correct," said Charlotte. "But Eliza, I truly believe you should consider the matter further. I know that your romantic disposition leads you to wish for true love and respect in a marriage. But how likely is it that you will find such a situation? Is there such a man out there who will meet your fanciful requirements in a husband?"

"I must believe there is, Charlotte. Otherwise, I am in danger of losing my faith in humanity."

Charlotte sighed. "Eliza, I truly believe that happiness in marriage is a matter of chance. In this instance, it is perhaps unfortunate that you know so much of the defects of your suitor in advance. I am convinced that for women like you and me, there is little chance of being swept off our feet by a man who loves us above all other things. So if there is little opportunity, then why should we not settle for security instead? Let the men behave as they will. We can be happy in our security, our children, and in our own integrity."

Elizabeth had never heard Charlotte speak in such a manner. Though Charlotte had never espoused such romantic ideals as Elizabeth did herself, they had often spoken of what qualities they wished in a husband and what they wished to experience in a courtship. Elizabeth could only surmise that the passage of time had jaded Charlotte, for she was now four and twenty and there were no real prospects for marriage in Meryton. Thus, when Elizabeth responded, she took care for her friend's feelings, while being certain to state her opinion in a manner which could not be mistaken.

"I understand what you are saying, Charlotte—I truly do. There is little for us here in Hertfordshire as the prospects are limited and our charms are all we have to recommend us. I *do* wish for marriage someday.

"But I could not wish for a marriage to such a man. To be constantly demeaned by his affairs with anything wearing a skirt? It would be insupportable, to say nothing of the way he treats me as an object and openly tells me how he will prohibit me from those activities which bring me pleasure. That is not a marriage. In my opinion that is tantamount to a prison sentence and one which is guaranteed to last the rest of my life."

"Perhaps he will leave you a widow," said Charlotte with a mischievous twinkle in her eye.

Elizabeth could only laugh. "Perhaps he will! But if wishing for a man's death is the only thing brought into a marriage, then it is better to refrain. Such a marriage cannot be agreeable."

"I find I must agree with Elizabeth," opined Jane, though in her typical diffident manner. "I have observed Mr. Pearce in company, and I find I cannot esteem the man. There have been times when he has looked at me . . . Well, let us just say that he made me quite uncomfortable."

"And I am certain that is the least of his offenses," said Elizabeth.

"Then you are determined," said Charlotte. "And I cannot find fault with your reasons, much though I disagree with them. I pray you will not regret your refusal if you end an old maid with naught but bitter memories to sustain you."

Waving such a thing off as unlikely—even spinsterhood would be better than a life tied to Winston Pearce—Elizabeth focused on Charlotte's words.

"I beg your pardon, Charlotte, but am I to understand that you would accept a proposal from Mr. Pearce?"

A wan smile came over her friend's face. "I cannot know until such an offer is made, but as I am staring at the prospect of forever being a burden on my father, I would not dismiss it out of hand. I do not possess the same romantic ideals as you do, Eliza. I would be content to be mistress of my own home and in the company of my own children. While I would not wish for a man who was unfaithful, I would endure it if it meant my security."

Though Elizabeth was astonished to hear Charlotte espouse such opinions, she was struck by the fact that Charlotte was, in this respect, much like Mrs. Bennet. Charlotte was much more intelligent and proper than Mrs. Bennet, but in the matter of marriage, their opinions were closely aligned.

"I hope you find your handsome beau who will sweep you off your feet, Charlotte," said Elizabeth warmly, "because to settle for such a life would be a tragedy, in my opinion."

"And I knew you would feel that way, my dear Elizabeth. I hope you are able to find yours as well."

From there, the conversation devolved into more desultory subjects, and it was not long before the event ended and the Bennets were once again on their way home. Elizabeth found she had much to think on. She had always known of her circumstances and the possibility that she would never marry, but the matter had never been canvassed with such openness before that evening. A pall seemed to settle over her as she prepared to retire, and she wondered if she would ever be happy in life. It seemed that Charlotte would not, unless she came into some very great fortune.

A knock on Elizabeth's door startled her, and knowing it was not her mother—Mrs. Bennet would simply have barged in, if indeed her voice would not have preceded her—Elizabeth called out permission to enter. As expected, Jane slipped into the room when the door opened.

"Lizzy," said Jane as she stepped forward, "I wanted to speak to you tonight, for I sensed that Charlotte's words might have upset you."

Elizabeth sighed and sank down on the edge of her mattress. She did not wish to think of the matter any longer. She wished they could all go back to the way they had been before Mr. Pearce had upset their family harmony. But such was not to be, and she could not deny Jane. They had been confidantes throughout the whole of their lives.

"She did upset me, Jane, though not because of her opinions. The thought that we—none of us!—have much hope of making a good match or finding happiness in our lives is upsetting, I confess. But I know that if I am not blessed with a man I can love, I will be happy with whatever life brings me. I do not think that Charlotte can boast the same."

"I think you are wrong, Lizzy."

Surprised, Elizabeth looked up at her sister, wondering at her meaning. Jane approached and sat on the bed next to Elizabeth, coaxing her to rest her head on Jane's shoulder.

"In fact, I believe that you will be unhappy in life if you do not find a man who loves you, regardless of what situation you find yourself in. Elizabeth, you have such an affectionate, happy disposition, you must be in a position to share the affection with a man who loves you in return to achieve happiness.

"Charlotte will regret her situation if she is not able to find a partner, but I cannot but think that her practicality of manner will not allow her to at least find some measure of fulfillment. In your case, I doubt you will be able to be any more than content. And it fills me with sorrow, Lizzy, for you have so much love to give. There must be someone able to see the precious gift you would be in their life."

Tears slipped down Elizabeth's cheeks to drip down on her nightgown and dampen the fabric. Elizabeth had told herself many times over that she would be happy with whatever life brought her. But now that Jane had brought the matter into the open, Elizabeth could not pretend that her sister was not correct. What a miserable fate awaited them both!

"That is why I must continue to have faith," said Elizabeth, fighting to keep her voice from trembling. "I must have faith for both of us. For you deserve such a man as much as I. More so, as you possess a sweetness of spirit that I do not."

"Sweetness is not a guarantee of good character, Elizabeth."

"No, but it surely cannot be a hindrance either."

The two girls giggled together, and their good humor was restored. Elizabeth could not imagine a better sister than Jane.

The sound of a raised voice and footsteps on the floorboards caused Elizabeth to look up to the door, and a moment later her bedroom door was flung open and in marched her mother. The woman paused in the act of opening her mouth to begin her diatribe, when she noticed Jane sitting with Elizabeth.

"Jane, what are you doing here?" Mrs. Bennet scowled at Elizabeth.

"I hope you are not filling Jane's ears with your nonsense."

"We are speaking together as we often do, Mama," said Jane, her serenity meeting her mother's tumult.

"Then mayhap you can talk some sense into your sister. I shall not have this, Elizabeth. You shall change your mind and accept Mr. Pearce and do your duty as you ought. I cannot— "

"Mama, perhaps you should leave this to me," said Jane.

She rose from the door and caught her mother by the elbow, turning an astonished Mrs. Bennet to the door and escorting her from the room. As they left, their voices floated back to Elizabeth from the hallway.

"I shall speak to Elizabeth tonight. You should retire, Mama, as you need your rest."

"You are correct, Jane. My nerves are bothering me again with all this commotion, and thus far your sister has not deigned to hear a word I say."

"Then it would be best for you to go back to your room. Leave it to me."

"You always were the most dutiful of my daughters, Jane. Make certain that girl listens to you, for she is stubborn and pigheaded."

"I shall, Mama."

Her mother's footsteps sounded along the hallway, and soon Jane entered the room again, closing the door behind her. When the two sisters' eyes met each other, they could not help themselves; they descended into giggles.

"I dare say Mama considers you to be her confederate in this matter," said Elizabeth in between her laughter.

Jane sobered immediately. "I feel sorry for misleading her."

"Only by omission," said Elizabeth. "You never once agreed with her or offered to take her part."

"I cannot stand aside and allow her to scold you again, Lizzy. You must have one peaceful night."

Rising, Elizabeth stepped up to her sister and enfolded her in her arms, relishing the embrace that Jane unstintingly returned.

"I am very fortunate to have you as a sister, Jane," said Elizabeth, giving voice to her earlier musings. "I do not know how I would survive in this house if I did not have you."

"We are each other's strength. And we must continue to be so."

Jane did not leave Elizabeth's room that night, instead, electing to sleep in Elizabeth's bed. It was comforting to have her there; they had often slept in each other's rooms since they were girls, sharing confidences and giggling well into the early hours of the morning. That night their conversation was serious, and there was little of their usual mirth. But when they finally went to sleep very late, Elizabeth was once again happy. She was not made for discontent.

"Elizabeth!"

The sound of a shrieking voice jolted both Elizabeth and Jane from their slumber, and a glance out the window told Elizabeth that they had slept far later than was their wont. Outside the sun was shining on the landscape, and the birds were chirping their joy for the new summer day. Already the room was becoming uncomfortably hot.

Jane, never at her best in the morning, attempted to pull the blanket over her head. "Perhaps you should lock the door, Lizzy. Tell Mama that I am still speaking with you."

Laughing, Elizabeth attempted to detangle herself from the bed. Locking the door would not have done her any good, as she was about to discover.

The door was once again flung open, much as it had been the previous evening, and Mrs. Bennet marched into the room, pulling up in surprise at the sight of her eldest daughter peeking out from under the blankets on the bed.

"Jane! What is the meaning of this?"

"I was speaking with Lizzy as we agreed, Mama. We fell asleep here after our conversation."

A grunt met her declaration, and Mrs. Bennet's previous excitement returned. "I hope you have been able to talk some sense into her, for he is here. Come, Elizabeth, you will get up now and put on your best dress, for he has returned."

"Who has returned, Mama?" asked Elizabeth, though she knew very well to whom her mother referred.

Mrs. Bennet peered at Elizabeth as if she was mentally deficient. "Why, Mr. Pearce, of course! He has returned to gain your acceptance of his suit. You must look your best!"

"It does not signify, Mama, as I do not intend to accept his proposal, now, or at any time in the future. You may tell Mr. Pearce that he may depart."

A positively poisonous expression settled over Mrs. Bennet's face. She darted forward and, grasping Elizabeth by the ear, dragged her from the bed. Crying out in pain, Elizabeth swatted at her mother's hands. With a cry, Jane leapt from the bed, and between the two of them, they managed to free Elizabeth from the harridan's grasp.

"You listen to me, Miss Lizzy," hissed her mother, "if you ever wish to be welcome in this house again, you will go downstairs, do your duty, and accept Mr. Pearce with as much dignity and pleasure as you can muster. You will not like the result if you defy me again.

"Jane, you will return to your room, this instant!"

Not waiting for her daughters' replies, Mrs. Bennet called out to the maid, who hesitantly entered the room, keeping her eyes firmly fixed on the floor.

"Millie, fix Miss Elizabeth's hair and dress in her green pastel gown. She is to be downstairs in the sitting-room in fifteen minutes and not a moment longer."

Then Mrs. Bennet swept from the room, oblivious to the daggers impaling her back from Elizabeth's glare. For a moment, she thought to flout her mother's instructions and go back to bed, but the obvious fear on Millie's face prompted her to reconsider. Millie was a good sort of girl, and it would not do to expose her to Mrs. Bennet's wrath.

"There appears to be nothing more to be done," said Elizabeth. "Come, Millie, please do my hair. A tight bun at the back ought to do."

The maid's eyes widened in surprise and fear, but Elizabeth only waved her worries aside. "I shall take the blame for it—you need not worry."

Though still uncertain, Millie stepped forward, and soon the soothing sensation of the brush pulling through Elizabeth's long tresses allowed the tension to lessen, though she knew it would not completely go away.

"Oh, Lizzy!" said Jane, dropping to her knees by Elizabeth side and grasping one of her hands. "Surely you do not mean to accept him!"

"I do not, Jane. But I might as well face him, as Mother will obviously not allow anything else."

"You have my support."

Elizabeth smiled affectionately at her sister. "Thank you, Jane. You should go prepare for the day. I have no doubt it will be an eventful one."

Nodding, Jane pressed a kiss to Elizabeth's hand and exited the room. Elizabeth settled back in her chair, noting the way the maid was proceeding as swiftly as she dared.

"Slowly, Millie. I would not wish for Mr. Pearce to think that I am at his beck and call. It will do him some good to be made to wait for me."

The girl's consternation was obvious, but it did not prevent a sudden grin—carefully and quickly hidden, of course—from appearing on her face. Still, she set about her work, slowly pulling the brush through Elizabeth's hair. Then, when that was completed, Elizabeth took her time at her closet, considering her dresses and the impression she wished to make. At length she finally chose her least favorite dress—a grey muslin with a hint of a lavender tone, which was more appropriate for mourning than receiving a proposal of marriage.

In all, it was nearly thirty minutes later before Elizabeth left her room, and even then she waited until the sound of her mother's voice echoed up the stairs before she finally began to descend, and she took the stairs down as slowly as she could from the perverse desire to cause her mother as much grief and vexation as she could.

Once she had reached the landing, she approached the door to the sitting-room, only to see it open, and Mrs. Bennet slipped out of the room. She took one look at Elizabeth and screeched in dismay.

"What are you wearing? And what has that girl done with your hair?"

"Millie has done exactly as I told her to do, Mama," said Elizabeth. "You shall not berate the girl when it was my doing."

Pursed lips met her declaration, and Mrs. Bennet seemingly decided that it was of no moment. Instead, she stepped forward and put herself directly in front of Elizabeth, and another warning was again issued.

"Do not test my patience, Elizabeth. I have the power to make your life miserable."

"Not as much as Mr. Pearce would possess should I actually be mad enough to accept him."

And with a final glare in her mother's shocked face, Elizabeth stepped around her and entered the sitting-room.

It seemed to Elizabeth that the fates were conspiring against her. On that day, of all days most troublesome, the sun was shining outside, there appeared to be not a hint of a breeze, and the outside world beckoned her with tantalizing promises of a peaceful walk in the countryside. But the glorious day would no doubt be denied her, as she was forced to deal with a libertine who would not accept her answer.

Mr. Pearce stood by the mantle, tall and erect, his bearing suggesting that he was the equal of the king himself. He regarded her as she entered the room with an insouciant kind of smugness, his eyes raking over her form with lascivious interest. Witnessing his reaction only made Elizabeth want to grind her teeth in frustration. The man was a leech! In fact, Elizabeth thought a leech would actually be preferable.

"You have spirit, Miss Bennet," said Mr. Pearce. His eyes bespoke his hunger, and Elizabeth was repulsed all over again. "I shall enjoy taming that spirit, I assure you. When we are husband and wife, this insubordination will not go unpunished."

"I had thought nothing less of you, sir," said Elizabeth in a tone designed to insult. "Which is precisely why your proposal offends me. I wish for a marriage of minds, hearts, and common purpose, not the slavery which you propose."

A shocked gasp revealed the fact that Mrs. Bennet was listening behind the door. But Mr. Pearce only smiled at her in a superior sort of way, and he said:

"Such comments show your naiveté, Miss Bennet. You are a woman, and women are not equipped to be the equal of men."

"Mr. Pearce. You obviously came with some design other than insulting and offending me. Perhaps you should come to the point. Otherwise, we have nothing left to discuss."

"Charming, indeed, Miss Bennet."

Mr. Pearce turned and began to walk toward her, his gait reminiscent of a fox she had once seen stalking a fat hare. His expression of haughtiness never wavered for an instant, and though he had to know that she would not oblige him, he seemed confident that he would eventually prevail.

When he reached her he lifted a hand to caress her cheek. Elizabeth snapped her head back, glaring at him for attempting to take such liberties with her. But Mr. Pearce only laughed.

"It appears like you still mean to fight against the inevitable, but I shall give you another chance to accept me. I require a wife, Miss Bennet, and I have chosen you for the honor of filling the role. What say you?"

"I am astonished, Mr. Pearce. It seems like this time you have actually remembered that the lady must be *asked* rather than just assuming that she will accept. It shows an intelligence I would not have expected of you."

Another gasp sounded from behind the door, but neither occupant of the room took any notice. Elizabeth continued to glare at the man, projecting all the contempt she felt for him through her gaze, and Mr. Pearce continued to watch her, as if he had never been more amused in his life.

"From your words, might I assume that you wish to answer in the negative?"

"How intelligent of you, sir. I would not have expected you to catch on so quickly. Perhaps you have learned something."

A startled cry was heard behind the closed door, but apparently Mrs. Bennet was unable to listen any longer without making her opinion known, for the door sprang open, and Mrs. Bennet surged into the room.

"Lizzy!" cried she. "You will take your words back this instant!"

"Mrs. Bennet," said Mr. Pearce, "it is obvious that Miss Bennet is out of sorts today. I believe it would be best if I was to return another day."

"Oh, Mr. Pearce, do not concern yourself. Elizabeth will be made to see the right of the matter."

"I am sure she will, Mrs. Bennet. But regardless, I shall take my leave. Perhaps when I come next I shall endeavor to arrive at a later time. It seems that a lack of sleep is affecting her judgment."

"There is nothing impairing my judgment, sir. I simply will not marry an odious man such as you."

Though her mother gasped again in shock, Mr. Pearce simply favored her with a faint smile before excusing himself. A silence settled over the room when he had gone, and Elizabeth expected her mother to immediately descend into a rant the likes of which Elizabeth had never before seen. But she seemed to be caught up in the shock of the lack of success in forcing her daughter to bend to her will.

But the blessed silence was not to last as the rapidly reddening of Mrs. Bennet's face presaged an explosion of anger. Elizabeth was not disappointed. The form of her response, however, caught Elizabeth by surprise, for instead of screaming or crying, Mrs. Bennet turned on her heel and stalked from the room.

Curious, Elizabeth followed her mother, wondering what she was about. Mrs. Bennet did not go far; she stomped down the hall to the master's study and threw open the door without a word, entering Mr. Bennet's sanctum. Elizabeth was shocked, knowing that Mr. Bennet had expressly forbidden his wife from entering without an invitation.

"Mr. Bennet, I insist upon being satisfied! Your daughter has refused Mr. Pearce again, and we cannot allow such willful disobedience."

"Madam, I have informed you of my opinion. Your daughter has shown a greatness of mind in refusing the man. He could never make her happy."

"I care not for her happiness. I care for her security. You will tell Elizabeth that unless she accepts Mr. Pearce, she is not welcome in this house again!"

There was a dreadful pause, and then her father spoke.

"Very well, Mrs. Bennet. If you wish it to be so, then so be it. We shall send Elizabeth to the Gardiners."

And with that, Elizabeth's world came crashing down. Her father had betrayed her.

Chapter III

Two days later, Elizabeth found herself on her uncle's doorstep with naught more than a small trunk with a few dresses and other personal effects in her hand. It had all happened so quickly that she hardly knew what to think or how to act. The memory of her mother's smug smiles at having carried her point still filled Elizabeth with revulsion. Though Elizabeth loved her mother, at that moment she could not truly *like* the woman. She was petty and demanding, thought nothing of demeaning Elizabeth's understanding or looks, and she was narrow-minded and inflexible.

Mrs. Bennet's vindictive streak had been on full display the previous day when Elizabeth had been packing her trunk for her forced stay with her uncle and aunt. In her spite, Mrs. Bennet had only allowed Elizabeth to take along a few dresses, and most of Elizabeth's personal possessions had been left at home as well. Jane had been a blessing as she had been able to smuggle some of Elizabeth's more treasured items to her just before she had departed for the coaching station in Meryton. Jane's farewell had also been poignant and heartfelt.

"Lizzy," said Jane, as she had walked with Elizabeth toward Meryton. "Do not worry for your future. Our mother will come to the right way of thinking if you give her long enough."

Elizabeth had shaken her head; Jane truly was incapable of anything other than putting the best possible interpretation on events, even concerning such goings on as had occurred in the past weeks in her family home. But Elizabeth was not about to disabuse Jane of her notion; privately, Elizabeth suspected that her sojourn in London would be of some duration, as she had no intention of bowing to her mother's demands.

"I hope so, Jane. Though I love Aunt and Uncle Gardiner, being banished from one's home is not an easy thing to take, especially when Mama has no compunction whatsoever about publishing the matter to everyone in the neighborhood."

Jane looked a little uncomfortable with such an observation, but she made no response.

When it came time for Elizabeth to board the coach, the sisters shared a tearful farewell, particularly on Elizabeth's side, as she knew not how long they would be parted and had not Jane's positive outlook.

"Give my love to Aunt and Uncle," said Jane as she embraced Elizabeth. "And be happy, Elizabeth."

"I will try, Jane, and I will make sure to write frequently."

A little tearful laugh escaped Jane's mouth. "I believe I shall depend upon hearing from you often."

And then Elizabeth boarded the coach and was gone.

And it was done. Elizabeth stared at the door in front of her—she knew that her uncle was busy in his offices, and thus she had sent him a brief note stating that she would hire a hackney to take her to Gracechurch Street, which he had accepted, though Elizabeth had been able to see the reluctance in his reply. It was still early afternoon, and she suspected that he was still in his offices. She had no doubt that she would be required to explain what had occurred, as her father had likely included no information other than the request to host Elizabeth for a time.

The door in front of her was solid and sturdy, and it struck her that there was nothing solid about her life at present. How easy it was to be a door! Open and shut, allow passage, and keep out the elements; there was nothing else to consider!

Shaking her head at that little bit of folly, Elizabeth steeled herself and grasped the door knocker, giving it three distinct raps. Within a brief moment—as if the woman had been standing in the foyer, waiting for her niece—Mrs. Gardiner opened the door.

"Lizzy!" cried she and put an arm around Elizabeth's shoulders, drawing her into the house. "I was about to go looking for you. I expected you a half hour gone."

"The coach was delayed slightly in Watford," said Elizabeth.

"It is of no moment. You are safely here, and that is all that matters."

Once inside the house, Elizabeth greeted the housekeeper, who had come to take her light pelisse, and Mrs. Gardiner quickly conveyed her through the house toward her room. It was a handsome house, decorated in all the latest fashions, tasteful and elegant. It was not large, though it was comfortable for the Gardiners, their four children, and the servants they employed. Elizabeth was aware that her uncle had purchased it for a good price, and it was deemed sufficient for his growing family. Certainly he had other concerns to deal with rather than trying to give the appearance of wealth.

That was one of the things Elizabeth had always loved about her relations—they were good, intelligent, honorable people, who were genuine and not concerned about impressing anyone. Mr. Gardiner was hard-working, intelligent, and astute. In fact, though she would never say as much to anyone else, she rather hoped that her future husband was a man more like her uncle than her father. Even if his domestic situation had not been so happy as it was, Elizabeth could not imagine Mr. Gardiner treating his wife the way her father treated Mrs. Bennet.

As for Mrs. Gardiner, Elizabeth had nothing but respect for her aunt. She was the intellectual equal of her husband, loving, kind, and possessed of the most genteel manners. She was the daughter of a country parson who, himself, had been the son of a gentleman, and as such she was versed in all the proper behavior. In fact, it was largely due the Gardiners' influence—and Mrs. Gardiner's in particular—that Jane and Elizabeth had become the ladies they were.

"I shall have Abigail put away your belongings a little later," said Mrs. Gardiner once she had escorted Elizabeth to her room. "For now, I suggest you rest, for you appear to be done in."

Elizabeth looked at her aunt in surprise. "What, is there to be no inquisition?"

Laughing at Elizabeth's irreverent remark, Mrs. Gardiner said: "Not until later. If I understand the tone of your father's letter correctly, it is no happy event which has brought you to us."

"No, indeed," murmured Elizabeth.

"Then I suspect you will only wish to relay the particulars once. That can be done after your uncle returns."

Grateful for her aunt's forbearance, Elizabeth retired. The previous nights had not been restful, so she found that she was able to sleep for much of the time before dinner. And thus, refreshed in body, if not in spirit, Elizabeth rose to prepare for dinner and made her way down the stairs.

"Ah, Lizzy," said Mr. Gardiner when he espied her entering into the sitting-room. "I see you have rejoined the land of the living.

Elizabeth's young cousins perked up at his words, and the three oldest all crowded around her, welcoming her and demanding to know what she brought them; the youngest was yet a babe in arms. Elizabeth laughed for what felt like the first time in days and greeted them with enthusiasm. Within a few moments the children had been sent to the nursery for their dinner, and Elizabeth sat down with her aunt and uncle to have a frank discussion.

"Your father's note did not contain much in the way of detail," said Mr. Gardiner, opening the discussion. He smiled. "I am certain you are aware of your father's habits where correspondence is concerned."

"I did not expect him to tell you much," said Elizabeth, and even she had to confess that her tone was a little petulant. "He does not like to write letters."

"Of that I am well aware," said Mr. Gardiner, ignoring Elizabeth's ill humor. "In light of that fact, perhaps you should inform us of what has happened and why you have been sent from your home."

So Elizabeth began her tale, telling her uncle of the appearance of Mr. Pearce in the events of the neighborhood, and how he had singled her out, the inconsistency of his attentions, and then how he had finally proposed, been rejected, and had proposed again. Elizabeth did not temper the disgust she felt for her mother, Mr. Pearce, or even her father, though she was careful to avoid stating her displeasure in so many words. When she had finished, she could see the disappointment in her relations' countenances, though she was certain it was not directed at her.

"I can well believe your mother's behavior," said Mr. Gardiner, shaking his head. "Fanny has often lamented the lack of a son, and I believe she would champion any match as long as it would provide security for your sisters."

"I rather think she is much more concerned for *her own* comfort than that of her daughters," growled Elizabeth with annoyance.

"That is most certainly a facet of her fears," agreed Mr. Gardiner, "but I would ask you to temper your words. This *is* your mother—and my sister—we are discussing."

"I apologize for speaking so, Uncle," said Elizabeth. "But I do not apologize for the sentiment. My mother has a right to fear for her future, but I do not particularly appreciate being the sacrificial lamb for the sake of her future security. She does not consider—and she does not care—what her daughters think of the matches she champions."

Mr. Gardiner sighed. "I understand your frustration, Elizabeth. There are times I have wished . . . Well, let us simply say that a little more discernment on your mother's part would be welcome." Then Mr. Gardiner fixed his eyes on Elizabeth and, with a pointed look, said: "The fact of the matter is that your mother is correct in one respect—while your father has not left you all completely destitute and my brother Phillips and I will do what we can to assist, should the worst come to pass, you and your sisters would be best served to be protected in honorable marriage."

"I understand that, Uncle. But am I to give up my principles and marry a man I do not like and cannot respect?"

Her uncle's demanding gaze pierced Elizabeth. "So far you have told us that you dislike this Mr. Pearce, but you have not told us the specifics. Is he truly as bad as you make him out to be, or do you just not like him?"

Huffing, Elizabeth sat back in the sofa and crossed her arms. "He is so much older than me, and he has no redeeming qualities. He is condescending and rude, proclaiming his desire to 'tame me' and his insistence that I give up those things which give me pleasure in order for me to be more 'ladylike.' It is said that he has fathered several children, and he lives for nothing more than chasing everything in a skirt."

"And are these rumors to be believed?" asked Mrs. Gardiner.

"There are enough to cast aspersions on his character," said Elizabeth. "Jane is uncomfortable when he looks at her, and though I cannot vouch for the veracity of everything said about him, of course, there are too many rumors to be ignored. And according to Phillip Goulding, who also knows many in Mr. Pearce's usual social circle, his reputation is even worse there, which is why I suspect he is searching in Meryton for a wife."

"Then why does he not go even further afield if his reputation is so poor?" asked Mr. Gardiner.

"I know not. But I cannot abide the sight of him, and I wish he would turn his attentions on some other woman who welcomes them. There are many such ladies who would be happy to marry, based on nothing more than prudence. Why must he focus on me?"

The two adults shared a look before they turned their attention back onto Elizabeth, and her uncle said: "I am sorry, Lizzy, but I wished to understand your reasons for refusing this man. It appears you have some legitimate objections. I commend you for your fortitude, my dear. I know my sister, and I know what it must have been like for you to defy her."

Though she did not show any outward reaction, inside, Elizabeth breathed a sigh of relief. She had never given any consideration to the possibility her aunt and uncle would not support her, but the conversation of the past few moments had allowed a little sliver of doubt to creep into her breast.

"What of your father, Lizzy?" said Mrs. Gardiner. "What has been his reaction to these events?"

Careful to regulate her words—for she was still upset with her father—Elizabeth said: "You know Papa—he only wishes for Mama to cease speaking of the matter and to be left alone."

"Then why did he send you to London?"

In fact, Elizabeth had direct knowledge of why she had been shipped away from her father's house, and it was not completely because of Mrs. Bennet's demands. Elizabeth knew enough of her father's character to know he would not force her to marry where she did not wish, especially when he had told her numerous times that she would not be happy unless she found a man she both respected and loved.

He had made his intentions known to her very soon after he had agreed with her mother to banish her from Longbourn. In his typical way, he had annoyed and teased his wife, even while agreeing with her that Elizabeth should leave the house, but it had been naught but thirty minutes after the decision had been made before he informed her of his real reason for sending her way.

Her mother had been ranting again, crowing over how she had induced her husband to agree with her over the opinions of his favorite, when Mr. Bennet sat next to Elizabeth on the sofa and spoke to her in a low voice.

"I hope you will be happy with the Gardiners for a few months, Lizzy."

Elizabeth turned and regarded him, trying to contain her displeasure, but her sense of betrayal was making it difficult for her to maintain her countenance. "It appears my banishment shall be for a much longer duration, Papa. I will not bow to my mother's wishes."

"I did not think you would. But consider this—if you sojourn in London for a few months, you shall be spared your mother's constant opinions on the subject, and the rest of us will be spared the worst of her displeasure as well. In time, Mr. Pearce will grow bored of waiting for your answer and find some other woman to pursue. *Then*, once your mother recovers from the disappointment, you may return, and other than a few ill-timed words of annoyance, the matter will blow over, and we will all be as we were."

Skeptical, Elizabeth said: "So this is a ploy to remove me from Mama's influence."

"And Mr. Pearce's, of course." Mr. Bennet's countenance darkened from annoyance. "I must say that I agree with you regarding that man. I do not like his look. You did well in refusing him."

"Why do you not tell him that?" asked Elizabeth, struggling to hide her exasperation.

"Because the man has never given me the chance to," said Mr. Bennet with a shrug. "He has spoken with your mother, but both of them have forgotten that a father's consent must be obtained for an engagement to be approved. I must say, they have provided me ample amusement. The only way this farce would be improved upon would be if Pearce came to me on the matter. I am certain his countenance upon leaving would be fierce indeed."

Elizabeth looked at her father, disappointed. It was one thing for him to watch the follies of those about him for his own humor, but in this instance, he was ignoring a matter which caused his daughter—and one he claimed was his favorite—an inordinate amount of distress.

"There!" said Mr. Bennet, waggling his eyebrows at her. "Are you not happy with how I have protected you?"

Then Mr. Bennet rose and quit the room, leaving Elizabeth on the sofa, stewing as she listened to her mother continue to exclaim over Elizabeth's banishment.

When Elizabeth explained these matters to her aunt and uncle, it was clear that they were not happy with how Mr. Bennet had behaved. However, they were both apparently mindful of disparaging the father to his daughter, so they allowed it to rest. Rather, the discussion turned to what Elizabeth might expect here in London.

"For our part, Lizzy," said her uncle, "Meredith and I are pleased to have you with us."

Mrs. Gardiner echoed her husband's sentiments, and Elizabeth was moved to the point of tears and accepted their hospitality with gratitude.

"You are in possession of a great deal of understanding and fortitude," said Mr. Gardiner, his tone affectionate. "The one thing I will insist upon is the appropriate level of respect for your mother. I understand your frustration, but she is your mother, and I will not have you disparage her."

"I understand, Uncle," said Elizabeth, nodding her head. "As far as I am concerned, the fact that you are willing to host me removes all need for me to speak of Mama. I will be content."

"That is well. Another thing we must speak of is what you can expect of your time here."

"Oh, I do not require anything special," said Elizabeth. "I am simply grateful for the roof over my head and the opportunity to eat a regular meal."

"You are a good girl," said Mr. Gardiner fondly. "A young girl your age wishes for amusement and novelty, and we shall do our best to provide what we can. But I must tell you that money will be tight for the nonce."

Surprised, Elizabeth could only wonder as to her uncle's meaning. She knew he was not a fabulously wealthy man, but she had thought his business was prosperous. Mr. Gardiner apparently saw her surprise and was quick to explain.

"The business is much as it ever was, but I am entering a critical time. Not only am I attempting to expand, but I have also entered into negotiations to merge the business with that of another. Only the man's untimely death has prevented it from happening ere now. I expect to meet with my former colleague's son very soon to continue the effort, after which I will manage the joint business while he assumes the role of a silent partner."

"This man does not wish to be involved with the business?" asked Elizabeth.

"His father wished to become a landed gentleman for many years. This merger is the means by which he may achieve that, as I will be purchasing a part of his business, thereby becoming the majority owner and managing partner. He will continue to see a large percentage of the proceeds, but I will have sole control over it. And as a large part of my funds will be tied up in purchasing those shares, there will not be much left over for frivolities."

Elizabeth smiled warmly. "Then I congratulate you on your growing business, Uncle. But you need not concern yourself for me. I shall be quite content. And in return for your generosity, I shall assist Aunt with the children."

"Thank you, Lizzy," said Mrs. Gardiner, moving so that she was close to Elizabeth and putting her arm around her shoulders. "Let us have hope that in time this will all be forgotten. In the meantime, I am glad to have you here with me. Your assistance will be much appreciated, I am sure."

And so it was done. In some ways, Elizabeth knew she would enjoy staying with her relations far more than she would have enjoyed her time at Longbourn. They were good people, welcoming, proper, and possessed of every virtue, and Elizabeth could not state her thanks in tones warm enough.

For the next few weeks, Elizabeth struggled to effect a cheery countenance and a contented façade. There was much for her to occupy her time in London, which was a blessing, as she did not have the opportunity to dwell on her woes. Instead, she was able to concentrate on life with the Gardiners, which in turn softened some of her disappointments.

The Gardiner children were dears, and she had always enjoyed her time with them, whether it was seeing to their entertainment, minding them while their mother was engaged in some other task, or assisting in teaching the eldest. They were four—the eldest, a girl of seven, then two boys aged six and three, and finally the youngest girl, who was less than a year old. They were all well behaved and intelligent, all eager to have their aunt play with them. Elizabeth did her best to devise games they could share, read to them, attended the older girl's tea parties and the boys' toy soldier wars, and kissed them on the forehead when she tucked them into bed at night.

In return, the children played with her, accepting her into their circle, listening with wide eyes and careful attention to her stories, and told her they loved her when she soothed their hurts and played their games. In the children, Elizabeth found the most pleasure and happiness during her time with the Gardiners.

Her aunt and uncle were everything solicitous, welcoming, supportive, and cheerful, and their presence helped to alleviate some of Elizabeth's distress. Elizabeth was certain the Gardiners were not fooled by her contented façade, and as she did not wish to worry them, she redoubled her efforts to appear happy. As they did not discuss the matter, Elizabeth was able to content herself in being at least partially successful in putting them at ease.

From Longbourn, Elizabeth heard very little; or perhaps it would be more correct to say Elizabeth heard very little she would wish to hear. Every week, Elizabeth was the recipient of a letter from her mother consisting of a long diatribe for her recalcitrance and a demand for her to return to Hertfordshire and do her duty. The first such letter was upsetting to Elizabeth, though as the weeks wore on she simply decided to ignore them, often giving them only a cursory reading, if she even opened them at all.

The first letter from her mother she made the mistake of actually responding to, with a polite, but firm statement that she had made up her mind and would not be moved from it. Within a few days of sending her reply, she received a response that was so angry in tone and insulting in word that she actually threw it into the fire, frustrated with her mother's tenacity. Needless to say, the rest of her mother's letters went unanswered.

As for the rest of the family, Jane wrote a few times, usually short letters written in secrecy, as Mrs. Bennet had decreed that Elizabeth was to have no correspondence from her sisters. Elizabeth was grateful for Jane's defiance, even if it was only done in Jane's typically passive way. From Mr. Bennet there was nothing but silence.

In order to keep herself busy and avoid dwelling on her misfortunes, Elizabeth also undertook some other tasks. Mrs. Gardiner was quite active with some of the local charities, and Elizabeth accompanied her, making herself useful wherever she could. In addition to this, Elizabeth would sometimes take messages for her uncle. Mrs. Gardiner was reluctant at first to allow her niece to go out in such a manner, but Elizabeth was able to argue her case successfully.

"Uncle's warehouses are just down the street, Aunt," said Elizabeth the first time she offered to go in a maid's stead. "If you are concerned, you may even watch me from the bay window in the front sitting room. I am certain nothing will happen."

Though Mrs. Gardiner appeared to be more than a little reluctant, she assented, and soon Elizabeth was dressed in her pelisse and swinging her arms as she walked down the street, enjoying the late August air. As she had not often had the opportunity to leave the house—other than the times she and the children's nurse had taken them to the nearby park—Elizabeth relished the freedom to walk, especially now that the activity was more difficult to indulge in than it had been at her father's estate.

When she arrived at her uncle's warehouse, she was escorted into her uncle's office by a clerk. It was a small and cramped space with walls full of shelves on which sat ledgers and books about every conceivable subject pertaining to business. Light from the bright sun outside streamed in through a window on the far wall and her uncle sat at his desk, working on some books, intent upon his task. The offices were obviously not intended for comfort—every available inch of space was devoted to her uncle's warehouse full of inventory.

As Elizabeth entered the office, Mr. Gardiner looked up, and he greeted her with a wide smile. "Elizabeth! What do you do here?"

"I have come to bring you a note from my aunt," said Elizabeth, handing him a small slip of paper.

Mr. Gardiner glanced at it while saying: "I am surprised that you managed to convince her to allow you to come yourself."

"She *was* hesitant, but I persuaded her. I was only walking outside for a few minutes."

"So you were. But your aunt frets over you." Mr. Gardiner sighed. "You may tell her that she may as well go ahead without me, for I doubt I shall be home in time for dinner. I have discovered there is an error somewhere in my records, and I must go through these ledgers and find it. I shall need an accurate accounting of my holdings to complete the negotiations with my new partner."

With interest, Elizabeth approached the desk and looked down at the books. They were standard ledgers with many figures running down them, and though they were more complicated than her father's books, they resembled them greatly.

"Can I be of assistance, Uncle?"

Mr. Gardiner smiled while shaking his head. "I am afraid not. Going through these numbers is not difficult, only tedious, for I must check each sum as I go along."

"I have often helped father with his books. I am certain yours cannot be much different."

Frowning, Mr. Gardiner looked up at Elizabeth, considering her offer. "Your mother would never forgive me if she found out that I was allowing you to help in my office."

"She does not like it when I help Papa either," said Elizabeth. "I do not wish to sound disrespectful, but I dare say that she cannot protest that which she does not know."

When Mr. Gardiner still hesitated, Elizabeth said: "It is clear you have other matters which need your attention. If you will show me what needs to be done, I am certain I can find your error and leave you to handle more important things."

"I am sure there can be no harm in it," mused Mr. Gardiner. "And there are some matters to which I must attend." He nodded. "If you are willing to take on the task, I will ask one of the stock boys to take a message to your aunt, so she does not worry for you."

"Of course, Uncle. I would be happy to be of assistance."

And so it was done. Within a few moments Elizabeth was ensconced at her uncle's desk, having been taught the basics of his bookkeeping. When he was happy with her level of understanding, Mr. Gardiner took himself back into his warehouse to accomplish a few tasks, while Elizabeth sat and pored over his ledgers. She was actually enjoying herself—while she did not enjoy keeping ledgers to any great degree, the feeling of being of use to her uncle filled her with warmth, such as she had not felt since arriving in London. On a few occasions her uncle's clerk happened to look up at her from outside the office across the room, and if his expression was disapproving, Elizabeth did not allow it to bother her. He could think what he wished.

When her uncle returned from his tasks in the warehouse, Elizabeth showed him the results of her investigation.

"What is this?" exclaimed her uncle with surprise. "You have found two additional errors?"

"Yes, Uncle," said Elizabeth. "The other two were so minor that they might not have mattered, but I have corrected them nonetheless."

"Very well done. You say you have helped your father in the past?"

Elizabeth smiled. "You know Papa. He focuses on his books, and when he can be induced to attend to matters of the estate, he does it in a hurried manner. I have been helping him with his ledgers since I was thirteen years of age."

"Astounding! You have saved me hours of work, my dear." Mr. Gardiner leaned close and, in a voice pitched low and a furtive manner, said: "In fact, the keeping of the books is a part of my work which I detest. I am grateful you have taken it off my hands."

"It is my pleasure, Uncle. I am simply happy I can be of some use."

"You have, indeed! Now, since your aunt will soon wonder why I have kept you so long, perhaps we should return to the house so that we might not keep dinner waiting."

Elizabeth assented, and soon they had left her uncle's office for the short walk home. By her side, Mr. Gardiner whistled a merry tune while they walked, clearly happy that he had been spared a tedious task. Elizabeth felt warm all over. Her mother might be infuriated with her, and she had been banished her from her childhood home, but she was of use to her uncle and aunt. It made her feel slightly better about the whole situation.

Chapter IV

Matters continued in a similar manner for the next few weeks. Elizabeth played with the Gardiner children, helping her aunt whenever she was able, spent some afternoons at her uncle's offices helping with his work, and in her spare time she helped herself to the works in her uncle's library and walked in the nearby park whenever she could. And through it all, she attempted to forget—or at least put behind her—the fact of her banishment. At times she did not know what to do with herself, but sitting down at the pianoforte would soothe her, or a book would take her mind off her troubles, and she would be content again for a while. The fact that she did not need to fight Mary off for control of the pianoforte was providential, and after some time, she actually saw an improvement in her proficiency.

The situation with her home and Mrs. Bennet did not change, unfortunately. She still received at least one angry letter from her mother every week, and she continued to ignore them. She treasured the few words Jane could send her, though they were often long overdue and far briefer than Elizabeth would have liked. She was grateful for them nonetheless.

On a bright September day about a month after Elizabeth arrived in London, she received a piece of intelligence from her uncle which was certain to provide some means of breaking up the routine. For that, she could not repine.

"I believe your social circle is about to be expanded, Lizzy," said Mr. Gardiner, "for on the morrow we expect a visitor to join us for dinner."

"Meeting new acquaintances is always welcome, Uncle," replied Elizabeth. "Who is this new and interesting person?"

"His name is Charles Bingley and he is to be my new partner in business, assuming, of course, everything proceeds as planned. He arrived in London from his home near York a few days ago, and negotiations have proceeded to the point where we must meet face to face to continue and resolve the final few issues standing in the way of our merger."

Elizabeth smiled. "And what sort of man is this Mr. Bingley?"

"I have not actually met the young man," said Mr. Gardiner. "But I can tell you his father was a sober, but jovial sort of man, inclined to be friendly with all he met. When I met with the elder Mr. Bingley only a few weeks before his untimely death, Mr. Bingley was in his last year attending Oxford. The elder Mr. Bingley passed away from a sudden apoplexy shortly after. His son, of course, has been in mourning, but now that the six month period has passed, he is determined to finish what his father started."

On the designated evening, Elizabeth waited with anticipation to meet the newcomer. He had met Mr. Gardiner at the warehouses earlier in the day and had toured the premises with her uncle. Her uncle declined the reciprocal offer, citing how he had previously seen Mr. Bingley's location with the man's late father. After spending some time in discussions at the warehouse, the two men arrived in good spirits.

Mr. Bingley was, in fact, everything her uncle said. When he arrived, he greeted them all with evident good cheer. His introduction to Elizabeth in particular was amusing to the entire company.

"Miss Bennet," said he in a tone of good humor, as he bowed over her hand, "I am so very glad to meet you. Your uncle has told me of your being in residence with him at present, but even though he was complimentary, he did not do your beauty justice."

Elizabeth laughed. "Methinks you are a charmer, sir."

A grin suffused Mr. Bingley's face. It was a handsome, though boyish, face, Elizabeth decided. He was tall and well-favored, and he appeared much like a boy just out of the classroom. His shock of reddish hair was styled and combed neatly, and his clothes were impeccably tailored and suited him in the pale cream pants and the dark blue jacket he wore. His eyes were his most intriguing feature, being a light shade of blue, the depths of which were akin to the clearest pool of water on her father's estate. Elizabeth imagined a woman might swoon, should the force of those eyes be turned upon her in passion.

"I merely speak as I find, Miss Bennet. Then he winked at her and leaned close, and in a low tone and with a furtive air, he said: "I hope you will not accuse me of insincerity. I would be crushed."

A gay laugh met his statement. "I am quite ready to accept your words at face value, sir. But I wonder what your reaction would be should you meet my sister, who far exceeds my own paltry claims at beauty."

"I believe I should like to meet this wondrous creature, if she is everything you say. If her beauty renders what I see before me nothing more than common, then she must be something to behold."

"She is my dearest sister, so I may be rightly accused of bias, but she is a dear sweet creature and is widely considered to be the beauty of Hertfordshire. I dare say she is an angel, Mr. Bingley, for I know no one better."

"You intrigue me, Miss Bennet. I believe I should like to be introduced to your sister one day."

"I am sure you shall, sir. I would be pleased to make the introduction."

"I shall hold you to it."

Once their prolonged greeting had been completed, the company sat for some time, talking about mundane matters. But Mr. Bingley was happy and intelligent and had the knack for rendering the most banal subjects interesting by nothing more than the force of his enthusiasm.

It was much the same when they went in to dinner. The conversation continued, mostly between Elizabeth and Mr. Bingley, though the Gardiners did add their own opinions on occasion. Elizabeth did not notice, however, as she found herself quite entertained by the man's conversation. After they had sat at dinner for some time, the conversation turned to books, and though Mr. Bingley was intelligent, she found that his intelligence was not necessarily due to being book learned.

"I will own that I am surprised, Miss Bennet," said Mr. Bingley after Elizabeth had related some observation about a volume she had recently read. "From all this discussion, I would hazard a guess that you are not a stranger to the pages of a book."

"Indeed, I am not, sir," replied Elizabeth. "My father allows me to peruse his library at will, and my uncle gives me the same freedom when I am here. I quite enjoy the delights of a good piece of literature."

"In that case, it is unfortunate you are not able to attend university. I am sure you would fit right in with the more bookish students at Oxford, where I attended."

"It is indeed regrettable, sir. I have often thought it would be something to attend classes in such hallowed halls."

"Lizzy," said Mrs. Gardiner, "perhaps such talk is better left alone. It is not ladylike."

"I am not offended, Mrs. Gardiner," said Mr. Bingley. "In fact, I am quite charmed. The fact that Miss Bennet has such intelligent opinions is refreshing, and that she has come to them on nothing more than the force of her own determination and study is nothing less than astonishing."

"You flatter me, sir," said Elizabeth, blushing a little.

"I do not, I assure you," replied Mr. Bingley. "You might be surprised to hear it, considering my own success in graduating, but I rarely read. There are far too many things vying for my attention, and though I have some few books in my collection, there are far more than I will ever look into!"

"A capital failing indeed, sir! Perhaps you should bring one by sometime and we can read it together. Such activities might serve to motivate you."

The entire company laughed at her suggestion.

"Perhaps I shall, Miss Bennet," said Mr. Bingley. "I am sure your opinions would render even something dreadfully tedious such as Fordyce to be interesting!"

"You should take care," said Elizabeth, disarming him with a smile, "for Fordyce has been my sister Mary's favorite author for this past year at least!"

"So long as you do not share the fascination, I believe myself to be safe."

"No, sir. I do not."

"Excellent!"

The conversation then turned and at length they arrived on the subject of the proposed merger. Mr. Bingley was as enthusiastic about this subject as he was about everything else.

"I must own that I am happy to be pursuing my honored father's wishes," said Mr. Bingley. He paused for a moment, clearly still affected by his father's recent death. "As far back as my grandfather, my family wished to ascend to the ranks of landed gentlemen, but the means never existed to do so. I am grateful to Mr. Gardiner, as it will allow me to fulfill my father's ambition."

"I am certain you shall do him proud, Mr. Bingley."

"Thank you, Miss Bennet. I appreciate the sentiment."

Mr. Bingley then turned to Mr. Gardiner and said: "Mr. Gardiner, I had thought to attend the theater since I am now in town, and I would like to inquire if you and Mrs. Gardiner, and Miss Bennet, of course, would consent to attend with me."

"I am sure we would be delighted, sir," said Mr. Gardiner. "Did you have a particular date in mind?"

"Would Tuesday next be acceptable?"

Mr. Gardiner looked at his wife, who smiled and said: "I believe next Tuesday is perfect, Mr. Bingley. We would be pleased to accept."

"Excellent!" cried Mr. Bingley. "I shall look forward to it."

Then Mr. Bingley turned to Elizabeth and said in a knowing tone, "I am certain Miss Bennet would be happy to attend a play. I will confess that the theater often serves as my own form of being lost in the pages of a book, for if I cannot devote the time to read Shakespeare, at least I may enjoy another's interpretation of it!"

"That is quite intelligent of you, Mr. Bingley," said Elizabeth, laughing at his antics. "I, too, am a devoted lover of the theater. There is something wondrous about seeing a favorite work play out on the stage."

"I cannot agree more, Miss Bennet. I try to go as often as I can. The performances near my home are not quite aso polished as those you might find in London, but they are pleasing nonetheless. Now, have you ever had the good fortune enjoy the vantage provided by a box?"

"I confess, I have not, Mr. Bingley," said Elizabeth. "Aunt and Uncle have taken me a time or two, but we have sat in the gallery."

"The gallery has its own advantages, of course. But there is something about a box which makes everything so much more delightful. There is more to be seen, and I sometimes wonder what part of the stage should claim my attention. It can be quite the conundrum!"

Elizabeth laughed. "Surely you overstate the matter, sir."

"Perhaps, but only a little. It is a wonderful experience, and I shall be happy to introduce you to it."

The remaining discussion expanded upon the wonders of seeing a play from a box and of Mr. Bingley's stories of his home near York where he had been raised. This, of course, led to other talk of Hertfordshire, as well as some of the places her uncle had travelled to. In all, it was an enjoyable evening, which ended too soon for Elizabeth's taste. She thought she might have enjoyed talking far later into the evening.

After Mr. Bingley departed, Elizabeth ascended the stairs to her room. She had soon, with the assistance of her aunt's maid, removed her gown in favor of her nightgown, and her hair had been braided for sleep. Not long after, a knock sounded on the door.

Upon her call to enter, the door opened, and her aunt stepped into the room. With a smile, she approached Elizabeth and said: "You are about to retire?"

"I had not decided if I wished to read a little before bed."

"In that case, I thought we could speak for a few moments."

Curious, Elizabeth readily accepted. It was not unusual for her aunt to wish to speak with her, but given her expression and the general gravity of her demeanor, Elizabeth wondered if Mrs. Gardiner had some unpleasant news to impart. Since the only thing Elizabeth could think of which would cause such consternation was the situation with respect to Mr. Pearce, she regarded her aunt with some trepidation.

Mrs. Gardiner, apparently seeing Elizabeth's hesitation in her countenance, laughed lightly and asked: "Is speaking with your aunt so daunting a task? I had not thought I was quite so fearsome."

Relaxing a little at her aunt's changed tone, Elizabeth sat on the edge of the bed and looked at her expectantly. "I was a little concerned, for you seemed to be more than usually serious."

"I apologize, Lizzy," said her aunt. "I had not intended to distress you. Rather I had thought to speak to you concerning your impressions of the evening and, perhaps more specifically, about our guest."

Elizabeth was nonplused. "About Mr. Bingley? I do not understand."

"The gentleman is an amiable one, is he not?"

"As amiable a gentleman as I have ever met," replied Elizabeth. "He possesses happy manners and an engaging way of speaking which cannot help but garner him friends, I think."

"And what of his person? Do you find him to be a handsome man?"

Frowning, Elizabeth considered the question. She was starting to understand her aunt's purpose for approaching her.

"I dare say he is as handsome as any man I have ever met."

"Then you like him."

"I do indeed, Aunt." Elizabeth looked at her aunt with some severity. "He has everything in his advantage—fortune, looks, happy manners and an engaging disposition. I cannot imagine there are many who would disapprove of Mr. Bingley."

Nodding, Mrs. Gardiner approached and sat on the bed, her fond smile making Elizabeth feel warm all over. This was the kind of nurturing love Elizabeth had always wished to receive from her mother.

"I understand you are far too intelligent to miss the reason for my questions, Lizzy."

"I will own they were a little blatant," said Elizabeth, smiling at her aunt. "Mr. Bingley is indeed an engaging gentleman, and I like him prodigiously well. I cannot tell you if I like him well enough for *that*, but I *do* like him very well indeed."

"Then that is fine for the present."

Mrs. Gardiner paused, as if thinking of what she wished to say next. When she did speak again, it was slowly and carefully, ensuring she was understood without a hint of doubt.

"I think you know that I will not push you at a suitor, Elizabeth."

Elizabeth looked skyward. "Unlike my mother." At her aunt's stern look, Elizabeth relented. "I know, Aunt, and I will not speak about my mother in a disparaging manner. I never thought you would force me on Mr. Bingley or anyone else."

"Good," said Mrs. Gardiner. "As long as you live with us and your father does not intervene, you will be free to choose your own path in life.

"However, I will say that I do like Mr. Bingley. He is, perhaps, still a little young to be thinking about a wife, but he is eligible, a good man, and would be a fine catch for any young woman. But though I think he would be a good suitor for you, I would not have you think you must attempt to secure him in order to avoid this Mr. Pearce."

"Nor would I do so," said Elizabeth firmly. "I wish to have something more in my marriage than to marry for purely mercenary reasons."

"That is commendable. But you must remember that practicality has a place as well. If Mr. Bingley took a liking to you and you to him, it would be a rather neat solution to your current problem."

"But I have still only met him."

Mrs. Gardiner smiled and rose to her feet, leaning over to kiss Elizabeth's cheek. "It is still early, of course, and I am not suggesting you throw yourself at his feet. We shall see much more of Mr. Bingley in the coming weeks, and I simply wish for you to consider the matter further. If nothing comes of it, so be it. But he is an amiable gentleman who would provide well for a wife and would always be devoted to her. It is something on which to ponder."

And with that, Mrs. Gardiner let herself from the room, leaving Elizabeth alone with her thoughts. And they were such that she was awake well into the evening, thinking on Mr. Bingley, Mr. Pearce, the differences between the two men and, perhaps most importantly, whether she had a hope of esteeming Mr. Bingley enough to accept a proposal, should he ever make one.

* * *

The next morning, Elizabeth awoke, feeling refreshed despite the late night. She had been largely happy at her uncle's house, though at times remembrances of her situation set in, turning her mood melancholy. But what she had not been was active, outside her trips to her uncle's office and the few times she could steal away for a walk in the nearby park. A night at the theater was exactly what she needed to liven up the doldrums of her existence.

Mrs. Gardiner was busy that day with some other concerns, and as her uncle did not require her assistance, Elizabeth was left largely to her own devices. She played with the children for some time in the morning and indulged in a book of poetry in the early afternoon. In all, it was a satisfying day.

Throughout it, however, thoughts of Mr. Bingley intruded as she considered her aunt's words, and she wondered what it might be like to be pursued by a man she could actually esteem. Mr. Pearce, of course, did not fill that requirement. And the more she thought about it, the more she decided she would enjoy Mr. Bingley's attentions, should he deign to offer them. She was still of two minds about truly loving the man, but she was willing to do as her aunt instructed.

Of course, thoughts of Mr. Bingley led to thoughts of the theater once again. Unfortunately, that was when reality came crashing down, for as Elizabeth looked in her closet at the dresses hanging there, she realized that there was nothing suitable for a night at Covent Gardens.

Chagrinned, Elizabeth took out her dresses one by one, examining them, wondering if she could alter them to make them acceptable. She had some pretty dresses with her, including a pale green muslin and a yellow dress of the same fabric. Some she thought looked fine on her, and she considered them to be pretty pieces indeed.

But her mother's vindictive refusal to allow her to bring any of her finer dresses meant that there was nothing for an evening in attendance to one of London's many attractions, though there was one or two which would be acceptable for an evening in company, as long as the company was not too fine. And try as she might, Elizabeth could not imagine any of her current dresses being pulled apart and made into anything which would allow her to attend.

Hot waves of disappointment coursed through Elizabeth. Were she to show up in one of these frocks, she would no doubt be derided as a lowly, frumpy maid without connections or fortune. It was in every way inconceivable.

The sense of inevitability settled over Elizabeth, and though she tried to affect a cheerful demeanor, the fact that she was to be denied even this amusement caused her mood to be quite morose. Her sudden disappointment was obviously visible to her relations, for soon after dinner started, Mr. Gardiner jokingly asked what had become of his normally cheerful niece. Swallowing her disappointment, Elizabeth gathered herself and made the communication she knew was required.

"I believe I will be unable to attend the theater. Would you be so good as to extend my regrets?"

"I am sorry, Elizabeth, but I do not understand why you would not be able to attend." Mr. Gardiner regarded her with open curiosity. "Is there some problem of which I was not aware?"

"Mama—"

Mindful of the previous conversation she had engaged in with her uncle concerning respect for her parents, Elizabeth swallowed what she was going to say about her mother's petulance. Instead, she grimaced and attempted to relay the facts, rather than her feelings concerning the matter.

"I have nothing I can wear to the theater, Uncle," said Elizabeth. "I have only a few frocks with me, and none are fine enough to be worn to an evening at Covent Gardens."

"Oh, I apologize, Lizzy," interjected Mrs. Gardiner, "but I neglected to mention that I have set up an appointment for us with my modiste for late tomorrow morning. If you would like, we can go to your uncle's warehouse in the morning and pick a bolt of fabric—he tells me there should be something suitable."

Elizabeth listened to her aunt with an open mouth, not understanding what she said. "An appointment with the modiste?"

"Of course. Otherwise, how shall we obtain a dress for you to attend the theater?"

"But—"

"Elizabeth," said Mr. Gardiner, his tone chiding, "you did not think I would allow you to miss Mr. Bingley's invitation because of a lack of appropriate clothing, did you?"

Fortunately, Elizabeth heard the affection in her uncle's tone, and she knew that he was not unhappy with her. She smiled, in a tentative sort of fashion, before she said: "But, Uncle, I had understood there were little funds available for frivolities. Is this not what you told me?"

"I did," said Mr. Gardiner. "But the matter of a single dress is rather inconsequential, do you not think? And the joy it will bring *you* and the ability it will give you to move in society, even if only for a night or two, is well worth the cost."

"I do not wish to be any trouble," said Elizabeth. "I am more than happy to not attend if it would cause hardship."

"It is no hardship, Lizzy," said Mrs. Gardiner. "We both thank you for considering our situation before your own, but you do not need to concern yourself."

"Indeed, you do not." Mr. Gardiner paused, and he reached across the table and took Elizabeth's hand in his own. "What you fail to see is that your help since you arrived in London has been invaluable. Not only have you helped your aunt with whatever she required and assisted with the children—all without complaint—but the assistance you have rendered with the ledgers at my business has been a true godsend. I dare say I should be paying you for the hours you have dedicated to my assistance!"

Elizabeth ducked her head, embarrassed at the praise, but Mr. Gardiner was not about to allow her to deflect it.

"And another thing you must consider. What would Mr. Bingley say if I were to inform him that my niece cannot attend because a lack of funds rendered purchasing a dress impossible? Would it not prompt second thoughts about our business merger if he were to think I could not afford such an inconsequential expense?"

"Uncle!" cried Elizabeth, though she was laughing at his words. "I was not suggesting Mr. Bingley be informed in such terms."

"I am aware of that, my dear," said Mr. Gardiner. "But Mr. Bingley is an intelligent young man, and I do not doubt he would understand more than we would choose to tell him. It is good business to ensure you are dressed properly for the theater."

"Besides," said Mrs. Gardiner with an expression of mischief mixed with studious innocence, "if we show you to your best advantage, perhaps Mr. Bingley will decide he cannot live without you."

"I pray you desist from this matchmaking!" cried Elizabeth. "I receive enough of it at home, and my mother is both less subtle and more aggressive than you can ever be!"

The Gardiners laughed at Elizabeth's joke, and she joined them. It was several minutes before their mirth subsided.

"I have already promised not to play the matchmaker," said Mrs. Gardiner. "But stranger things have been known to happen, and you *are* a beautiful young woman, Elizabeth. There is no harm in helping Mr. Bingley understand that fact."

"What, is there matchmaking occurring under my roof, and I was not aware?" asked Mr. Gardiner.

"Please, Uncle, no more!"

"Then I shall desist. And I thank you, Elizabeth, for your discretion—

I understand it is difficult to hold your tongue in the face of your mother's provocation, but I appreciate it nonetheless.

"I must say that I am anticipating the theater keenly. From what I understand, Mr. Bingley is a young man who is quickly enamored with comely young ladies, and I doubt he will be able to resist your charm, my dear. The dance between you two—Mr. Bingley advancing and you retreating—should be a sight to see."

Mrs. Gardiner laughed at her husband's sally, and Elizabeth had no choice but to join them. And so, the rest of the evening passed with discussions between Elizabeth and her aunt concerning the dress to be made for her and with the occasional gentle tease from Mr. Gardiner. Elizabeth attempted to be stern with him, but the twinkle in his eye caused her to laugh so often that it was no wonder none of her warnings or claims of retribution were taken with any seriousness.

Chapter V

The rest of the week and the ensuing weekend were spent pleasurably and with keen anticipation, and for the first time since leaving her father's house, Elizabeth thought she could lay claim to happiness. The next day, as promised, Elizabeth accompanied her aunt to her uncle's warehouse where they quickly located a bolt of lovely green fabric they decided would be used for Elizabeth's dress. It was a fine muslin which would be accentuated with lace and some deeper colors from the modiste and would turn out to be the most beautiful creation Elizabeth had ever worn.

The modiste was enthusiastic, and the time Elizabeth spent in Mrs. Marsten's shop was interesting and amusing. The woman was middle-aged and garrulous, clucking over Elizabeth and exclaiming over her coloring, her hair, her eyes and lashes, and anything else which entered her mind. Elizabeth was often embarrassed by the woman's compliments, but she accepted them with as much grace as she was able to muster. The woman had been Mrs. Gardiner's modiste for many years and Elizabeth had met her before, so she knew that she was not simply flattering her for the sake of increasing her custom.

"This will be a lovely design for you, my dear," said Mrs. Marsten when they had decided on a pattern for her dress. "I have some fine

Belgian lace with which we may accentuate your neck line, which I believe would look exquisite."

Elizabeth only stifled a groan, instead saying: "I would prefer a simpler design."

"You should not concern yourself, Lizzy," said Mrs. Gardiner with a laugh. "We shall not drown you in lace."

At Mrs. Marsten's curious glance, Mrs. Gardiner was motivated to explain. "Elizabeth's mother has a penchant for lace, and she tends to prefer much more of it be attached to Elizabeth's dresses than she prefers."

"That is an understatement," muttered Elizabeth.

At the same time, Mrs. Marsten clucked her tongue and said: "Oh, no, that will not do. Your niece is quite lovely as she is, Mrs. Gardiner. There is no need to resort to artificial means to enhance that which is already fine. I must agree with you on this matter."

Mrs. Gardiner laughed at the rosy hue which spread over Elizabeth's features, but Elizabeth allowed a little self-conscious laugh to escape her lips nonetheless. At least she could be certain her wishes would be adhered to in the matter of her own attire.

"Now," said Mrs. Marsten when they had decided on the details for the dress, "I will have your dress ready for the final fitting on Monday next, which will allow time to make a final few adjustments if required."

"Thank you, Mrs. Marsten," said Elizabeth quietly. "I do appreciate your assistance."

"Of course, my dear. We would not have you appear before your beau in anything but the most exquisite of dresses, now would we?"

Once again embarrassed, Elizabeth stammered out a denial, which the modiste simply waved off.

"Perhaps this young man is not your beau yet, but if he is an amiable man, you had best snap him up before some other opportunistic young woman manages to capture him while you are making up your mind."

There really was nothing Elizabeth could say to such a statement. So, with her aunt watching on, attempting to control her own laughter, Elizabeth thanked Mrs. Marsten for the dress and the advice, and within moments she and Mrs. Gardiner had left the shop.

"Mrs. Marsten does give excellent counsel, does she not, Lizzy."

A glare only served to increase Mrs. Gardiner's amusement, so Elizabeth decided it was not worth pursuing the matter. Instead she focused her attention on the passing scenery and attempted to ignore her aunt's amused chuckles as they travelled back toward the house on Gracechurch Street.

* * *

And so it was that Elizabeth stepped from the Gardiner carriage the next Tuesday evening, feeling every inch the fairy princess in her pretty new evening gown, all anticipation for the upcoming evening. Mr. Gardiner had complimented her when she descended the stairs that evening, telling her how beautiful she was and how Mr. Bingley would hardly be able to take his eyes off her the entire evening. Elizabeth thanked him while attempting to control her embarrassment.

It seemed, however, that Mr. Gardiner was correct in his suggestion concerning Mr. Bingley. As soon as they entered the foyer of the theater, Mr. Bingley, who had been waiting for them, hastened to them and welcomed them in his usual cheery tone. To Elizabeth in particular, however, were reserved his especial greetings.

"Miss Bennet," said he, bowing over her hand, "I cannot recall when I have seen such loveliness as has appeared before me this evening. You look very beautiful indeed."

"Thank you, Mr. Bingley," said Elizabeth, though she hardly knew how she managed to answer. "I thank you for your invitation tonight. I have hardly been able to contain my excitement."

Mr. Bingley grinned. "I am happy you have all accepted my invitation. I do not doubt we shall be a merry party tonight."

They stood in the foyer of the theater for some little time, Mr. Bingley gallantly offering to bring some punch for their consumption. As they stood and discussed the upcoming performance, Elizabeth observed the foyer and noted those personages present. She thought there was little in the way of higher society in attendance, and as the little season had not truly started, it was not surprising. Mr. Bingley, it seemed, did have a few acquaintances, as several came up to speak to him. It was the same with her uncle. But those Elizabeth thought were of a higher level of society did not approach.

When they adjourned to the box, they arranged themselves, Mr. Bingley seated beside Elizabeth while her aunt and uncle sat together on Mr. Bingley's other side. Soon the performance began and Elizabeth concentrated on the stage.

It was as Mr. Bingley had suggested, exquisite and with a much better vantage point from which to watch the story unfold. Everything could be seen from where she sat, and there were no ladies with feather headdresses or men with tall hats in front of her to block her view. It was the most marvelous experience Elizabeth had ever had at the theater.

There were two intermissions, and during the first, they descended to the foyer to partake of refreshments, while during the second they decided to eschew descending in favor of staying in their box and conversing amongst themselves. It was then that through conversation with Mr. Bingley, Elizabeth came to understand more of the man himself. She also came to understand that while he was amiable and attentive, he held no particular attraction for her.

"Do you have family in town?" asked Elizabeth after they had discussed her home circumstances—a little about her family, though Elizabeth was careful to avoid any mention of Mr. Pearce and her mother's current displeasure.

"My parents have both passed on, as I am certain you are aware," said Mr. Bingley.

A ghost of pain passed over his face at the remembrance of his father, who Elizabeth knew had passed away only months before, but it was quickly gone in favor of his cheerfulness.

"I have two sisters, but other than an aunt and two uncles, no other close family."

"And your sisters?" prompted Elizabeth. "Are they out yet?"

"Yes, both of them," said Mr. Bingley with a laugh. "Louisa, my older sister, has been married less than a year to a Mr. Hurst. Mr. Hurst's father owns a prosperous estate in Lincolnshire. It was, you understand, a fortunate connection for her."

Elizabeth inclined her head. This was one of the things she admired most about Mr. Bingley; he had no illusions about where he was from and did not attempt to be something he was not. He was aware that his family's fortune would buy him little in the way of acceptance from most of society, and the matter bothered him little. He was much like her uncle in that regard.

"My younger sister, Caroline, is but nineteen years of age," continued Mr. Bingley. "She has not been presented in London yet, but she has been out in York society for more than a year. We hope to be able to find some member of society willing to sponsor her so that she might make a curtsey before the queen."

"And your family remains in York at present?" asked Elizabeth.

"Caroline is currently with my uncle in York. He has built up his own shipping company there—it is mutually beneficial, you understand; my father purchased our wares and my uncle shipped them. I believe Mr. Gardiner intends to make use of that connection in the future.

"Regardless, Caroline is still there. Louisa and Hurst are at his family's estate at present. But I expect them to join me before the end of October. We have never been in a position to attend the events of the season—though Hurst is not unknown in town—and I believe my sisters to be anticipating it keenly."

"I can understand why they might be excited at the possibility of such amusement, sir. I hope their journey is safe and comfortable."

"Thank you, Miss Bennet. I shall be happy to introduce them to your acquaintance once they arrive. In fact, I intend to invite you and your aunt and uncle to dinner once Louisa is able to serve as my hostess."

"I believe my uncle and aunt will be happy to accept."

Their conversation continued in a more desultory manner for some minutes, and Elizabeth attempted to watch Mr. Bingley as they spoke. The fact that he was amiable had already been acknowledged, and he continued to show himself adept at the art of speaking of inconsequential things. What Elizabeth thought he was missing was a certain something a young man who admired a young woman might display.

There were little clues two people would give each other when interested in a closer relationship, and if the person was astute enough, those clues could be recognized for what they were. A bright smile could mean more than simply good humor or an appreciation for a point one had just made, and other things, such as the touch of a hand, the propensity to smile at the most inconsequential statements, a sparkle in the eyes when regarding one for whom a person has tender feeling—all these things bespoke regard.

In Mr. Bingley's case, he was pleasant and animated when he spoke with Elizabeth, but nothing of his demeanor spoke to anything more than good humor and pleasant company. Elizabeth felt certain that despite her aunt's wishes, Mr. Bingley would not be paying court to her.

And Elizabeth decided that for her part, she could not repine his lack of interest. He was a good sort of man, intelligent, obviously caring and considerate, but he did not excite any depth of feeling in her either. She thought she would be quite content to simply remain friends with him.

In fact, the more Elizabeth considered it, the more she began to wonder whether Mr. Bingley would in fact prefer Jane. The thought was not a surprise in and of itself, as Jane was admired wherever she went. But in the case of Mr. Bingley, Elizabeth thought that should he ever meet her, there was a good chance he would see beyond the beauty of her face into the person behind the calm manners. She thought they might be a very good match indeed.

"Your father's estate is quite close to town, Miss Bennet?" asked Mr. Bingley at one point near the end of the intermission.

"No more than four hours from Gracechurch Street, sir," said

Elizabeth. "It is near the town of Meryton, north of London, but as it is not on the main road north, it is a little less known than some of the other market towns."

"I should like to see it someday," said Mr. Bingley. "I believe Mr. Gardiner has informed you that I am looking for an estate?"

"He did indeed, sir."

"I hope to be settled at an estate sometime in the next few months," said Mr. Bingley. "But I am having difficulty finding one which meets my requirements."

Elizabeth arched an eyebrow at him. "Are your tastes so exacting and your requirements so narrow that there is not an estate in England which will satisfy you?"

A laugh met her statement. "No, indeed. But I would not wish for one so large as to overwhelm me, nor one so small as to present a negligible challenge. And, of course, it must be near London."

"That is indeed a rigorous list. But I do not understand, Mr. Bingley—the size I readily understand, but would an estate in Gloucestershire not be so agreeable as one in Kent?"

Mr. Bingley fixed her with a grin. "Perhaps you might have noticed that I am a sociable fellow. The close proximity to town is due to my desire to partake in society, and my sisters will demand it for the same reason."

"Then perhaps you should consider Netherfield Park," said Elizabeth.

"Netherfield?" asked Mr. Bingley. "I do not believe I have heard of such an estate."

"It borders my father's estate Longbourn," explained Elizabeth. "It is a fine estate and boasts a house which is easily the largest in the vicinity. And yet, the estate has been empty for longer than I have been out."

Mr. Bingley regarded Elizabeth thoughtfully. "It sounds very like what I have been searching for. You say it has stood empty for some time? Is there some deficiency with the property which has kept it from being let?"

"I do not think so, though it is possible that time and neglect have affected it adversely. The family who owns it, the Hansons, moved to Sussex when Mr. Hanson inherited a larger estate. My father would know more about the state of the property than I would. Perhaps you could speak with my uncle. He can provide an introduction to my father, who can certainly tell you more. In addition, my uncle Phillips is the solicitor in Meryton and has been involved with attempts to lease it in the past."

"Very well, I shall speak to him." Mr. Bingley flashed her a dazzling smile, and Elizabeth almost felt as if it would be something to have the regard of this man. "It sounds much better than any of the other properties I have toured in the past months. They have all been either neglected or there has been some insurmountable problem which would cost far more to repair than I am willing to pay."

"I hope Netherfield meets your needs, Mr. Bingley. I believe the people of the neighborhood would be happy to have you."

"And I would be happy to join them. You see, Miss Bennet . . ." Mr. Bingley trailed off and some emotion seemed to come over him, which he immediately shook off and forced a smile. "That is to say, it was my father's wish to purchase an estate and become a gentleman. Had he survived much longer, he might have realized his dream."

Elizabeth was filled with compassion for this man, and she reached out with a tentative hand, resting it on his arm. "And now it is left to you to fulfill your father's dream."

"Yes, it is, Miss Bennet. And I assure you that I consider no other promise as sacred as that which I made to my father before his untimely death. I wish to make him proud of me and ensure future generations of his progeny are raised to the level of society which he worked all the years of his life to attain."

"I am sure your father cannot be anything but proud of you," said Elizabeth, favoring him with a warm smile.

"That is my hope," said he, and he appeared reflective, which in the time Elizabeth had known him was unlike his normal cheerful demeanor. "I do hope so very much."

That night at the theater was a wonderful change for Elizabeth. Not only had she experienced the play from a box for the first time, but she had also enjoyed the attentions of a handsome young man, and if he did not see her as a potential marriage partner, she was still enchanted by the magic of the evening and the happiness it engendered. Though Mrs. Bennet continued her assault of words through the post, Elizabeth was able to cheerfully ignore her mother and concentrate on the good fortune of living with her aunt and uncle and to feel useful in the tasks she performed on their behalf.

It was unfortunate the euphoria of that night was not destined to continue.

A few days later, Elizabeth was with her aunt and uncle in the sitting-room on a bright, warm autumn morning in late September. The previous days had been so good that she found herself in high spirits and was thinking of visiting the park that morning. Mr. Gardiner had not yet departed for his offices, and the three sat in the room speaking, their banter playful and happy. The shadow that came over their happy routine was one which was destined to last for some time.

It began with the ringing of the doorbell. When it sounded, Mr. Gardiner stood and looked at his wife and niece with evident fondness.

"I believe that is the signal for my departure."

"You would leave Lizzy and me to the mercy of whatever caller is about to descend upon us?" demanded his wife. The brilliance of her eyes and her laughing countenance belied the severity in her tone.

"I am completely confident in your abilities, my dear," replied Mr. Gardiner. "I have tarried for longer than I ought this morning, so I shall greet our visitor and leave you to your visiting."

"I am shocked, Uncle," said Elizabeth in a teasing tone. "I had not thought you this unsociable."

Mr. Gardiner grinned at Elizabeth. "I am not in general. But there is something about a drawing room when the ladies are clucking like hens that sets me on edge. I had much rather work in my office."

"That is a pretty picture you paint of me!" cried Mrs. Gardiner. "I shall have you know that I am nothing like a hen!"

"I would not dare suggest such a thing," said Mr. Gardiner. He leaned over and kissed his wife's cheek. "However, I cannot say the same about some of your acquaintances."

Whatever Mrs. Gardiner would have said in reply was lost, for at that moment the door opened, and the housekeeper led the visitor into the room.

"Mr. Winston Pearce to see Miss Bennet, Mrs. Gardiner."

And there, in all his glory, strutting like a peacock, Mr. Pearce strode into the room.

Elizabeth was shocked. She had not for a moment thought the man would actually seek her out in London. In fact, she had thought that he would have given up on her by now to pursue some other unfortunate woman.

"Miss Bennet," said Mr. Pearce in a low tone. "How lovely to see you."

Shocked as she was, Elizabeth was unable to reply for a few moments. When she finally found her voice, her reply was not one which showed good breeding.

"Mr. Pearce. What are you doing here?"

While Mrs. Gardiner appeared a little annoyed that Elizabeth would treat a guest in her house in such a manner, Mr. Gardiner only watched the man warily. For his part, Mr. Pearce favored Elizabeth with the barest hint of a smile.

"Still as charming as ever, I see. Can you not divine my purpose yourself?"

Elizabeth gathered herself for a stinging retort, but Mrs. Gardiner, apparently seeing her displeasure, intervened.

"Lizzy, will you not do us the honor of performing the introduction?"

Mr. Pearce turned a sneering glare on Elizabeth's aunt. "Is it not customary, madam, for the higher ranking to ask for an introduction to the lower?"

"Perhaps you are correct, sir," interjected Mr. Gardiner. "But when you arrive at my home uninvited, you must expect to be introduced. I believe it to be only good manners to request it upon arriving. If you do not wish to be known to me, then you may depart without delay."

"Do whatever you wish," said Mr. Pearce with an airy wave of his hand. "I am here to speak with Miss Bennet, so if an introduction is what you require, an introduction is what you shall have."

Though reluctant—she did not wish to show this man *any* courtesy—Elizabeth stood and indicated the man who stood insouciantly just inside the door, seemingly wishing for all the world that he was anywhere else.

"Aunt, Uncle, this is Mr. Pearce from Hertfordshire. Mr. Pearce, my aunt and uncle, Mr. and Mrs. Gardiner."

Rather than being offended by Elizabeth's intentional reversal of the introductions, Mr. Pearce turned an amused eye on Elizabeth.

"My, but you are a feisty one, are you not? I shall not claim that you do not understand the protocols of society, since I am well aware of your intentional insolence."

"I quite understand protocol, sir," said Elizabeth through clenched teeth. "I simply do not believe you deserve such notice."

Mr. Pearce chuckled while shaking his head, but Mrs. Gardiner was most certainly not amused.

"Now, Lizzy. Let us at least make an attempt at civility." Mrs. Gardiner then turned to Mr. Pearce and said: "Will you not sit, sir? I shall call for tea."

Again, the man waved his hand in that disrespectful manner of his. "Do not trouble yourself, for I do not mean to stay any longer than necessary. I have come to speak with your niece. You may leave so that we may have a moment's privacy."

"There is no reason for us to speak alone," said Elizabeth. "There is nothing you can say that anyone else cannot overhear. Say what you will and depart."

For a moment Elizabeth thought he would attempt to insist, but a glance at her uncle revealed Mr. Gardiner's stony countenance. It was clear that Mr. Gardiner was not inclined to allow him to have his way, and Mr. Pearce seemed to sense that. In his typical manner he discarded the matter as irrelevant and turned his attention on Elizabeth.

"If you wish to have every person in London as witness, that is your prerogative. But I have come to gain the promise of your hand, and I shall have it."

"You shall *not* have it, sir. I will not bestow it, I assure you."

"Your mother has promised me you shall."

"My mother is not my father. As he has refused to enforce his will upon me, there is nothing my mother can do."

"And yet you have been banished from your home." Mr. Pearce regarded her with some scorn. "You have been reduced from the daughter of a country gentleman to one out of favor with her mother, living in squalor with those who are beneath you. Surely you can see that I can give you a good home. Why must you resist?"

"I must confess, Elizabeth," said Mr. Gardiner, interrupting her rejoinder, "that I now see why you are determined to reject this man. I believe I would have questioned your sanity had you accepted him."

Elizabeth was astonished at her uncle's words—he was almost unfailingly a genial and polite man, not given to antagonistic behavior, regardless of the situation. But again Mr. Pearce declined to take offense, showing more fortitude and patience than Elizabeth would have given him credit for. He did glance at Mr. Gardiner with distaste, but he quickly turned his attention back on Elizabeth with an expectant air.

"Well, what say you?"

"I believe I have already made my sentiments known, sir. You could not offer me your hand in a manner which would tempt me even for an instant to accept. Your suit is futile, sir. I suggest you give it up and leave."

"Do you not understand all that I can give you?"

"I understand the degradation of being married to you. I am also astonished at your behavior. Why must you persist in insisting I accept you? What man would wish a wife who will endure any fate as long as she is not forced to marry him?"

"My reasons are of no concern to you. Suffice it to say that I have decided that you will be my wife, and I will not be gainsaid."

"I am sorry to bring you disillusionment and disappointment," said Elizabeth in a scathing tone, "but in this I am afraid you will need to become accustomed to being contradicted. I will not marry you."

Shaking his head, Mr. Pearce regarded Elizabeth like she was a recalcitrant child. "It is unfortunate that you persist in taking this stance, my dear. But I shall cease to importune you for the moment."

"Cease to importune me forever!" exclaimed Elizabeth.

"I will return anon," said he, ignoring Elizabeth's words. "Hopefully by that time you will have acquired the necessary maturity to realize my proposal is in your best interests."

Then without another word of farewell, Mr. Pearce turned and left the room, and within a few moments, the sound of the door closing behind him echoed from the entrance. Silence reigned in the room.

All at once it became too much for Elizabeth. All her good mood, all the contentment she had achieved, all of her aunt and uncle's help and support suddenly dissipated like the sweet scent of roses blown away by an onrushing wind. And though Elizabeth had always fancied herself strong enough to meet any intimidator with courage, she collapsed on the sofa, tears spilling from her eyes in ragged sobs.

"There, there, Elizabeth," said her aunt, her tone comforting.

Feeling Mrs. Gardiner's gentle arms wrapping around her, Elizabeth allowed herself to be drawn into her aunt's embrace. It was soothing, though it did nothing to stop the tears. Elizabeth did not know what to do.

When at last her tears subsided, Elizabeth continued to lean on her aunt's shoulder, drawing comfort from the simple contact.

"Do not worry, Lizzy."

The voice of her uncle startled her, and Elizabeth looked up to see him sitting close by, an expression of utter compassion directed at her. She had not realized he was still present.

"I cannot imagine your father giving his consent to such a man," continued Mr. Gardiner. "You know he has always said you require a man you can respect. A man like that Pearce fellow can inspire little more than contempt, I am sure."

Elizabeth chuckled, a watery sort of sound. "He does at that. I dare say he is adept at that particular talent."

"That is the spirit!"

"Lizzy," said her aunt, "your uncle and I are in agreement that you may stay as long as you like. We now understand why you have refused him. You will have our support regardless of what comes."

Rubbing his chin thoughtfully, Mr. Gardiner said: "In fact, I believe I will write my sister directly and let her know of Pearce's behavior. She should know what kind of man he is."

"Thank you, Uncle, but it will do little good. Mama sees only his five thousand a year and his house in town. I cannot imagine your account of his behavior will move her from her position."

"Perhaps not," agreed Mr. Gardiner with a bit of a rueful chuckle, "but she should still know of it, nonetheless. For that matter, your father should know of it too. He might not do anything concerning Pearce, but it will make him less likely to submit to my sister's constant caterwauling just to obtain some peace."

"And this is how you speak of my mother?" asked Elizabeth with a raised eyebrow.

"She is *my* sister and I am an adult, so I may speak the truth if I wish," said Mr. Gardiner with a wink. Then with compassion in his countenance and in a tone of gentle affection, he continued: "Do not worry, Lizzy. Eventually this will all blow over. I cannot think his insistence will survive your continued refusal. Though it seems insurmountable now, I believe all shall turn out well.

"But I am afraid I have been away from the office for too long," said Mr. Gardiner, as he rose to his feet. "Perhaps you should take the opportunity to rest, Lizzy. I do not think there is anything that requires your attention at present."

"I believe I shall." Elizabeth favored her uncle with a wan smile as he repeated his farewells and departed a moment later, leaving Elizabeth alone with her aunt.

"Lizzy," said her aunt, once her uncle had left the room, "you are far too sensible to allow this to affect you. Your uncle and I shall allow nothing untoward to occur in our house, and I very much doubt your father will force you to return to Hertfordshire. It is hard, but the best thing to do is to forget this episode and continue on as you were."

"I shall try."

In truth, Elizabeth was not certain she could promise anything, but she would think on the matter once she gained the privacy of her room. At present she was simply tired—so very tired. She wished for nothing more than to lie down.

"Go ahead and retire, Elizabeth," said Mrs. Gardiner. "I shall see to it that you are not disturbed."

Taking her aunt's advice, Elizabeth climbed the stairs to her room. But though she lay down on the mattress almost immediately, sleep did not find her. Thoughts and remembrances of Pearce's behavior and threats ran through her mind, and she could get little rest. Her relations' words were comforting, but the sight of Pearce's disinterested face filled her mind, at odds with his seeming determination to have her. She wanted to believe Mr. Gardiner when he said that Pearce would eventually lose interest and give up, but she thought it was more likely he would persist. Whatever was she to do?

Chapter VI

The ensuing weeks were miserable. There was little joy to be had in Elizabeth's daily life and much to fear, and Elizabeth found herself spiraling down into a well of anger and despair. The one thought she held onto with a desperate strength was that she would not be forced to marry Pearce, no matter what happened. She would rather run away to America than to be subjected to such demeaning circumstances for the rest of her life!

The situation affected Elizabeth to the extent that for several days after her confrontation with the man, she was afraid to go outside. It was silly, she knew, but in her mind, images of the man appeared, phantasms ready to snatch her and carry her away to his manor, filled with horrors she could not begin to imagine. Elizabeth doubted he was lying in wait to capture her the moment she stepped from the house—he possessed far too much confidence in her eventual capitulation to resort to any such stratagems. But that did not stop Elizabeth from imagining all sorts of fates at the man's hands.

Mr. and Mrs. Gardiner were sympathetic to her plight, and they supported her whenever they were able. Elizabeth knew they suspected the extent of her despair, but it seemed like they understood that endless discussion on the matter only made her more upset, and they desisted, contenting themselves to an encouraging word here and there when they felt like she most needed it. Elizabeth was grateful for their forbearance and attempted to be happy, though she knew it was a miserable failure.

Her mother's continuing diatribes over the post only exacerbated the situation, of course, and much as Elizabeth had predicted, her uncle's letter to her mother did not help the situation. In fact, it might even have made it worse. Mrs. Bennet's next letter after the event was filled with accusations; she accused Elizabeth of misleading the Gardiners and inventing fanciful narrations of the man to bring Mr. Gardiner to her side of the conflict and demanded yet again that Elizabeth do her duty. Elizabeth did not even finish half the letter before she threw it into the fire in a fit of pique. All other letters were similarly treated—she would not stand for her mother's abuse.

Mrs. Gardiner was shocked when she discovered what Elizabeth was doing with the letters. The very next letter to come after her mother's abusive diatribe was mere days after the first, and Elizabeth, after being handed the post, casually looked at the paper, noted the sender, and moved to the fire, dropping it in without a second look.

"Lizzy!" said Mrs. Gardiner with a gasp. "Did you just throw your mother's letter in the fire?"

"I did, Aunt," said Elizabeth in a tone bereft of emotion. "My mother can see fit to do nothing but berate me, so that is the only treatment her words deserve."

As scandalized as Mrs. Gardiner appeared, she paused before speaking. Elizabeth thought from her countenance that Mrs. Gardiner was in agreement in substance, though she certainly was not happy with the perceived disrespect Elizabeth was showing.

At length her aunt sighed and moved to sit by Elizabeth. "I do not know that throwing your mother's letters into the fire is the proper way to handle this, Lizzy. If she were ever to find out, I do not doubt she would be offended and rightly so."

"And am I not offended by her continual attacks? She thinks nothing of accusing me of being selfish, saying that I will ruin the family, telling me that I am worthless, and generally laying all the family's misfortunes at my feet. If I am rendered uncivil by discarding her letters, then I suppose I shall have to be so. I will not read them."

Mrs. Gardiner hesitated for a moment, before she looked at Elizabeth and began to speak, though slowly. "I understand why you have refused the man, Lizzy. I imagine there are many women who would marry him for his situation alone, and though I have never wished to behave so myself, I can understand the lure. You have always been cut from a different cloth from your mother, so it is not a surprise you would wish for something more from your marriage.

"But you must understand the way of the world. As a young woman, you are completely at the mercy of your father until you come of age. You are fortunate your father is not a man to force his daughters against their will; many fathers would not even ask your opinion and would have compelled you to the altar whether you wished it or not."

Elizabeth sighed. "I know that, and I am grateful to Papa, Aunt."

"You must also understand that to many, your refusal *is* selfish, Lizzy."

When Elizabeth tried to protest, Mrs. Gardiner held up a hand, silencing her. "It is the truth. Your family is in a precarious situation. If your father died today, your family would be homeless, and at present it would be difficult for your uncles to assist. In a few years, when Mr. Gardiner's business has hopefully become profitable, we would be much better positioned to help support your mother and sisters. By marrying Mr. Pearce, you would be assuring their security. Mr. Pearce is certainly not the best of men, but he could provide for them."

"Do you think he would?" asked Elizabeth, feeling a little sullen at her aunt's words.

"I cannot say, of course." Mrs. Gardiner smiled a little ruefully. "My first impression of the man was not at all favorable, of course, but I cannot say that he would be unchristian and refuse to support them. But that chance is far better than what your family is facing now."

"So you think I should marry him."

A frown came over Mrs. Gardiner's face, and she regarded Elizabeth, making her feel as if she was a petulant child. At that moment, she did feel like one, though she thought she had the right.

"I have not said that, have I?"

Blushing, Elizabeth murmured that indeed her aunt had not.

"Your uncle and I understand you would be miserable in a marriage to a man such as Mr. Pearce. Regardless, it is not *our* decision to make. But we offer whatever support we are capable of giving. I understand why you have refused Mr. Pearce, but there is always more to consider than one's own point of view, and the situation of your family is one other consideration."

"Should my father and my mother not be responsible for the welfare of my family?" asked Elizabeth a little plaintively. "Why should it fall to their daughters to save them?"

With a sigh and a rueful smile, Mrs. Gardiner said: "You are correct, of course. It is that, along with the knowledge of how little contented you would be in marriage to him and our regard for you which induces us to support you. I do not blame you for refusing Mr. Pearce. In fact, I think I might have refused him myself. He truly is a loathsome man."

Elizabeth giggled. "He is indeed." She then turned a serious eye on her aunt. "I want you to know that I *do* understand what you are telling me. I am not insensible to my family's situation, nor do I misunderstand what is likely to happen, should none of us make a good marriage. But self-respect also has a place in my decision. I would be miserable with him; of that I am certain."

"I know you would be, Lizzy. But try to remember your mother's position in all this, and think on her fears for her future. Do not dismiss another's opinion just because it does not agree with your own."

"I will do my best," replied Elizabeth. "But I will not read my mother's letters. They all say the same thing anyway."

"Just do not consign them to the fire in my presence. What you do with them is your own business, but I do not wish to witness it."

Elizabeth felt a little better after her discussion with her aunt. Mrs. Gardiner had always been a true, steady presence in Elizabeth's life, and she knew she was blessed to have an uncle who was willing to assist.

From that day forward, the situation became a little easier to bear. Elizabeth began to again resume her previous schedule, though walks in the park figured a little more prominently than they had before. She felt that she required the solitude to think about her life and situation, and though she would venture out alone, she agreed with her aunt that if she was going to walk further than the nearby environs which were visible from the house, she would take a maid or footman with her. She never needed to abide by this stricture as she was careful to stay close to the edge of the park where she could be seen.

Mr. Bingley was much in evidence in those days, as he could often be found at the warehouse meeting with Mr. Gardiner, or at the townhouse visiting. He would often stay for dinner, and when he did, he would laugh and jest at how much he was imposing on his friends' hospitality.

"I dare say it will take me a sixmonth to overcome my debt to you, Mrs. Gardiner," said he one evening after he had once again dined with the family. "When my sisters arrive, I shall have to be entertaining you every week in order to reset the imbalance which has sprung up between us."

"I think we can dispense with that, Mr. Bingley," replied Mrs. Gardiner with a laugh. "A bachelor like yourself, living alone in London, would no doubt subsist on the fare offered at your club, or at certain eating establishments, where you would not likely eat a hearty meal. I am happy we are able to assist you."

"And I appreciate it very sincerely," said Mr. Bingley. "The townhouse is a lonely place at present, and I have been busy trying to hire servants for it. I wish to have everything ready for when my sisters arrive."

"That does you credit, sir," said Elizabeth. "I can imagine there would be nothing so tedious to a woman who has not partaken in London society as to have to spend her days hiring servants."

Mr. Bingley laughed. "I can tell you with certainty that it is. After all, I am naught but a *man* who finds himself in the same situation. I should much rather attend a dance!"

"You are fond of dancing, sir?"

"I am indeed. There is something appealing about a dance floor where one may lose oneself in the steps and engage in conversation with charming young ladies. I never miss the chance to dance."

"Then you must come to Meryton and attend our assemblies. There is almost always a scarcity of gentlemen, so you would be quite welcome."

Mr. Bingley replied that he would be happy to and the subject changed. As the man continued to speak with her aunt and uncle, Elizabeth watched him, and she noted that very little in his manners had altered. He was still happy and amiable, and he paid every attention to Elizabeth when they were in company. Only it was easy to see that he did not do it from a sense of admiration—rather he seemed to be the same with everyone whom he met. He was simply a garrulous sort of man.

Though Elizabeth was not disappointed in his lack of further interest, she thought her aunt and uncle were. She knew they considered it to be an easy solution to her problem, but they were not about to influence the matter, and when it became evident nothing further would develop between them, they subsided with good grace, though they were not above teasing Elizabeth for the handsome man who engaged her in lively conversation whenever her was able. Elizabeth laughed along with them, but almost never said anything further.

Life continued in this manner through the rapidly shortening days of October. The weather deteriorated as time wore on, and Elizabeth began to feel hints of the onset of winter, though for the most part it remained pleasant.

On a day in late October, Elizabeth felt restless and unaccountably unable to focus on her usual pursuits. Having nothing else to do, she thought to take a walk in the park. But also feeling unequal to the thought of being alone, she determined to take her youngest cousin—Miss Emily Gardiner—along with her on her excursion.

When informed of her intention, Mrs. Gardiner looked at her carefully, but she was apparently satisfied with what she saw, as she simply waved Elizabeth away.

"Emily has been as restless as you have all morning, so perhaps it is for the best that she goes out with you. Make certain to bundle up, as the wind is a little chilly."

Agreeing, Elizabeth gathered the child to her and wrapped her in her clothes with extra blankets for added warmth. Then, donning her own outer gear, she slipped out the door and turned down the street, making for the nearby park. It was indeed a little cool as her aunt had suggested, and though the wind was nothing more than a light movement of air, it was still in her face and rendered her cheeks rosy as she walked. Elizabeth clutched little Emily to her breast to ensure she was not adversely affected by the wind as she walked.

When they gained the park, Elizabeth wandered about her usual haunts for a time, appreciating the freedom to walk as she chose. The trees were largely now bare of their verdant summer mantle, and the blanket of leaves, a riot of yellows, reds, browns, and even a hint of greens, eddied in the breeze, forming little whirlwinds of colors where the air currents made themselves known.

In her arms, Emily giggled and babbled happily as Elizabeth showed her the sights. Elizabeth longed for the wonder and excitement of the newness of the world, without determined suitors and odious men disturbing her peace. Would that it could all be so simple again.

At length the child tired and promptly fell asleep in Elizabeth's arms, and feeling the burn of holding her for so long, Elizabeth sought out a park bench whereby she might rest for a few moments before returning to the house. There were several benches along the boulevard at the edge of the park, and Elizabeth chose one at random, gratefully easing onto its surface and allowing the child to settle into her lap. Though Emily squirmed a little in protest for being disturbed, she once again settled in, continuing to sleep without a care in the world.

As she sat, Elizabeth glanced around, taking in the sights all about her. They were in the middle of one of the busiest cities in the world, and there was evidence of humanity all around her. She longed for the open fields and woods of her home. But such was denied her at present. There was little to be done.

As she sat, the frustrations which had been stewing in her mind came to the fore, and she found herself feeling peevish all over again. And the sudden need to speak of her hurt and anger found release in speaking to the sleeping child in her arms. At least the baby would not judge, would not berate her for selfishness or demand she do her duty.

"I do not know what to do," said Elizabeth to the child.

The baby stirred slightly in her arms, but she went on sleeping.

"Oh, to be as free as you are," said Elizabeth. "Nothing but the wonders of nature and the newness of everything in life to consider. I doubt *your* mother will ever berate you for not doing your duty or insist you marry a loathsome man for nothing more than the wish to secure her own security."

Elizabeth sighed. "There I go again. I am being unfair to Mother. She is assuredly thinking of us all when she insists I marry Mr. Pearce. But she does not understand that she is not being fair to me. She does not understand that not all people have the same opinion of security and happiness as she possesses herself.

"The fact of the matter is that Mr. Pearce's proposal *is* an eligible one. The man possesses an income of two thousand five hundred per annum, and when he inherits his relation's estate, he will have another three thousand at his disposal. That sum is not insubstantial. If father's estate brought in half that amount, I am certain he would be very well pleased. Perhaps he might even have provided for us all better than he has."

Falling silent for a moment, Elizabeth thought of the situation and her objections to it, and when she spoke again, her voice carried a hint of pensive annoyance.

"Aunt is right; there are many young ladies who would jump at the chance to marry a man who could provide for them in such a manner. Why does he single me out and insist, over my protests, that it must be me? Even Jane would accept him, I am sure, as she would no doubt feel it her duty to provide for her family."

Then a sensation of extreme distaste settled over Elizabeth, and she shuddered at the mere thought. "Of course Jane cannot marry him, and I would not allow her to make such a decision. She would be even more miserable than I would, and her gentle disposition and reticence would not allow her to take her husband to task for his poor behavior.

"It is well that Mr. Pearce does not understand the weapon he could wield against me. If he turned his attention on Jane, I would capitulate for no other reason than to spare her the indignity of being bound to such a man. Let us hope that he never realizes this."

The flow of words exhausted for the moment, Elizabeth fell silent.

The sounds of the bustling city assaulted her ears, and the slight wind kissed her cheeks. She gathered the sleeping child closer to her breast to shelter her from the wind. It would be time to return to the townhouse soon, but Elizabeth could not face it at the moment.

"I simply cannot do it. The man's money means nothing to me. The fact that he is a philanderer of the worst sort, that he fathers children at will and then pays to send the women away with his loathsome progeny, his insulting words and his disgusting pride render it impossible to ever marry such a man. Were he as rich as Midas, still I could not force myself to marry him. That way leads to misery and an unhappy life. I will not live like my mother, laughed at and disrespected at every turn by my husband.

"I simply do not know how I shall cope. Winter comes and by all indication it looks like it might be a long and hard one. Mother, vindictive as she is, has permitted me only a few worn dresses and this thin autumn coat. What will I do if I am confined to uncle's house for the winter because I have no garments to keep me warm? I am certain I shall go mad."

With a sigh, Elizabeth looked down at the child in her arms fondly. Little Emily was sleeping soundly, her mouth slightly open. She appeared angelic in repose.

"It is not as if I do not wish for children, you know," said Elizabeth. "In fact, I would be happy with an entire brood of little ones pulling at my skirts, demanding treats, that I sit and play and read to them. As long as they are all as beautiful as you, I know that I shall have no reason to repine. I simply believe I should have some say in determining the identity of the father of those children."

A sudden gust of wind broke Elizabeth from her reverie and she looked up, startled. The sky had grown gray as she had sat, and the wind had grown stronger. It was time to return home.

Carefully readjusting the child in her arms, Elizabeth rose to her feet. With a quick glance around the area, she made to depart, when the sight of a man watching her caused her to freeze in her tracks.

He was a tall man, a shock of dark hair arranged haphazardly on his head, and his piercing blue eyes seemed to see right through her. He stood no more than a few yards from the bench, and though he had not approached and did not regard her in a menacing fashion, his very being screamed an ability to intimidate should he choose to do so. And yet, his face was finely chiseled, almost aristocratic in form, and his bearing was regal. This was an important man, and one who was used to dictating his will upon others.

When he said nothing, Elizabeth began to feel uncomfortable, and she dropped into a hint of a curtsey, saying, "Sir," under her breath, before she turned and began to walk away. The feeling of his eyes hard upon her back stayed with her as she walked, making her uncomfortable, wishing she could run all the way back to her uncle's house. She thought she almost would have, if she thought she would not look like a silly girl, frightened of her own shadow.

After she had walked for some moments, Elizabeth, feeling an almost unbearable tension, risked a glance back at the man. The place where he had stood was empty.

Elizabeth let out a great breath of air she had not known she was holding and chided herself for being such a silly little girl. The man had obviously looked at her when she had arisen and not because of any interest or ill intent.

Feeling better, Elizabeth hurried along her way, arriving at the house within a few moments.

"Elizabeth!" exclaimed her aunt as she entered. "I was about to go looking for you. You were gone much longer than I had anticipated."

"My apologies, Aunt," said Elizabeth, feeling chastened, though she knew that was not her aunt's intention. "I believe I lost track of the time. But I am grateful for it. Emily and I enjoyed ourselves immensely, though your youngest betrayed me by falling asleep in the middle of our walk."

Aunt Gardiner smiled. "I am happy you took her, for she seems to be much more content now than when you left. Perhaps she will take after you, my dear, in your penchant for walks. I must own that I am not certain that is precisely desirable."

Laughing, Elizabeth handed the baby—who was just beginning to wake—to her mother. "I will be quite happy to impart all I know to your daughter, should she wish it. It would be great fun to have another so like me."

"Heaven help us!" said Mrs. Gardiner.

Then she leaned forward and kissed Elizabeth's cheek, before turning and departing with her daughter, leaving Elizabeth to remove her outer wear and leave it in the capable hands of the housekeeper.

Feeling fatigued, Elizabeth climbed the stairs to her room and refreshed herself in the basin of water waiting for her. It was chilly, but she appreciated it nonetheless. Then she went to her bed and lay down on the top, grateful for its softness.

Almost against her will, Elizabeth's thoughts meandered back to the man she had seen as she was leaving the park. Though such matters had almost passed unnoticed in the surprise and consternation of the moment, Elizabeth recalled the man's dark hair and blue eyes, and the strong jaw and prominent cheekbones, and she realized that he had been quite a handsome man. In fact, she thought that he was quite the handsomest man she had ever met and one she would enjoy receiving the attentions of.

Then Elizabeth chastised herself for such thoughts. There was more to a man than a handsome mien, upright bearing, and broad shoulders; Mr. Pearce possessed all those virtues, after all. For all she knew, the man in the park possessed pride which would put Mr. Pearce to shame. There was nothing about the man that suggested he was of good temper or that he would even consider paying any attention to a penniless country miss who was at present not even in a situation to call herself the daughter of a gentleman. For that matter, Elizabeth could not even be certain the man was a gentleman himself.

But try as she might, Elizabeth could not shake the thought that the attentions of such a handsome man would be something indeed. And when she fell asleep, she saw the bluest of eyes in her dreams, thought herself to be in heaven when the man professed his love and whisked her off to his estate, where the name "Pearce" was never spoken. For a while, Mr. Pearce, her mother, odious marriage proposals, and banishments, were purged from her mind in favor of pleasanter dreams.

Chapter VII

As promised, Mr. Bingley invited the Gardiners to dinner later in October, laughingly claiming that he was repaying in some small measure all the meals he had enjoyed with them at Gracechurch Street. Though the Gardiners were adamant in insisting that Mr. Bingley did not owe them anything, Elizabeth knew they were anticipating the event keenly, curious as to the sisters and brother-in-law of whom they had heard so much, as was Elizabeth herself. Perhaps more importantly, the evening at Mr. Bingley's house was a release of sorts from the continual drudgery of Elizabeth's situation and a welcome relief from her brooding.

At the appointed time, Elizabeth donned the evening gown that her uncle had provided for her and entered the carriage with her relations for the journey to the Bingley townhouse. There was a smattering of conversation as they rode, with much of it speculation concerning what they would find with the Bingleys that evening.

"The address is a fashionable one," said Mr. Gardiner as the carriage rolled through the streets. "Mr. Bingley's father has indeed been successful over the years to allow him to purchase such a residence."

"So the Bingleys live amongst the cream of society, do they?" asked Elizabeth.

Laughing, Mr. Gardiner replied: "I do not believe they live amongst dukes and duchesses, Lizzy. But though they do not live in an *exclusive* area, it is still closer to high society than Gracechurch Street. I believe Mr. Bingley's father was in business for many years, which enabled him to afford such extravagance."

"And you hope to do the same?"

"There is more to life than simply climbing the ladder of society," said Mr. Gardiner. "While I hope to be able to provide for my wife and children, so that they will never want, the attractions of high society are limited to me. I appreciate the convenience of my house to my warehouses, and our frugal way of living has made possible the business merger which should increase our consequence."

"We would like to purchase an estate someday," interjected Mrs. Gardiner. "As you know, my father, though a parson, was the third son of a gentleman, and as such, I do possess some connections to the gentry."

"I hope that all your dreams come true," said Elizabeth sincerely. "I believe you would make a fine gentleman, Uncle."

"Perhaps," said Mr. Gardiner, displaying a cheery grin. "But it shall not come to pass for some years yet. For now I am firmly ensconced in the concerns of my business, and I am quite happy here, I assure you."

As Mr. Gardiner had predicted, Mr. Bingley's house was in a fashionable district, and if it was not one of the imposing townhouses which housed London's elite, still it was a handsome building. As the coach pulled up, a footman stepped forward to open the door, and Mr. Gardiner stepped out before turning to assist first his wife and then his niece. There, on the front step of the house, stood Mr. Bingley, along with a tall woman who greatly resembled him.

"Mr. Gardiner!' cried Mr. Bingley as he strode up to greet them. "Welcome to my humble abode. I cannot tell you how happy I am to finally be able to receive you here."

"Thank you, Mr. Bingley," said Mr. Gardiner, as he shook the younger man's hand. "We were happy to accept your invitation."

"Excellent!"

"Charles, shall we not invite our guests into the house?" asked the woman by his side. "This wind is biting."

"But of course," said Mr. Bingley. He turned and offered his arm as an escort to Elizabeth, with his sister on his other arm. "We can perform the introductions once we attain the warmth of the house."

The interior of the house was pleasant, yet Elizabeth could discern its age as well. The tiled floors had been laid with care and had withstood with test of time admirably, but the wallpaper in places was a little faded, and the furnishings appeared a little worn. If Elizabeth had to guess, she would have said that Mr. Bingley's father had purchased the house not long before his death, and little had been done to update it to a more current style. Nonetheless, it was an attractive abode, spacious and airy, and Elizabeth thought it suited Mr. Bingley. No doubt he would wish to entertain his friends, and he could amply do so with the space available.

The party stopped at a door down the hall toward the back of the house, and when a footman opened the door, they stepped into a large sitting room where two others awaited them. The woman was much shorter than the woman on Mr. Bingley's arm, and though handsome, her countenance appeared disinterested. The man was a little corpulent, though obviously not much older than Mr. Bingley, and he was a little homely.

"Well, now that we are all here, please allow me to perform the introductions." Indicating Elizabeth and her relations, Mr. Bingley said, "Hurst, Louisa, Caroline, this is Mr. Gardiner, Mrs. Gardiner, and their niece, Miss Elizabeth Bennet. Mr. Gardiner, Miss Gardiner, Miss Bennet, my relations, Mr. Humphrey Hurst, Mrs. Louisa Hurst, my sister, and my younger sister, Miss Caroline Bingley."

A chorus of "delighted to make your acquaintance" filled the room, and the newly acquainted eyed one another in the manner of those who have just been introduced and do not know how to proceed with conversation. By the order of the introductions, Elizabeth thought that Mr. Hurst must be a gentleman, or at least the son of a gentleman. If he was in trade like her uncle, she thought that the introductions would have been reversed.

Once she was able to truly take stock of Mr. Bingley's relations, Elizabeth was able to form some quick opinions that she was by no means certain were actuality. Mr. Hurst did not say much, and if his glass of amber liquid, which Elizabeth assumed to be brandy, was any indication, he preferred to keep it close at hand. The Bingley sisters were handsome women, though the elder plainer than the younger. She was also only about Elizabeth's height, while Miss Bingley stood several inches taller. They both shared Mr. Bingley's distinctive shock of red hair, and at least in Miss Bingley's case, little fashion sense—though the woman was impeccably attired, the color of her dress was a rather unattractive shade of yellow which clashed with her hair. Elizabeth thought the woman would appear to much greater advantage if she wore shades of green or even blue.

"Well, this is a fine to do!" exclaimed Mr. Bingley after a short period in which little was said. "I had expected at least *some* conversation. Anyone seeing us might think that we did not possess a tongue amongst the lot of us."

General laughter erupted, though Elizabeth thought it was a little forced in the case of his sisters—Mr. Hurst contented himself with a grunt, reinforcing Elizabeth's rapidly forming opinion of the man being a bit of a bore. She felt it incumbent on herself to respond, to further the conversation.

"That is the way it is amongst those newly acquainted, is it not? We must take stock of one another and discover subjects which are safe to canvass before we may speak freely."

"Perhaps," said Mr. Bingley, "but in a group which contains you and me, Miss Bennet, I would hope that we are able to find ample topics on which to converse."

"You *are* adept at such things, Charles," said Miss Bingley, speaking up for the first time.

With that, conversation did begin to spring up, and the company naturally gravitated to two groups centered on the three gentleman and the four ladies. Thus, though Elizabeth was unable to gain much more of an opinion about Mr. Hurst, the sisters became less of an enigma as the night wore on.

"I understand your husband has been in business for some time, Mrs. Gardiner," said Miss Bingley.

"Yes, he has," replied Mrs. Gardiner, "though not so long as your family. His father left him with an inheritance which he used to lay the groundwork of his current success. But his father was a solicitor, not a man of business."

"The Bingleys have been in the import business for more than fifty years," said Mrs. Hurst. She did not say anything else and her tone indicated a considerable disinterest for the subject.

"Then your father, and perhaps his father before him, possessed considerable business acumen."

"I believe he did," said Miss Bingley. "But it has been his particular wish that we join the ranks of the landed, and only his early death prevented those dreams from being realized. We wish to leave the sphere our father inhabited behind."

"A commendable goal," said Mrs. Gardiner. "I wish you every success. Elizabeth's father is the proprietor of an estate which has been in his family for more than two centuries."

Miss Bingley appeared to be impressed with that bit of intelligence, and she looked at Elizabeth with a little more interest than had characterized her attentions before. But before she could say anything more, the housekeeper entered to announce dinner, and the company moved into the dining room.

The dinner was exquisite—a four course meal which Elizabeth's mother would have felt acceptable. The flavors were exquisite, the soup excellent, and the pheasant roasted to a turn. Elizabeth's aunt set a good table, even when it was only the family dining together, but clearly this was a formal meal, and Elizabeth thought it had been presented with the intention to impress. This opinion was confirmed when Mr. Gardiner complimented Miss Bingley on the fare and was rewarded with the woman's preening response.

"We have engaged a French cook for our London house. I expect that we will be entertaining often, and I do not doubt Charles's connections will soon result in some very lofty acquaintances indeed."

Elizabeth was impressed with her uncle for the way he ignored her self-congratulatory and supercilious statement by smiling and saying: "Your cook has prepared a magnificent meal. I thank you for inviting us this evening."

"Merely a trifle, Mr. Gardiner."

Elizabeth raised her napkin to her mouth to hide the smile which threatened to break forth at the woman's absurdity. She appeared to think she was the very queen herself, rather than the daughter of a tradesman whose brother had not yet even purchased an estate. Elizabeth knew that Miss Bingley was the lowest ranked person in the room, by virtue of her single status and the fact that Elizabeth was the daughter of a gentleman, but to hear her speak, one would almost think she considered herself to be the highest. Her behavior only worsened as the night wore on.

It was after dinner when the gentlemen and ladies separated that Elizabeth began to take the true measure of her hostess, and the more she learned of the woman, the less impressed she was. Miss Bingley had begun the evening speaking civilly to them—as well she might, for it was Mr. Gardiner's business acumen and money purchasing part of the Bingley business which would make it possible for Miss Bingley to ascend to a higher sphere. But as the night wore on, her questions became more intrusive, and her manners became less friendly.

"So you are the daughter of a gentleman, Miss Bennet," said Miss Bingley.

Elizabeth thought the woman had been waiting for an opportunity to bring up the subject. As Mrs. Gardiner was in conversation with Mrs.

Hurst, she was able to speak with Elizabeth without interruption.

"Yes, Miss Bingley," said Elizabeth. "My father has been master of the estate as long as I remember. He was born quite late in his father's life and inherited as a young man."

"And where is your father's estate located?"

"Near the town of Meryton in Hertfordshire. It is west of the great north road which means it receives less traffic. But it is still a goodly sized town, and there are a number of estates nearby."

Miss Bingley seemed to consider, and when she spoke again it was with a hesitant, almost searching quality.

"And the estate will then be inherited by your brother?"

"I have no brother, Miss Bingley."

"Oh, my apologies, Miss Bennet. I did not mean to offend."

"I am not offended. But I am the second of five daughters. My eldest sister, I believe, is about your age, and a sweeter, more angelic woman you could not find."

Though the smile on the woman's face did not alter, Elizabeth thought she detected a cooling in the woman's manners, as if something she had said had caused Miss Bingley to think less of her. She pondered Elizabeth's statement for some moments, before she smiled and said:

"That must make for a chaotic household. Why, I remember times when my antics with my sister would push our mother to her wits' end. I cannot imagine having three more sisters as part of the bargain."

Laughing, Elizabeth confirmed her words, saying: "It can be tumultuous at times. My youngest sisters are only fourteen and twelve and they are already high-spirited girls. My father often seeks refuge in his study when the din becomes unbearable. He is to be pitied, being the only man in the house."

"It must be difficult," said Miss Bingley. "Surely a man wishes to have an heir to whom he might teach and raise in a manner which would be a credit to him."

"I am certain my father wishes he had been so blessed."

"But surely your sister shall remain close after her marriage? I assume the estate will become part of her dowry."

This was the crux of the conversation, Elizabeth was certain, and though the question was a little crass, it was clear Miss Bingley did not think enough of her to warrant a subtler line of questioning.

"My father's estate is actually entailed away on a cousin, Miss Bingley."

"Ah, perhaps that is best. In many cases, estates have been broken up to provide for younger siblings. Your father was wise to have instituted such a restriction."

Though Elizabeth knew the entail was actually from her great-grandfather's time and it would end with the inheritance of the next proprietor, she decided it was not worth it to illuminate Miss Bingley any further concerning the state of her family's situation. The conversation digressed from that point and several moments were spent in more general discourse. However, the topic soon turned under Miss Bingley's subtle guidance to another which must have some interest for the woman.

"It was my father's specific wish that my sister and I attend school with all the young ladies of the sphere which he meant to raise us to," said Miss Bingley when the subject of education had arisen. "As such, Louisa and I both received the best education and made several valuable connections."

In spite of herself, Elizabeth was curious. As she had never attended school herself, she had often wondered what it would have been like, and as there were few in the area around Meryton who *had* attended, she had not been able to learn much.

"Where did you attend?"

"At a large seminary in Oxfordshire." Miss Bingley preened, and leaned forward, as if imparting a great secret. "It is an exclusive school, you understand, Miss Bennet. Many daughters of the elite are sent there to complete their education."

"And how did you find it? I can imagine it was a great honor to attend with such ladies."

A shadow passed over Miss Bingley's face, and Elizabeth had to laugh to herself. Miss Bingley's father might have wished his daughters to gain the best education he could purchase, but if her guess was correct, Elizabeth thought those daughters of influential men had been less than enthusiastic about accepting the daughters of a tradesman.

"It was wonderful, Miss Bennet," said Miss Bingley, seemingly pushing aside any such unpleasant memories in much the same way one would swat at a fly buzzing around one's head. "I have learned all the modern languages, honed my skill on the pianoforte and the harp, and gained all of the accomplishments deemed necessary by high society."

"Then I congratulate you," said Elizabeth. "Diligence is required for such skill to be attained."

"Great diligence indeed." Miss Bingley paused and looked at Elizabeth, asking: "And what of your experiences? Where did you attend school?"

"I did not attend, Miss Bingley. My father saw to my education, and

I am most grateful to him, for he imparted to me a love of the written word."

Miss Bingley seemed shocked. "You did not attend? What of your need to learn of languages, what of your skill on an instrument? Surely your father could not teach you all of this."

"Father is fluent in several languages," said Elizabeth. "I am well versed in French and Italian, though I will own that reading Latin can be a trial. German has always been a little incomprehensible, though I can muddle through if necessary. As for the pianoforte, I never wanted for masters when I showed the interest. I have improved my playing substantially while staying with my uncle, as there are fewer demands on the pianoforte than at my home."

"But what of drawing, painting, netting purses, embroidery, and all those other things which comprise accomplishment?"

"Of drawing and painting I have little interest, and less skill. As for the others, I can do any of them with passing skill, though they are not activities which I enjoy to any great degree."

As Elizabeth spoke, Miss Bingley's countenance became ever frostier, and by the time Elizabeth was finished speaking, Miss Bingley was positively looking down her nose in disdain. The only word which passed her lips after Elizabeth finished speaking was a clipped, "I see." After that, she turned back to Mrs. Gardiner and her sister and began speaking of their journey to London. It was only a few moments later when the gentlemen entered the room and greeted the ladies cheerfully. Or at least Mr. Bingley and Mr. Gardiner did—Mr. Hurst went straight for the brandy decanter and poured himself a healthy portion before sitting beside a table and amusing himself with a selection of sweetmeats which sat thereon.

"You ladies appear to be getting on splendidly," said Mr. Bingley as he approached.

"Quite," said Miss Bingley, and though she refrained from looking at Elizabeth, Elizabeth could nonetheless feel the scorn directed at her.

But Mr. Bingley remained oblivious and after a few moments called for some music. Elizabeth was pressed to go first, and she did so after a little coaxing. She chose a piece she knew well and thought she acquitted herself well when the end of the song arrived. Mrs. Hurst and Miss Bingley succeeded her at the instrument, and Elizabeth thought that in this matter, Miss Bingley's pride was not overstated. The woman's playing was fine indeed.

It was not long after that the Gardiners stated their intention to depart and thanked their host for a wonderful evening. Their host and hostess walked them to the door where the farewells were completed and wishes for future meetings were stated.

"I hope to have our gathering repeated many times in the future," said Mr. Bingley, grinning as was his wont. "Caroline and I were happy to have you with us this evening, were we not, Caroline?"

"Quite," said Miss Bingley, her only response.

Mr. Bingley appeared to be oblivious to his sister's thinly veiled disdain. "I anticipate a close relationship, now that we shall be partners. And I could not ask for a better man with whom to share the burdens of business."

"I, too, am impressed with you, Mr. Bingley," said Mr. Gardiner. "You are a good man, as your father was before. I believe he would be quite proud."

A sense of loss, coupled with a feeling of gratitude, seemed to come over Mr. Bingley, and even his sister did not appear to be impervious to the compliment. Mr. Bingley stepped forward and grasped Mr. Gardiner's hand, clutching tightly.

"Thank you, Mr. Gardiner. I would do anything to know that my father was proud of the way I have handled his concerns. It means much to hear it from a good man and a man of business such as yourself."

"You are very welcome, Mr. Bingley, but it is only the truth. Let us hasten the final agreement so that you will be free to focus on your father's wish of becoming a gentleman, eh?"

Laughter bubbled from Mr. Bingley's lips. "I agree. And thank you again."

The final farewells were said, and the Gardiner party stepped into the carriage. Soon, they had pulled away from the Bingley residence.

"Well, Lizzy?" said Mr. Gardiner once they had travelled some distance down the road. "What did you think of the evening?"

"Very interesting. Mr. Bingley was as amiable as ever, but his sisters are quite different."

"I had no doubt you would discern that," said Mr. Gardiner, his eyes twinkling in merriment.

"You were speaking with Miss Bingley for some time," said Mrs. Gardiner. "Do you care to share the substance of your conversation?"

Elizabeth laughed. "I believe Miss Bingley was attempting to determine if my connections and accomplishments were grand enough to warrant her approval."

"Surely not!" exclaimed Mrs. Gardiner.

"I assure you it is not far from the truth, Aunt. She wished to know of the state of my family and our connections, and she was not happy to learn that though my father is a gentleman whose estate has been in the family for many years, I have no brother and that estate is entailed. Furthermore, she seemed quite proud of the fact that she attended an exclusive seminary and contemptuous of my education which was provided by my father."

Mr. Gardiner shook his head. "Mr. Bingley did mention that his sisters—especially the younger—were sometimes a trial."

"It matters little, Uncle," said Elizabeth with a dismissive wave of her hand. "I was not offended by Miss Bingley's airs, only amused. Little though she may wish to acknowledge the fact, *she* was the lowest ranked person in the room tonight, which renders her conceit even more humorous."

"I expect that once Mr. Bingley cedes control of the operation of the business to me, we shall see his sisters but little."

"That would be agreeable to *me*," said Elizabeth with a laugh. "Mrs. Hurst seems like she is not a bad sort, but both she and her husband seem to be quite dull. But of Miss Bingley's society, I believe a little goes a long way."

Laughter filled the carriage and the subject was changed. Soon, they had arrived back at Gracechurch Street and had retired for the evening.

The days of Elizabeth's residence at Gracechurch Street lengthened, and Elizabeth found herself settling into life with the Gardiners again. The circumstances were not forgotten, but once the immediacy of Mr. Pearce's behavior faded, she found herself able to shunt it to the back of her mind.

In those days, though Elizabeth had often thought the inclement weather of autumn threatened, it remained stubbornly fair, and if a chill wind did blow at times, it was nearly always followed by cheery days of sunshine and warmth.

Elizabeth could not but be grateful for Mother Nature's forbearance, as it afforded her the continued opportunity to escape the house. The oncoming winter was still a concern, as she was still possessed of few dresses and no appropriate winter clothing, but she decided, with a philosophical bent, that she need not worry about things which were beyond her control.

Her uncle, however, when he learned of Elizabeth's fears by chance one day, was quick to admonish.

"You can sometimes be as silly as a goose, Lizzy," said he, a stern expression fixed on her, though Elizabeth could easily tell it was mixed with amusement. "Did you think that I would allow you to go cold this winter, should you reside with us throughout?"

"But, Uncle, I do not wish to be a burden."

Shaking his head, her uncle said: "You must remove such a notion from your mind, Lizzy. You are family. You are most certainly *not* a burden."

Mr. Gardiner reached forward and touched the sleeve of her dress which she noticed had begun to fray, and he continued: "For that matter, do you think your father would allow his favorite to go without?"

"He banished me here," said Elizabeth, a sullen sort of despair welling up within her.

"In order to remove you from your mother's censure," replied Mr. Gardiner. "I have been corresponding with him, and he has sent some money which you may use to properly attire yourself for winter."

All at once Elizabeth felt her throat tightening up with emotion. "Papa has sent money for me to purchase dresses?"

"Yes, he has, child."

"But what of Mama?"

Mr. Gardiner only regarded Elizabeth with exasperation. "Since when does your mother have anything to do with Longbourn's budget, other than to request more money from your father than she ought?"

A tentative smile settled on Elizabeth's face. "Never."

"Then I am certain your father can arrange to have some money sent for you, while not informing his wife. Now it is not enough to afford an entirely new wardrobe, Lizzy. Your father was not expecting the expense of clothing a daughter, when she already possesses a suitable wardrobe. But there is enough to provide you with the ability to purchase items which will keep you warm for the winter and, perhaps, a few new dresses as well. I suggest you purchase another evening dress and a few for everyday use."

"I will make an appointment with the modiste," said Mrs. Gardiner cheerily.

Through teary eyes, Elizabeth smiled at her uncle and stepped forward to embrace him, relishing the feeling of his strong arms settling around her.

"Thank you, Uncle, for taking such prodigious care of me."

"You are welcome, my dear. Please repay me by attempting to be happy. I would appreciate the return of the effervescent Lizzy who existed before coming to London."

"I shall try."

And so it was that on one of the last days in October, Elizabeth, clothed in a new dress with her new winter pelisse providing warmth, stepped out of the Gardiners' townhouse and made her way from the house, intending to take a turn about the nearby environs of the park. There was almost no wind that morning, and Elizabeth walked at a quick pace, enjoying the feel of the light autumn breeze and the way the cooler air served to dampen the smells of the city, which were sometimes unbearable in the summer months.

Soon, Elizabeth entered the park, and as she walked along the now-familiar paths, she thought of her life and her present circumstances. What she wished for most was some news from home, but no doubt due to her mother's decree, she had not heard from anyone other than Jane and her father, Jane writing in secret, while her father jotted down a few lines here and there whenever he felt the urge. Mr. Bennet had never been a great correspondent.

What of Charlotte? What of the rest of the Lucases, the Longs, the Gouldings? Elizabeth had not had any news for so long she wondered what was happening in the lives of her friends and neighbors. Of course, since Jane was required to write in secret, Elizabeth could not respond and ask for news, not that Jane would be able to write much in any case. But that did not stop Elizabeth from wishing she was able to do just that

"Excuse me, Miss."

Startled to be thus addressed, Elizabeth turned to look at a tall man who was standing nearby watching her. It was the man she had seen in the park the day she had come with Emily.

Chapter VIII

So startled was Elizabeth that for a moment after the man spoke, she thought to flee. Common sense reasserted itself, however, and she looked the man over, noting how he was watching her with intensity written on his brow, but no intimidation or any other quality which might cause her to fear for her safety. In fact, though he was a tall man and held himself with a self-assured air, he appeared to be nervous, if the twisting of his walking stick and the way he watched her through lidded eyes were any indication. Almost immediately, Elizabeth relaxed—she had no reason to be afraid.

"Yes?" replied she politely. "May I help you?"

Her words seemed to relax the man, and he approached a few steps, saying: "I am sorry for speaking, miss. I understand it is not precisely the proper way to be introduced, but as we have no common acquaintance to perform the office, I had thought to stretch propriety a little."

It was *not* completely proper, Elizabeth knew, but as they were standing inside a park where anyone could see, she decided it would not hurt. As she was certain this man was of a higher social sphere than Elizabeth inhabited herself, it was up to her to introduce herself first.

"My name is Elizabeth Bennet, sir."

"Fitzwilliam Darcy, at your service," said the man, and he bowed to Elizabeth's curtsey.

When he straightened, Elizabeth looked him in the eye, and apparently the question was writ upon her face, for he began speaking.

"I have no doubt you remember me from last week when you walked in the park with a babe in your arms?"

"Yes, I do, sir. The child is my aunt's youngest."

"I had inferred that," said Mr. Darcy, nodding. "I have returned to this park daily since then, hoping to meet you again, since I had not the wit to approach you that day."

Astonished, Elizabeth could only blurt out: "You have searched for me?"

Mr. Darcy released a self-deprecating laugh. "I have indeed. I also rode along the street in the direction you walked, hoping to catch sight of you. I had almost despaired of seeing you again, but it appears all my attempts have been worthwhile, considering our meeting here today."

As surprised as she had been before, Elizabeth could only gape. The man had been searching for her? For what purpose? But when she finally managed to ask—in language which was only just coherent—he demurred, pointing to a small café not far down the street.

"I shall explain all, but if you please, will you not take some coffee or tea while we speak? I believe the inside of the café will be much more comfortable."

Elizabeth hesitated for a moment—her aunt was not expecting her to return just yet, so there was no difficulty with respect to time. But as improper as it might have been to introduce themselves to each other, spending further time in one another's company could only be less proper, especially without the sanction and presence of her uncle.

But as Elizabeth thought of these issues and gathered herself to deny his request, she looked in his eyes and saw something she had not expected. Mr. Darcy was a strong, confident man—this she could tell by nothing more than the way he carried himself. However, he was watching her, an expression of hope fixed on her which almost seemed pathetic. She did not know why it was so important that he speak to her, but it suddenly felt like it would be churlish to deny him. And so she found herself speaking the words she knew she had perhaps better not.

"Very well, sir."

Elizabeth was taken aback by the brilliantly beaming smile he directed at her, and she thought that a man as handsome as Mr. Darcy must cause women to swoon all around him by the force of nothing more than his smile. Gathering herself, Elizabeth rested her hand lightly on his offered arm, and they made their way down the sidewalk. As they walked, Elizabeth's curiosity got the better of her, and she looked up at him and said:

"Excuse me, sir, but I infer that you are not a resident of this area. Is that correct?"

"No, indeed, Miss Bennet. In fact, my home lies in the Mayfair district. The offices of my solicitor are not far from here, which is why I was in this area the other day."

Elizabeth's eyebrows climbed her forehead in shock. Mayfair was in actuality quite close to the Bingley townhouse, but it was even further removed from Mr. Bingley's home than his home was from Mr. Gardiner's. The cream of society lived in Mayfair. This man must possess wealth and connections aplenty if he resided in such an exclusive area.

"I cannot imagine what a man who lives in a place like Mayfair could want with a girl like me," said she. Then she clasped her hand to her mouth when she realized her thoughts had actually come out through her lips.

Mr. Darcy only smiled. "I shall explain all, Miss Bennet. But first I hope you will indulge my wish to know you a little better."

There was nothing else to be done at this point, so Elizabeth readily agreed. The entered the café and sat at one of the tables by the window looking out onto the street, and Mr. Darcy, proving himself to be a gentleman, ensured she was comfortable in her seat before taking his own.

The proprietor emerged from behind the counter, and upon noticing Elizabeth—she had stopped by the café several times with her aunt since arriving in London—looked at her askance. Elizabeth merely shook her head slightly to let the man know she was well, and though he did not appear to understand, he did not make an issue of her presence with an unknown man.

"What is your preference, Miss Bennet?" asked Mr. Darcy. And then when he noticed her looking at the selection of chocolate, chuckled and gestured to the proprietor. "Chocolate for us both, sir, and a selection of your cakes."

"Very good, sir," said the man, and he left to fill the order.

"I have never actually had the chocolate before, sir," said Elizabeth, feeling unaccountably shy.

"Then prepare yourself for a treat," said Mr. Darcy. "It is not something I would wish to drink often, as it is quite rich, but it is good. My sister adores it, and I try to indulge her on occasion."

"You have a sister?"

"I do. She is but thirteen years of age and very shy. But she is my only immediate family, and I care for her greatly."

"An ideal elder brother, then," said Elizabeth, "for you are both indulgent and careful. And though I do not know when these events occurred, may I offer my condolences for the passing of your parents?"

A little incline of the head met her statement, and Elizabeth thought she detected some measure of the man's emotions. "I thank you, Miss Bennet. My mother has been gone these past eleven years. She never fully recovered from the birth of my sister and passed when Georgiana was but two years of age. My father . . ."

Mr. Darcy appeared to choke up a little at the mention of his father, but he quickly mastered himself and smiled. "My father passed only two years ago. I apologize, but the pain of losing him has not yet left me."

"I understand, Mr. Darcy. I cannot imagine losing my father." Elizabeth paused, searching for something else to say which would be appropriate to the situation. "Have you any other family?"

"My uncle and his family, as well as an aunt on my mother's side. I am not close to most of them, save for a cousin who is of age with me and his younger sister. On my father's side I have only some distant cousins."

"Quite alone in the world, then," murmured Elizabeth, wondering what she would do without her family. Even though she was now estranged from most of her immediate family, at least she still had the Gardiners.

"I cannot be unhappy with my lot, Miss Bennet," said Mr. Darcy, drawing her attention back to him. "My sister is everything I could wish for, and I share a deep understanding with my cousin. In addition, I have inherited an estate to be proud of, and have never needed to want for the material things in life. I am . . . content with my situation."

Perhaps it was an inflection in his voice or the pause when he spoke, but Elizabeth had the distinct impression that contentedness did not extend to happiness. This was a man who felt deeply, she thought, and had not experienced so much joy from life as a person ought. It made her feel a little better about her own situation; yes, she was estranged from her family, and yes, her mother could be a trial at times, but she had not been unhappy at Longbourn. Quite the contrary, in fact.

Mr. Darcy apparently saw her attention, and he smiled at her. "I can see you are quite observant, Miss Bennet, and I will not sport with your intelligence by refusing to give you a full account of my hesitance."

A sigh fell from his lips, and he looked down for a moment, raising his eyes again once he had come to some resolve.

"The fact of the matter is that though I am wealthy, wealth does not bring comfort, and indeed at times it can be more of a curse than a blessing. Since I am now master of my own estate and possess connections to the highest echelons of society, I find myself hunted. My mourning for my father ended over a year ago and I have been the target of every matchmaking mother of society and all their calculating daughters.

"I am not of the most outgoing disposition, Miss Bennet, as I am certain you have already apprehended." He chuckled when Elizabeth indicated her understanding of that fact. "You see? You have already determined much more about me than most young ladies would see or care. That makes you different and very interesting to one such as I."

For a moment Elizabeth had an inkling of Mr. Darcy's purpose, but he abruptly changed the subject, not allowing her to pursue that line of thought.

"What of you, Miss Bennet?" asked Mr. Darcy. "Can you tell me something of yourself?"

Their order arrived, and Elizabeth busied herself pouring the chocolate for them both, savoring the rich, sweet scent which rose from the steaming liquid. At Mr. Darcy's prompting she chose a delectable cream pastry and settled it on her plate. Then she raised the cup to her lips, blowing on the hot liquid briefly, before taking a sip of the dark concoction.

Elizabeth almost groaned with pleasure as the sweet beverage flowed through her lips, over her tongue, and settled on her taste buds. She had experienced a bit of chocolate on occasion, but nothing had prepared her for the sheer decadent pleasure of the treat in the form of a drink. It was so delicious, Elizabeth thought she might swoon from the almost sensual pleasure.

Once she mastered her reaction to the explosion of flavor, Elizabeth became aware of the fact that Mr. Darcy was watching her, and she glanced up to see his lips rise slightly in amusement. When he saw her looking at him, he said:

"Can I infer you like the chocolate?"

A little giggle slipped from Elizabeth's mouth, and she nodded in agreement, attempting to be a demure, sophisticated woman. She thought her act was a miserable failure.

"It is . . . Well, I am not certain I possess the words to describe it. It is quite delicious, sir."

Mr. Darcy nodded. "*That* I could see. And I am treated to the same reaction every time I see my sister indulge in chocolate. I believe you and she would be great friends, should you meet."

Though made uncomfortable with the suggestion, Elizabeth shunted it to the side for now. She still did not know what this man meant by approaching her; his purpose was a mystery.

"I believe you were about to tell me something of yourself?" prompted Mr. Darcy a moment later, as Elizabeth was about to ask him what he wished of her.

"I am from Hertfordshire, sir," said Elizabeth, deciding to oblige him for the moment. "My father's estate is near the town of Meryton. I am the second eldest of five daughters."

"Five daughters?" asked Mr. Darcy. "So you have no brother? And does your eldest sister inherit the estate?"

"No, Mr. Darcy," said Elizabeth, feeling an atypical reticence steal over her. "Longbourn is entailed on my father's distant cousin, though I believe he has never met the man."

"Ah, that explains much then."

Puzzled, Elizabeth said: "Pardon me?"

Mr. Darcy sipped his chocolate and nibbled a little on the side of his pastry before he focused on her once again, and Elizabeth thought he was a little uncomfortable.

"I must confess, Miss Bennet, that I heard something of your soliloquy the other day in the park."

"Oh," said Elizabeth, feeling her cheeks heat up.

"It was because of that I decided to seek you out. Your story intrigued me, as it is not anything like the behavior I have observed from members of society."

"I am not a member of London society, sir. I have only attended events in Meryton, which cannot be considered grand by any means."

"That is not a detriment in my opinion, Miss Bennet."

Elizabeth looked at him askance, but Mr. Darcy did not appear inclined to elucidate on his statement any further.

"Regardless, I would wish to know more of this situation which necessitates your residence in town. Will you not tell me?"

Hesitating, Elizabeth considered his request. She knew nothing of the man; why should he wish to hear of her misfortunes? What could they possibly mean to him? Elizabeth knew that most in society would consider her to be foolish for refusing a man of Mr. Pearce's consequence—did he mean to join in the chorus?

Surely not. Mr. Darcy had proven himself to be a gentleman. A man of his consequence and importance would surely not go out of his way to ridicule a gentlewoman who had made a foolish choice.

"I am sorry, sir, but I cannot help but wonder why you would wish to hear such a tale. What possible interest can you have in a young woman's folly?"

Mr. Darcy leaned forward and looked her in the eye. "What I heard, Miss Bennet, did not sound like folly. It sounded like a young woman in a difficult circumstance standing up for her beliefs. Will you not tell me?"

Though Elizabeth could never state with a certainty, she thought it was the compassion in his eyes and voice which undid her and prompted her to respond.

"It is simple, Mr. Darcy. I received a marriage proposal from a man I cannot accept, and when I refused, my mother became very distressed." Elizabeth paused, uncertain how much to say about her home and her mother's behavior. She decided it would be best to be truthful but vague. "My mother is fearful for her future, due to the entail on the estate. She believes her daughters must make good marriages to secure not only our futures, but her own."

Nodding, Mr. Darcy said: "Understandable, if perhaps a little misguided. Security is indeed something to be desired. But happiness in marriage is of equal importance, in my opinion. My parents were happy together. I believe my mother's early passing led to my father's death, at least in part."

A sigh escaped Elizabeth's lips. "My parents have never enjoyed felicity in marriage, Mr. Darcy. That is why I refuse to enter a marriage with a man I do not esteem and cannot respect. Perhaps it is foolish of me, but I cannot act otherwise."

"Why is the man so objectionable? Is there some deficiency in him?"

"Many deficiencies, I assure you," said Elizabeth, feeling the fire of indignation ignite once again in her breast. "Mr. Pearce can provide for a wife adequately, and his prospects are such that his wealth will grow. But he is more than twice my age, and he is proud, deceitful, and lacks integrity. It is well known that he is a libertine and a seducer, and that he has fathered many children, none of whom he has deigned to acknowledge. Should I marry a man I know will be unfaithful? Should I attempt to teach my children to respect a man so undeserving of respect? I shall not."

Mr. Darcy looked on her with compassion, and Elizabeth felt the resentment fade away in favor of her former feeling of abashment.

"Then I commend you, Miss Bennet. I think there are many young ladies of your situation who would not think twice about accepting such circumstances for the opportunity of wealth and security. You are to be commended, indeed."

"Thank you, sir," whispered Elizabeth.

They fell silent then, Elizabeth lost in her thoughts, and Mr. Darcy seemed to be equally affected. The fact of recounting her story to someone who was not a relation was in some way cathartic. To know there was a young man in the world who did not think her a silly girl to be clinging to such romantic notions of love and affection warmed her heart. Perhaps there was some hope after all that she might find someone she could esteem.

The small clock on the wall of the establishment in which they sat chimed the hour, and Elizabeth looked up at it, knowing her aunt would soon wonder where she was. It was time for her to depart.

"I thank you for your company and the chocolate, sir," said Elizabeth, smiling at the gentleman whose attention was now focused on her. She favored him with a shy smile. "The chocolate was superb, and I appreciate your allowing me to try it. But my aunt will soon become concerned at my absence. I believe I must return."

Mr. Darcy paused, as if thinking of something, before a resolve settled over him like a mantle. He turned to look in her eyes and he said: "If I might have your indulgence for one more moment, please."

Intrigued, Elizabeth motioned for him to continue.

"I would like to further our acquaintance, Miss Bennet. To further that goal, I would like to request your permission to call on you for the purpose of courtship."

Elizabeth gaped at him. "Courtship?" she finally managed to ask, though it came out as a squeak.

"Indeed, Miss Bennet." Mr. Darcy's lips curved up in a wry smile.

"But why?" asked Elizabeth.

"For the usual purpose. When a young woman interests a man, it is the usual practice to enter into a courtship, so as to further become acquainted, is it not?"

"I am well aware of the customs of our society, Mr. Darcy," said Elizabeth, feeling a little annoyed at his levity. "What I wish to know, is why me in particular?"

"Do you not think yourself worthy of receiving the attentions of a gentleman? Or is it your fate to be importuned by the Mr. Pearces of the world?"

Elizabeth regarded Mr. Darcy as if he were daft. "I do believe I am worthy, sir. However, the estimation of worth from one person to the other can be a gulf so wide as to be impossible to cross."

Mr. Darcy frowned, but Elizabeth would not allow him to speak until she had voiced her thoughts. "I may be speaking out of turn, Mr. Darcy, but you have told me you are a man of great consequence. Is that not the case?"

"It is, Miss Bennet."

"Then why would you focus on a young woman like myself? We have not canvassed the subject of my family's situation, but let me tell you that not only is my father's estate entailed upon another, but my sisters and I possess little in the way of dowry and no connections which would be tempting to a man of your importance. In fact, at present I am not sure if I even have a family.

"Furthermore my uncle is a man of trade, and my aunt, though she does have some connections to the gentry in the past, is the daughter of a country parson. I am not what a man of your influence would be expected to marry. Unless I am very much mistaken, I believe you are in a position that to aspire to a daughter of a noble would not be a presumption. Am I correct?"

Mr. Darcy was silent for a moment, and Elizabeth almost thought she had offended him. But when he spoke, he did not immediately answer those questions Elizabeth had asked in her diatribe. Rather, it quickly became evident that he was, after a fashion, defending her own connections and situation in life.

"Miss Bennet, you are the daughter of a gentleman, correct?"

"I am, sir, but that is hardly the point."

"It is exactly the point." Mr. Darcy leaned forward and faced her, his eyes boring intently into hers. "As you have surmised, I do possess connections to the nobility, and the daughter of an earl would not be an unreasonable expectation for my future wife. But the fact remains that I am naught but a gentleman—a wealthy gentleman, but a gentleman nonetheless. As you are a gentleman's daughter, by this estimation I must consider us to be equals. Can you refute this?"

Though she was tempted to speak on the relative importance of their maternal relations, Elizabeth was forced to acknowledge that he did indeed speak the truth.

"Very good," said Mr. Darcy. "Now, you mentioned your uncle. The way you have spoken of him, I have inferred that he is a good man, industrious, caring, and diligent. The fact that he has taken you in and given you shelter in spite of your mother's protests speaks well to his character. Am I incorrect?"

"No, sir," said Elizabeth. "My uncle is a good man, and my aunt is all that is lovely, proper, and pleasing. I cannot repine having them as relations, though they are not of the fashionable set."

"Excellent!" said Mr. Darcy. "Now that we have dealt with all of these things, let us canvass your other objections. Your lack of dowry concerns me not for an instant, as I am well able to provide for you and any children with which we might be blessed, even if we should have a dozen daughters. And as for connections, I have more than I know what to do with at present. The loss of a few more does not deter me. In fact, it might even spur me on."

Mr. Darcy sighed and he massaged his temples briefly. "Tell me, Miss Bennet, you mentioned that you are not a member of London society—I assume this means you have spent almost no time in London drawing-rooms?"

"Virtually none at all, Mr. Darcy," replied Elizabeth. "In fact, my father hates town and refuses to come here except when we visit my aunt and uncle. The only society which I have ever been exposed to is that of my home, and the few gatherings I have been to with my uncle."

Nodding, Mr. Darcy said: "Your father is a wise man. I postulate that the reason he hates society is because of the insipidity, the artificiality, the outright greed shown by most of its members. London society is not for the faint of heart, Miss Bennet. I believe I will like your father exceedingly, as I espouse the same opinion of society in general."

"This all may be true, sir," said Elizabeth, becoming exasperated with this conversation. "But the question remains: why me? What do I have to tempt a man like you?"

"Integrity," responded Mr. Darcy without a hint of a pause. "Hearing your story, told to a sleeping babe in arms, intrigued me. Knowing more of you today has only firmed my resolve. I am not looking for an heiress, Miss Bennet. I wish for something more than wealth and connections. I wish for a true meeting of minds with my partner, a woman I can love and cherish, while hopefully exciting the same feelings from her in response.

"I am convinced it is possible between us. At the very least, I know you are not a fortune hunter. A woman who would not accept a man who is worth more than five thousand a year cannot be one who is seeking to marry for wealth."

"I may simply be holding out in hopes of attracting a man of higher consequence," said Elizabeth.

Mr. Darcy smiled, and Elizabeth felt her insides flutter at the sight; he truly was a handsome man.

"I believe you delight in espousing opinions which are not your own in order to play devil's advocate, Miss Bennet. Given the situation you have related to me, I cannot imagine you are that foolish. If your family's situation is at all similar to what you have said, even attracting a man with an income of five thousand a year is not likely. You are too intelligent to turn the bird in hand away in hopes of snaring one larger."

"You will eventually regret me," said Elizabeth weakly, though she wondered why she was still protesting. "Many in society will think you a simpleton to be trapped by a country miss, and my acceptance will be difficult."

"If you think that gives me a moment's pause, you are mistaken," replied Mr. Darcy, his voice as firm and immovable as a mountain. "I despise most of the ton, and those with whom I do associate will accept you on nothing more than my recommendation. In time, it is your own qualities which will guarantee the approbation of the rest, that and the Darcy name.

"I think we would do well together. I see in you an intelligent woman who, while still young and inexperienced, is capable of conversing with a man like myself with something other than an agreement to everything I say. I want that in a wife, Miss Bennet. And you are not unattractive either—quite the contrary, I assure you."

Mr. Darcy's scrutiny began to make Elizabeth feel uncomfortable, though he was not looking on her with disfavor.

"There is something remarkably fine about your eyes," continued Mr. Darcy, almost speaking to himself. "They are well shaped and of a lovely shade, and your beautiful long lashes perfectly complement their exquisite appeal. Even on a short acquaintance, I find myself entranced by your beauty, Miss Bennet. Now we have only to discover if we are well matched . . . unless, of course, you cannot find anything good in my countenance."

This last was said in a playful tone, and Elizabeth, knowing that Mr. Darcy was well aware of his handsomeness, could only smile in demure response.

What could she say to such flattering words, especially when she knew in an instant that he meant every word of them and did not intend them to be mere flattery? Elizabeth had never had any illusions or aspirations toward beauty—Jane was the pretty one of the family, not Elizabeth. She had never understood what it could feel like to hear a man speak such words of admiration and know that he was speaking the absolute truth. It was like a heady wine which played about her senses, wreaking havoc with her equilibrium.

Thus, there was only one answer for Elizabeth to make.

"You may call on me, sir, with my uncle's permission." Then a feeling of mischief stole over her, and she grinned impishly at him. "Of course, since my elder sister is the beauty of the family and is sweetness personified, you may ultimately regret your choice."

"I believe I am willing to take that chance, madam."

Elizabeth could not completely stifle a giggle, and he laughed too, an open, hearty sort of sound.

"Shall I accompany you back to your uncle's house then?" asked Mr. Darcy.

"You do not believe in procrastination, do you?"

"It seems best to settle the matter immediately. Do you not agree?"

There was no response to be had. They finished their chocolate—Elizabeth was not about to allow such a divine treat to be wasted, even in the smallest measure—and then they stood to depart, Elizabeth accepting his offered arm. What a change in circumstances this was! She did not know how she could assimilate it in so little time.

Chapter IX

There was something solid and dependable about Mr. Darcy, Elizabeth decided. The man was tall and sturdily built, with broad shoulders and an erect bearing. But even more than this, he exuded competence and confidence, an ability to see to the heart of a problem and the fortitude to take the appropriate action to correct it.

While this was all conjecture—she really did not know him yet—the strength of his arm where her hand was resting lightly was unmistakable. He stood much taller than she, the top of her head not even reaching up to his chin, and she, though somewhat dainty, was not an excessively diminutive woman either.

Elizabeth led them down the street toward her uncle's home, and in her mind she wondered at what had just occurred. She had lived almost as an orphan being supported by relations for more than two months now, so much that it had almost become true in her own mind. To go from a homeless waif, dependent upon others for her daily bread, to the object of courtship of a wealthy and influential man was almost too much for her to take in! She wondered what her aunt would make of her sudden arrival on her doorstep with Mr. Darcy in tow.

She was soon to find out, as within moments they had arrived at the house. Gesturing, Elizabeth led them to the front door, saying:

"My uncle's home. He will be at his offices right now, but if you wish to speak with him without delay, my aunt will send for him."

"I believe it is best, Miss Bennet," replied Mr. Darcy. "Our acquaintance thus far has not exactly been proper. I would prefer to have your uncle's sanction to my calling on you bestowed as soon as possible."

Elizabeth nodded and led them up the stairs to the front door, letting herself in as she normally would. A maid soon entered the room to take her winter clothing, and the girl stopped short at the sight of the tall gentleman by Elizabeth's side.

Seeking to put her at ease, Elizabeth smiled and said: "Abigail, is Mrs. Gardiner in the sitting-room?"

"Yes, she is, miss," said the maid.

The simple act of speaking to her seemed to restore the maid's equilibrium, and she stepped forward to take Elizabeth's pelisse and gloves, and she received Mr. Darcy's hat, coat and gloves at the same time. She made to leave to stow them, when she stopped and looked at Elizabeth.

"Would you like me to call the housekeeper to announce you?"

Exchanging a glance with Mr. Darcy, Elizabeth decided she would take the task upon herself.

"No, thank you. I will see Mr. Darcy to the sitting-room."

"Very good, miss," said the maid and she departed.

"Courage, Miss Bennet," said Mr. Darcy. "Surely your aunt cannot be so fearsome."

Directing an expression of mock severity at the man, Elizabeth retorted: "I will have you know, Mr. Darcy, that every attempt to intimidate me merely prompts my courage to rise in response. I shall not be afraid of my aunt."

A laugh escaped Mr. Darcy's lips. "I shall remember that for the future, should I ever attempt to frighten you."

"Frighten me?" asked Elizabeth, an eyebrow raised. "Should I reconsider my acceptance of your suit? I do not think I would appreciate a husband who was continually attempting to frighten me."

"I do not know why you should," replied he. "You may tear any attempts I might make to shreds on the force of your will alone. What have you to concern yourself with?"

Heartened by their lighthearted banter, Elizabeth beckoned Mr. Darcy forward, saying: "Come, Mr. Darcy. I shall introduce you to my aunt."

At the same time she heard her aunt calling out to her: "Lizzy? Do you have someone with you?"

Turning an expressive look on Mr. Darcy—which prompted a smile from the man—Elizabeth led him to the door and opened it. Her first sight of her aunt betrayed Mrs. Gardiner's worry, which quickly turned to surprise at the sight of the tall gentleman entering behind her.

"Lizzy?"

"Aunt, please allow me to introduce you to Mr. Darcy. Mr. Darcy, this is my aunt, Mrs. Meredith Gardiner. Mr. Gardiner is my mother's brother. Aunt, this is Mr. Fitzwilliam Darcy."

"Delighted, madam," said Mr. Darcy, bowing to her aunt's curtsey. "I thank you for receiving me into your home without prior notice."

It could not be said that Mrs. Gardiner was one who was not able to adapt to unexpected situations. She quickly recovered and offered Mr. Darcy a seat, which he accepted with thanks. Mrs. Gardiner then called for tea and returned to sit with Elizabeth and Mr. Darcy, regarding them with expectation, clearly wishing for an explanation. Mr. Darcy took the hint with alacrity.

"I must apologize for intruding on you in such a manner, Mrs. Gardiner. I had seen Miss Bennet in the park previously, and when I saw her again today, I could not allow her to depart without introducing myself to her."

"For what purpose, sir?" asked Mrs. Gardiner.

"I wish to call on Miss Bennet for the purpose of courtship."

Her jaw almost dropped to her chest in her shock, and all Mrs. Gardiner could do was stare. If Elizabeth had not been so unaccountably nervous, she might have found the sight amusing. As it was, she watched her aunt anxiously, wondering what she would say. Of all her relations, at present Elizabeth wished for the good opinion of her aunt and uncle, and she hoped this episode would not damage her in their eyes.

"Courtship?" managed Mrs. Gardiner in an incredulous tone after a few moments had passed.

"Yes, Mrs. Gardiner. After hearing something of your niece's history, I believe that she and I would suit."

"I believe I should have my husband summoned from his offices," said Mrs. Gardiner.

"If you please, I would very much appreciate it."

Mrs. Gardiner gazed at Mr. Darcy for several moments, as if trying to determine if he was making sport of her. She soon seemed to be convinced of his sincerity, and she rose to have a word with her housekeeper.

Petrified, Elizabeth sat on the sofa, feeling stiff and almost afraid to move, wondering what trouble she had brought for herself. Her uncle was certain to throw Mr. Darcy from the house, and she would be confined to her room for a month!

"Do not be alarmed, Miss Bennet."

The words brought her from her stupor, and Elizabeth turned to see Mr. Darcy regarding her.

"Your aunt is surprised—and rightly so—but I believe she will come around soon. Now, where is that vaunted mettle of which you earlier spoke?"

Though relaxing only slightly, Elizabeth turned a stern glare on him. "These are people whose opinion means much to me, sir. And my aunt is not attempting to intimidate me."

"That is the spirit," replied Mr. Darcy. "And you are correct that she does not attempt to intimidate. You should remember that she loves you and wishes for your happiness. The surprise will fade quickly, I dare say, leaving nothing but hope for your—for *our*—future."

The truth of Mr. Darcy's words penetrated Elizabeth's mind, and her nerves settled, allowing her to favor Mr. Darcy with a grateful smile. He returned it but only had the time to whisper "Good girl!" before Mrs. Gardiner returned.

"My husband will return before long, sir. I shall allow him to speak to you concerning the genesis of this matter, though I will expect an accounting from my niece later tonight."

Her expression suggested that Elizabeth *would* be expected to inform her as to the goings on which had led to Mr. Darcy's extraordinary application. Elizabeth resigned herself to the inquiry which was certain to take place. In fact, she welcomed it, as she had not yet determined in her own just what had happened and would appreciate Mrs. Gardiner's wisdom in helping her understand.

"Of course, Aunt," was the only thing Elizabeth said.

Satisfied for the moment, Mrs. Gardiner turned back to Mr. Darcy. "Excuse me for the impertinence, Mr. Darcy, but are you at all related to the Darcys of Pemberley."

Almost immediately, Elizabeth could see Mr. Darcy stiffen at her aunt's question. After a moment, however, he relaxed and was able to answer Mrs. Gardiner's question with equanimity.

"At present, Mrs. Gardiner, my sister and I *are* the Darcys of Pemberley."

Mrs. Gardiner nodded. "I apologize for the impertinent question, Mr. Darcy. You see, I am quite familiar with that area of the country, and in times past, I had heard much of your family."

This seemed to pique Mr. Darcy's interest. "You are familiar with Derbyshire?"

"I am, sir. I spent most of my youth living in the village of Lambton, with which I believe you must be intimately familiar."

"Why, that is not five miles from Pemberley!" exclaimed Mr. Darcy. "Does any of your family still live in the district?"

"None of my immediate family. My father was Mr. Blake, who was the pastor of Lambton parish."

"I remember Mr. Blake very well indeed!" replied Mr. Darcy. "He was a good man and an excellent minister. The district mourned his death exceedingly."

"Thank you, Mr. Darcy. I believe he was."

Mr. Darcy paused for a moment, seemingly trying to remember something. Then he spoke up again and said:

"But that must mean that you are related to The Blakes of Dewberry Fields."

"Yes, sir," said Mrs. Gardiner. "The current master of the estate is my uncle. My father was his youngest brother."

"Dewberry Fields is a fine estate, Mrs. Gardiner. It is not so large as Pemberley, but it is well-maintained, and Mr. Blake's flock of sheep produce some of the finest wool in the country. My father was a close confidante to Mr. Blake."

"Yes, I had heard that your father had passed on. You have my condolences, Mr. Darcy. Your father is very much missed, I believe."

"He is indeed," replied Mr. Darcy, his voice quieter, introspective. He soon shook himself from his thoughts and smiled. "It is a fortuitous chance to meet you here, Mrs. Gardiner. Though my family has traditionally attended church in Kympton, we are quite familiar with Lambton as well. It is a splendid town."

"I think it the dearest place in the world, Mr. Darcy. When Mr. Gardiner is in the position to purchase an estate, I have insisted that it be as close to Lambton as can be arranged. I still have many friends in the area, you understand." Mrs. Gardiner smiled, turning a mischievous eye upon Mr. Darcy. "I do not suppose you would be willing to give up Pemberley, would you?"

Mr. Darcy laughed. "Unfortunately, I cannot see my way to selling the home of my ancestors. But you may be assured that I shall be happy to assist you in whatever manner I am able in your quest for an estate on Lambton's doorstep. I would be delighted to have you as neighbors."

As the conversation continued, Elizabeth watched as her aunt and

Mr. Darcy spoke of Derbyshire, Lambton, and of some common acquaintances of the area, wondering at the change which had come over her suitor. Her suitor! How strange it was to think of *any* man in such a fashion!

Shaking her head clear of such thoughts, Elizabeth turned her mind back to the gentleman seated by her side. When they had first entered, though Elizabeth had been too nervous to think on the matter much, Mr. Darcy had in fact been quite rigid and formal. He had tried to put her at ease, but she now recognized that he was ill at ease himself. She thought back to the things they had spoken of in the café, and she recognized that not only did he feel hunted by those in society, but he was actually uncomfortable with those with whom he was not acquainted.

Now, however, he appeared to be speaking with true pleasure, completely without concern. And it was her aunt's questions and comments which had done the trick. Elizabeth, of course, had no knowledge of Mr. Darcy's character, though her initial impression was a positive one, but she thought to file the information away for future reference, as it might become useful at some point.

The three sat together for some time speaking of various matters—though, in truth, Elizabeth listened to Mr. Darcy and her aunt more than spoke—and after a while, Elizabeth began to wonder why her uncle had not appeared yet. The question seemed to be answered when he finally arrived and joined them in the sitting-room.

The three fell silent when the sound of the front door opening and closing was heard, and the master's voice speaking to the maid drifted in through the open door. Mr. Gardiner's voice preceded his entrance into the room.

"Meredith!" called he. "I was meeting with Mr. Bingley. I hope this was important enough to pull me from those discussions."

Stepping in through the door, Mr. Gardiner stopped abruptly at the sight of an unknown gentleman, sitting on his sofa, speaking with his wife and niece as if he had known them for many months.

"As you can see, it is quite important, Edward," said Mrs. Gardiner, rising from the sofa.

Mr. Darcy and Elizabeth also rose, and after a moment of studying the young man before him, Mr. Gardiner approached, though he did not say anything. Mr. Darcy seemed to understand the situation.

"Mrs. Gardiner, will you do me the honor of introducing me to your husband?"

"Of course, Mr. Darcy. Mr. Darcy, this is my husband, Edward Gardiner. Husband, Mr. Darcy, who is visiting with us today on a mission of *particular* importance."

It was impossible for Mr. Gardiner to miss his wife's emphasis on the word "particular" and he glanced at Elizabeth, who could only blush in response.

"Well, well," said Mr. Gardiner. "It appears I was needed at home indeed. Welcome, Mr. Darcy, and I am pleased to make your acquaintance. Shall we sit and converse for a time, or do you wish to speak of this business at once?"

"If it is no imposition, I would prefer to speak of it immediately. I have been from home for some time, and my sister will likely be wondering what has become of me."

"Very well, sir. Let us retire at once."

Nodding, Mr. Darcy turned to Elizabeth and, grasping her hand, bowed over it. "Miss Bennet, I shall farewell you once I have spoken with your uncle."

"Thank you, Mr. Darcy. I wish you every success in your endeavors."

A smile lit up his face, and Mr. Darcy bowed again before quitting the room in Mr. Gardiner's wake. Elizabeth could only stand and watch as he departed. She decided then and there it would be something indeed to be this man's object of interest.

There are times in one's life when a lesson is learned which impacts the learner profoundly, and this was one of those times. Though he had thought much of Miss Bennet in the time since he had seen her in the park, and he had quickly made the resolution to seek her out if the opportunity presented itself, Darcy had not known what he would discover when he finally found her.

Her situation had been clear, simply by what he had managed to overhear that fateful day. She was undoubtedly the daughter of minor country gentry, if her mother was so afraid for her future as to insist that her daughter marry an objectionable man. Either that, or she was some impoverished lord's daughter, though that was not as likely, as a member of the nobility would almost certainly arrange her marriage without even consulting his daughter.

When Darcy had originally heard Miss Bennet claim a man of trade as a close connection, it had been all he could do not to react with distaste. He had had dealings with the trade class before, and had found many of them to be just and upright men—good men, regardless of their backgrounds and professions, little though he wished to associate with them. But the woman whose story he had become immediately fascinated with was more important than some objectionable relations, so he had swallowed his response and focused on what was truly important.

As the daughter of a man who had himself been the son of a gentleman—and the Blakes were good people, just and upright, and without fail exceedingly proper—Darcy had not expected Mrs. Gardiner to be anything other than what she was. Mr. Gardiner, however, was a man who had never been connected to the gentry—other than by marriage through his sister—and Darcy had not known what to expect of him.

And thus, the reason for his chastening was made clear. Only a few moments in Mr. Gardiner's company and Darcy knew that he was a good and industrious man, but also a man with impeccable manners, well-versed in all proper behavior. Mr. Gardiner could easily have passed himself off as a gentleman and none would have been the wiser. There was only one other man whom Darcy personally knew who would have had as much success as Mr. Gardiner in such an endeavor, and while *that man* possessed all the manners and none of the substance, Mr. Gardiner possessed both. Darcy realized in an instant that he would be happy to call Mr. Gardiner a relation, though Darcy's own relations would almost certainly be less than pleased with the connection.

"Can I get you anything to drink, Mr. Darcy?" asked Mr. Gardiner when they were seated.

"I thank you, no," said Darcy. "I truly should be going as soon as our discussion is concluded. I do not wish to seem like I am anxious to leave, but I should return to my sister."

A nod met his statement. "Very well then, sir. Perhaps you should state your business so that you might return."

"My purpose is clear, Mr. Gardiner. I wish to be given permission to call on your niece for the purpose of courtship."

Mr. Gardiner was quiet for some moments, looking upon Darcy with open curiosity.

"Given what I saw in the sitting-room, it seems inevitable that you would make such an application. But I must confess that I am shocked. Can I assume, sir, that you are one of the Darcys of Derbyshire of whom I have often heard my wife speak?"

"I am, sir. Your wife informed me that she grew up in Lambton, which is only five miles from my estate at Pemberley. My family has attended church in Kympton for generations, but for all other business we deal in the larger town. We are well known in Lambton."

"So you are, sir." Mr. Gardiner hesitated, no doubt thinking of what he should say next. "If my wife's tales are to be believed, you are of great consequence, sir. Assuming that is so, are you aware of my niece's situation, both her current situation and that of her family?"

"I know she is in London because her mother insisted on her acceptance of a man she cannot abide. I am also aware that her father is a country gentleman, and though we did not canvass the subject openly, I surmise that his estate is small, and he is not able to provide much in the way of dowry for his daughters."

"And yet you are determined to pay your addresses to her?"

"I am."

Mr. Gardiner was again silent, digesting what Darcy had told him. Darcy was patient—this application must be so unexpected, so far from what the man's niece could expect, that he was naturally at a loss. When he finally did speak, he spoke slowly and concisely, apparently in an effort to ensure he was not misunderstood.

"I must own that I do not know quite how to respond, sir. You say you understand Elizabeth's situation, but I wonder if you truly do. She is not what members of your set would typically require in a wife."

"Mr. Gardiner," said Darcy, "I have spoken with Miss Bennet at some length, and I believe I understand much of her character and what she would bring to a marriage. You are correct that many of higher society would expect a large dowry and connections, but I must tell you that I am not one of those men.

"In fact, it is precisely those qualities which draw me to Miss Bennet. My position in society is a constant source of frustration, Mr. Gardiner. I am continually hounded by fortune hunters and those seeking to curry favor, and though I know I am painting all of society with broad strokes of a brush and it does not necessarily apply to all, I am rarely with those who wish to know me rather than connect to me. I do not like most of society, and choosing a wife from amongst the insipid heiresses is a duty I have until recently been reluctant to perform.

"Your niece is like a breath of fresh air. She is genuine, caring, happy, engaging, and possessed of the highest character and integrity. I already have proof she is not a fortune hunter, else she would have accepted this other man's suit. Though I will grant you I do not know her well as yet, I am certain we can find much more than a typical society marriage together. I want that, sir. My parents had it, and I would follow their example."

Mr. Gardiner's continued silence irked Darcy. Most men would be falling all over themselves in an effort to assure him they were quite happy to give their daughters or nieces to him, especially one who was essentially penniless and had been banished from her home. Yet Mr.

Gardiner appeared to be deep in thought. But knowing anger would not serve his purposes, Darcy held his tongue, waiting for the man to speak.

When the man finally responded, it was with a wry smile. "I know we should all be grateful for your application, Mr. Darcy, and I assure you both my wife and I are. Elizabeth's situation has weighed heavily on our minds of late, and the solution always seemed so simple, and yet so difficult. Your offer resolves my worry, which I appreciate. Your name is familiar to me, sir, and it is always spoken with the highest of respect for your integrity.

"For myself, I am happy to grant you the permission to call on my niece, though you must understand that it is her father who will need to give permission for a courtship, as he has not ceded that authority to me. However, there are some impediments of which you must be aware."

Just when Darcy had begun to feel better about Mr. Gardiner's response, talk of impediments startled him. What impediments could there possibly be?

Mr. Gardiner nodded. "I can see you are surprised, sir, and I cannot fault you. Yours is a very eligible offer, and I know we should be jumping at it. But my brother is not a usual man, you see, and he counts Elizabeth as his favorite daughter."

"If she is so, then should he not be happy that I would provide for her?"

"If that was all it entailed, I think he would be very happy."

Mr. Gardiner must have seen something in Darcy's countenance, for he sighed and leaned forward in his chair, placing his clasped hands on the desk, and he looked seriously at Darcy.

"I am not certain how much Lizzy has told you of her family situation, but allow me to elucidate. Mrs. Bennet—my sister—I do not think will be a problem. The fact that your income is significantly higher than Pearce's will guarantee her approbation." Mr. Gardiner paused and seemed to hesitate for a moment before he continued to speak: "You must understand something about my sister, Mr. Darcy. She is not an intelligent woman, and as the estate is entailed away from her daughters, thoughts of her future security occupy her constantly."

"Security is something I can provide."

"I do not doubt it, sir," said Mr. Gardiner. "But she is also a silly woman, single-minded, and unable to understand felicity in marriage, much less why a man of your importance would prefer her second daughter over her eldest, who is considered to be the beauty of the family, and the focus of all her hopes."

"But that is absurd! I have never even met her eldest."

"No, you have not. But in her mind, the sight of Jane would cause all thoughts of Elizabeth to disappear from your mind. I am not trying to warn you off, just to inform you of what you might hear her say when you meet her.

"As I said, my sister is not the problem. This matter with Pearce is, and I cannot predict what my brother will do."

"What do you mean? Why would her father prefer a man she does not even like." Darcy decided to avoid the matter of the other suitor for the present.

"He would not prefer the man, I am sure. However, your estate being situated in Derbyshire would put her three days journey away, and my brother might balk at the distance."

"Surely not!" said Darcy.

"I do not think he would ultimately refuse his consent for such a reason," said Mr. Gardiner, spreading his hands out to either side. "But he might be reluctant, as he and Elizabeth have always been close."

"And this fellow Pearce? What of him?"

"He is nothing but persistent," said Gardiner with a distasteful grunt. "He is one of the most unpleasant men I have ever met, and I disliked him within a few minutes of making his acquaintance. If you will forgive me, he behaved more like what I would imagine a man of *your* importance would be expected to act like."

"Proud? Disagreeable? Haughty?"

Laughing, Mr. Gardiner allowed it to be so.

"I *have* been called that in the past," said Darcy with a shrug. "My natural reticence is often taken as pride. But it is a trait I have never repined, as it protects me from some of the worst machinations of the ladies of society."

"I am surprised even that is effective."

Darcy frowned. "It is not for the more determined. But the timid ones tend to leave me alone when I scowl at them."

Silence descended on the room. As he considered the matter before him, Darcy thought of Mr. Gardiner's words and the possible ramifications. Clearly the key was Miss Bennet herself. If she was her father's favorite as Mr. Gardiner said, then it was likely that Mr. Bennet could be persuaded to allow the courtship just because she wished it. Thus it behooved Darcy to determine how serious he was about this courtship, and to convince Miss Bennet that she wished for it too. The more immediate problem, however, was this other suitor, who, it appeared, could not be dissuaded.

"Do you think this Mr. Pearce will be induced to desist?"

A sigh escaped Mr. Gardiner's lips. "I do not know what to think of the man. As I said, he is proud and disagreeable, looking down on Mrs. Gardiner and me, at least. His suit is eligible, of course, but Elizabeth's accounts of his activities and propensity to father children wherever he goes are worrisome. I cannot speculate on any other vices—I had heard nothing of the man before his proposal to Lizzy, and I decided it was not worth it to investigate him, as Bennet was not inclined to approve of his suit."

"Do you have any inkling of why the man is so persistent?"

"Nothing I can state. He is proud enough that it may simply be because he is not happy being denied by a young woman he considers to be his inferior. I cannot think of anything else."

"Then do you have any suggestions?"

"I do," said Mr. Gardiner, nodding his head decisively. "Keep your courtship informal. I believe I have enough authority to approve it in those terms. Once you have decided that you wish to offer for her, then go to Longbourn and seek her father's permission. When it is a fait accompli, Pearce should give up and look for someone else."

Darcy nodded slowly. "That is prudent, Mr. Gardiner. If you are in agreement, I will court your niece informally for the present."

Mr. Gardiner offered his hand, which Darcy shook. "Very good, Mr. Darcy. I will make sure the staff is instructed regarding your intentions to visit Elizabeth."

"And you will inform me if Pearce importunes Elizabeth again?"

"What do you mean to do about it?"

Darcy smiled in a particularly mirthless manner. "Leave Pearce to me. If he does not show himself, then there is nothing to be done. But I have many connections which may be brought to bear against the man should he prove to be a problem. I do not intend to allow him to stand in my way and will take the appropriate action should it be required."

A shrewd look came over Mr. Gardiner's face, and he nodded. "Very well, Mr. Darcy."

Chapter X

It was a week after first meeting Mr. Darcy that Elizabeth sat in her room in the Gardiner townhouse and thought of the first days of her courtship. Elizabeth had always imagined the first such days would be sublime, filled with feelings of love and laughter, the bliss of knowing she was the focus of a man's attention. Perhaps she was a little fanciful—she had owned that to Jane on more than one occasion—but the image had always stayed in her mind.

Courtship with Mr. Darcy was nothing like she had imagined. For one, she did not love him, and she was well aware that Mr. Darcy did not love her. He had approached her on nothing more than a whim brought about by an overheard conversation with an infant, of all things. All he had spoken of thus far was an intention to determine their compatibility and ability to coexist with peace and harmony. These were not the words a young girl inclined to romance wished to hear from the man who was courting her.

That was not to say that she thought Mr. Darcy incapable of such feelings. He was a reticent man, it was true, and he rarely used two words when only one would convey that which he wished to say. He was also thoughtful and intelligent, and his opinions were formed and well-considered. Furthermore, he was scrupulously proper, insisting upon all the appropriate forms of courtship, which included where and when he could see her, that chaperonage was present, and that they never strayed to improper subjects during the course of their conversations.

Despite all this, Elizabeth was convinced that given the right encouragement, Mr. Darcy would be an agreeable suitor, and perhaps more importantly for a young woman considering matrimony, a passionate lover. There was something about him, some measure of the way in which he regarded her, which caused a stirring of . . . well, something, to well up within her. Elizabeth could not quite determine what it was. All she knew was that he watched her intently, and rather than seeming to see her flaws, he appeared to be quite happy with what he saw.

Of his seriousness, Elizabeth was of two minds. In her mind's eye, she had always had the picture of her future suitor as a man of a sociable, genial nature, and though she had not, as yet, seen Mr. Darcy in any company other than that of herself and her relations, she was confident that he was not a gregarious man. In fact, it sometimes seemed to Elizabeth like it was a trial to induce anything more than the barest hint of a smile from him.

But it was also evident that Mr. Darcy's gravity of nature, though naturally borne, was further augmented by his father's early death and his inheritance of a large estate, the care of a much younger sister, and the society into which he had been thrust. Though he had not yet told her explicitly, Mr. Darcy had alluded to his struggles with society and the unwanted attention his inheritance had brought him. A particular conversation only the day before had given Elizabeth much to think on, and she felt that they had both exchanged confidences which allowed them to understand the other better than they had before.

When Mr. Darcy had arrived at the Gardiner townhouse, Elizabeth had been waiting in the Gardiners' sitting room, attending to her embroidery. It was not a task she enjoyed, but it allowed her to calm herself when she became nervous. She was becoming accustomed to Mr. Darcy's calls, but they still caused her a little anxiety.

"Miss Bennet," greeted Mr. Darcy when he had entered the room.

As was his custom, he approached her directly and bowed over her hand. Elizabeth received him with pleasure, murmuring her welcome. In her mind, however, she was considering what it would feel like should he actually press his lips to her hand. Butterflies began fluttering in her midsection.

"It is a fine day today. Shall we not walk in the park?"

Elizabeth glanced over at her aunt, who was watching their interactions with interest.

"I have no objection, Mr. Darcy," said Mrs. Gardiner.

After she retrieved her outer wear, Elizabeth accepted the offer of Mr. Darcy's escorting arm and they proceeded down the steps from the house and out onto the street. They walked, saying little of substance, and Elizabeth was happy to see that Mr. Darcy was correct—it was indeed a fine day, and the little wisps of wind that tickled her cheeks only served to make them a little rosy. Elizabeth was happy to once again be out of doors.

They had almost reached the park when Elizabeth noticed that Mr. Darcy was watching her. That in and of itself was not unusual—he often watched her. What was different was the slightly upturned lips and the mirth in his eyes.

"Does something amuse you, sir?" asked Elizabeth, feeling a little self-conscious.

"Not so much amusement as happiness, Miss Bennet," said Mr. Darcy. "You seem to be so young and carefree as you walk. The previous time, when we walked from the café to your uncle's house, I do not recall paying attention to you, for I was far too nervous."

"Nervous, sir? You appear to be far too self-assured for apprehension."

A faint smile met her declaration. "I do consider myself to be a confident man. But you must recall, Miss Bennet, that I have never asked for a courtship with a lady before. I expect such feelings are natural when faced with such a life-altering conversation."

"I suppose you are correct, sir," replied Elizabeth.

Mr. Darcy regarded her for several moments before he spoke again. "I do not believe we have canvassed the subject of your age yet, and the sight of you enjoying yourself has struck me with the thought that you are very young. Will you tell me your age?"

"I am seventeen, sir," said Elizabeth.

"And your birthday?"

"July."

"It is still many months before your eighteenth birthday, then," said Mr. Darcy. Elizabeth had the impression he was speaking more to himself than to her.

Then his eyes focused once again on her and he said: "I believe you said you have several sisters?"

"Four, sir."

"And you are the second?"

"Yes. My eldest sister, Jane, is now nineteen. My younger sisters are sixteen, fourteen, and twelve years of age."

Mr. Darcy seemed to consider that. "Since you are obviously out in society, can I assume that you follow country customs? Your next youngest sister is also out?"

"That is correct, sir. Not only do we follow country customs, but you must also remember that my mother insists upon all of us being married as soon as may be, and for that we must show ourselves to greatest advantage and do so as soon as we are of a proper age. To my mother, that means the age of fifteen."

"Fifteen is full young," said Mr. Darcy. "I understand how matters work in the society of small towns and have seen many young ladies introduced to such gatherings at the age of fifteen or sixteen. However, as my society is that of London, I doubt my sister shall be allowed to enter it until she is eighteen years of age. In London, Miss Bennet, even someone of your age might almost be considered to be too young, though since you will be eighteen soon after the end of next season, it would be acceptable."

"I understand," said Elizabeth, thinking of her sisters. Kitty and Lydia, while still very inexperienced, did not display manners which gave Elizabeth any comfort that they would be ready for society when her mother was almost certain to insist they join it. Neither had much interest in any kind of learning, and they were as yet loud and uncouth, and unless her father took them firmly in hand, she did not doubt they would not improve before their coming out.

"However, that is something we should probably be preparing for," said Mr. Darcy.

"What should we prepare for, sir?" asked Elizabeth.

"Your curtsey before the queen," said Mr. Darcy in an offhand manner. "Your future position in society as my wife will necessitate your introduction to the queen. You will require a sponsor, but I do not doubt we shall overcome that hurdle in time."

By the way he was talking, Elizabeth could almost detect some future trouble. She was not allowed to think on the matter further as Mr. Darcy soon spoke again.

"Have you attended many functions in London since your coming?"

"Only a few, sir, and certainly nothing to which you would be accustomed. I have been invited to a few dinners with my aunt and uncle, but for the most part we have stayed comfortably at home. My uncle, you understand, has been focused on his business of late, and he has had little time for the frivolities of life."

Mr. Darcy nodded. "Your uncle is a good and industrious man.

"In fact, it is good that our courtship is taking place at this time," continued Mr. Darcy. "As the little season is all but over, we will be able to come to know one another without being required to submit to the scrutiny of the ton."

Not sure whether to feel affronted, Elizabeth only looked up at him, attempting to mask her thoughts. Her attempt appeared to be less than successful, however, as he noticed her expression and was quick to apologize.

"I did not mean to offend, Miss Bennet. There are two reasons why I believe it is best that we stay out of the public eye at present. The first is that I am not fond of society, and the more attention I receive, the worse my temper becomes."

"Oh, I was not aware of that, Mr. Darcy," said Elizabeth, drawing on her sense of humor. "What have I done? Am I to be courted by a man who is prone to tantrums?"

Chuckling, Mr. Darcy said: "I think not. But I have been told—mostly by my cousin, who delights in teasing me—that when my temper deteriorates my visage becomes positively fearful. It is often useful when I wish to fend off the undesirable, but the disadvantage is that I am rumored to be a proud, foul-tempered sort of man."

Elizabeth laughed. "I am happy you have informed me, sir. I had begun to think you without defect. I will attempt to remain unintimidated when you display this terrifying scowl."

The grin which appeared on his face positively transformed him. Elizabeth had thought him handsome from the first time she had seen him, but it was clear that his true attraction lay when he smiled. If only she could induce him to do so on a more frequent basis!

"I hardly think I could intimidate you, Miss Bennet. You have given me far more reason to smile than anyone else save my sister.

"The other reason the lack of scrutiny is to be desired is that I am well-known. The ton can be a merciless place to those who are new. I would prefer to attend to our courtship without being required to defend your honor, both from the ladies, who will undoubtedly resent you for stealing my attention away, and from the rakes of society who would see you as fair game for their schemes."

Had Elizabeth not already been acquainted with him, she might have thought he was being more than a little conceited in his comments of how the ladies of society would react to their courtship. But Elizabeth knew that he was only telling the absolute truth, and it was accompanied by nary a hint of vanity. It spoke well to his character, she decided, as she thought that many who were the object of such attentions might think very well of themselves.

"I will trust your judgment on this matter, sir," said Elizabeth. "I am not unhappy to be out of the public eye, so the lack of attention does not concern me in the slightest."

"I am glad to hear it."

They walked on in silence for several moments, during which Elizabeth attempted to pluck up the courage to ask him several questions about himself. Again, Mr. Darcy proved adept at reading her thoughts.

"Do you have something you wish to ask me, Miss Bennet?"

Elizabeth turned to look at him, and the expression of openness on his visage allowed her to release her trepidation.

"I was merely wondering your age sir. After all, I have allowed you to know mine."

Smiling, Mr. Darcy said: "I am five and twenty, Miss Bennet. Not so old as to be fearsome, I should hope."

Elizabeth laughed. "No, sir. I believe five and twenty is quite acceptable. Mr. Pearce is five and thirty, if he is a day. I think I far rather prefer a man who is eight years my senior to one who is more than double my age."

A raised eyebrow met Elizabeth's statement. "Is that the *only* reason why I am more acceptable than this other man?"

"Perhaps," said Elizabeth, showing her companion a mischievous smile.

Mr. Darcy returned her laugh. "To be rendered more agreeable by nothing more than the fact that I am younger is a hard thing to accept. You, Miss Bennet, are adept at taking a man's pretensions and exposing them as nothing more than hubris."

Elizabeth allowed herself to chuckle with him, and they strode on in silence. Perhaps Mr. Darcy was not so serious as she had first thought if he was inclined to smile and laugh with her. He did take his responsibilities with earnest care, but was that not to be wished for in a man? Although Elizabeth loved her father, she did not wish to be married to a similar man. She would much rather spend her life with a man who was diligent in performing his duties. She had only known Mr. Darcy a week, and she already knew he was responsible.

"Will you tell me what sorts of things you enjoy doing, Miss Bennet?" asked Mr. Darcy. "I had thought we could plan an outing."

The subject was agreeable to Elizabeth, and she turned to him and began to speak of the theater, their tastes in music, Elizabeth's wish to visit museums, art galleries, and other such delights. Mr. Darcy appeared to approve of what she told him.

"It sounds like you are quite knowledgeable concerning the arts, Miss Bennet," said he when they had turned back toward the Gardiner townhouse. "Your father appears to have instilled a love of such things in you."

"He has to a certain extent, sir," said Elizabeth. "My father loves reading and literature above all other things. But he detests London more than he likes society or the arts, so I have never attended a play or seen an exhibit in his company. Those sorts of activities have always been undertaken in the company of the Gardiners.

Mr. Darcy only nodded. "Do any of your other sisters enjoy similar pursuits?"

"My older sister, Jane, has many similar interests to myself. As for my younger sisters . . ." Elizabeth trailed off, uncertain how to explain without giving him a poor impression of her family. "Their tastes are as yet unformed. My sister Mary is the only other who is out in society, and her tastes tend to run toward music and sacred text."

"Perhaps her interests will form as she partakes more in society."

"I hope so," said Elizabeth, thinking of Mary. She was a good girl, but she tended to be a little too somber for Elizabeth's tastes. Of the three sisters who were out in society, Elizabeth thought Mary to be the one who would have benefited the most by waiting. Though a pretty sort of girl, it was often said she paled in comparison to the others, and Elizabeth thought she felt the insult keenly. She tried to soothe the worst of the hurts and protect her sister, but as she and Mary had little in common, it was difficult to get close enough to the girl to provide any support.

"My mother, of course, cares little for such things," continued Elizabeth. "If only her letters were full of the doings of Meryton . . ."

Elizabeth trailed off, her cheeks blooming. She had not meant to make such statements, and wished she had thought before speaking.

"Your mother is a source of concern?" asked he, when Elizabeth was reluctant to continue.

Sighing, Elizabeth looked up at him and said: "I am the recipient of a letter from my mother every few days. She does not scruple to inform me that I am a disobedient child and a disappointment."

A frown fell over Mr. Darcy's face, but Elizabeth hastened to reassure him.

"It does not signify, Mr. Darcy. I have long been my mother's least favorite child, and with the matter of Mr. Pearce still looming, her behavior is not unexpected."

"That still does not give her the right to constantly harass you."

"Maybe not. But I have stopped listening to her, so it matters little." Elizabeth paused and giggled, and her companion regarded her, a question evident on his features. "Before we met in the park, I had become so frustrated with my mother's rants that I consigned a letter to the fire, in front of my aunt, no less."

Mr. Darcy laughed. "May I suppose Mrs. Gardiner was shocked at your actions?"

"You may. She understood when we talked of it, but she asked me not to do such a thing in her presence again."

"And what becomes of the letters you receive from your mother now?"

Elizabeth looked at him with a coy smile. "I will not suggest that they all remain intact, but I certainly do not read them. The most I ever do is skim through them, for they are all the same and I do not wish to be continually importuned."

"And does your father write to you?"

"My father is a dilatory correspondent at best." Elizabeth sighed. "My uncle Gardiner has often lamented the fact, especially when he manages some small investments for my father and must often wait for some time for answers to letters he sends my father.

"As for me, I have had only a few short notes from him since I came to London. He has told me, in his droll manner, that he was forced to bar his wife from his study, as she would not let up on her demands for him to force me to come home. Since she is vocal in other parts of the house, I think my father mostly stays in his study now."

It was not precisely what she wished to be speaking of with her suitor, but Elizabeth did not want him to pursue her under false assumptions. Her family was quite ridiculous at times, and he must understand that if he wished to continue on this path. Fortunately, Elizabeth was quite accustomed to her family's ways and had largely been inured to their behavior. While she thought Mr. Darcy took her words in stride and had chosen to ignore them for the most part, Elizabeth was beginning to dread his actual meeting with them. She did not know if his regard—whatever there was of it—would survive.

"You mentioned that you are your mother's least favorite daughter?"

"Indeed, I am, though I think Mary is likely close to my level in my mother's eyes."

"Is it because of this situation with Mr. Pearce?"

"No, sir," said Elizabeth. "This long predates his appearance in our lives. In fact, my mother does not like my 'wild ways.' She does not consider my love of literature to be ladylike, and my propensity for walks and other such nonsense can only make it more difficult for her to marry me off.

"I am my father's favorite, for precisely those reasons. I am content. I know my mother does love me, regardless of her inability to show it, and as I have always had my father to support me, my mother's occasional criticism may be taken in stride."

Though Mr. Darcy appeared to wish to discuss the subject further, he allowed it to drop. She could tell the thought of her receiving her mother's constant censure displeased him. Again, Elizabeth thought it would be wonderful to have such an eager protector in Mr. Darcy.

Of course, if she returned home on the arm of Mr. Darcy, Elizabeth did not doubt her mother would explode with raptures and Mr. Pearce would be entirely forgotten. If Elizabeth was honest with herself, she was not certain which she preferred—her mother's censure, or her mother's raptures. Each seemed equally daunting in different ways.

For Darcy, the week in Miss Bennet's company was a delight. Though still full young, as he had discovered, he found her to be intelligent, thoughtful, proper, and possessing of all the necessary social graces he would want in a prospective wife. She would no doubt experience some criticism from those of society, but so would any newcomer who had deigned to attract a man of the first circles. Darcy had no doubt she would soon win over the naysayers. Or at least she would win over those who were open to being won over; those who valued position above all else and those young ladies who had wished to attract his attention to themselves would no doubt withhold their approval regardless. But as there were few in society who would openly disparage her—the Darcy name carried much weight—Darcy decided it did not signify.

In fact, Darcy had rarely met someone like Miss Bennet. There were others with whom he was acquainted who were open, jovial, possessed of happy manners and estimable characters, but there was something about Miss Bennet he could not quite explain. She was so carefree and lighthearted, and her ability to laugh at her family's foibles and not take offense at her mother's constant attacks was truly commendable. Darcy could not help but think that she brought a ray of much needed sunshine into his life.

It was something which he desperately needed, Darcy decided, after contemplating their courtship. The fact of the matter was that Darcy had not been happy these two years since his father's death. Mr. Robert

Darcy had been a tower of strength in Darcy's life, fulfilling the role of father, mentor, teacher, and many others besides. Darcy did not think he had ever been closer with another human being than he had been to his father.

Robert Darcy had been in steadily declining health up until the day he had died, and though the end had been expected, it had still left Darcy feeling unprepared to take up the mantle of ownership of his estate and all the responsibilities which came with being a Darcy. It was fortunate his father had been diligent in teaching his son his responsibilities, for though he had thought up until the very end that his father's health would improve and he had never expected to inherit at such a young age, it was not to be; his father had perished before he had even attained fifty years of age, leaving Darcy with a much younger sister to care for, a large estate and several satellite estates to manage, and an image in society to uphold.

They had been heavy burdens, and at times Darcy had wished they had fallen on the shoulders of another. His sister, while everything good and proper, was a struggle to care for. What did he, a young man of five and twenty, know of the needs of a young girl of thirteen? How could he possibly know how to show her how she must behave, teach her what she must learn to become an adult? It was in every way inconceivable. And his relations pressuring him to marry, not only to ensure the succession of the estate, but also to expand the family connections, had not helped in the slightest.

Darcy shied away from thoughts of his relations, knowing it would do no good to dwell on them. None of his relations' reasons for pressuring him to marry had spurred him to think more of matrimony—rather, it was the thought that he would have assistance in rearing his younger sister. For if he took a wife, even if the woman was inexperienced, she would undoubtedly know more about raising a young girl than he did himself. At the very least, a wife would be able to draw on her own experience, helping his younger sister navigate the difficult waters and avoid the more dangerous shoals which sometimes appeared along the river of a young girl's life.

Enter Elizabeth Bennet. On the day he had first caught a glimpse of her, Darcy had written her off as a governess or a young mother to be walking with such a small babe in her arms. It had been truly nothing more than chance which had led him to be close enough to hear her words, as his hat had blown off by a gust of wind, taking him close to her side. It was a measure of the tumult of her thoughts that she had not noticed him there until she had risen.

But he had been instantly captivated by her story. There were few who would not jump at the chance for instant advancement and wealth, and yet she refused to bow to her mother's insistence and act in a manner which was contrary to her character. And her artfulness, her happiness in the face of tribulation, her appreciation for life, and her happy disposition were all traits Darcy did not possess and wished for more of in his life. Though he had not the wit to approach her when he had first heard her story, he could only be happy he had managed to meet her yet again. She was the breath of fresh air lacking in his life.

Though Darcy had kept his courtship with Miss Bennet to himself for the first week he had called on her, he soon decided it was time to tell his sister of Miss Bennet. Not only would Georgiana benefit by an association with the young woman Darcy esteemed, but he wished to share some measure of happiness with her. That Georgiana could benefit from Miss Bennet's disposition too, he was certain.

They were seated in the music room after dinner that night, Darcy listening with pleasure as Georgiana played for him. Even at the tender age of thirteen, she was already becoming quite proficient on the pianoforte, and she took to the instrument with an enthusiasm which sometimes necessitated a reminder that she had other studies which required her concentration. Regardless, Darcy was happy she had something she enjoyed so much, and as her playing led to his own enjoyment, he counted it a double blessing.

After she had played a few pieces, Darcy beckoned for her to join him on the sofa by his side, which she did with enthusiasm. Though still naught but a slip of a girl, Georgiana was tall for her age and slender, with a willowy sort of figure which was just beginning to develop. Her countenance was pale and free from most blemishes, except for a few freckles which would appear on her nose during the summer months. And her hair was spun gold, flowing in long, shimmering waves down her back when free from constraint. Darcy acknowledged that he was most likely biased, but he thought she would be the epitome of beauty when she attained her majority.

Perhaps more importantly, she was a sweet girl and eager to please. She had never given him a moment's trouble; her behavior had been always demure and proper. If she had one flaw, it was her lack of confidence which manifest itself in an almost crippling shyness with anyone other than those of her immediate family.

And perhaps even some of those, thought Darcy ruefully.

Focusing on the task at hand and shaking his head free of such extraneous thoughts, Darcy concentrated on his sister, favoring her with a smile.

"As always, your playing is lovely, my dear. You have practiced that piece diligently, it would seem."

"Oh, yes, brother," replied his sister. "It is one of my favorites, so it is no hardship to practice it."

"I believe practicing is not a hardship regardless," said Darcy. "You take to it with enthusiasm."

A shy smile met his words. "I am not so very fond of scales and the like, but I do enjoy playing."

"I am glad you do."

Darcy paused, wondering how to break the news to his sister. In the end, he decided to simply come out and tell her, as he thought she would be happy with such news and with the prospect of gaining a sister.

"I have something to tell you, Georgiana. You see, I have begun calling on a young lady."

Georgiana gasped. "You are courting someone?"

"I am. She is delightful, happy and pleasant. I believe you will like her very much indeed."

"That is wonderful!" cried Georgiana, almost bouncing up and down in her seat in her excitement. "I can hardly wait to meet her. I am sure, if you have chosen her, she must be a worthy young lady!"

Darcy laughed. "I am not infallible, Georgiana."

"I have always thought you were." Georgiana looked at him with a mischievous smile. "At least, I have never been witness to anything in your character resembling a fault."

"Will you force me to enumerate my many imperfections to disprove your words?"

"No, Brother," said Georgiana. "I am quite happy to continue to think of you in such a manner."

Shaking his head, Darcy allowed the subject to drop.

"Do I know her, Brother? Does she live close by?"

"I doubt you have ever met her, even in passing, dearest," said Darcy. "Her name is Miss Elizabeth Bennet, and she is currently living with her family on Gracechurch Street. Her father's estate is located in Hertfordshire, and I believe it is an easy distance from town."

A frown settled over Georgiana's face. "Gracechurch Street? But is that not in Cheapside, Brother?"

"*Near* Cheapside," corrected Darcy.

"So she is not of our level of society?"

"She is not, Georgiana, but to be honest, I count that as a point in her favor, rather than the reverse. She is clever and quick, bright and inquisitive, and she is kind and thoughtful to all. I believe that you will like her very much indeed."

Though Georgiana still seemed surprised, her manner quickly turned enthusiastic. "Since you recommend her, I must believe she is an estimable lady indeed." Suddenly overcome by shyness, Georgiana regarded him through lowered lashes. "When am I to meet this lady of whom you speak so highly?"

Darcy smiled at her enthusiasm. He had no doubt Georgiana would be comfortable with Miss Bennet as soon as Miss Bennet had the opportunity to charm his sister from her reserve.

"I will attempt to arrange a meeting as soon as may be. I am certain she will be happy to make your acquaintance."

At that moment the door opened and his cousin, Captain Fitzwilliam stepped into the room. Darcy had not seen his cousin for some time, and he rose to greet him with true pleasure, along with Georgiana, who let out a squeal and launched herself into Fitzwilliam's arms.

"Cousin! I had no notion that you were back in town. When did you arrive?"

"Only last night," said Fitzwilliam. "I have been reassigned to General Douglas's staff, along with a promotion to major."

"Well done!" exclaimed Darcy, at the same time Georgiana said, "Does that mean you shall not be sent to France any longer?"

Fitzwilliam smiled indulgently at his young cousin. "There are no guarantees, sprite. But I believe I am less likely to be called to such action while I hold this post."

Truly happy to once again be in company with his cousin, Darcy invited Fitzwilliam to sit and visit with them. Unfortunately, the first words out of Georgiana's mouth were those which Darcy had not yet been ready to share.

"Do you have any news?" asked Fitzwilliam after they had taken their seats on the sofa.

"The best news of all!" cried Georgiana. "For Fitzwilliam is calling upon a young lady. I dare entertain hope that I will have a sister before long."

"He has been?" asked Fitzwilliam, turning to raise an eyebrow at Darcy. "Is this a recent change in your brother's status?"

"Quite recent, I believe." Georgiana turned to Darcy and asked: "How long have you been calling on her, brother?"

"Only a week," said Darcy, wishing that he had asked his sister to keep the matter to herself. Though Fitzwilliam was all that was good and had many times derided the notion that the accident of birth accounted for the worth of a man, he was still a product of his father, who was a proud man. Darcy would rather have continued to visit Miss Bennet outside of his family's knowledge and to share the news when he deemed it appropriate to do so. At least he thought he could induce Fitzwilliam to stay silent concerning the matter.

For the next half hour Georgiana conversed with her cousin, speaking of her studies, her newly learned pieces on the pianoforte, and anything else which crossed her mind, with Darcy adding a few comments where appropriate. But while Fitzwilliam listened attentively, complimented where appropriate, and asked pertinent questions, he often attempted to turn the conversation back to Miss Bennet. And with each new revelation related to Elizabeth's standing in society and her likely connections, his expression became all that much more pensive. His frequently raised eyebrows in Darcy's direction were irksome, and Darcy wished he would desist.

At length, Georgiana excused herself to seek her bed, but not before she turned to Darcy and said: "I will hold you to your promise of an early introduction to your young lady, Brother."

"I hardly think she is *my* young lady at present, Georgiana."

"Perhaps not. But I cannot but think that the fact you have begun to call on her means that it will not be long before she is. You rarely engage in something half so important as the matter of your future wife without meaning to see it to its conclusion."

And with that, Georgiana leant to give both Darcy and Fitzwilliam a kiss on the cheek, and she excused herself, leaving the room.

"Well, it is evident that your sister knows you very well indeed," said Fitzwilliam.

Darcy could only allow it to be so.

"Now, what say we adjourn to your study and speak more of this Miss Bennet?"

"You just wish to partake of my brandy," grumbled Darcy, though his tone was nothing more than a good-natured tease.

"And I own it without disguise," agreed his affable cousin.

Retire to his study they did, and when they were ensconced with their glasses, Fitzwilliam fixed him with a long contemplative stare.

"Now, will you not tell me of this young lady?"

"If you wish," said Darcy.

Darcy then began to speak, telling his cousin of the past week, how he had met Miss Bennet, and how he had determined to call on her. He did not precisely gloss over her background or her recent struggles, but he still was not so explicit as his cousin wished. When Fitzwilliam pushed further, Darcy opened up with a few more tidbits of information, which still did not satisfy him, but he left over digging for more information in favor of beginning the expected teasing.

"I must hand it to you, Cousin," said Fitzwilliam, chortling into his glass. "You have described your life at times as predictable and even boring, but you have managed to inject a measure of excitement into your existence. Well done! I did not know you had it in you to be so impulsive!"

Darcy only shrugged. "It seemed better to be decisive, given the situation. If I had delayed, there was no telling if I would ever have found her again. And it is only a courtship. It may be ended at any time, should we decide that marriage is not what we wish."

Fitzwilliam pierced him with a skeptical look. "Do you actually think this young woman will willingly allow you to withdraw your suit, now that she has induced you to extend it?"

"I do," replied Darcy, allowing for no hint of disagreement. "Miss Elizabeth Bennet is perhaps the least pretentious girl I have ever met. She will not agree to marry me if it is not what she wishes, and her reasons will be quite unrelated to my fortune or standing, I assure you."

The pointed glare with which Fitzwilliam regarded him could not be misunderstood. "And how can you know this?"

Pausing, Darcy wondered if he should reveal Miss Bennet's circumstances to his cousin. Though it was not precisely a secret, he knew she would not wish for them to be bandied about like so much gossip. But Fitzwilliam's look told Darcy that he would not subside easily. Perhaps it was for the best if Fitzwilliam knew. He could help soften the blow when the earl was informed. Furthermore, Darcy trusted his cousin, perhaps more than any other in the entire world, and he was confident Fitzwilliam could be trusted with the true story of her recent history.

"I know she is not a fortune hunter as she has already refused a proposal from an eligible man, for no other reason than an inability to abide him."

"Truly?" asked Fitzwilliam. Darcy sensed that he was still more than a little unconvinced, though impressed in spite of himself. "And how do you know of this matter?"

"Because she informed me of it herself," replied Darcy.

"And you did not think to confirm the matter for yourself? That is most unlike you, Darcy."

Chuckling, Darcy turned a smug smile on his cousin. "I believe I have anticipated you, Fitzwilliam. Though we have spoken on the subject and her uncle informed me himself when I first met him, I first learned of it when she was speaking of the matter to her little niece."

Still Fitzwilliam was unmoved. "How do you know that she was not speaking for your benefit?"

"Come now, Cousin!" scoffed Darcy. "She was speaking for my benefit? There is no way she could have known if I was even there, let alone that I was close enough to hear. And how could she know that I would speak to her? That I would offer a courtship? Is that not a little too much for anyone to expect from a simple overheard conversation."

Putting out his hand in surrender, Fitzwilliam said: "When you put it like that, I suppose it is a little too much to plan in advance."

"I do put it like that," said Darcy. "Miss Bennet is no fortune hunter. I would stake my very reputation on it."

"You have staked your future happiness on it. I hope you are right."

Darcy was silent as he thought on the matter. The very idea that Miss Bennet was a fortune hunter defied all logic. In fact, when he thought of her . . .

"There is something artless about her manner. She is happy and carefree, and yet she is intelligent, thoughtful, and feels deeply, I believe. I have never met anyone like her. She is . . . I believe she will be the making of me."

"Then I believe she deserves you, Darcy."

Darcy started and looked at his cousin. He had not even realized that he had spoken aloud.

Laughing at his cousin's confusion, Fitzwilliam leaned forward in his chair. "When am I to meet this wondrous creature?

Chapter XI

Elizabeth was nervous, as her rapid pacing would attest to. She had become accustomed to meeting with Mr. Darcy, and she was starting to gain an appreciation for the quiet gentleman. Mr. Darcy was more than Elizabeth would ever have believed when she first met him. The first week of their courtship had been characterized by probing conversations, questions, and hesitance, as they learned more about each other. In recent days, however, they had begun sharing anecdotes which were more personal in nature. And though she had sometimes wondered if she could make a life with such a quiet gentlemen, she now knew that whatever else might happen in the future, she could not imagine refusing him on such grounds alone. In fact, with her more outgoing character, they seemed to be quite well matched indeed.

What Mr. Darcy thought of her, Elizabeth could not be quite certain. It was evident he enjoyed her company, as he was more animated with her than he was with her uncle and aunt, for example. And Elizabeth often found that Mr. Darcy watched her with a steady, earnest sort of gaze which appeared to be slightly contemplative in nature. Whether this was an attention to her looks, her character, or to something else altogether, she could not say. But much could develop from such a beginning.

But today marked a completely new element in their relationship. For the first time, Elizabeth was to be introduced to the formidable Miss Georgiana Darcy.

The thought almost caused Elizabeth to stop her pacing and laugh at her own ridiculousness. Whatever Elizabeth had heard of Mr. Darcy's sister, "formidable" did not seem to be an adjective which could be used with any great accuracy. In fact, Mr. Darcy had confided in Elizabeth that his sister was shy and afraid of doing wrong. Whatever else she was, Elizabeth did not expect to meet a young woman who would look down on her and demand her brother give up his unseemly infatuation with such an unworthy woman.

That was not what was concerning Elizabeth. It was the fact that the man was now comfortable enough in her company and desirable of furthering their understanding sufficiently to recommend a meeting with his much younger sister, of whom he was quite protective. Elizabeth did not wish to make a poor impression upon his sister—she knew the girl would likely approve of her based on her brother's recommendation alone, but as the elder, she would wish to be a proper example. Elizabeth doubted she was capable, given her upbringing in a much lower sphere.

"Elizabeth!" exclaimed Mrs. Gardiner. "You have been pacing the floor these past ten minutes at least. Shall you not sit for a while? I am afraid you will wear right through the floor boards!"

Though with fond affection, Elizabeth rolled her eyes at her aunt, receiving a laugh in response.

"Come, my dear. Sit on the sofa and let us speak of this."

Reluctant to leave her pacing, Elizabeth nevertheless approached her aunt and sat by her dutifully. Mr. and Mrs. Gardiner had been pillars of strength to her these past weeks. This was not the first time Mrs. Gardiner had called her niece to her side to calm her. It most certainly would not be the last.

"I believe you are fretting a little too much this time," said Mrs. Gardiner when Elizabeth was seated by her side.

"And I have not fretted too much any of the other times?"

"I would not say that. But this time seems a little different."

"I am to meet the man's sister!" exclaimed Elizabeth. "His much younger sister, whom he does not introduce to many. I believe I am entitled to a bout of nerves."

Mrs. Gardiner grinned with true delight. "It is at times like this, Elizabeth, that I am reminded how much you are your mother's daughter."

Though shocked, Elizabeth regarded her aunt with an expression of mock affront. "Like my mother indeed!"

"Can you deny it? You pace the floor as if you are about to meet the queen herself, when it will be nothing more than the shy younger sister of the man who is courting you. Do you think he would arrange for this meeting if he did not think you would be a good influence on his sister?"

"Of course not. But since I am meeting her, I will be expected to provide her with a good example of genteel manners and impeccable comportment. How can I provide such an exemplary model?"

"By simply being Elizabeth Bennet," said Aunt Gardiner.

Elizabeth watched her aunt for a moment, wondering if she was making sport with her, but Mrs. Gardiner only smiled gently.

"You have agonized over every detail of this courtship far too much, Elizabeth. It almost makes one wonder if your feelings are already engaged."

These words were spoken with a raised eyebrow and a hint of a smile, and Elizabeth found herself blushing in response.

"I do not believe so, Aunt. Not yet at least. But I do find him . . ."

"Amiable? Handsome? Agreeable?" asked her aunt when she did not immediately reply.

Shaking her head, Elizabeth said: "I do not know that Mr. Darcy can be called 'amiable,' though he has always spoken respectfully and pleasantly to me. I believe he can be quite severe."

"And yet, by your own admission, he has never been that way with you," reminded Mrs. Gardiner with a pointed look.

"No, he has not. But I do not believe my feelings are engaged. It is far too early for that."

"But you desire his good opinion."

"I do."

They were silent for a few moments, and Elizabeth's thoughts returned to when Mr. Darcy had made the request to introduce his sister. They had been visiting in the Gardiners' sitting room only two days before, and their conversation had been a little sparser than it normally was. Elizabeth had thought something was on the man's mind, and while she tried to induce him to speak, she was also mindful of allowing him the benefit of his thoughts. Thus, the application had been quite a surprise.

"Miss Bennet," said he, speaking up quite unexpectedly, "I know we have only been meeting for these past few days, but I wonder if I might introduce my sister to your acquaintance."

Taken by surprise, Elizabeth was unable to say anything for a brief moment after his request. She soon marshalled herself for a response, however, which was delivered with at least tolerable composure.

"I would be happy to make your sister's acquaintance, Mr. Darcy. Everything you have told me of her suggests she is a lovely girl."

"She is, Miss Bennet. But I believe your vivacity would be a perfect counterpoint for her reticence. I cannot but suppose she would benefit greatly from an acquaintance with you. And I believe we have reached the time in our courtship where introducing you would be desirable."

"Then I shall wait with anticipation, Mr. Darcy."

At the time, Elizabeth had wondered if he had seen through her nervousness. Mr. Darcy had endeavored to once again steer the conversation as Elizabeth had been too full of thoughts for the upcoming introduction, and she had been grateful for his assistance. Now, as she remembered the ensuing conversation, she remembered little anecdotes he had shared with her of his sister, and she thought they might have been designed to make his sister appear less imposing.

And yes, Mrs. Gardiner was right—Elizabeth found that Mr. Darcy's opinion of her was important. She could not yet say that she loved him or that she even wished to be in love with him. But his good opinion was important, perhaps more important than any other man's she had ever before met.

A movement by Elizabeth's side caught her attention, and she looked at her aunt, noting Mrs. Gardiner's continuing amusement, which was tempered with a hint of serious reflection.

"Just remember to be the Lizzy Bennet your uncle and I know and love. If you are, I believe you have nothing about which to concern yourself regarding Mr. and Miss Darcy. She cannot help but love you."

Elizabeth smiled at her aunt, grateful for Mrs. Gardiner's steady guidance.

At that moment, the door chime rang, and Elizabeth reflexively looked at the door. They had arrived; the moment had come.

Within a few moments, the visitors had been led into the sitting-room by the housekeeper, and Elizabeth was able to receive her first impression of Georgiana Darcy. She was a typical girl of thirteen, she thought, with long flowing blonde locks, which had been pinned to the back of her head in an elegant style. In brother and sister there was a marked resemblance—she possessed some of his strong jaw and his prominent nose, though softened due to her femininity. Elizabeth thought the girl would be uncommonly pretty when she was fully grown.

She also hung back a little as they entered, eyes darting this way and that, in the manner of a startled doe. When the girl's eye alighted on Elizabeth, they settled on her for an instant before they looked down at her feet, her face blooming with color. And so, all Mr. Darcy's assertions concerning his sister's reticence were confirmed.

"Miss Bennet," said Mr. Darcy. He approached and bowed over her hand, bestowing a significant look on her which made Elizabeth feel warm inside. "I thank you and Mrs. Gardiner for welcoming us today."

"It is no trouble, Mr. Darcy," said Elizabeth, remembering her manners. "We are quite delighted to make your sister's acquaintance."

Mr. Darcy smiled, though it was understated, and gesturing to his sister, said: "Miss Bennet, Mrs. Gardiner, I would like to introduce you to my sister, Georgiana. Georgiana, Miss Elizabeth Bennet, and Mrs. Meredith Gardiner. Miss Bennet is the young lady I have been calling on these past weeks, and Mrs. Gardiner is her aunt."

"I am delighted to meet you, Miss Darcy," said Elizabeth, dropping into a curtsey which was mirrored by the young girl.

Miss Darcy likely said something in response, but whatever it was, Elizabeth would be surprised if it was audible all the way to the floor, which was where her mouth had been pointed. Bashful did not even begin to state Miss Darcy's behavior.

The young girl's obvious shyness incited Elizabeth's sympathy, and she determined to draw the girl out.

"Shall we sit and call for tea?" asked Mrs. Gardiner.

"Thank you," said Mr. Darcy, and he led his sister to a sofa, ensuring she was seated next to Elizabeth, before taking his own seat on her other side. There, Miss Darcy surprised Elizabeth by exerting herself to speak, when moments before she had seemed almost incapable of doing so.

"M—my brother has told me of you, Miss Bennet," said Miss Darcy, her eyes travelling up Elizabeth's person, though stopping before they reached her eyes.

"I hope he was not too severe, Miss Darcy," replied Elizabeth, with an arch look at Mr. Darcy.

In apparent shock, Miss Darcy's eyes darted up to Elizabeth's face. "Severe?" squeaked she. "That has not been the case at all! Quite the contrary, I assure you!"

"Then I am happy to hear it," said Elizabeth, smiling at the girl and attempting to put her at ease. "For when he speaks of you, Miss Darcy, I hear nothing but pride and affection in his voice. It is clear that he quite thinks you are the best sister in the entire world."

Suddenly shy again, Miss Darcy's eyes dropped to the floor before she once again turned to Mr. Darcy. For his part, Mr. Darcy appeared to be amused, and his affectionate look at his sister confirmed her words. All these things happened within an instant, but they appeared to serve to calm her; she smiled shyly before she turned back to Elizabeth and actually met her eyes without having to be shocked into it.

"And I believe that William is the best of brothers. I have been blessed."

"William?" asked Elizabeth, directing a raised eyebrow at Mr. Darcy. "I thought your brother possessed some dignified and imposing name, designed to infuse respect and admiration from all those with whom he comes into contact. And yet you refer to him with a more familiar moniker?"

At this, Georgiana Darcy actually giggled. For his part, Mr. Darcy directed a frown at Elizabeth. "A dignified name it might be, but I assure you that I do not use it as a weapon."

"It is also too much of a mouthful," said Miss Darcy. "I much prefer to refer to him using the shorter form."

"And it also eliminates confusion," added Mr. Darcy. "My cousin, Major Fitzwilliam, is typically referred to by his surname. His elder brother, of course, is referred to by his title, as he is a viscount."

Filing this information aside for later contemplation, Elizabeth focused once again on Georgiana Darcy. The girl was sitting demurely beside her brother, but Elizabeth caught a glimpse of her eyes flicking up to her a few times, as if the girl did not quite know what to make of her.

"I will share a secret with you," said Elizabeth, leaning forward as if to share something of such a profound nature that it could not be said aloud. "I have no brothers, only five sisters. I cannot tell you how fortunate you are to have a brother."

Once again Georgiana Darcy giggled. "I should have liked to have a sister."

She looked like she wished to say more but lacked the courage, so Elizabeth took up the conversation yet again.

"Sisters are wonderful for sharing confidences and discussing subjects in which gentlemen have no interest. But there are drawbacks to sisters too. There tends to exist a rivalry, of sorts. In my case, as my elder sister is the sweetest tempered lady I have ever met, and quite five times as pretty as the rest of us, there truly is no competition."

"I believe you exaggerate, Miss Bennet," ventured Miss Darcy. "I find you quite lovely. I am certain my brother does too."

Though given an opening to voice his opinion, Mr. Darcy said nothing. But the way he smiled at his sister and then the manner in which he turned a frank gaze on Elizabeth left her quite breathless and filled with anticipation, though for what she could not say.

The conversation continued, focused on general matters, though the subject of Mrs. Gardiner's childhood living in Lambton once again came up, and the three discussed some remembrances of the area and a few stories about common acquaintances. Mrs. Gardiner even told Miss Darcy about having met Lady Anne Darcy when she was young, enthralling the girl with tales of her charitable works and her beauty of form and feature and of character.

By the time tea had arrived, Elizabeth was quite on the way to knowing this young, shy girl, and she could not but be happy with the acquaintance. As the daughter of a wealthy man, she was well aware that Miss Darcy could have been insufferably proud and haughty. In short, she could have been another Caroline Bingley, though with much greater reason for feeling superior.

But she was nothing of the sort. She was shy and sweet and genuine, and Elizabeth felt certain that should her courtship with Mr. Darcy proceed to its natural conclusion, she would be able to love her new sister with tolerable ease. There was something endearing about her which prompted a protective streak in Elizabeth. She was not much different from Jane, in essentials, though Jane's reticence was more borne of simply a quiet nature, whereas Miss Darcy was overly shy. Elizabeth thought that should they meet, Jane and Miss Darcy would get along famously.

At length, the tea service was delivered, along with a few cakes, and they all settled in to have afternoon tea. Conversation continued, and by the end of their teatime, Elizabeth thought she had become fast friends with her suitor's sister. It was an auspicious beginning to her relationship with the young girl, and she was happy with how it had gone.

Near the end of the Darcys' visit, a chance remark alerted Elizabeth to the knowledge that one member of Mr. Darcy's extended family had already been made aware of her courtship with Mr. Darcy.

"Oh, yes," said Miss Darcy with enthusiasm. "My cousin, Major Fitzwilliam, has returned to London. When he came to visit us a few days ago, we spoke of the matter. I believe he is anticipating meeting you."

"Is he now?" asked Elizabeth, turning a questioning gaze on Mr. Darcy.

"Fitzwilliam is my dearest friend," said Mr. Darcy by way of explanation. "I believe he will be happy to make your acquaintance."

Elizabeth nodded. "With a recommendation such as that, I shall be quite happy to be introduced to him."

It was not long afterwards when the Darcys rose to take their leave, and Elizabeth walked them to the door at the suggestion of her aunt. The visitors gathered their gloves and coats and prepared to depart, but as they were walking out the door, Miss Darcy paused and turned back to Elizabeth, a bashful sort of smile on her face.

"Miss Bennet, if you . . . if you would not mind . . ." The girl paused, clearly embarrassed. When she spoke, her words came out in a rush. "May I refer to you by your Christian name? I would be happy if you would call me 'Georgiana.'"

Heart melting at the earnest entreaty from this young girl, Elizabeth smiled and grasped her hands. "Of course you may. My sisters call me 'Elizabeth' or 'Lizzy,' and my close friend calls me 'Eliza.' I think I would prefer either of the first two."

"Elizabeth it is," said Georgiana, a beaming smile coming over her face. "I have no nicknames, but it would please you if you would call me 'Georgiana.'"

Elizabeth laughed. "You mean no one has ever called you 'Georgie?'"

The other girl joined her in laughter. "No, but if you insist upon it, I shall not mind."

"Well, for the present I shall stick to your full name. But I warn you I might revert to the more familiar at some point. I and two of my other sisters all have nicknames, and the others don't simply because they have boring, short names."

Georgiana giggled. "In that case, those of us with longer names must be allowed to make our names easier for others to remember."

"Except when we are vexed with one another!" cried Elizabeth. "Then the use of the full name is required!"

The two girls collapsed against each other giggling. Elizabeth, who happened to be facing Mr. Darcy, who was behind his sister, looked up at the man, noting his indulgence with his sister. When he saw Elizabeth looking at him, he nodded to her, Elizabeth thought in thanks. She could only flush with pleasure at the sight and return his nod. His sister truly was a precious creature, and befriending her was no trial at all.

Then the Darcys went away, leaving Elizabeth alone to her thoughts. There truly was something infinitely estimable about the Darcys. For the first time, Elizabeth began to feel like she had been very fortunate to have come to Mr. Darcy's attention.

Though meeting the man's sister had been preceded by Elizabeth's pacing the floor, it was nothing compared to the return visit which took place a few days later. Before they left, Elizabeth and her aunt had fixed the time when they would return the favor, and though she tried not to think of it, Elizabeth spent the intervening time worrying concerning the upcoming visit.

It was fortunate indeed that Mrs. Gardiner was so calm and rational, for she was able to see to the crux of the matter in a way Elizabeth had not.

"Do not focus upon the house, Lizzy."

Curious as to her aunt's meaning, she cocked her head to the side and watched her aunt as she chuckled and understood Elizabeth's question.

"You are feeling a little intimidated by the thought of seeing Mr. Darcy's large home. Am I correct?"

Elizabeth murmured that she was indeed, and her aunt smiled at her again. "Mr. Darcy's house might be a large house, lavishly decorated with all the latest styles, and displaying Mr. Darcy's wealth. But in the end it is nothing more than a house. I suggest you focus on the people living in that house: Mr. Darcy, with whom I believe you have become quite comfortable, and Miss Darcy, who is as sweet a creature as I have ever met—these should be your focus."

"But are my fears not rational?" asked Elizabeth, a hint of complaint which she could not suppress entering her voice. "I have not been brought up to manage such a place as I expect Darcy house to be, and Pemberley, from what you have told me, is very grand indeed."

"Are you not an intelligent girl? Have you not been brought up as a gentleman's daughter? The difference is in the scale.

"Furthermore, you should remember that Mr. Darcy's mother passed on more than twelve years ago. In all that time, there has been no mistress to oversee either property, which suggests the housekeepers possess a great deal of autonomy. With no mistress in all that time, it is possible the house is not done up in the latest fashions. Watch for such things, as they will make the house appear more manageable, and less imposing than before."

The discussion left Elizabeth with much to think about, and by the time they finally entered the Gardiner carriage for the journey to Mayfair, she had managed to compose herself tolerably.

They passed through many neighborhoods on the way to the Darcy townhouse, and on one street, Elizabeth thought she recognized the location as one which was near to Mr. Bingley's townhouse. She was not certain, so she did not mention it to her aunt, but the thought that the Bingleys were not very far from the Darcys helped Elizabeth to further come to terms with the impending visit.

That was where the similarity ended. The carriage finally pulled up in front of a large, three story townhouse which sat on the corner of a picturesque district. The stone façade was imposing in the manner in which it loomed out over the street. Across the street from the house stood a large park with many lovely walkways—Elizabeth looked at it longingly, wishing she could explore its environs. She consoled herself with the knowledge that should she marry Mr. Darcy, she would no doubt become intimately familiar with it.

Though the locales were not truly a great distance from each other, Mr. Darcy's house was further removed from Mr. Bingley's house than Mr. Bingley's house was from Gracechurch Street. It truly was an imposing building, and all of Elizabeth's insecurities once again began to well up within her.

A footman was on hand to assist Elizabeth and her aunt from the carriage, and soon they had alighted and stood on the stairs where Georgiana was waiting for them. The girl beamed brightly in greeting, stepping forward to curtsey to Elizabeth, and then grasping her by the hand and tugging on it, leading her into the house.

"Oh, Elizabeth! I am so glad you have come today!"

Elizabeth watched the girl through bemused eyes, noting how the shy creature she had first met the day before seemed to have been replaced by this enthusiastic young girl. Elizabeth could not be happier at the transformation; the friendship of Mr. Darcy's sister was not to be taken lightly. It would no doubt smooth her way into effectively becoming mistress of the house if she had the support of his only sister.

"We were truly happy to come, Georgiana," replied Elizabeth. "You have a lovely home."

"It is *home*," replied the girl, "though I believe William would agree that it is Pemberley which is truly our home. Still, I have fond memories of this house, and I am glad to show it to you.

"William extends his apologies, but he has been detained by a matter of business. He shall join us later."

Though feeling a sense of disappointment, Elizabeth nodded and allowed Georgiana to lead her and her aunt into the house.

When they entered the vestibule, Elizabeth looked around with interest. The foyer was large, the ceiling high, and it could obviously be seen as the home of a wealthy man. The floors were covered in a marble tile, which also sheathed the stairs leading to the second floor, and over the entire area hung an enormous crystal chandelier, which would undoubtedly be difficult and time-consuming for the servants to light.

Fortunately, there were also wall sconces spaced around the room to provide light; Elizabeth suspected the imposing chandelier was only lit on special occasions, such as when the Darcys were hosting a ball. If Elizabeth's guess was in any way correct, she suspected that they had not hosted such an event in many years.

That final thought brought her up short for a moment; if she married Mr. Darcy, surely *she* would be responsible for planning such an event someday. The mere thought almost caused Elizabeth's carefully held nerves to once again run amuck.

Calm yourself, you silly goose! Elizabeth told herself sternly.

Even if she was required to do such a thing, surely it would not be for some time, at least after she had had a chance to grow into her new role a little. There was no sense in fretting over such things.

"Come, Elizabeth, Mrs. Gardiner," said Georgiana. "I wish to introduce you to our housekeeper, Mrs. Mayberry, and our butler, Mr. Johnson."

It was then that Elizabeth noticed a stout woman of middle years and a tall, severe man standing patiently to one side, studying her. Putting on a smile, Elizabeth allowed herself to be led forward, and she greeted them with perfect composure and exchanged a few words.

"Mrs. Mayberry has been the housekeeper of Darcy house since I was a girl," said Georgiana. "She and Mrs. Reynolds at Pemberley are the best housekeepers in all of England! And Mr. Johnson has been here since my father was a boy!"

Though the pair listened to the praise with stoic patience, Elizabeth thought she detected a hint of a blush on the woman's face. It was not evident in her manners, however, as she spoke with Elizabeth, answering questions and apparently filing what she saw of Elizabeth away for future reference.

"I have worked at Darcy house since I was a girl, Miss Bennet," said Mrs. Mayberry when asked. "I started as a junior maid and worked my way up to my present position. I was fortunate in that old Mr. Darcy approved of his servants learning, and thus I was taught to read and do my sums."

"And I can see that you perform your position excellently," said Elizabeth, looking around the foyer. It was true—she could see no deficiencies in the way the work had been completed. Everything fairly gleamed in the morning sun.

"I thank you, Miss Benet," replied Mrs. Mayberry. "The house has run smoothly on our established practices for many years. I do naught but direct the servants and ensure that everything we have always done is continued."

There was just a hint of question in the woman's voice. After a moment, Elizabeth understood; as the woman the master was courting, she would have a great deal of influence on Mrs. Mayberry's position. A poor or demanding mistress could make the servants' lives difficult, and the woman would no doubt be wondering if she would be inclined to make changes to her already carefully managed domain.

"Everything appears to have been done magnificently, Mrs. Mayberry. You and the rest of the servants have done outstanding work."

A true smile of pleasure lit up the woman's face. "Thank you, Miss Bennet. Now, I believe Miss Darcy has mentioned something about a tour of the house?"

Agreeing, Elizabeth allowed herself to be led away by the housekeeper, while acknowledging the butler's bow as he moved off into a different part of the house. The man was almost as stoic as Mr. Darcy, for he had not said more than two words. He might have been equally likely to disapprove of Elizabeth as he might be to write an anthem of praise to her for all she could see in his manners.

As they walked, Elizabeth felt her aunt grasp her hand and squeeze it with gentle affection, and she noted her smile of approval.

"Well done, Elizabeth," said Mrs. Gardiner in a soft voice. "Your installation into this house will be much more easily accomplished if Mrs. Mayberry is friendly with you."

As they were just about to be led into one of the many rooms, Elizabeth did nothing more than smile her thanks.

"This is the music room, Elizabeth," said Georgiana with an absolutely effervescent fervor. "It is my favorite room in the house."

What followed was a dizzying display of the house's most prominent features. All of the rooms were decorated finely, with costly materials and well-built and finely crafted furniture. It was not long before Elizabeth realized it would take some time before she would ever know the house intimately, though she surely understood it must be nothing to Pemberley.

"How exquisite!" exclaimed Elizabeth when they were led into the library.

It was a long, rectangular room, with shelves situated on every available space along the walls, and which were literally groaning with the weight of a great bounty of books. There were more books in this room than she had ever seen in one place, even the bookseller's in Meryton. Elizabeth knew immediately that she could spend many happy hours in this room. If her father ever visited, it was not certain he would ever leave!

"This is the smaller of our two libraries," said Georgiana. "The library at Pemberley takes up two floors, each of which is double the size of this room."

Eyes wide as saucers, Elizabeth looked at Georgiana with disbelief. "Your library at Pemberley is four times the size of *this*?"

Georgiana shrugged in an offhand manner. "Approximately. William would know better than I. but it is a large and handsome room, and when he is in residence, he spends much time there. His study is in an adjoining room, which allows him easy access to some of the books he uses to manage the estate."

"It must be wondrous indeed," said Mrs. Gardiner. "But you must remember, Lizzy," continued she, directing a mock glare at Elizabeth, "there are other things to life than reading."

"You may need to remind me of that fact on occasion," said Elizabeth to Georgiana with a little laugh. "Should I ever see the library at Pemberley, I might just forget the rest of the world exists."

Georgiana smiled, a smug quality inherent in it. "William is the same way."

Deciding it was best to allow that to pass, Elizabeth approached one of the nearby shelves, looking at the titles on the spines of the books. On instinct, she raised her hand and ran her fingers across the spines, tracing the titles, and relishing the feeling of the leather, breathing in the scent of so much accumulated knowledge. She felt in that moment she might be willing to marry Mr. Darcy on the recommendation of his excellent library alone!

When the other three ladies were finally able to pull Elizabeth from the books, they continued the tour of the principle rooms, ending up in the main sitting-room, where Georgiana called for a tea service. It was indeed a handsome house, Elizabeth thought, and she was happy her friend had shown it to her.

But a curious thing had happened as they had proceeded on the tour. Though the rooms were obviously decorated with the best items money could buy, it was still functional—elegant, yet comfortable, like she would expect a home to be. Furthermore, what her aunt had said about the interior of the house lacking recent updates was correct. Everything was cared for in an impeccable manner, but still Elizabeth had seen certain places where the wallpaper was a little faded, or the corner of a sofa had seemed a little worn.

It was clear the work of decorating the rooms had been completed by

Lady Anne Darcy, which meant that it was more than a dozen years old and likely quite a bit older. That she would need to make the decisions on new décor was a little intimidating to Elizabeth, but what she saw was more than a little comforting to her. And as she sat in the sitting room with Georgiana and her aunt, sipping tea and speaking of inconsequential subjects, she decided that she would not allow her insecurities to get the better of her again.

I will be perfectly courageous, thought Elizabeth to herself. *I will not allow myself to be intimidated. In fact, every attempt to intimidate me shall be met with greater fortitude and perseverance!*

They had been sitting in this attitude for some moments when a gentleman wearing regimentals stepped into the room and approached them. He was a tall man, with brown hair of a lighter shade than Mr. Darcy's, possessing broad shoulders and an erect bearing. His size was truly intimidating, especially to a small woman like Elizabeth, as he was truly a bear of a man, standing even taller than Mr. Darcy. But the genial look in his eyes and the expressive smile on his face told Elizabeth he was also a happy, contented man, one who was kind to all and sundry, as long as one did not make an enemy of him.

"Georgiana!" boomed he as he approached them. "I see you are entertaining friends today."

With a smile of true delight, Georgiana sprung up from her place on the sofa and threw herself into the man's arms.

"Anthony! You know very well the lady William is courting is visiting today. Is that not why you have come yourself?"

The major turned piercing blue eyes on Elizabeth, and for a moment she thought he was about to disapprove of her. Then his brow crinkled with amusement, and he disengaged from Georgiana's arms, favoring her with an affectionate grin.

"I did not come specifically to meet William's young lady, but I will not refuse an introduction should you choose to favor me with one."

"Oh, Anthony!" cried Georgiana. "Can you not ever be serious?"

The major gave Georgiana an outrageous wink. "Not if I can help it, my dear."

Elizabeth could not help but laugh. "A man after my own heart!"

The introductions were performed and within moments, the major was ensconced with the ladies, drinking tea and prompting their laughter at his stories. Elizabeth could not tell if the man actually led such a colorful life or if he was just an excessively talented storyteller, but she could not remember another time when she had been so ably entertained by a gentleman. Most of the rest of the visit passed in this agreeable manner.

It was near the end of their time there when Elizabeth found herself cornered by the major. She could not determine how he had managed it, but Aunt Gardiner and Georgiana ended up across the room looking at a painting—Elizabeth was given to understand it was a depiction of fabled Pemberley—and the major began to ask her questions.

"I understand you live in Hertfordshire, Miss Bennet?"

"Yes, sir," replied Elizabeth. "My father's estate is near the town of Meryton, only about four hours distant."

The man rubbed his chin in thought. "Though I have never stopped in Meryton, I have ridden through on occasion."

"I dare say it is not the most exciting place in the world," said Elizabeth.

"And your father is a gentleman?"

"Yes. My family has held our estate for more than two centuries, and though the estate is not large enough to provide us entry into the upper echelons of society, it is well maintained and prosperous."

"I understand you have several siblings?"

"Four sisters."

The major frowned. "And your father's estate is entailed away?"

"On a distant cousin, sir."

A brief silence ensued while the major considered what she had told him. Elizabeth supposed that she might feel annoyed at his persistent questioning, but in truth it was nothing less than she expected from his family. In fact, based on some of the few things Mr. Darcy had said since he began courting her, Elizabeth rather thought this was only a taste of what would ensue when his uncle was told.

"Miss Bennet, may I be frank?"

Though startled at the directness of the question, Elizabeth could only nod; perhaps it was for the best after all.

"Thank you." He paused and smiled, she thought in an attempt to disarm her, for all she also suspected it to be genuine. "I would not speak in this manner unless prompted by the sincerest concern for my cousin. I believe you must apprehend that you are not precisely what society would expect my cousin to focus on."

"I do understand. However, I do not believe I am any less worthy than any other young woman due to nothing more than the fact that I do not possess a large dowry or connections to a duke."

Major Fitzwilliam barked in laughter. "Well said, Miss Bennet. Well said, indeed. You will find that I agree with you. I have met many a man during my time in the regulars who possesses the finest credentials, but lacks something intrinsic in his character. You will find that I tend to judge people on their merits. This has, at times, put me at odds with my father and my brother.

"What I truly wish to determine is your intentions, specifically with respect to my cousin. He has suffered unduly these past years, and it has changed him, almost beyond recognition. He deserves happiness in his life, and I would not see him bound to a woman who does not care for him."

Elizabeth nodded, but she did not respond immediately. This was important, she sensed; to gain the major's approval, the relation to whom Mr. Darcy was closest, would be no small matter in gaining the approval of his other relations.

"I do understand your meaning, Major," said Elizabeth. "I am aware of the obstacles standing in my way, and I know that I will be looked down on for daring to raise my sights to someone of your cousin's standing.

"The fact of the matter is that I do not know what my intentions are." The major raised an eyebrow at that admission, but Elizabeth only nodded. "It depends on how my relationship with Mr. Darcy develops. If it progresses to the point where we can each boast a sincere attachment to the other, then I will gladly accept a proposal from him."

"And if it does not?" challenged the major. "Will you give up Darcy's wealth because you do not love him?"

Elizabeth sighed. "I am well aware of my position and Mr. Darcy's ability to care for me and any children I might be blessed with. I am not insensible to prudence, sir. But I believe I will not allow it to rule me."

Elizabeth stopped for a moment, eying the major while debating how much to tell him. In the end, she decided she gained nothing from keeping silent, so she determined to tell him everything which motivated her.

"Can I assume Mr. Darcy has told you little of my specific circumstances?"

"No, in fact," replied the major with a wry grin. "He was rather close-mouthed about you, though he did tell me some more general information."

"I expected as much. In truth, Major Fitzwilliam, I have not had much of a good example of matrimony, at least from my parents. My mother is a silly woman, who, though I love as my mother, is not the epitome of sense. By contrast, my father is a learned, erudite man, who I believe married on the strength of sudden infatuation. Theirs is not a happy marriage, and is one I would not emulate.

"I believe that love in a marriage is to be desired, and I wish for nothing less for myself. Respect is equally important. If I can find these things with Mr. Darcy, and if he chooses to propose to me, then I believe I will accept him. But I do not believe I can make any promises at this time."

Elizabeth paused and favored the major with a saucy smile, which prompted a laugh. "Will that suffice, sir?"

Still chuckling and shaking his head, the major turned the first genuine smile Elizabeth had seen directed at her. "I believe you will do, Miss Bennet. I believe you will do. I could not wish for anything more for my cousin."

"I am glad I meet with your approval, sir," replied Elizabeth. "I cannot imagine what I would have done should I have been unable to gain the support of one as important as you."

The sound of the major's delighted laughter rang throughout the room.

Chapter XII

Never had a delay due to business been more vexing to Darcy. Knowing that Miss Bennet was to return his sister's visit today, Darcy had wished to be available to greet her and show her his home. But an urgent request for a meeting had come from his solicitor, requiring Darcy's presence at the man's office. That it was situated near to Gracechurch Street meant that Darcy would be passing Miss Bennet somewhere along the way, and though he watched out the window, hoping to catch a glimpse of her along the way, he had not espied her, leaving him in an annoyed mood.

The matter with his solicitor had taken some time to deal with, but when it was finally at an end, Darcy bounded from the office into his carriage with a terse command to return to the house as quickly as possible. The return journey was an opportunity for Darcy to think on the situation, and especially his own reaction to his inability to be at his house that morning.

As Darcy could readily confess to himself, he enjoyed the time he spent with Miss Bennet, and he keenly anticipated their next occasion to meet. Furthermore, showing the woman he was courting his house for the first time was an opportunity to witness her reaction. He did not know why it was so important to him already, but her approval was something to be sought after. He could not explain it any more clearly than that.

When Darcy thought back on the past weeks, he was surprised that Miss Bennet had wormed her way into this heart and his consciousness. She had a joy of life, a happiness and ability to look at the positive which Darcy knew he lacked, particularly in the years since his father had passed away. Darcy did not know what madness had possessed him to approach her, but he was now happy he had. He wanted that optimism to be part of his life.

As soon as the carriage pulled up to the house, Darcy stepped out without waiting for the footman to open the door for him. He leapt up the stairs two and three at a time and entered the house, to be greeted by his faithful butler, who stood by the open door ready to take his hat and coat.

"Are Miss Bennet and Mrs. Gardiner still visiting my sister?"

Johnson nodded. "They are in the sitting-room with Miss Georgiana and Major Fitzwilliam.

Darcy frowned that that last piece of intelligence. He had not expected his cousin that day, and he had a suspicion that Fitzwilliam's presence was anything other than unplanned. Darcy trusted his cousin, but he could not imagine him passing up the opportunity to interrogate Miss Bennet in Darcy's absence.

"Thank you, Johnson. I shall join them directly."

"Very good, sir." The butler paused for a moment, as if thinking of something, then he looked back at Darcy, his expression unreadable as usual. "Miss Bennet is a happy young lady. It seems Miss Georgiana is excessively fond of her."

Then with a bow, Johnson retreated, leaving Darcy staring after the man with amazement. Though his words had been brief and almost prosaic, to Darcy, who had known him since his earliest years, they were nothing less than a ringing endorsement.

Shaking his head, Darcy headed for the sitting-room and, pausing at a mirror to make sure there was nothing amiss with his appearance, stepped into the room.

And he was immediately displeased. Georgiana, along with Mrs. Gardiner, was on one side of the room while Fitzwilliam was in close conference with Miss Bennet on another. His pique was lessened when his cousin threw back his head and roared with laughter; apparently Miss Bennet had worked her magic in charming Fitzwilliam, who, though he was adept at his own brand of charm, was still quite protective of Darcy and Georgiana. Regardless, Fitzwilliam should never have presumed to importune her in such a fashion.

"Darcy!" exclaimed Fitzwilliam when he espied Darcy crossing the room. "Come join us, man. I have been speaking with Miss Bennet, and have found her to be an agreeable and intelligent conversation partner indeed."

A long look passed between Darcy and Fitzwilliam, and Darcy decided to ignore the matter for the nonce; his cousin's words were nothing less than his own approval of Miss Bennet. At least he had not attempted to intimidate her.

"She is indeed, Fitzwilliam."

When he had stopped in front of them, Darcy bowed over Miss Bennet's hand in greeting, bestowing a smile on her in which he attempted to show her his growing regard.

"Miss Bennet, I am happy you were able to visit with Georgiana today, and I apologize for my own absence."

"It is quite all right, Mr. Darcy," said Miss Bennet. "We had an agreeable visit with your sister. I must say you have a lovely home."

"Why do you think I stay here so often, Miss Bennet?" asked Fitzwilliam. "Not only are my rooms well-appointed and comfortable, but my cousins' society is superior to anything else I might find in London."

"Not to mention how much you enjoy my brandy," replied Darcy.

Fitzwilliam laughed. "Indeed! We must not forget that!"

Miss Bennet turned a raised eyebrow on Fitzwilliam. "So you prey on your cousin's good will for nothing more than the reward of his brandy? Strange that you did not see fit to mention that to me."

Laughter once again echoed throughout the room. "Darcy, I think I must withdraw my approval of this young lady," said Fitzwilliam through his laughter. "She sees through my paltry attempts at obfuscation far too readily. How am I ever to maintain any hint of credit?"

"Perhaps you should try practicing more honest behavior," was Miss Bennet's sly reply.

"Nonsense! Where would be the fun in that?"

The conversation continued for several moments, and though it was lively and fast paced, Darcy had very little part in it. For two such animated and intelligent people, it was nothing less than their usual behavior, but Darcy was of a more serious and sober disposition. In truth it was not long before he began to feel irritated with his cousin and, perhaps, even a little with Miss Bennet. Fitzwilliam never missed an opportunity to charm, and Miss Bennet seemed to be more than willing to allow herself to be charmed. For a time, Darcy actually wondered if she preferred his cousin.

It was as the ladies were leaving that Darcy found out how ridiculous he was being. When Mrs. Gardiner declared their need to depart, the company rose and farewells were exchanged. Fitzwilliam, perhaps sensing Darcy's mood, joined Mrs. Gardiner and Georgiana as they walked through the house toward the door, leaving Darcy to escort Miss Bennet.

The young woman, seemingly unaware of his less than desirable mood, chatted happily, enthused about seeing his house and meeting his staff. He listened to her, making only the barest of comments, happy that at least she had liked what she had seen. Darcy was reminded of his thoughts that morning and how it had been important to him that she approve of the house.

When they arrived at the entrance, Miss Bennet turned to him, and by her shy smile she thought she was feeling a little bashful.

"Thank you for welcoming me into your house, sir. It is beautiful and comfortable. I know your lady mother must have put a great deal of thought into its appointments."

"I believe she did, Miss Bennet," said Darcy, thinking of the import of her words. There was no false flattery about how the rooms had been decorated in a costly way; rather, she seemed to be more interested in comfort, which meshed very well with his opinion of her tastes. "My mother redecorated many of the rooms when I was a boy. I remember it very well indeed."

"She had impeccable taste, sir. I think . . ."

Miss Bennet paused and colored slightly, turning her face away for a moment. Then she squared her shoulders with a visible effort and turned to look him in the eye. The courage in her countenance almost took his breath away.

"I understand what an honor it is that you are considering me to succeed your lady mother, and I am very sensible of the gesture. I simply wished to say that I will do everything in my power to be worthy of her and of you if you decide you wish to pursue this courtship to its natural conclusion."

Stunned and speechless, Darcy gazed at this young woman, wondering at his great fortune in finding such a gem. Her words were heartfelt and earnest, but they also contained a searching quality, seeming to speak to her insecurity.

Of course she would feel inadequate! Darcy almost groaned at the thought he had not considered her feelings on the subject before. The

Gardiners' house, while handsome, was small, and he suspected her father's estate was nowhere near the size and fineness of even the townhouse. That she was able to push past her fears and act with such courage told him more about her character than any number of walks in the park.

Her countenance as she spoke also softened his prior irritation with her and Fitzwilliam. She was calm and earnest, but her eyes betrayed a hint of a beseeching quality, which called out for him to reassure her. That, he hastened to do.

"I have the fullest confidence in your abilities, Miss Bennet," said Darcy, injecting all the warmth of feeling he felt for this woman into his tone. "I do not doubt you will fill the position with flair when we come to that point."

Cheeks blooming at the inference inherent in his words, Miss Bennet curtseyed and stepped into the carriage with his assistance, and soon it departed, the clatter of the horses' hooves and the carriage wheels against the cobblestones announcing their going. The three relations stood on the steps watching them, Darcy with anticipation for the next time they should meet, Georgiana, unless he missed his guess, ecstatic at the thought of gaining a sister, while Fitzwilliam appeared to be satisfied.

Darcy's earlier pique with his cousin returned.

When the carriage had disappeared, those remaining returned to the house, and Georgiana left, stating a need to return to her studies. Darcy watched her go, noting her erect bearing and the slight spring in her step. Miss Bennet was good for her. She was becoming a young woman, and Darcy knew he would need to start thinking about putting her in a school for girls her age and society. After that he would need to hire a companion. For a young woman of Elizabeth's age to suddenly take over his sister's education and nurture would be difficult, especially when she would be focused on learning to be the mistress of his homes. A companion would be for the best.

"I am required back at the barracks before long," said Fitzwilliam, interrupting his thoughts. "Shall we adjourn to your study for a brief conversation?"

Agreeing, Darcy led the way to his study in silence. Fitzwilliam had obviously seen the signs of his annoyance, unsurprising, given how close they were. He was normally not a man who felt the need to explain his actions, but in this instance, Darcy thought he wished to make his case.

"Now, before you become upset with me," said Fitzwilliam as soon as they had entered the room, confirming Darcy's suppositions, "I must tell you that I heartily approve of the girl. She is calm and poised, yet lively and intelligent. Such traits will only serve her well in society."

Darcy nodded, but he speared his cousin with a baleful glare, the sight of which only caused Fitzwilliam's mirth.

"You have no need to flay me with your gaze in such a manner, Darcy," said Fitzwilliam. "You know it does not affect me."

"Then perhaps I should make myself clear," replied Darcy, in a tone which brooked no dispute. "I shall not tolerate anyone treating Miss Bennet with disrespect. That stricture holds for anyone, including those in the family."

"Which is precisely why I wished to visit today and take the measure of her," said Fitzwilliam. All trace of his normally irrepressible spirts was gone in favor of a serious mien. "Darcy, you know the mild inquisition I subjected her to this morning is but a taste of what she will experience from society. That is to say nothing of what my father will say."

Grunting, Darcy was forced to agree with his cousin's assessment. "Do you think there will be any chance of convincing him?"

Spreading his arms wide, Fitzwilliam sat back in his seat. "I know he will not wish to expose a rift in the family, but he will not wish to meet her. He will tolerate her presence when necessary, but I doubt you should expect any warming of his feelings toward her."

"It is as I expected," replied Darcy. "Of more import at present is your mother. Do you think she will agree to sponsor Elizabeth in society?"

Fitzwilliam snorted. "If you insist, perhaps. But you know her disapproval will be plain for all to see, whether or not she takes the trouble to attempt to hide it."

A sigh escaped Darcy's lips. These were just a few of the obstacles which would stand in their path. There would be those who would look down on Miss Bennet for nothing more than the fact that she was not one of them, to say nothing of how the matchmaking mothers and their hopeful daughters would treat her. Darcy had no doubt that on merit alone Miss Bennet was more than acceptable. Members of the ton, unfortunately, rarely considered others on their merits. Wealth and connection were all that was important.

"Perhaps Charity could help," said Fitzwilliam, as he tapped a finger against his lips in thought. "Rachel is a lost cause, as I am certain you well know; ever since her marriage to duke what's-his-name, her nose has been so far in the air, I am concerned a good gust of wind will blow her out to sea."

A short burst of laughter left Darcy's lips, not that he disagreed with his cousin.

"And you know James is as much of a stick-in-the-mud as my father, and his wife is no better. But Charity has always been more tolerant of others and she numbers several ladies of less than impeccable pedigree as her close friends. With her marriage, she is in a position to assist. It might be best if you arranged an introduction at some point and watch to see how they get on."

Darcy thought about it for a moment and then nodded. Charity truly was the best hope he had of his family approving of Miss Bennet.

"If Charity approves of her, she can speak to her friends on her behalf, and your Miss Bennet will gain the acceptance of at least some members of society. I am certain your friends will approve of her on nothing more than your recommendation. As for the rest, the need to avoid insulting Darcy house is too important for most to disparage her in your presence. I suspect with her qualities, she will win at least the grudging acceptance of most, if not their approval."

"That is all I can really ask for," said Darcy with a slow nod. "It matters not to me if people I detest approve of her. All I require is their respect."

"And I am sure you shall have it. Eventually.

"Well, I must be off. I wish you luck, Darcy. She is a wonderful girl, but I do not envy the storm this shall raise."

With a nod, Fitzwilliam departed, leaving Darcy to his thoughts, which included, in no small measure, a petite and pretty woman who was working her way into his affections, and the society which could go to the devil if they did not see her worth as he did.

A few days after Miss Bennet had come to Darcy house for the first time, Darcy made a most interesting acquaintance.

After spending some time with Miss Bennet, again at the park near the Gardiner home, he escorted her back to her uncle's house, where he was invited to enter and take a little refreshment. Though he was of a mind to return to his home directly, the thought of a little more time in Miss Bennet's company was enough to induce him to acquiesce.

They had been drinking tea and talking with Miss Bennet's aunt in the sitting-room when Darcy heard the sound of a door opening and closing. Within moments, Mr. Gardiner stepped into the room, followed by a young man. He was tall and slender, likely a few years younger than Darcy himself, and from the smile on his face, he appeared to be gregarious and happy. His most defining feature was the shock of curly reddish hair upon his head.

"Mr. Darcy," greeted Mr. Gardiner upon espying him, "I did you know you were visiting today."

Darcy stood and shook Mr. Gardiner's hand, and noting that the man had not offered to introduce his companion, decided the man was of a lesser standing and requested an introduction.

"Certainly, sir," said Mr. Gardiner. "Mr. Darcy, please allow me to introduce my friend and future business partner, Mr. Charles Bingley. Mr. Bingley, this is our Elizabeth's suitor, Mr. Fitzwilliam Darcy."

Beaming with pleasure, Mr. Bingley soon proved Darcy's impression of him to be the truth, as he offered his hand and said with a smile: "I am happy to finally make the acquaintance of Miss Bennet's suitor. I have heard much of you, sir, and though I have not seen Miss Bennet much recently, it has not been difficult to see her happiness even on the few occasions I *have* been in her presence!"

A little bemused, and noting Gardiner's grin, Darcy returned the gesture. "I am happy to make your acquaintance, sir. So you are investing in Gardiner's business?"

"It is much worse than that, I assure you," replied Mr. Bingley, leaning forward as if to impart a secret, "In fact, I own another business which is being merged with Mr. Gardiner's business. As my father long wished to enter the ranks of the gentry, it is my intention to pass our joint businesses to Mr. Gardiner's direction and search for an estate."

"Very commendable," said Darcy. "I wish you the best of luck. There should be many such estates available for purchase. If I might offer a piece of advice, however, you might wish to lease an estate first. Then if the estate is suitable, you could purchase, or look for a new one if it is not."

"Excellent!" enthused Mr. Bingley. "I shall keep your good advice in mind when I am looking."

"Mr. Bingley," said Mrs. Gardiner, "shall you not join us for tea?"

For a moment Darcy thought Mr. Bingley might demur, but instead he smiled and agreed, and soon was ensconced with the company. Darcy found himself enjoying the man's company exceedingly. He was garrulous and open, speaking of any subject readily, and laughing more often than not. Darcy suspected that he was not the most perceptive of men, and perhaps not as scholarly as was Darcy himself, but on the whole he was quite happy for the acquaintance.

"I am curious," said Darcy after they had been sitting in that attitude for some minutes, "I do not think we have ever canvassed the exact nature of your business, Mr. Gardiner. Can I assume you and Mr.

Bingley are not competitors?"

"Perhaps you men should take any talk of business back to the study!" said Mrs. Gardiner with a laugh.

"Shall we, gentlemen?" asked Gardiner.

Darcy readily agreed and after saying farewell to Mrs. Gardiner and bowing over Elizabeth's hand, he followed Gardiner, accepting a glass of port when offered.

"Mr. Bingley and I are both in the same line of business," said Gardiner after a moment. "We are both importers, but where I import primarily from the Far East, Mr. Bingley's family has built a profitable trade importing from the continent and the Americas."

"It appears to be an excellent combination of matching interests," said Darcy.

"It is," enthused Mr. Bingley. "Furthermore, it allows me to become a gentleman and yet maintain my interest in the business, which still provides me with my wealth. With the sale of part of my assets to Mr. Gardiner, my yearly income will decrease, but that should be offset by the income I will receive from the rents of an estate."

"As long as you choose well when deciding upon the estate to purchase," said Darcy, rubbing his chin in thought. "There are many estates on the market at present. It will take some discernment to know which will be a good investment, and which are being sold for other reasons."

Mr. Bingley appeared a little worried. "I have considered that problem. The man I have hired has assured me that he will do his due diligence, but it is still a concern nonetheless."

Thinking for a moment, Darcy decided that he liked Mr. Bingley very well indeed. "If you will, I will be happy to assist, wherever I have knowledge to do so."

Eyes widened slightly, Bingley nonetheless responded with pleasure. "I welcome the offer, sir. If I have any questions, I shall seek you out. I do not anticipate my decision will be immediate, though there are several I have been looking into, all of which appear to be excellent opportunities."

From there the conversation turned to other matters, most of which consisted of Gardiner and Bingley's plans to merge, the work which needed to be done to combine their inventories, and the profits they expected to make. It had been clear from the start that Gardiner made a comfortable living, in spite of the fact that most of his liquid capital was currently tied up in this merger. But Darcy was impressed with the figures the two men discussed. With wealth such as they were speaking of, Darcy wondered how long it would be after their companies were merged before Gardiner himself began investigating the possibility of purchasing an estate.

"The only issue remaining is the extent of my warehouse space," said Gardiner as the conversation turned to other matters concerning their partnership. "I do not have enough in my present location to house all our combined goods. There is a building on the far side of my warehouse which I could demolish and add additional space to my existing warehouse, but there is not enough capital to allow for such a purchase, and I am hesitant to take on further debt with the bank."

"Will not the sale of my existing warehouses allow for such an expenditure?"

Gardiner shook his head. "The issue is I would still need space I currently do not have to house the goods, and I would not have the space to store it until the addition is complete."

"What if I was to invest in your company?" asked Darcy.

The offer was a spur of the moment decision, but the moment he made it, Darcy knew it was the right one to make. Not only would he stand to profit handsomely from the investment, the way the two men were speaking, but he wished to help these industrious men.

"I thank you for the offer, Darcy," said Gardiner, clearly surprised at the offer. "But I would not wish to embroil you in our business, any more than you would be connected to us through marriage to Elizabeth."

"It is no trouble, and I would not have suggested it if I was not in earnest." Darcy paused, gathering his thoughts. "The fact of the matter is that the world is changing, gentlemen. The wealth of the world used to rest in a very large part with those who owned land. That is not the case any longer. In fact, smart, hard-working men such as yourselves are quickly making large fortunes through trade, the invention of new machines, and the promotion of ingenious ideas.

"I have long thought my portfolio must be diversified in order to weather any storms which might come in the future. In particular, though our current strife with Napoleon seems to be eternal, at some point the war will be over, and prices will fall. Investing in your business, among others, will help my family continue to grow our wealth, rather than suddenly seeing our standard of living decrease because of it."

Mr. Bingley let out a laugh. "It appears that you are well versed in matters of economies, sir. I have tried to explain exactly what you have just said to several gentlemen in the past, and all I have received were condescending looks and patronizing responses."

Shrugging, Darcy said: "I am not surprised. Many gentlemen would much rather bask in their own superiority than acknowledge that which they do not wish to be true. My uncle and my cousin are two such men. Though they are family, I cannot but anticipate the day when all I have tried to tell them is proven correct. Neither are dissipative, but both are exceedingly proud of their status in life and loath to accept new ideas."

"To be honest, sir," said Mr. Bingley, though he hesitated before speaking, "I must own that I am surprised you have entered into a courtship with Miss Bennet, for precisely those reasons."

Darcy nodded, completely unsurprised. "I believe I might have surprised myself. My cousin certainly had no compunction against teasing me for my impulsivity. But I hope that I am able to see when a woman is worth more than the rubies she might bring as a dowry."

"Well said, sir!" exclaimed Mr. Bingley. "Well said indeed."

The discussion turned to matters of business, and the three sat for some time discussing the extent of Darcy's involvement in the scheme. In the end, Darcy was satisfied with the outcome. He would provide the money for Gardiner to purchase the building in question and build another on the site. In exchange he would receive a fair share of the profits from the endeavor, which would certainly improve his portfolio. If the estimates were in any way correct, he thought his income from the endeavor would outstrip the interest he would have made on the money by a significant margin.

When the negotiations were complete, Gardiner sat back in his chair and directed a grateful smile at Darcy. "Thank you, sir," said he. "Not only will this make the logistics much easier, but it will also make the movement of goods much less expensive. I am glad to have this matter resolved."

"I am happy to be of assistance. I will, of course, discuss this matter with my solicitor and my banker, but I cannot imagine either would find any fault with what we have decided here today."

"I believe it will be acceptable on all our parts," said Mr. Bingley, raising his glass in toast.

Darcy drank, and after a moment he turned to his new acquaintance. "Since we are to be business partners, I wonder if you would join Gardiner and his wife, and Miss Bennet, at my house for dinner. We have planned it for next Tuesday, though the date can easily be modified should that day not be agreeable."

A true beaming smile of pleasure came over Bingley's face. "I would be happy to, sir. Might I inquire if my sisters and my eldest sister's husband might be included in this invitation?"

"Of course," said Darcy.

He passed over his card to Mr. Bingley, indicating the address, and then the men stood to depart. Though he had not intended to make a new investment that day, he was content with what had been decided, and happy to make Mr. Bingley's acquaintance.

Chapter XIII

It seemed to Elizabeth like it was a week in which she would meet more of Mr. Darcy's formidable relatives, though since she had not yet met the earl and countess, she had not truly passed through the fire. Late that week after she had met Major Fitzwilliam, Elizabeth received a note from Georgiana Darcy, requesting her to visit the next day in order to be introduced to Charity, the major's youngest sister.

As of yet, Elizabeth had not heard much of the Fitzwilliam family. She knew he had an elder brother and at least one sister, but other than that, her information was rather spotty at best. What this particular invitation might portend Elizabeth could not state with any surety, but she thought that they would not choose to introduce her to one who was disposed to be severe on her so early, and as a result, decided that Lady Charity was likely of an amiable disposition. Thus, Elizabeth went, determined to be pleased with the new acquaintance, and perhaps more importantly, resolved to maintain her recent vow of meeting all new situations with courage.

When the invitation arrived, Elizabeth showed it to her aunt, requesting her presence at Darcy house. Her aunt, however, only laughed and demurred.

"I believe you may go yourself, Lizzy," said Mrs. Gardiner.

Elizabeth frowned, but her aunt continued, saying: "It is time you began to mingle with these people without relying on me as a crutch. They will be *your* family should you marry Mr. Darcy, and you must learn to carry yourself with confidence in their presence. I will only be a hindrance."

"Surely not!" cried Elizabeth. "Everyone who meets you must find you to be the epitome of good breeding."

"I have enough pride in myself to believe that to be the case," said Mrs. Gardiner with no little affection. "But I well know my present status. I might be the granddaughter of a gentleman, but I am also naught more than the wife of a tradesman. I am quite happy with my position in life, I can assure you."

Though inclined to once again beg her attendance, Elizabeth decided her aunt was determined, and as such, she desisted. Therefore, to Darcy house she was to go, this time unaccompanied.

When the next morning arrived, Elizabeth dressed carefully, and after breakfast, she stepped into the Gardiner carriage and set off for Darcy house and the anticipated meeting. As was common for a weekday morning, the streets in the vicinity of Gracechurch Street were teeming with activity, as carts laden with goods vied with carriages and pedestrians for seemingly every available inch of the road. Her uncle's carriage driver deftly navigated the congested streets with the flair of one long accustomed to driving in such conditions, and soon they had left the hustle and bustle of the busier districts behind and entered some of the quieter streets where the higher members of society lived. It was not long before the footman was handing her down from the carriage in front of Mr. Darcy's house.

With instructions for the driver to return to collect her in an hour's time, Elizabeth climbed the stairs to the front door and was about to use the knocker when a voice interrupted her from behind.

"Well, hello. What do we have here?"

Turning, Elizabeth espied a young man approaching Darcy house, his long legs carrying him up the stairs two at a time. He was tall and handsome—though neither so tall nor so handsome as Mr. Darcy, Elizabeth thought—with a head full of neatly groomed dark brown hair, deep brown eyes, and an infectious smile. His frame was lean, much as the sapling of a newly planted tree, and though he appeared to possess strength in that frame, he was not nearly so broad-shouldered as Mr. Darcy.

When did I start comparing every young man I meet to Mr. Darcy? thought Elizabeth.

It was an idle thought which did not survive the young man's next words:

"You are visiting with Miss Darcy, I presume?"

"Yes sir," said Elizabeth, just remembering manners, though she had not as of yet been introduced to this man.

Then mindful of how Mr. Darcy thought it better to keep their unofficial courtship as yet unknown, Elizabeth said: "I have been acquainted with Miss Darcy for some time now."

A brilliant grin overspread the man's face, and Elizabeth was almost forced to reassess her earlier assessment of Mr. Darcy's superiority. Almost.

"I have been acquainted with the Darcys all my life. Miss Darcy is an especial favorite, as I watched her grow, almost as an elder brother, and devoted hours to her entertainment when she was young."

"You grew up on an estate near to Mr. Darcy's?"

"Actually, I had the very great fortune of being raised at Pemberley itself, at the late Mr. Darcy's knee." The man dropped into an exaggerated bow, saying: "George Wickham, at your service, madam."

"Elizabeth Bennet," replied Elizabeth, not knowing what else to do.

"Excellent! I look forward to knowing you better, Miss Bennet. Perhaps you might start by telling me a little of yourself? I have the feeling we shall be great friends indeed!"

Something about this young man struck Elizabeth as being a little off. He was handsome and charming, and seemed to be aware of the devastating effect of his smile. There was nothing in his manners which warned her off, but for whatever reason, Elizabeth sensed that it was best to be cautious.

To have such a discussion while standing in front of the door of the man who was courting her did not seem completely proper, so she reached for the door knocker and rapped thrice.

"I am happy to make your acquaintance, sir," said Elizabeth. "But Georgiana is expecting me, so I would not wish to make her wait."

Eyes slightly widened, Mr. Wickham said: "You must be a dear friend indeed, if you are given the privilege of using Miss Darcy's Christian name."

Elizabeth cursed her own careless tongue and smiled at Mr. Wickham in what she hoped was a disarming fashion. "She is a dear girl, and I sometimes forget myself. I apologize. For one as well-connected with the Darcy family, I believe you must know what a high emphasis they put on the proper etiquette."

"Indeed, I do, Miss Bennet. I shall not share your slip with anyone—

you may count on me!"

Turning away at the sound of the door opening, Elizabeth decided it was best to simply enter the house. The man's flattery was beginning to wear on her.

When Johnson, the butler opened the door, he bowed to Elizabeth, but when he rose he caught sight of Mr. Wickham to her side, and all expression fell from his face.

"Miss Bennet," said Johnson. "Miss Darcy is waiting in the sitting-room for you to join her."

"It is quite all right, Johnson," said Wickham with a cheerful grin as he stepped into the house passing by the surprised butler. "I am well aware of where the sitting-room is located. I shall escort Miss Bennet there."

"I believe, sir—" began the surprised butler, but Mr. Wickham just waved him off.

"Do not concern yourself. It has been some time since I last met with Miss Darcy, and I would be happy to see her again."

"I believe you should apply to me first."

Startled, Elizabeth looked across the hall to see Mr. Darcy watching them. While Elizabeth could not yet claim to be an expert in interpreting the man's inscrutable expressions, she thought he regarded them with nothing short of displeasure, though she did not think it was directed at her. Johnson, though mirroring his master's demeanor, nevertheless appeared more than a little relieved at Mr. Darcy's appearance. For his part, Mr. Wickham's genial smile never wavered.

"Darcy! It has been far too long!"

For a brief moment, Elizabeth thought Mr. Darcy would not answer Mr. Wickham's words, and his eyes almost appeared to be attempting to bludgeon the man where he stood. After a brief pause, however, he deigned to say: "Indeed."

Then he turned to Elizabeth and his mien softened. "Miss Bennet, we are happy you have joined us today. Georgiana and Charity await you in the sitting-room."

Turning to Johnson, Mr. Darcy said: "Please convey Miss Bennet to my sister, and then report to my study."

"Very good, sir."

Knowing she was being dismissed, but not quite understanding exactly what was happening, Elizabeth turned to leave, but she was prevented from it when Mr. Wickham, still sporting a charming smile, grasped her hand and said:

"It was a pleasure, Miss Bennet. I hope it will be repeated in the near future."

Then Mr. Wickham bowed, but as his head descended, she thought he might kiss her hand, and unaccountably reluctant to allow him the honor, she pulled it from his grasp.

"Thank you, Mr. Wickham," said she, and she allowed herself to be led away by the butler.

That did not stop Elizabeth from feeling the sensation of Mr. Wickham's eyes upon her back as she departed. She could not remember being so uncomfortable, except perhaps when Mr. Pearce had watched her in a similar manner.

As Darcy watched Miss Bennet walk away, his mind was caught up in the agreeable pleasure of seeing her arrive at his home, welcoming her to the place he was becoming increasingly certain she would one day be mistress. In truth, he wished to be with her at that moment, watching as she employed her arts to charm another of his relations. But there was an interloper to be dealt with, and thus, Darcy turned and directed a glare on Wickham.

The man only laughed. "There is no need for you to turn your inscrutable glare on me, Darcy."

"Wickham," said Darcy, though it came out more like a grunt. "What are you doing here?"

"I see you have lost none of your charm."

Unlike a moment before when he was speaking with Miss Bennet, Wickham's voice exuded a sardonic contempt which Darcy had experienced too many times to mistake. He had also seen the man's expression change from charming to lascivious far too often, and he was well aware that Wickham's taste in women would make Miss Bennet a target, should care not be taken.

"I have no charm to spare for the likes of you," said Darcy. "I distinctly remember informing you that all connection between you and my family was at an end."

"Did you really think you would be rid of me so easily?" asked Wickham. "I *was* your father's favorite, after all."

Darcy snorted. "Your influence with my father was far less than you imagine."

"You were always jealous of me, Darcy. I had the love of your father, while you only had the duty of living up to his expectations."

Eyeing the man with distaste, Darcy shook his head at Wickham's willful blindness. "I know what you think Wickham, and I know it is pointless to try to make you understand. You had hoped my father would bestow a gentleman's income on you, but you never realized that my father was a creature of duty. He never would have broken up the family holdings for anything other than a second son."

"Then why did you not tell him?" asked Wickham. Whatever geniality had existed when the man had come was now gone, replaced by nothing more than cold hostility. "He was every bit the prude you are. Would he not have written me out of his will? Or perhaps you knew he would take my word over yours . . ."

"I did not inform him because I did not wish to upset him when ill health came upon him." Darcy glared at Wickham with derision. "Do not think he would not have believed me."

"You are deluding yourself."

"Enough!" declared Darcy. "I tire of this. It is time you leave."

"I shall, once I have stated my business."

Darcy watched the man, wondering what game he was playing. Though he could order Wickham to be thrown from the house if he so chose, something stayed his hand. It would be better to hear his plea and disabuse him of all further notion of making any further entreaties for money or whatever else he had come for.

"Very well."

Turning, Darcy began walking away from his erstwhile friend, knowing all the while that though Wickham would chafe at the necessity of following on Darcy's sufferance. And follow he would; whatever he came to obtain would not be had without making his case.

They encountered no one on the way to the study, which suited Darcy quite well; Wickham was known in Darcy house, and though Darcy thought he would not have any friends left here, he could not be certain. When they entered the study, Darcy moved behind his desk and sat there, steepling his fingers on the desk in front of him. Wickham watched him as he did so, a glare disguised as scornful amusement on his face. He sat in one of the chairs for a moment looking around the room lazily, before he turned his attention on Darcy once again.

"Where are your manners, Darcy? Do you not offer port to a visitor who has come to discuss business with you?"

"Do not make me laugh, Wickham. We both understand what this meeting will devolve to, and I shall not dignify it by calling it 'business.' Now state what you came for or leave me be."

"Charming to the last, Darcy," said Wickham. He watched for a moment and then said: "Very well, then. I have come for what you owe me."

"Owe you? I owe you nothing."

"What of the living promised to me in your father's will? I understand the incumbent is not expected to live much longer." Wickham let out a bark of laughter. "Old Gregson was ancient even when we were boys. He must be positively decrepit by now."

"And you think you are suited to caring for the spiritual wellbeing of others."

"I am not perfect Darcy," replied Wickham. "But I am no worse than the next man."

Darcy ignored the man's words, sorely tempted though he was at the thought of laughing in his face.

"What of the compensation you received in lieu of that living?"

"Come now, Darcy, you well know that the living is worth much more than what you paid me. Why, I might earn that much by holding the living in a matter for a few years. Clearly you have not executed the spirit of your father's will."

"I will have you know that my uncle derided my decision to pay you as much as I did. He doubted the living was worth half as much as I paid you for it.

"But it matters not," said Darcy, interrupting Wickham when he would have spoken again. "I have, in my safe at Pemberley, the contract which you signed, resigning all right to the living and any future compensation."

Wickham scowled. "It said nothing of the sort."

"I assure you it did. You were so eager to receive the money, you did not take the trouble to read it. Tell me, Wickham, what has become of the money you received?"

Though his jaw tightened, Wickham ignored Darcy's question. "I shall bring suit against you."

This time Darcy actually laughed at the man. "You will use your experience in the law to assist you in extorting more money from me? If you wish to try, then go to it. I wish you good fortune." Darcy paused and directed a scornful look at his nemesis. "How *is* your study of the law proceeding, Wickham?"

"Well enough," replied Wickham shortly.

The two men stared at one another. Darcy had kept track of Wickham's movements for a few months after their last meeting, and he was well aware of how Wickham had been occupying his time. He did not doubt there was nothing left of the money he had received and that the man's circumstances were desperate.

"Then I wish you the best in it. But this conference is over. You will leave, Wickham and you will not importune me on the matter again."

"I am warning you, Darcy—"

"You will warn me of nothing!" said Darcy, standing in response to Wickham's belligerence. "You are nothing more than a wastrel and a libertine, and no more Darcy money will be squandered at your hands."

At that moment, Johnson appeared in the doorway, accompanied by two burly footmen. Darcy glanced at the men and nodded grimly—Johnson had chosen well indeed. Both men had reason to have no love for Wickham for various reasons.

"Excellent timing as always, Johnson," said Darcy. "Mr. Wickham was just leaving. If he should return again, the family will not be home to him."

Having said this, Darcy turned to Wickham, raising his eyebrow, daring Wickham to take issue with the commands he had given his staff. But though Darcy had rarely seen Wickham restrain himself, particularly when it concerned something he wanted, his discretion seemed to tell him that the odds were not in his favor in this particular instance. Thus, though he directed a poisonous glare at Darcy, he stepped away from the desk and toward the door.

But just when Darcy thought he would go away quietly, Wickham paused and hissed: "You shall regret this, Darcy. I will have what is mine, or I will ensure you suffer for your betrayal."

"Do what you must," said Darcy. "But remember that I still hold the receipts for your debts in Lambton and Cambridge. Try my patience, and I will bury you in the deepest hole I can find."

Though reluctant to give his former friend any credit, Darcy had to acknowledge that Wickham was not lacking in courage or resolve. He flicked not an eyelash at the threat in Darcy's words, and his stare continued to bore into Darcy, as if trying to impale him by the force of his displeasure.

Wickham said nothing further, however, allowing himself to be led away by the butler. Darcy followed, wishing to ensure the libertine was gone from his house. As luck would have it, however, Wickham was not allowed to leave the house without a confrontation with one he truly feared. For as they walked through the foyer the door opened, and Major Fitzwilliam was admitted to the house.

"Wickham!" exclaimed he. "I have not seen you in many years, man. How are you occupying yourself?"

To anyone who did not know the major, they might have mistaken his greeting for one of pleasure due to being reunited with a companion he had not seen for many years. Darcy, however, witnessed the dangerous glint in his cousin's eye, and the way his smile seemed far more predatory than genial. Fitzwilliam had always been of the opinion that Wickham was a cur who needed to be treated as such.

It was clear Wickham understood the undertones of Fitzwilliam's greeting as well as Darcy did himself. He blanched and his eyes widened with alarm, and as a reply, he only managed: "Captain!"

"Major," corrected Fitzwilliam, an almost offhand indifference inherent in his voice. "It is a new promotion, which you would not be familiar with, as we have not met in some time."

"Ah . . . Well then . . . Congratulations are in order, I suppose . . ."

"I will take your words in the manner in which they were intended."

Nodding nervously, Wickham continued to walk to the door where Johnson opened it for him, and then closed it after he had left, with a little more force than was strictly necessary. Darcy nodded at his butler in thanks.

"My strictures are to be passed around to all of the staff. If Wickham should return, he is to be denied entrance, and if he should happen to find his way inside, I want him arrested for trespassing."

"Very good, sir," said Johnson, his eyes betraying just a hint of his satisfaction with such an order. The man then bowed and stepped away, leaving Darcy alone with Fitzwilliam.

"That mongrel should have been dealt with long ago, Darcy," growled Fitzwilliam. "He goes around blasting lives and ruining others."

"And it might come to that, if he continues to make a nuisance of himself," said Darcy. "But I owe it to my father to give him every opportunity to make something of his life."

Fitzwilliam was not impressed with Darcy's rebuttal. "Why was he here, Darcy? Trying to extort more money from you?"

Though Darcy did not say anything in response, Fitzwilliam nodded once, clearly seeing something in Darcy's face which confirmed his suspicions.

"Your loyalty to your father's memory is commendable. But you have given Wickham far too many chances already, and he has never had a chance he did not squander. Leaving him to prey on others like this is irresponsible. I suggest you think long and hard about what ought to be done about him, and do not allow sentimentality or your father's memory to prevent you from doing what you know to be right."

And with a significant glare, Fitzwilliam turned and strode toward the sitting-room, Darcy following closely behind. As he walked, Darcy reflected on this situation. He could not help but reflect that everything his cousin had said was nothing less than the truth.

* * *

As she was leaving the foyer, Elizabeth happened to look back at the two men, and though her back was to Mr. Darcy, rendering it impossible to see his face, Mr. Wickham's was clear, and she did not like what she saw there. He was watching Mr. Darcy with an expression of mixed amusement and contempt, his eyes dead and lifeless. She shivered—clearly the two men were not friends, and given what Elizabeth knew of Mr. Darcy's character, she suspected that Mr. Wickham was not a good man. Elizabeth resolved to avoid him, not that she thought there would be much opportunity for her to be in his company.

Only just able to put the matter of the man from her mind, Elizabeth entered the room where she was greeted by Georgiana and a woman who resembled her greatly. The woman was perhaps a little taller than Georgiana, her hair a slightly darker shade of blonde, and her air more poised and confident. Elizabeth thought she was perhaps three or four years Elizabeth's senior, which made the gap between her and the girl by her side even more pronounced. Even more importantly, Elizabeth thought from the woman's open curiosity and bright demeanor that she was a friendly, happy sort of person.

"Elizabeth!" greeted Georgiana when she espied her entering the room.

The girl rose from her seat on the sofa quickly and crossed the room, dropped into the barest of a curtsey, and then grasped Elizabeth's hand, pulling her toward the sofa where the other woman had risen. Her smile of indulgence suggested to Elizabeth that she truly was fond of her younger cousin and cemented her amiability in Elizabeth's eyes.

"I see your friend has arrived, Georgiana. Will you do me the honor of introducing me?"

"Of course, Charity."

Georgiana turned and dragged Elizabeth a little further forward, eliciting a laugh from Elizabeth for being so manhandled.

"Cousin, this is Miss Elizabeth Bennet, the young lady that William is courting. Elizabeth, this is my cousin, Lady Charity Spencer. Charity is my cousin Anthony's younger sister."

"Lady Charity," said Elizabeth, dropping into a low curtsey. "I am happy to make your acquaintance."

The other woman looked at her for a moment before a bright smile broke out on her face. "And I am happy to make yours. Our Georgiana has had nothing but praise to say about you. I believe I must thank you for being such a good friend to her."

"It is nothing!" said Elizabeth, laughing at Georgiana's embarrassment. "She is quite easy to esteem, so it is no trouble to do so!"

"Elizabeth!" scolded Georgiana. "Do not speak of me as if I were not here!"

The two girls laughed, and Lady Charity looked at them with indulgent amusement.

"I must say that I am quite impressed with your effect on my cousin already, Miss Bennet. She is a shy creature; for you to be laughing and talking with her so easily on such a short acquaintance speaks well of you."

"Charity!" exclaimed Georgiana. "Now *you* speak of me as if I am not here!"

A laugh burst forth from Lady Charity's lips, and she turned on her cousin with fondness. "Did you not know that it is sometimes the prerogative of those of us who are elder to speak in such a fashion concerning the younger?"

"I am not *that much* younger than you."

"No, dear," said Charity, "but you *are* younger, so you must endure it nonetheless."

Elizabeth decided then and there that she liked Georgiana's cousin very well indeed. Here was another member of Mr. Darcy's extended family she thought she would get on with, and with little effort.

It seemed that Lady Charity guessed something of Elizabeth's thoughts, for she turned a bright smile on her and said: "It appears Miss Bennet has been told something of our family, for she seems surprised that I can speak with her easily and without ensuring my nose is higher in the air than hers."

Though a laugh wanted to escape, Elizabeth fought it back, instead saying: "I *have* heard something of your family, Lady Charity, but since I have met your brother, the major, I cannot give credence to all that I have heard. You are both amiable indeed."

"I flatter myself that I am, Miss Bennet," said Charity, accompanied with a chuckle. "But do not allow your opinion of us give you the wrong impression of the rest of my family. My father and my eldest brother *are* impressed with their situations in life, and my eldest sister, Rachel, can no longer take the time for those of us who are lesser than she. And since I married naught but a gentleman, she considers herself to be so much better."

By this time, Elizabeth was laughing along with her new acquaintance as she spoke of her family. While it was clear she loved them despite their foibles, she was not blind. In that way, she was much like Elizabeth with respect to her own family.

"And my mother," continued Lady Charity, "is amiable enough, but she cares for nothing but her status as one of the leading ladies of society.

"You might find it shocking," said Lady Charity, leaning forward as if to impart some great secret, "but she wishes to be recognized alongside Lady Jersey and Lady Castlereigh as one of the ladies who look down upon the masses and decree the strictures of proper behavior, determine who will be allowed into the hallowed and tedious halls of Almack's, and how many times those of us who are of lesser stature must genuflect towards her every day."

"Surely not!" cried Elizabeth at the same time Georgiana exclaimed: "Oh, Charity, if Aunt Susan heard you speaking thus, she would be quite offended."

Lady Charity's eyes positively danced with amusement. "Perhaps I have exaggerated a little, but *only* a little. And I am certain I can count on you ladies to keep a secret, can I not?"

They readily agreed—simple in Elizabeth's case, as she was not actually acquainted with the lady—and soon they were ensconced in the sitting-room, speaking in a lively fashion and sharing anecdotes from their childhoods. Elizabeth was diverted exceedingly by her new acquaintance. Lady Charity was not only genuine and forthright, but she was also intelligent and an excellent conversationalist. Elizabeth thought she would like her very well as a cousin, though some of the anecdotes about her other family members gave her cause for alarm. Astute as she was, Lady Charity saw Elizabeth's consternation on a number of occasions, and after taking the opportunity to tease her a little more, attempted to ease her dismay.

"In all truth, Miss Bennet," said she, directing a kindly smile at Elizabeth, "I may have embellished my family's eccentricities a little."

"Only a little?" demanded Georgiana.

"In some ways, yes," replied Lady Charity, a glint of humor shining through in her eyes. "However, I believe you have little to fear from them. I doubt many of them will wish to be friendly with you, but my mother will at least be kind, and the rest civil. James's wife's behavior I cannot predict with any degree of confidence. She is far haughtier than even Rachel, but whereas she sometimes possesses a sharp tongue, she will often instead simply choose to ignore 'interlopers.'"

"I have no doubt that Miss Bennet will be able to dispense with my brother's wife with ease," said a new voice, and Elizabeth looked up to see the major standing just inside the door, with Mr. Darcy entering just behind him; she had not heard the door open.

Major Fitzwilliam favored Elizabeth with a devilish smile before he continued, saying: "You might not know it, Charity, but Penelope is not the brightest woman of my acquaintance. I believe her propensity for delivering cutting remarks—which she doubtlessly practices in front of a mirror for several hours a day—have given her the false reputation for wit."

By this time the three ladies were giggling in a vain attempt to stifle their laughter, but the major merely continued on, a grin etched upon his face the entire time.

"In truth, all Miss Bennet will need to do is speak something of current affairs, or literature, or of anything which is not contained within the pages of a fashion magazine, and Penelope will no doubt be so confused that she will not dare say a single word to Miss Bennet's detriment!"

With the major's words, the entire company dissolved in laughter, and even Mr. Darcy was chuckling at his cousin's words. When the hilarity began to subside, however, he was quick to interject his own opinion in the matter.

"I shall not allow anyone to disrespect Miss Bennet, Charity. The Darcy name is not to be trifled with."

"No, William," replied Charity, her previous mirth giving way to seriousness. "That is not the way to handle society. I had not known Miss Bennet for two minutes before I knew that she is quite capable of handling the Penelopes of society. You would do much better to allow her the right to her response without stepping in every time someone makes some unkind comment."

Mr. Darcy frowned. "Do you suggest I allow Miss Bennet to be abused in my presence?"

"I suggest nothing of the sort. I merely believe that when other ladies make comments, you should allow Miss Bennet to deal with them. Otherwise, she will gain the reputation of one who must rely upon her husband to protect her. She never will gain any measure of respect unless she earns it for herself.

"Of course," said Charity, directing a sly grin at Mr. Darcy, "your fearsome scowl is likely enough to make many behave in your presence. I would not suggest you dispense with that at present."

The major chortled. "I am certain that is something our Darcy can handle admirably."

Though Mr. Darcy looked at his cousin with exasperation—something Elizabeth thought was a regular occurrence—he turned back to Charity and bowed a little insouciantly. "Perhaps I shall take

Penelope's example and practice my 'fearsome scowls' in the mirror so that they might be more effective."

Once again the company laughed, and the major exclaimed: "I hardly think that is required. If it was any more effective, they might run for the hills!"

Mr. Darcy glared at his cousin, but the mirth this comment engendered rendered his expression irrelevant. Faced with no choice, Darcy allowed himself to join in. And so the visit continued for some time, with lively conversation, laughter, and good company. Elizabeth reflected that she enjoyed visiting with Mr. Darcy's relations very well indeed. If she had not already been aware of their situation in life, she would have never thought them anything akin to the scions of an earl.

At length, Lady Charity stood to leave, citing another engagement, and Major Fitzwilliam also rose, stating his own need to depart. Elizabeth rose as well, as she knew the carriage would be coming to collect her soon.

"It has been a pleasure meeting you," said Lady Charity as she rose. "I hope to have it repeated in the future, and I believe it will, assuming a certain . . . desirable event comes to pass."

Though Elizabeth understood quite well Lady Charity's meaning, she also knew the other was teasing her, which allowed her to resist the impulse to be a little bashful in her presence. "I hope to meet with you again, Lady Charity. The pleasure has been all mine."

The lady smiled brilliantly at her and said: "Miss Bennet, if you will allow it, I would prefer to dispense with the formalities. Shall you not call me by my Christian name, and leave off this 'lady' nonsense?"

Elizabeth returned her smile with pleasure. "It would be an honor. I thank you."

"Do not thank me, Elizabeth. I have high hopes for you. With the exception of my overly jocose brother here, we Fitzwilliams tend to be somewhat of a somber bunch. I rather hope you will help inject some life into us which has been sorely lacking."

"She has already managed to inject some life into Darcy," said the major.

"Quiet, Fitzwilliam," said Darcy.

"I believe that all Mr. Darcy needs is a bit of practice," said Elizabeth. "Perhaps your family might do the same."

"Perhaps," said Charity, eyes sparkling with mirth. "But I believe your excellent example is required to show them how."

"I shall do my best."

With those words, they parted. Elizabeth was about to depart herself when Mr. Darcy strode up to her.

"Miss Bennet, might I have a moment of your time?"

Though surprised, Elizabeth readily agreed. They departed the sitting-room with the others, but whereas Georgiana walked on ahead with her cousins, Darcy stayed back and walked slowly with Elizabeth.

"I wished to speak with you regarding the man you met when you arrived," said Mr. Darcy with a directness Elizabeth had come to expect from him.

"Mr. Wickham, was it not?"

"Yes." Darcy paused and smiled. "Your memory is quite precise as usual."

The smile quickly fell away from his face, and he turned a serious gaze upon her. "Might I inquire if you noticed the hostility between us?"

"I must confess, I did. Mr. Wickham spoke of living at your estate and being acquainted with you from childhood, but his words of friendship rang hollow when I saw the way he looked at you."

"That much is true," said Mr. Darcy. He paused for a moment, then stopped walking and turned to Elizabeth and regarded her intently. "Miss Bennet, I must insist that you do not speak with Mr. Wickham again."

Though surprised at the high-handedness of his sudden statement, and more than a little irritated by it, Elizabeth considered her response carefully. It had become clear that Mr. Darcy had become accustomed to ruling over his domain and issuing orders that he expected to be obeyed, but Elizabeth did not wish to be constantly directed, though as a husband, he might reasonably be expected to behave in such a manner. However, she sensed that he was not attempting to be officious; in fact, he likely had very good reasons for making this request, and what she had witnessed of the man in question suggested that it was prudent.

"I do not believe it is necessary to demand such a thing, Mr. Darcy," said Elizabeth cautiously. "It is clear that you and Mr. Wickham are no longer friends. I doubt I will have any opportunity to come into contact with him, nor would I wish to know him better."

Mr. Darcy studied her. "That may be true, Miss Bennet, but I would not put it past Mr. Wickham to seek you out."

Frowning, Elizabeth said: "For what reason, sir?"

Rather than respond directly, Mr. Darcy began walking again, though his pace was slow and he was clearly deep in thought. When he finally spoke, it was with a hint of uncharacteristic uncertainty.

"Wickham's father was my father's steward. He was a good, upright man, who was not only my father's employee, but also his friend.

George, however, was not cut from the same cloth as his father—I knew this by my twelfth birthday. As he has grown into a man, his character has become ever more vicious, as his manner of living has become more dissipative."

Once again, Mr. Darcy stopped, and he turned to look at her. "Seduction is one of his worst vices, Miss Bennet, and I have no doubt he has gained some inkling of our current relationship. As he is quite angry with me now, it is possible he might use any means available to gain his revenge upon me. I do not doubt he would use you to such ends, if he should be given the opportunity."

A chill passed through Elizabeth, and she swallowed thickly. "Very well, sir, I will ensure I will not speak to him, even should he approach me."

"Thank you," said Mr. Darcy. Then he stood for some moments watching her, and then said: "In fact, I think it would be better if you do not walk out alone again, even to your uncle's warehouse or to the nearby park."

Elizabeth frowned, annoyed that he would wish to take such freedoms from her. "Surely Mr. Wickham will not be that intent upon seeking me out. I am sure he does not even know the directions to my uncle's townhouse."

"Perhaps not, Miss Bennet," replied Darcy. "But you must understand that though we have managed to keep word of our courtship from the tongues of London's gossips, eventually word *will* get out. I am prominent enough that when it does, it will be all over the city." He smiled, affection evident in his eyes. "This is what you agreed to when you allowed me to call on you, and your life will change because of it. May I assume that it is not too onerous a burden to be connected to me, even if you must accept an escort when you go out walking?"

His words were spoken with lightness and humor, but Elizabeth could still see the uncertainty behind them. She was not sure what she felt for this enigmatic man at present, but she knew that his attentions were anything but onerous.

"No indeed, sir," said Elizabeth with a shy smile. "I have been very happy to receive your calls. In fact, I believe that we are getting on splendidly."

The smile on Mr. Darcy's face changed into something more brilliant and alive at her words, and Elizabeth, for the first time, realized that she was gaining a power over this man. It was not surprising, then, to know that *he* also had power over *her*.

"I shall take a maid along when I go out, sir, if I am not in the company of my aunt or uncle."

Mr. Darcy nodded, but his hesitation suggested he was not quite pleased with her arrangements.

"I believe, Miss Bennet, a sturdy footman would be preferable. I will speak with your uncle—if he cannot spare a man, I will assign one of the footmen employed at Darcy house to his home for your use. I would not curtail your freedom, but we must ensure your safety."

The only thing Elizabeth could do was to agree with his request. And soon, when she had reached the entrance, she said her farewells to Mr. Darcy and to Georgiana, who was waiting for them, and departed.

But as she went, she looked back and saw Mr. Darcy watching the carriage as it pulled away. And in that moment their eyes met, and no matter what Elizabeth did, she could not pull her gaze away. She knew then that something was building between them.

Chapter XIV

Soon the night of the dinner engagement at Darcy house arrived. By this time, Elizabeth had visited Darcy house several times and had become familiar with it, and she was now comfortable with Georgiana, and increasingly so with the master of the house. Thus, she was not overly concerned for the evening, knowing that everything would be lovely.

Still, Elizabeth, though she had never been vain about her appearance—who could be vain next to such a stunning creature as her sister Jane?—took care with her appearance. She had thought long and hard about Mr. Darcy, and she still did not know exactly what she felt at present, she knew it was growing and developing. Could this be the much longed-for love she wished to feel for her partner in life? Elizabeth was still uncertain, but she now knew she was eager for the joy of that discovery.

As the maid was putting the finishing touches on Elizabeth's hair, Mrs. Gardiner entered the room. "Thank you, Marie. I shall finish Miss Bennet's preparations. You may have the rest of the night to yourself."

When the maid had departed, Mrs. Gardiner inspected Elizabeth's hair and, apparently finding everything in order, smiled at her. "You look wonderful tonight, Elizabeth. Mr. Darcy will not be able to take his eyes from you."

"Thank you, Aunt," replied Elizabeth, though feeling a little self-conscious. "I hope he is pleased."

Mrs. Gardiner directed a level look at Elizabeth. "You do not think he will be anything but, do you?"

"I believe that . . . I think that Mr. Darcy is a man who knows his heart and mind, and I think he is coming to respect me more and more."

"And does he love you?"

Elizabeth shook her head. "I do not know, Aunt. It is clear he likes my company a great deal, but he is a private man and infuriatingly difficult to read."

"It is not easy to know what *any man* is thinking, Elizabeth," said Mrs. Gardiner with a laugh. "I am more interested in the contents of *your* heart, my dear. Have your feelings for him grown as well?"

"I do not think that is in question," was Elizabeth's wry reply.

"Then you do esteem him."

"Of course. I do not know at present if my esteem tends to love, but I have always respected him, and the more I come to know him, the more I understand that he is a good man, one who cares deeply and who is serious about his responsibilities. In that way, he is much like Uncle Gardiner."

"That is true," agreed Mrs. Gardiner. Then she turned a shrewd eye on Elizabeth. "Perhaps you also esteem him because he is *unlike* your own father."

Elizabeth dropped her gaze to the floor. "I love my father, Aunt. But I have never wished to marry a man like him. I wish to be loved and esteemed, to know that the man I marry will be diligent in providing for me and my children. My father is a good and intelligent man, but he has not upheld his responsibility in this matter."

A sigh escaped Mrs. Gardiner. Elizabeth looked up and noted her resignation. "I do not wish to disparage your father, Elizabeth, but I wished to determine whether you had thought of this matter. I believe that Mr. Darcy would be quite good for you, and one of the reasons is because of that precisely. You need respect, love, and all the typical facets of a marriage, but I believe it is equally important for you to know without a doubt that your husband will provide for you, protect you, and lift you up when necessary."

Nodding, Elizabeth thought back to their conversation concerning Mr. Wickham. Mr. Darcy might be accustomed to directing all those within reach, but she would never need to worry that he would leave her alone to fend for herself. Quite the opposite, in fact.

"I do not know if you love Mr. Darcy yet," said Mrs. Gardiner, eyeing Elizabeth with a faintly mischievous smile, "but I believe you have made a charming start of it. True love takes time to develop and is built upon mutual esteem and respect. In most cases, it is not like the novels you are sometimes fond of."

Elizabeth giggled at the reference, and her aunt laughed along with her.

"Now, I believe a certain young man is waiting for you to arrive. It would not do to make him wait longer than necessary. Let us depart."

Simply put, Miss Bennet was a vision. She exited the carriage where Darcy met her, marveling at the way her hair was twisted into an elegant knot, while little curled ringlets hung down the sides of her face, dancing along her cheek as she moved. She smiled when she saw him, a smile he knew came directly from her heart and was meant for him alone. And then when they entered the house and she passed her pelisse off to the butler, her elegant evening dress caught his attention as he noted the way it clung to her as she moved, showing her figure to the best advantage. It was all Darcy could do to rein in his sudden well of longing which sprung up within him for this young woman.

And young she was, he forced himself to remember. A member of a privileged class, Darcy knew that a young woman was brought up to be an innocent until the day of her marriage, and though Miss Bennet's intelligence sometimes gave the impression of her being far more experienced and worldly, she was as yet still a girl of seventeen and quite naïve. Darcy would need to take care to avoid frightening her with his passion, which was building for her. Passion would come in due time.

"Elizabeth!" exclaimed Charity and Georgiana almost in unison when they entered the sitting room where the rest of the party was waiting.

Darcy watched as Miss Bennet shared happy greetings with Darcy's two female relations, noting the way they were already in each other's confidence. The Gardiners were introduced to Charity and Gerald Spencer, her new husband, and the group soon sat down to visit in anticipation of the final party to arrive.

Unfortunately, that presence seemed to dim a little when Bingley and his relations arrived, and it was almost entirely due to the actions of one of the party.

They were led into the room by the housekeeper, and Bingley, in what Darcy had come to understand was his usual manner, approached Darcy with a hand outstretched and a grin on his face.

"Darcy. Thank you for inviting us tonight. We are happy to be at your home."

"You are welcome, Bingley. I am happy you could join us this evening."

The introductions were made, and it seemed to Darcy that everyone was happy to be acquainted with one another. It was unfortunate that Fitzwilliam had not been able to join them that evening, as he possessed the gift of making conversation and helping others be comfortable, even if they were not well known to one another. Charity was in her element, speaking with the ladies as if they were old friends, and the gentlemen were similarly gathered around Bingley, who, it was apparent, was comfortable in any situation. That Mr. Gardiner was also a verbose man, and Spencer was able to hold his own, assisted in keeping the conversation flowing.

It was Miss Bingley who was the problem. Upon first being led into the room, it was clear that the woman was nearly speechless at the sight of his home—it was not nearly the sense of intimidation which his sister had reported Miss Bennet had felt, which had quickly turned to pleasure when she realized the Darcys did not tend toward ostentatious shows of wealth. Rather, this was a speechless surprise at the mere *sight* of wealth.

And she clearly coveted that wealth, for it was not moments after the company's arrival that Darcy happened to be looking at her as she allowed her gaze to roam over the room, and he saw the exact moment when a calculating sort of leer came over her face. Darcy did not know the woman as of yet—he had not made her acquaintance until that evening. But he could easily understand that she was not at all like her brother. He only hoped that she was proper enough in manner to maintain some semblance of control over the suddenly burgeoning stratagems he knew must be going through her mind. Darcy had seen her kind far too many times.

Her first words to him that evening only proved Darcy's assumptions. Before long, Darcy had managed to maneuver Miss Bennet into a position in which they could converse, and though he still felt utterly charmed by everything about her, he was beginning to control his reaction better.

"May I say how beautiful you look this evening, Miss Bennet?" said Darcy once he was certain he had her full attention.

"Thank you, Mr. Darcy. You are looking rather well yourself."

Darcy was disappointed; she was becoming so accustomed to his presence that it was more difficult to elicit the reaction he wished from her—that of her fetching blushes. Determined to do better, Darcy said:

"I was hardly able to hold my countenance when I saw you. You are a lovely young woman. I would be required to fend off the men of society if they were able to see you tonight."

Rather than the expected blush, Miss Bennet only arched an eyebrow. "Then it is well that I dressed with you in mind, sir. I have no desire to impress any other young man at present."

Darcy arched an eyebrow of his own, enjoying their banter immensely. "At present? With that choice of words, I might wonder if I might have some competition in the future."

Laughing, Miss Bennet replied: "I doubt it, sir. If you continue on in such a charming manner, I doubt I shall ever be able to focus on any other man."

"I am happy to hear it." Darcy leaned forward, and in a tone low enough to only reach her ears, said: "You know not what you do to me, Miss Bennet. I assure you the thoughts I entertained when you entered were not fit to be shared with polite company."

Perhaps these words were a little too bold, but they achieved their intended effect as Miss Bennet flushed from the top of her head all the way down to her neckline. But even then, rather than stammer out a response, she gathered her fortitude, which delighted him so well, and looked him in the eye.

"I did not know I was allowing such a rake to call on me, Mr. Darcy. Perhaps I shall have to reconsider."

"I think not," replied Darcy. "If I was pushed, I would have no recourse but to throw you over my horse and ride for Gretna Green. If compromised in such a manner, I doubt you would have any choice other than to marry me."

An understated smile crept over her face. "In that case, I shall grant you a reprieve, sir. But only if you promise to follow up the passion in your voice with action."

"When the appropriate time arrives, Miss Bennet, I believe I shall have no difficulty whatsoever in keeping that promise."

The spell between them was broken when the sound of Miss Bingley's voice floated to them from where she had approached.

"Oh, Mr. Darcy, we are so happy you have asked us to join you this evening."

Feeling a little startled—and noting that Miss Bennet was in the same straits—Darcy stepped back a little and watched the woman approach. She was eyeing him much as a wolf would eye a juicy hare, though when her eyes flicked to Miss Bennet, it was accompanied with a gaze which seemed to size her up, no doubt attempting to measure the competition.

Darcy could not be certain if Bingley had told his sister about his courtship with Miss Bennet, but from what he could see, he suspected she would think it to be little impediment to her ambitions.

"You have a very lovely home, sir," continued Miss Bingley. Her eyes turned away from Miss Bennet, seeming to discount her altogether. "I was astonished at the elegance, the veritable cornucopia of style and taste which exudes from every room, from every detail, which has been so painstakingly chosen to produce the greatest effect. It is in every way wonderful."

Darcy bowed shortly, hoping he could induce this woman to be gone. "I thank you, Miss Bingley, but I cannot take credit for it. My mother decorated these rooms many years ago when I was a boy."

"She had exquisite taste, sir," enthused Miss Bingley. "I cannot imagine any arrangements so fine or so perfect. I understand your estate is in Derbyshire?"

"Yes, Miss Bingley; that is so."

"Charles has told me it is very fine."

"That is interesting, Miss Bingley," said Miss Bennet, "for I do not believe your brother has ever seen Mr. Darcy's estate. I cannot comment myself, as I have not yet had that opportunity either, but according to my aunt, who lived many years in the neighborhood, there are few which can compare with it."

Miss Bennet turned to Darcy, a knowing smile writ upon her brow, and continued: "And, of course, you and your sister have told me much of it as well. From your description, I feel like I already know it intimately."

"I am certain one day you shall, Miss Bennet," replied Darcy warmly. "It is a wonderful place, if I do say so myself."

"It cannot be anything but!" cried Miss Bingley. "And though you are correct that Charles has never before seen . . ."

"Pemberley," supplied Darcy, though he almost wished there was some way to keep it from her.

"My, even the name is all that is elegant, invoking wondrous expectations of what to expect when visiting. Since we are all the best of friends, I hope to one day see it. I am certain words do not do it justice."

"I can only agree with that, Miss Bingley," said Darcy. "I can do it little justice myself."

It was a strange conversation, Darcy decided. Though they continued to speak in an amiable manner, Miss Bingley punctuated their words with comments about his person, his home—which she had owned to never having seen—his sister, his relations, and even his clothes. Miss

Bennet, for her part, clearly understood Miss Bingley's intentions and was amused by her comments, even as she attempted to draw more details about Pemberley from him. Darcy was frustrated by Miss Bingley's insistence upon intruding in their conversation, while at the same time feeling charmed that Miss Bennet was so interested in his home, rather than a large building finely furnished.

The conversation turned a little later when Miss Bingley, apparently sensing she was not making much of an impression in complimenting his person, decided to change tack.

"Miss Bennet," said she, turning to Elizabeth and addressing her for the first time since joining their conversation, "I understand you have been away from home for some time. I am certain you must miss it by now."

"Indeed I do, Miss Bingley," replied Miss Bennet. "It is a dear place, though it is not in the peak district like Mr. Darcy's home."

"I am sure that it cannot in any way compare. The north *is* far superior in beauty, though London is a wondrous place. My family is from the area of York, and is thus quite close to Mr. Darcy's home. Have you ever visited York, Mr. Darcy?"

Darcy regarded Miss Bingley for a brief moment, wondering if simply ignoring her would be ungentlemanly. Though he was sorely tempted, he knew he could not behave in such a manner to a guest in his home. He did resolve, however, that Miss Bingley would not be invited to his home with any frequency.

"I have visited York, Miss Bingley. In fact, I am quite familiar with it, as I own a small estate within a day's travel of the city."

If anything, Miss Bingley's eyes grew wider and the avaricious gleam within grew even stronger. "It is a wonderful place," said Miss Bingley, "but I have always observed, when passing through Derbyshire, that there is something . . . undefined about it; something inherently lovely and estimable, though there are parts which are rather untamed and far too wild for my taste."

Miss Bennet's smile was positively dancing at the woman's words, alerting Darcy to the fact that she was almost certainly about to make some witty response. She did not disappoint.

"Actually, Miss Bingley, I rather suspect that the wildness of Derbyshire is the precise reason why most of its inhabitants declare it to be the best of counties. Though I have never seen it, I can well imagine the beauty of the peaks, the pristine freshness of landscapes untouched by man. It is as nature intended it to be."

A sneer came over Miss Bingley's face, and her responding words were just short of insulting. "That is a rather . . . interesting assertion for one who has confessed to never seeing that of which she speaks."

"The substance of our thoughts is remarkably similar, Miss Bennet," said Darcy, before Miss Bennet could respond. "In fact, my home is not distant from the peaks, and they can be seen on a clear day. My home has largely been left to nature's hand, as she is a much better steward of the land than I can ever be."

"But, Mr. Darcy," exclaimed Miss Bingley, her tone incredulous and even a little alarmed, "surely you do not mean to say that you have no formal gardens at your estate."

"No, Miss Bingley, I did not say that. We have formal gardens enough to satisfy even the most ardent lover of flowers. We have topiaries, a hedge maze, and many other things designed to offer peace and tranquility. But beyond our gardens, the park has been left to nature, with a few well defined paths which allow one to take in its glories. I prefer it that way, as have my ancestors before me. In my opinion, man's hand on nature only distracts from its beauty."

It was clear Miss Bingley did not know what to say to such an assertion, though Darcy could almost see the exact instant in which she decided it did not signify, which was, of course, accompanied by thoughts of what changes she would implement when *she* became mistress of the estate.

The conversation continued in this manner until dinner, and as Mr. Darcy spoke with Miss Bennet most of all, he began to see Miss Bingley's frustration that he was paying so much attention to her rival. She began to make little cutting remarks at Miss Bennet's expense. Though Darcy was irritated by the woman's behavior, only the manners his father had long ago instilled in him allowed him to refrain from reprimanding her. By contrast, Darcy's admiration for Miss Bennet grew apace when he saw how she parried the woman's attacks with an aplomb worthy of someone several years her senior.

When the housekeeper entered to announce dinner, Darcy thought Miss Bingley must have been watching for the announcement, counting the minutes, as she moved almost before Mrs. Mayberry began to speak. In her haste, she shouldered in front of Miss Bennet, knocking her slightly to the side, and latched onto Darcy's arm as if she was a leech.

"How wonderful, sir," said she, accompanied with a batting of her eyelashes. "Shall you escort me to dinner?"

Before Darcy was able to respond, his cousin Charity's voice interrupted them. She stepped forward and smoothly transferred Miss Bingley's hand from Darcy's arm to her husband's other arm, saying:

"We have decided to dispense with formality this evening, Miss Bingley. I would value your attendance, as we have not had an opportunity to speak."

Miss Bingley's distress was palpable, but she resigned herself to her situation, and within moments she was even sporting a sly smile at Miss Bennet, clearly thinking she was being favored by Darcy's female relations. Darcy snorted at the mere thought; Charity's glance at him suggested that he owed her for distracting his predatory admirer.

"Well, Mr. Darcy," said Miss Bennet, "I believe you are left with the indignity of escorting me."

"'Tis no indignity, Miss Bennet," said Darcy, charmed all over again. "Quite the contrary, I assure you."

The day after the dinner, Elizabeth was engaged to shop with her aunt and Miss Darcy. Charity had been forced to decline the invitation as she had other engagements that day, but the three ladies gathered together and visited the shops on Bond Street, enjoying one another's company immensely.

Elizabeth had never been precisely fond of shopping, though that was likely as much due to her mother's propensity for dominating her purchases with styles she found unappealing. This day however, was engaged mostly in browsing, and though the ladies did make some small purchases, on the whole, they enjoyed one another's company rather than concentrating on buying.

The previous evening had been all Elizabeth had hoped for. Mr. Darcy had made his admiration for her plain, and Elizabeth had spent the dinner hour in earnest conversation with him. And if Miss Bingley watched her with a smug expression every time Charity said something to her or glared at Elizabeth if she thought she was engaged in speaking too much with Mr. Darcy, Elizabeth could do nothing but laugh at the woman's absurdity and ignore her glares. And Miss Bingley had learned how much esteem Charity had for her in a manner which could not be misinterpreted, which had put her in ill humor the rest of the evening.

After dinner had been consumed, the ladies had risen to leave the gentlemen to their port and had returned to the sitting-room. There, Elizabeth had had the opportunity to once again speak with the hostess, which she had been denied most of the evening.

"Did you enjoy dinner?" asked Charity at the first opportunity.

"Very much," said Elizabeth, suppressing a hint of laughter. "I enjoy speaking with your cousin, and Georgiana is such a dear girl.

Charity only directed a level look at Elizabeth; it seemed she was not about to allow Elizabeth to forget what she had willingly endured for her sake.

"Then it is well, though the conversation at the foot of the table was not quite so . . . scintillating." "I do not know," said Elizabeth, by now barely holding her laughter, "it seemed to be quite animated at times."

There was only time for her friend to direct a severe look at her before they were joined by the woman of whom they were—obliquely—talking.

"Lady Charity!" exclaimed Miss Bingley, "I cannot tell you how wonderful dinner was. You created a memorable culinary experience and made us all feel so welcome. And all at such a young age too!"

It was almost too much for Elizabeth when Charity rolled her eyes at Elizabeth; Elizabeth was not even certain Miss Bingley was unable to see it!

"I thank you, Miss Bingley. But my mother *is* a countess, after all. She would not have raised a daughter who was incapable of performing as a competent hostess."

"And her efforts have been an admirable success! You are to be commended."

"Dinner truly was lovely, Charity," said Elizabeth. "I would love to obtain the recipe for the dessert when convenient. My mother would adore it."

"Perhaps, Miss Bennet," interjected Miss Bingley, in a manner overflowing with dismissive scorn, "you have not been raised in polite society. The daughter of an earl must be referred to with the title 'lady' applied to her name."

"That is true, Miss Bingley," said Charity, her tone hard and her manner suggesting that she had endured quite enough of Miss Bingley's poor behavior, "but such formalities may be dispensed with when both parties are in agreement."

The fact that Miss Bingley's jaw dropped in amazement did nothing to improve her appeal, and Elizabeth could not help but feel a hint of satisfaction at the woman's set down.

"Oh . . . of course . . . I . . . well, I would be pleased, since we are all . . . friends here, if you would . . . also call me by my Christian name."

By the end of her response, Miss Bingley's former supercilious manner had returned, but she was destined to be disappointed, as her declaration was met by nothing more than silence from the woman with whom she wished to ingratiate herself.

Instead of responding, Charity turned back to Elizabeth and said: "I believe Darcy would be delighted to share the recipe with you, *Elizabeth*.

But I doubt it will be needed. After all, I do not think it will be long before you will be able to claim it for your own."

The look of horror and consternation on Miss Bingley's face was comical, and Elizabeth was required to exercise iron control to avoid laughing out loud. "It might be a little early for such expectations, but I thank you regardless."

Having experienced enough humiliation, Miss Bingley excused herself and soon took up a position by her sister's side, and if the whispered conferences and pointed looks at Elizabeth were any indication, Elizabeth thought she had made an enemy that evening.

"You cannot imagine the indignities I have suffered tonight, Elizabeth," said Charity in a quiet tone.

Elizabeth made the mistake of looking across the room at Miss Bingley as she giggled. The woman's countenance tightened at the insult—it was obvious they were laughing at her—and Elizabeth thought that had the superior society not been present, Miss Bingley might have attacked her. As it was, she turned once again to her sister and their whispered conference continued. Mrs. Hurst, for her part, had made no outright declarations that evening, but it was clear that she supported her sister in whatever she wished.

"Miss Bingley, you see," said Charity, pulling Elizabeth's attention back to her, "is a rather peculiar mix of haughty self-importance and a desperate need for approval from those she considers to inhabit the level of society to which she wishes to ascend. I could hardly keep my countenance when she bestowed the most outrageous compliments upon me in one breath, and in the next boasted of her achievements. One might think her to be the most accomplished lady of society with such talk."

"It seems clear that she has had a change of heart and does not consider you to be a rung on the ladder she wishes to climb."

"Good," said Charity with a snort. "Then perhaps she will leave me alone. I have had all I can stomach of Miss Bingley tonight, I assure you."

Even thinking on the matter now, Elizabeth could not imagine why Miss Bingley had acted the way she had or why she might think such behavior was welcome. It was possible that many of those of higher society might wish to be treated with such exaggerated deference—and among that number Elizabeth thought that several others of Mr. Darcy's relations might be included, given what she had heard of them. But one only had to speak with Charity, Major Fitzwilliam, or Mr. Darcy for the space of a moment to realize they would not suffer such behavior. And yet Miss Bingley had persisted.

The subject being distasteful, Elizabeth turned her mind back to the evening with Mr. Darcy, and she could not be happier with the way their relationship was progressing. There was something real and tangible between them, and it was not any less real for her inability to name exactly what it was. At this point, she almost preferred to be unaware of what exactly it was—it made the discovery all that much sweeter, and the anticipation greater.

They stopped for luncheon in a small café near the shopping district, and after they had finished, they made their way to a museum which stood up the street, yet within easy walking distance. There, they were met by the gentlemen, Mr. Darcy and Mr. Gardiner, their arrival having been prearranged. Greetings were exchanged with pleasure, and soon they were walking through the hallways, examining the exhibits and exchanging opinions. The others, cognizant of the desire for the young, still unacknowledged lovers for privacy, walked on ahead, while Darcy and Elizabeth lagged a little.

"I trust you are enjoying your outing today?" asked Mr. Darcy, as they walked through the halls.

"I do not as a rule enjoy shopping, Mr. Darcy."

Elizabeth giggled when he raised his eyebrow at her. "I *have* enjoyed the *company*, sir, but the activity is not what I would normally prefer. It is sometimes a necessary evil, but I usually prefer to complete it as soon as possible."

"Is that so?" asked he. His eyes darted furtively around them, and noting no one in close proximity, he once again spoke quietly, saying: "Then if we marry, I need not worry about you spending all our income on frivolities."

"I think that highly unlikely, sir," replied Elizabeth.

"But I thought all women were eager to spend as much of their husband's money as possible."

"That might be true for *some* women, but I pride myself on the fact that I do not require a new wardrobe whenever the style changes slightly. I think it a silly affectation, to be honest."

"A thrifty wife is much to be desired," said Mr. Darcy.

"Or perhaps I simply prefer to purchase much more expensive items, Mr. Darcy," replied Elizabeth, a hint of a challenge in her tone.

Mr. Darcy favored her with one of his devastating smiles. "I believe I shall be quite happy to give into your whims, Miss Bennet, even if it should result in our destitution."

They both collapsed in laughter at Mr. Darcy's statement, the absurdity of the conversation finally catching up with them. Beaming with delight, Elizabeth could only say:

"I believe we are getting on quite well, sir. There is nothing more indicative of felicity than the ability to laugh together at silly conversations."

"I cannot agree more, Miss Bennet."

They continued on, and the longer they spoke, the more powerful a feeling was building up in Elizabeth's breast. Mr. Darcy was calm and considerate, solid and dependable, and yet possessed an understated sense of humor and a knowledge of the world which was appealing. Their opinions of the art they examined was not always complementary, but they discussed their differences frankly, and Elizabeth thought she was quickly coming to a more complete understanding of this gentleman. And she could not help but be happy with what she saw.

Chapter XV

It was later the day of the outing to the museum when Darcy went to his club, accompanied by Bingley. Though he had not yet known the man for long, Darcy almost felt like their acquaintance had been of some duration, as Bingley's open manners were entirely conducive to quickly becoming friends. He had become so comfortable with Bingley that he had agreed to sponsor him at White's, and they met there for a drink and to have a little discussion.

As they sat across the table, Darcy watched his new friend, noting the man's easy manner with all and sundry. Though Bingley was not known to anyone, Darcy was at least known by sight to many, and there was a steady stream of gentlemen who stopped by for a word, a brief conversation, or just to greet him as they passed by. Though there were some whom Darcy would have wished not to know at all, the majority of those with whom they spoke were actually quite well known to him, and of this group, those to whom Darcy introduced Bingley accepted him with pleasure, as he had known they would; Darcy was not in the habit of surrounding himself with those who believed themselves to be above their company.

When the stream of those who wished to greet Darcy dwindled, Bingley sat back in his chair, and though he was as affable as ever, he had a slightly startled air about him.

"I say, Darcy," said he, though his voice was moderated substantially, "I had no idea you were such an important man of society. I knew you possessed connections, but I think I counted no less than three earls and a duke who stopped by our table in the past thirty minutes!"

In fact, one of the earls and the duke were people whom Darcy would prefer never to meet again, but he did not think he needed to mention such a thing to Bingley. The earl was an associate of his cousin, the viscount, and thus not one with whom Darcy would wish to associate, and the duke led a faction in parliament of which his uncle was a member. He also had high hopes of recruiting the Darcy family to his cause. Darcy, unfortunately for the duke, had no intention of supporting him.

"My uncle *is* an earl, Bingley," said Darcy, "though I have never aspired to gain such social prominence myself."

"I almost think you might be successful should you wish it."

Darcy nodded but did not elucidate. There had been occasions in the past when prior Darcys had refused titles. The Darcy name was not defined by a title; it was built upon generations of hard work, fair management of their land, and unshakable integrity.

"It also seemed to me like most were not disgusted by my presence, as I might have thought."

"The fact that you are leaving trade behind has something to do with that," replied Darcy. Bingley was right, but there were several who would have refused to acknowledge Bingley if it had not been Darcy introducing him.

"Perhaps," said Bingley. "However, I find myself indifferent to the approval of society. My father always wished to become a gentleman, and I will confess I am anticipating it myself, but I do not care for the approbation of society."

Talk from there turned to other matters, and soon they were discussing their experiences at university, from which Bingley had graduated only months earlier.

"You say you attended Oxford?" asked Darcy.

"It was originally my intent to study at Cambridge," replied Bingley, "but in the end my father and I decided on Oxford."

"I shall try not to hold that against you," said Darcy, prompting a laugh from his new friend.

"I thank you, sir!"

Thoughtful, Darcy considered his friend. Given that Bingley had only finished months before, their time at school would have overlapped by one year.

When Darcy said as much to Bingley, he added: "Had you attended Cambridge as you had intended, it is possible we might have met ere now."

Bingley laughed. "It is quite possible indeed! It is strange that we should meet now in such circumstances. And had you not been courting Miss Bennet, we still might not have met."

"Or had your father not decided to merge with Mr. Gardiner."

"That is true. Sometimes life takes the most intriguing turns, which we might not have expected."

"Indeed it might."

Darcy was thinking of Miss Bennet and his sudden decision to pursue a courtship with her. Darcy had always prized integrity and trust above all other traits, and nothing more than an overheard conversation with a sleeping child, of all things, had alerted him to these qualities in Miss Bennet. It was the stuff of novels.

After leaving the club, Darcy returned to his house, his mind full of thoughts of how his life had changed these past weeks. He had often lamented the paucity of his friends, those whom he could trust, and yet in recent weeks, he had met Mr. Bingley, a jovial man and true friend, and been introduced to Mr. Gardiner, who possessed similar qualities.

But these paled in comparison with Miss Bennet, the lovely and genuine young woman he had recently begun courting. And something in Darcy's heart told him that courtship was only the beginning, and that he would ultimately lead her to the altar. She was to be priced above the costliest jewels, of more worth than all the gold in the world. Part of Darcy could not wait until he was once again in her presence, basking in the radiance which was such a part of her.

When he arrived at the house, Darcy retired to his study and quickly wrote a letter of business to his solicitor, and once that was complete, he left his study to go in search of Georgiana. He did not need to look far, as he heard the sound of the pianoforte almost as soon as he left the room.

Though he thought to enter the music room in silence and listen to his sister as she played, she espied him as he entered almost immediately, and rather than continue to play as she normally would, she rose to join him by the door. At once, Darcy was put on his guard by the troubled expression with which she regarded him.

"Is aught amiss, Georgiana?" asked Darcy as she stepped up to him and accepted a kiss on the cheek.

"Brother, I had wondered . . ."

When Georgiana fell silent, Darcy prompted her: "What is it?"

Seeing her discomfort, Darcy took her arm gently and led her to a nearby sofa, sitting her close by his side. He grasped her hand and stroked it gently, once again asking her to share her distress with him.

"I was wondering, is your courtship with Elizabeth proceeding well?"

Darcy frowned at the question, wondering what had brought Georgiana to concern herself with his relationship with Miss Bennet. He was also becoming a little annoyed that both Charity and Georgiana had been given the privilege of calling her by her Christian name, while Darcy was still relegated to the use of her surname. But knowing such feelings were not only improper but silly, he put them from his mind, instead focusing on his sister.

"It is proceeding very well, Georgiana. But I must confess I am surprised. Given what I have observed, I had thought you to have the highest opinion of Miss Bennet."

Eyes widened with almost comical distress, Georgiana blurted: "Oh, no, William! I love Elizabeth and would not wish for a better sister."

"Then what has brought on this distress?"

For the briefest of moments, Georgiana withdrew into herself, considering her words, he thought, before she turned to him, the words coming out in a flood.

"Miss Bingley visited, and from her words she led me to believe that you would soon be changing your attentions and focusing on *her* rather than Elizabeth."

"What?" demanded Darcy, his temper rising instantly.

Georgiana did not notice his sudden pique, as she was passing from uncertainty to her own annoyance before his very eyes.

"Soon after I returned from my outing with Elizabeth and the Gardiners, and after you left for your club, Miss Bingley called on me. Is that not more than a little . . . presumptuous, Brother? I am not yet out, and I have only met her once. Should she be calling on me?"

"No, Georgiana, she should not be," said Darcy. "What did she say?"

"Well, she seemed put out that you were not at home," replied Georgiana, speaking slowly, "but she quickly recovered and suggested that we visit for a time."

Georgiana shook her head, and he thought he saw a hint of anger in her countenance. "Her conversation was nothing but unconcealed flattery, Brother, and I knew in an instant that she would not have even glanced at me a second time had I not been your sister. She was so insincere."

"Go on," said Darcy, when she did not continue to speak. Inside he was growing angrier by the moment, but he would keep his temper in check for his dearest sister's sake.

"We spoke for a time, and then we spent time in this very room, where she insisted on praising every note which issued forth from the pianoforte." Georgiana smiled shyly and said: "A few times I even made mistakes on purpose, and even that did not halt her fawning. And it is all so silly, as she is quite accomplished herself, and she plays much better than I do.

"She is also several years older than you are," said Darcy.

Georgiana merely waved him off with imperious impatience. "I know, William. I do not feel inadequate next to her. What I feel is pity. She covets your position and society so much that she is willing to sacrifice her self-respect in order to obtain it. Her words about Elizabeth . . ." Georgiana paused, a pained expression on her face. "She did not say anything direct, of course, but she made several comments to the effect that Elizabeth was not a suitable companion for me, or a suitable wife for you. I almost told her exactly what I thought of her when she persisted in saying such things."

Darcy was surprised at hearing his sister make such an observation, but he was pleased that she had seen to the heart of the matter so easily—if she showed half this much perception after her debut in society, she would do very well indeed.

"I was afraid she would never leave," said Georgiana. "She was finally induced to depart only a half hour before your return, and even then it was only because I pointedly told her I had to complete my studies. Mrs. Jenkinson was not happy with her persistence."

Mrs. Jenkinson was the lady who had been his cousin Anne's companion before her passing, and in thanks for her years of faithful service, Lady Catherine had recommended her to Darcy to assist with Georgiana's upbringing. She was originally brought on as Georgiana's governess, but now that Georgiana had attained the age of a young woman, that was not precisely accurate any longer. She still maintained responsibility for Georgiana's education, but Darcy thought the woman would not wish to become her companion as she was becoming quite elderly. Hence the need for a new companion within the next few years.

"I believe you handled the situation as well as you were able, Georgiana," said Darcy. "Miss Bingley should not have presumed to call on you based on so slight an acquaintance, she should not have called in the afternoon, and she certainly should not have imposed upon you for more than two hours."

"Do you suggest we do not admit her next time she comes?"

After a moment's thought, Darcy shook his head. "Bingley is a good man, and I have become friendly with him. I would not wish to shame his sister by denying her entrance.

"But I cannot condone her behavior either. I will speak with Bingley and inform him of what his sister has done. I do not doubt he will take action."

"Very well," said Georgiana, seeming relieved by Darcy's words.

Darcy smiled at her, feeling proud of her all over. "Again, I wish to emphasize how proud I am of how you handled her. If there is a next time, ask her to leave as soon as you can and inform me of the matter. Hopefully I shall be able to speak with Bingley before it happens again."

"I shall." Georgiana then giggled, saying: "I shall need to relate the afternoon to Elizabeth. We shall laugh so at such absurdity!"

A chuckle escaped Darcy's lips, and he was forced to agree with her assessment. "I believe you are entirely correct, my dear. Elizabeth would be diverted by Miss Bingley's ridiculous behavior."

Feeling altogether better, Georgiana soon rose from the sofa and entertained Darcy with several songs. For his part, though Darcy enjoyed the performance, the greater part of his attention was focused upon the woman his sister had spoken of with such partiality. Darcy was feeling no less fondness, and his pique with Miss Bingley was all but forgotten.

It was only the day after Elizabeth's shopping excursion with Miss Darcy and the visit to the museum when the idyllic pleasure of her courtship was shattered by the detested person of Mr. Pearce.

In the company of her aunt, Elizabeth was at the pianoforte in the sitting-room when the gentleman was admitted, and so surprised was Elizabeth at his appearance that her playing stumbled to a halt. She rose in consternation, wondering at his sudden entrance—her mother's continuous letters notwithstanding, having gone so long without hearing from the man, Elizabeth had hoped that he had given up on his pursuit of her. Apparently that had been nothing more than wishful thinking.

The man took in her appearance and, in a sneering sort of voice, said: "Well it seems your improved state of dress attests to your father's inability to deny you. I should not have believed your mother's insistence that her husband would not bother to send you money for additional dresses. It seems he cannot resist providing for his 'favorite daughter,' when he should be insisting that you do your duty."

"Why are you here, Mr. Pearce?" said Mrs. Gardiner.

The man eyed her with disdain written all over his brow. "You will be silent. You are nothing to me, and I do not have the inclination to debate with you. I have come to speak with your niece, and I will not be kept from my design."

Having spoken, Mr. Pearce turned from Mrs. Gardiner, ignoring her as if she was nothing more than an insect. Though she was focused on Mr. Pearce, Elizabeth did not miss her aunt quickly walking to the door behind him and summoning the housekeeper. What the discussion consisted of Elizabeth could not say, for her attention was focused on the belligerent figure of Mr. Pearce.

"I had thought that a little time to think of your situation would be enough to ensure your compliance," began he, his tone almost conversational, "but apparently I have underestimated your obstinacy, Miss Bennet."

"You have underestimated quite a lot if you still believe that I shall relent and marry you."

"Oh, I will gain what I want. I always do."

Elizabeth laughed out loud, a harsh, grating sound, designed to provoke his displeasure. Though she had never managed the feat before, she felt a savage sense of triumph, for his countenance darkened noticeably.

"As you can see, Mr. Pearce, I am quite happy living with my aunt and uncle. There is no reason for me to capitulate."

"You are happy living with those who are so far beneath you?"

"They are not beneath *you*. They are far above you in everything that matters, Mr. Pearce. They are kind and amiable, sensible and intelligent, good and caring, and everything that you are not."

"Are you completely witless? To imagine that some . . . *tradesman* and his wife are above me is the most absurd thing I have ever heard."

"I imagine you must be accustomed to it, sir, given the continued absurdity of your attentions after my repeated, emphatic refusals."

"Why can you not bow down to your fate?" cried Mr. Pearce.

"Why can you not accept the reality that your suit is doomed to failure?"

Elizabeth returned Mr. Pearce's stare with one of her own, and his eyes narrowed. Affecting a calm she did not completely feel, Elizabeth watched him, waiting for him to speak once again. Mrs. Gardiner had come to stand with her to face the antagonist. For a moment, Elizabeth almost thought the man would throw up his hands and depart. But he did not.

"What will it take to induce you to see reason?"

"Nothing," replied Elizabeth, holding her head high. "I would not agree to marry you should you be the only man on earth. I suggest you surrender to the inevitable."

"I shall not!" exclaimed Mr. Pearce. He stalked toward Elizabeth, fury overtaking his countenance. "I shall have you, Miss Bennet. Of that you may be certain. This recalcitrance of yours is at an end. I shall have your pledge to marry me at the earliest opportunity, and you shall give it to me now!"

"Never!" cried Elizabeth.

The rage which settled over the man's face was in no way comparable to what Elizabeth had witnessed before, and Elizabeth actually began to be afraid of his becoming violent. Mrs. Gardiner apparently sensed the same, as she moved in front of Elizabeth, putting herself in between her niece and the angry man stalking her.

"I must ask you to leave, Mr. Pearce!" said Mrs. Gardiner, her voice high and shrill. "You are not welcome here any longer."

"I shall leave when I have obtained that which I came for," said Mr. Pearce, though his voice came out more like a snarl.

Seeing the man approaching them, Elizabeth cried out with the only thing she could think of to try to delay him.

"I am already being courted by another man!"

Eyes widening with astonishment, Mr. Pearce yelled: "That cannot be! Mr. Bennet has made no mention of it."

At that moment, the door behind Mr. Pearce opened and her uncle hurried in, followed by a burly footman. The two strode forward quickly, Mr. Gardiner stepping in front of his wife, while the footman took up position behind the interloper.

"What is this? Why are you threatening my wife and niece?"

Seeming to sense that he was now outnumbered, Mr. Pearce subsided a little, but with evident ill grace. He ignored Mr. Gardiner's questions, however, in favor of asking his own.

"Why is your niece claiming a fictitious courtship? Had she actually been receiving the calls of a gentleman, her mother never would have been able to contain her crowing."

Elizabeth glared at the man for insulting her mother, though she knew his assertions were essentially the truth. Mr. Gardiner's response, however, showed no such restraint.

"That is something you must take up with my brother. Now, you will leave my house immediately. Do not return, sir, as you will not be allowed to enter again."

"I shall not until you answer my question!"

At Mr. Gardiner's nod, the footman stepped forward and tapped Mr. Pearce on the shoulder. "The master has asked you to leave. *Now*, sir."

Mr. Pearce stepped to the side, glaring at the footman for daring to lay hands on his person, but he soon seemed to realize this was not a fight he was about to win. But he did not move immediately; instead he paused and studied Elizabeth, as if he was trying to fathom the reason for her continued defiance.

For her part, Elizabeth did nothing more than glare at him in return, allowing him to see all the contempt she held for him. Though she had felt the quivering of her insides when the man had first entered the room, the fire of indignation had welled up within her, bolstering her courage and filling her with determination to continue defying him.

A short bark of laughter told her what Pearce thought of her boldness. "It seems you have some pluck, Miss Bennet, and I cannot help but admire you for it. But it shall all come to naught."

Turning, Mr. Pearce stalked across the floor, opening the door, which he allowed to crash against the wall behind, and then exiting the room, the footman following behind, ensuring he departed as he ought. For the briefest of moments, there was silence in the room, which was only broken when Elizabeth's sigh rent the air.

"Sit here, my dear," said Mrs. Gardiner, guiding Elizabeth to a nearby chair.

Elizabeth allowed herself to be led, though she directed a wan smile at her aunt once she was situated comfortably. "Thank you, Aunt. But I am quite well indeed."

"It seems you have garnered an even greater fortitude these past months, Lizzy," said Mr. Gardiner, his face shining with the force of his approval.

"I know not, Uncle. But I do know that I cannot capitulate to that man. I am unable to fathom why he is so insistent on having me for a wife, but I will not allow him to intimidate me, and I will *definitely* not be prevailed upon to marry him."

"Good girl, Lizzy," said Mrs. Gardiner.

Mrs. Gardiner directed a significant look at her husband, which he understood with a nod.

"I shall have Mr. Darcy summoned immediately."

As he moved away to write a note to Mr. Darcy, Elizabeth reflected on how the very thought of the gentleman filled her with confidence.

Mr. Darcy would never give her up to the likes of Winston Pearce.

Only an hour after the incident, and less than half an hour after receiving word of it, Darcy strode into the Gardiners' sitting room, anxious to see Miss Bennet and confirm for himself that she was well. The message was concise, yet it lacked any significant detail, leaving Darcy guessing as to what exactly had occurred. All he knew was that Pearce had once again appeared at the Gardiner townhouse and demanded Elizabeth marry him. If he had harmed one single hair on her head . . .

The moment he entered the room, Darcy could see that she was well. Mrs. Gardiner had ordered a tea service, and the two ladies were seated on the sofa together, calmly sipping their tea. By contrast, Mr. Gardiner was pacing the floor, muttering imprecations under his breath.

"Miss Bennet," said Darcy as he entered

He strode forward, kneeling by her side, inspecting her for any harm to her person. She was as he had ever seen her, cheeks rosy, eyes bright, and a calm sort of contentedness. But as he looked at her, he realized she had changed from the girl he had first known. She was more mature, for one, and there existed about her person a . . . firmness of purpose, for want of a better term. She exuded confidence. Darcy had never found her as beautiful as he did now.

"You are well," asked Darcy, though he knew it was not required.

"I am," replied Miss Bennet with nary a hint of hesitation.

"What happened?"

Darcy took her hand gently, content to do nothing more than hold it in his. With a firmness of manner and voice, Elizabeth told him exactly what she had experienced with the reprobate Pearce, and as she spoke, Darcy felt his ire rise higher and higher. By the time she had finished her recitation, he knew exactly why Mr. Gardiner had been pacing the floor. Darcy felt the need for a little pacing himself, lest he ride immediately for Hertfordshire and call the man out!

"What manner of man is this?" demanded Darcy. "With behavior and pride such as this, he puts my cousin the viscount to shame."

"I know not, Mr. Darcy," said Mr. Gardiner. "But I have never seen the likes of Mr. Pearce, and I have had dealings with gentlemen from all levels of society."

Mr. Gardiner looked at Darcy for a long moment before he appeared to come to some decision. "It would seem the time for action has come, Mr. Darcy. I do not believe you have the luxury of waiting any longer, for I do not doubt Pearce will head directly for Longbourn to accost my brother. I am certain you can imagine what will happen next."

"Once Mrs. Bennet hears of it," added Mrs. Gardiner, "Elizabeth will be allowed no rest until she accounts for her time in London."

"And if she does not force Elizabeth's return home," said Mr. Gardiner, "Bennet will almost certainly wish to know what has been happening and begin to ask questions himself."

"That is," said Mrs. Gardiner, "if you still wish to proceed with this courtship, Mr. Darcy."

If Darcy had been asked even a few days earlier he might not have known his own mind and heart enough to answer that question. As it was, however, he did nothing more than smile at Mrs. Gardiner—and he noted her own grin, like she was already aware of his answer—and turn to Miss Bennet.

"Miss Bennet, I understand we have truly only had a little time to come to know each other, but I find that my esteem for you is beyond anything I have ever experienced. I believe the time has come to formalize our courtship. Do I have your consent to call on you for the purpose of courtship?"

"Of course, Mr. Darcy," said Miss Bennet. "I wish for nothing more."

"In that case, I shall ride to Hertfordshire on the morrow and obtain your father's consent."

"I wish you luck, sir," said Miss Bennet, this time showing a smile of true amusement. "I hope your resolve survives my mother's display of enthusiasm."

"My business is with your father, is it not?" asked Darcy, a grin threatening to break through his calm façade. "I shall speak with your father and allow him to cope with your mother's effusions on the subject."

"Well played, sir!" exclaimed Mr. Gardiner. "If you are able to develop such effective stratagems, no doubt you will be able to withstand my sister very well indeed."

Darcy acknowledged Mr. Gardiner's sally. He thought that he would be quite happy indeed to have Mr. Gardiner as an uncle.

The moment past, Darcy turned his attentions to more practical matters. "Mr. Gardiner, I know you indicated that your staff was able to provide for Miss Bennet's safety, but I wish you would reconsider. With Pearce's threats, there is no telling what he might do. I propose that I assign a footman to Miss Bennet's protection. I have just the man in mind, and I have no doubt he will do very adequately indeed, being both an intimidating specimen and versed in many forms of combat."

Mr. Gardiner nodded without hesitation. "That would be acceptable, Mr. Darcy." He then turned to Elizabeth and said: "Lizzy, I realize you do not appreciate having your freedom curtailed, but I believe what Mr. Darcy proposes is not only sensible, but the very least we must do."

"I have already agreed to this stricture with Mr. Darcy, Uncle. I shall not protest."

Smiling with affection, Gardiner reached out and patted his niece's shoulder. "I was aware of that, Lizzy. Thank you for allowing us to protect you."

"Is there anything else?" asked Darcy of the company. "Any specific recommendations for how to approach Mr. Bennet, what I should say, anything I should emphasize would be helpful."

"Speak of your affection for Lizzy, Mr. Darcy," said Mrs. Gardiner. "She is unquestionably his favorite, and though he will be reluctant to part with her, he will do so without hesitation if he believes she will be cherished."

A few more comments were raised by others, but in essence they were similar to what Mrs. Gardiner suggested. Confident he could approach Mr. Bennet with a reasonable expectation of success, Darcy turned to Miss Bennet and smiled, which she returned.

"Mr. Gardiner, may I beg for a few moments of conversation with Miss Bennet in private?"

"Of course, Mr. Darcy," said Mrs. Gardiner, answering for her husband. "We shall leave you alone for ten minutes, so you might make your good byes."

Grateful for her forbearance, Darcy thanked her, and the Gardiners withdrew, leaving Darcy alone with Miss Bennet. They regarded each other for several moments, neither seeming inclined to say much. Though he could not guess at Miss Bennet's thoughts, by expression she seemed to be feeling a modicum of mirth. For his own part, Darcy was reflecting upon the very great pleasure a pair of expressive, beautiful eyes in the face of a pretty woman had the power to bestow.

"Come now, Mr. Darcy," said Miss Bennet at last. The mirth he had seen in her face was echoed in her voice. "I believe we must have some conversation. Perhaps you should comment on the good condition of the roads you shall traverse tomorrow, while I might wish you a quick and easy journey."

Darcy raised an eyebrow. "Is this the sort of banal conversation I might expect as a rule once we are married?"

Miss Bennet flushed delightfully, but she bravely lifted her chin and said: "I cannot say, sir. Is it not a wife's prerogative to wish her husband a swift journey and speedy return?"

"I suppose it is. But I would wish for your intriguing conversation to continue once we are married, Miss Bennet. I wish for a companion in life."

"Not one who would expand your ego?"

"Are you willing to take on the office?"

Miss Bennet laughed. "Perhaps on occasion. If you wish for someone to do it on a continuous basis, I suggest you marry Miss Bingley. Surely she is an expert at the art."

A grimace settled over Darcy's face, causing Miss Bennet to laugh ever harder. "Do not even suggest such things, Miss Bennet. Besides, once she managed to get her hooks into me, I doubt her flatteries would continue. Why flatter when she has already achieved her heart's desire?"

"Why indeed?"

"You will take care, will you not?" asked Darcy, turning to more serious matters.

"I shall," said Miss Bennet, nodding. "You need have no fear in that quarter."

"That is well. I would not expect this Pearce to attempt anything so soon, but we should be diligent. I . . ." Darcy paused, hardly knowing what he wished to say. "I cannot bear the thought of losing you to that, or any other, man. I must depend on the knowledge that you are protected before I may venture away on the morrow."

At his declaration, Darcy thought he detected again the well of regard in the depths of her eyes. "Do not worry, for I shall be well. I cannot fail to be well, with such a promise of devotion."

What a wondrous creature she was. Darcy could hardly wait for their life to begin. For the first time, he did not doubt they did have a future together.

Chapter XVI

In order to return the same day, Darcy left early the following morning. Though it was already late November and the colder days of late autumn had descended upon London, the weather was, in fact, still fine, with little snow dusting the ground. As such, Darcy considered simply riding out to Hertfordshire on his stallion, knowing it would reduce the time for his journey. In the end, however, he decided against it; the extra time the journey would take would be worth it in the end, not only because of the potential dangers of such a plan, but also because it would allow him time to think more on how he would approach Mr. Bennet.

Before he left that morning he ensured the footman Jack Thompson had been dispatched to the Gardiner townhouse with very specific instructions on his duties there. Jack was a big, brawny man, standing even taller than Fitzwilliam and possessed of a massive frame. Most men were intimidated just by looking at him, but Jack was also an expert pugilist and was familiar with many types of weapons. He had also been with the Darcy family for many years, being only a few years older than Darcy was himself, and was trusted implicitly. Anything short of an army would have a difficult time harming Miss Bennet if Jack was nearby.

When that task had been completed, Darcy sat back in his carriage for the ride to Longbourn and thought of Miss Bennet and what he would say to her father as the miles sped past. So pleasurable were his thoughts that they reached and passed through the town of Meryton almost before Darcy was aware of it, and only moments later the carriage pulled up the drive to a modest estate, and door was opened for Darcy to descend.

Darcy's first impression of the estate was a positive one. The house was not large, consisting of only two stories, and was built from a faded reddish brick. For all that, however, it appeared to be well cared for, as the signs of neglect, which would be so visible to the discerning eye, could not be seen. The drive was well maintained and what little snow there was had been cleared. To the left, Darcy could see what seemed to be a small park in behind the manor house, in which the trees were well pruned, and the pathways, free of brambles and other obstacles. Just based on what Darcy could see, he thought the estate likely produced between two and three thousand pounds, which was a respectable amount for a small land owner.

After disembarking, Darcy approached the door, noting several young ladies pressed up against the glass of one of the windows watching him. Thinking they must be Miss Bennet's sisters—and disapproving slightly of their less then decorous behavior—Darcy tipped his hat at them, smiling when they tittered and disappeared back into the room.

The door opened before Darcy had a chance to knock on it, and an elderly man, though still tall and straight, greeted him and asked his business.

"Mr. Darcy to see Mr. Bennet," said Darcy, handing the man his card.

His first impression of the man—the butler, Darcy presumed—was that he was very similar in essentials to Johnson, Darcy's longtime London butler. He glanced down at the card, noting the information it contained, and then invited Darcy inside, taking his coat, hat, and gloves, and then asking Darcy to wait while he informed the master. The butler then went to a door a little way down a hall which led off from the entryway, and after knocking, was admitted, returning a few moments later.

"Mr. Bennet will see you, Mr. Darcy."

Nodding his thanks, Darcy allowed himself to be led into the room and announced, where a man had risen to greet him.

Miss Bennet's father was a man of average height, perhaps fifty years of age, with dark hair dusted with gray. A pair of spectacles sat on his nose, giving him the look of a scholar, or one of Darcy's professors from Cambridge. The room in which he sat was lit through a large window on the far side. It overlooked the back gardens of his house, which were more extensive than Darcy would have thought for an estate of this size. The room itself was large and airy, with bookshelves lining the walls, and almost every available space was used for the storage of books.

It was clear Mr. Bennet was a bibliophile of the first order, and in that, at least, Darcy thought he would have a common interest with the man. Given the way he had handled the whole Pearce affair with his daughter, as well as Miss Bennet's comments made from time to time, Darcy was not certain what to think of Mr. Bennet. However, he was willing to give him a chance to prove himself, based on what happened in the next few minutes.

"Mr. Darcy, is it?" asked Mr. Bennet, extending his hand.

Darcy stepped forward and shook it. "Fitzwilliam Darcy, at your service, sir."

The man's only response was to peer at Darcy for a long moment. "If you will have a seat, you may state your business with me."

Nodding, Darcy sat in a nearby chair, watching the other man as he settled into his own.

"The reason for my journey here today is to request your permission for a courtship with your daughter, Miss Elizabeth Bennet."

"My Lizzy, you say."

"Yes, sir."

Again, Mr. Bennet was silent for a long moment, watching Darcy as if uncertain what to make of him.

"When Pearce showed up yesterday swearing and demanding I tell him the truth of my daughter's courtship, I had to chuckle at Lizzy's ingenuity. I thought she had concocted the story in order to induce him to leave her be. But I see now that I was mistaken."

"As you see," said Darcy. "I have been calling on Miss Bennet for more than a month now, and I wish for our courtship to be formalized."

"And has Lizzy given her consent?"

"She has, sir."

"Free of any outside pressure? This situation with Pearce, for example—she has not accepted you as a way to be free of his attentions?"

At Mr. Bennet's first question, Darcy almost felt offended, but with the second he better understood the other man's words, much though they still annoyed him.

"For her specific motivations, I am afraid you will need to speak to your daughter, Mr. Bennet. But I do not believe she has accepted my offer for any other reason than unalloyed inclination."

"Hmm . . . So you say. And yet, Elizabeth is not present for me to question her on the matter. I have nothing more than your assurances. Perhaps you should share with me how this all came about, as other than Pearce's storming into my room, blathering about how he had been betrayed, your statement is the first I had heard of it."

Ready to oblige him, Darcy nevertheless paused. "Can I assume from your tone that you never meant to acquiesce to Pearce's demands?"

Mr. Bennet snorted. "Of course not. The man is a womanizer, and I would not wish such a life for my Lizzy. I would never force her to marry against her will."

"Then why have you not told him that?"

"You assume I have not, Mr. Darcy. I have told Pearce several times that he had best give up his suit, as Lizzy would not have him. He has persisted in spite of that. I told him when he first applied to me, and I have informed him at nearly every meeting since. I sent Lizzy away from Longbourn in order to remove her from her mother's presence, as Mrs. Bennet would not have allowed the matter to rest."

"From what I have heard, she still has not."

"No, but at least Lizzy has not been required to bear her constant diatribes on the subject. In London, she may ignore the letters and be thankful that Mrs. Bennet has not the power to persuade her writing paper to complain in her stead."

Darcy could only laugh at such a silly observation. "From what I understand, your wife's letters have provided a great amount of fuel for the Gardiners' fireplaces."

A smile of delight spread over Mr. Bennet's face. "Good for you, Lizzy. I will refrain from informing my wife, as she would be highly insulted by her daughter's actions.

"Now, I would like to hear of how my daughter has gained you as a suitor, sir."

Feeling more at ease than ever, Darcy began the tale of his courtship with Miss Bennet, thinking that while he would not act the same in Mr. Bennet's place, he could like the man's dry wit very well indeed. It was important that Mr. Bennet know exactly how it all came about and was made aware of all Darcy's dealings with his favorite daughter, so Darcy left nothing out. He covered the chance meeting at the park where he had overheard her words, the ensuing week in which he had tried to find her, meeting her, asking for the courtship, the Gardiners' reasons for advising him against seeking Mr. Bennet's consent immediately, and the subsequent events which had led him to this point. Several times during his recitation, Mr. Bennet made comments or laughed at what Darcy had related, but in the end he understood.

It was clear, however, that he was still amused at how Darcy had sought his daughter out. "I commend you, sir," said Mr. Bennet, still chuckling. "I cannot think of half a dozen men who would have acted as you did. To overhear her words in the park and then seek her out without the benefit of an introduction—I might almost think it fiction, rather than the true sequence of events."

"I could hardly believe it myself, Mr. Bennet," replied Darcy. "And I lived it!"

Shaking his head, Mr. Bennet's manner sobered, and he peered at Darcy. "How can I be assured that your attachment is sincere? You did not know anything of my Lizzy before seeing her in the park. Such circumstances seem to be less than conducive to falling violently in love with my daughter."

"I cannot claim such emotions at present, Mr. Bennet," said Darcy, though he wondered if his statement was completely true. Setting it to the side for the moment, he continued: "But I have come to esteem her greatly in the time I have been calling on her. And is that not the purpose of a courtship? To come to know a woman in order to make an informed decision on whether she will suit to be your wife?"

"But a courtship is tantamount to an engagement, sir. Though not impossible to put aside, your honor might be engaged should you publish the fact of this courtship abroad."

"I understand that, sir. But I have no reason to believe that your daughter will be anything other than a fine wife. I believe I have enough of the measure of her character to know that much."

Mr. Bennet nodded, and he dropped that line of conversation. His eyes moved to Darcy's card, which had been sitting on the edge of the desk, and he picked it up and examined it. He did not speak for a few more moments, and Darcy thought he was attempting to reconcile Miss Bennet's choice. Soon, however, he sighed and looked up at Darcy again.

"From the quality of this paper, and from the aspect of the carriage my daughters were tittering over when you arrived, I believe you to be a man of some substance. Will you explain your situation in life to me?"

"Certainly, sir. I am the proprietor of an estate in Derbyshire, which is the main family estate, as well as a few other, lesser estates in different places in the country. My family has lived at Pemberley since the time of William the Conqueror."

"I assume then it is a great estate?"

Darcy nodded. "The park is ten miles around, and the annual income is in excess of ten thousand pounds per annum."

Eyes widened, Mr. Bennet said: "And this is only your main estate?"

"Yes, sir."

Mr. Bennet shook his head. "I can already hear the cries of 'ten thousand a year' echoing through the halls of my home, Mr. Darcy. Your coming here will cause great upheaval, I am sure."

"Perhaps. But you will know your daughter will be cared for all of her life."

A grunt was Mr. Bennet's response. "That may be so, but it is not the only—or even the most important—consideration. Now, have you anything else to tell me of?"

Shrugging, Darcy said: "There are many men to whom I would speak of my uncle, the earl, or my connections to my godfather, who is a duke, and other such concerns. But I have the impression that does not truly concern you."

"That is correct, Mr. Darcy," said Mr. Bennet. "As one who detests society myself, the prospect of my daughter moving through those circles, where many will look down on her for her 'common' origins, and immersing herself in a society I consider to be immoral, is not exactly a recommendation."

"And I cannot disagree with you, sir. I have no high opinion of society myself, though I *do* have obligations which must be fulfilled. You are correct about most of society, and even some of my extended family are proud, though for the most part not immoral. However, Miss Bennet has been introduced to my sister and two of my cousins, and they already love her as if she had been known to them all of her life."

Darcy paused and smiled. "In fact, my sister, who is twelve years my junior, would almost certainly mutiny if I did anything other than marry your daughter. She is shy and reticent, but I have seen her blossom during her association with Miss Bennet. She is waiting eagerly at home for news of my success."

Mr. Bennet laughed. "That's my Lizzy. She could charm the birds out of the sky, if she chose."

"I believe she could, Mr. Bennet."

"I must own that you have impressed me, Mr. Darcy," said Mr. Bennet, his gaze fixed on Darcy as he considered the matter. "In fortune you are far more than any of my daughters could ever hope for; I am well aware of that fact. And your story of how you approached her speaks of your determination. Besides," said Mr. Bennet, his eyes shining with amusement, "I doubt a man would confess to such a story if he did not already esteem the woman in question."

"I esteem her, sir."

The low tone of Darcy's words seemed to catch Mr. Bennet's attention, and he regarded Darcy in silence, one foot tapping lightly on the floor beneath his feet. After a moment, he leaned forward, his eyes never leaving Darcy's face.

"Others would call me mad for refusing an application such as yours, Mr. Darcy. I do not deny that. But I shall inform you here and now that if my Lizzy decides against you, I shall not force her hand."

"I had already expected as much."

Mr. Bennet nodded once, the motion curt. "The fact of the matter is that Elizabeth requires something more in marriage than a large house, jewelry, fine carriages, and more pin money than she can ever spend. She requires love and respect, a man she can look up to as her equal in every way. *This* is why I did not insist she marry Pearce—she could never hope to respect him, and love was out of the question. It is why I will not force her. I wish for her to be happy in life, and if it means rejecting the hand of every love-crazed suitor from here to Penzance, I shall do it.

"On the other hand, if you truly esteem her and respect her, then I shall not stand in your way. It shall be *Elizabeth's* decision, even if it comes after six months of courtship. If she decides that she will have you, again, I will not stand in her way."

Pausing to consider his words, Darcy was forced to reflect on the fact that he understood Mr. Bennet, and he respected him for putting the happiness of his daughter before other, more material concerns. It was not the most prudent, as the man had already acknowledged, but it was admirable.

"As I previously stated, Mr. Bennet, I cannot promise anything at present. I do esteem your daughter—very much. She is different from any other young woman I have ever met, and that is what led me to seek her out, when I might have been called daft for doing so. I will give you my word, however, that if I cannot offer her those promises you have mentioned, I will not propose to her. I shall only do so if I know in my heart that I can love her. Respect is not in question; she has amply shown her character to be worthy of respect, and I have never felt anything else for her."

Mr. Bennet was silent, and Darcy thought he sensed a hint of sadness playing about the man's eyes. Whether it was the knowledge that he might be forced to give away his daughter Darcy could not say. But he appreciated how giving her into the care of another man might be difficult.

"In that case, there is nothing more to be said. I approve of your courtship and all that it entails. I only request that you abide by the commitments you have made here today."

"I shall, sir," said Darcy, extending his hand. "You have my promise."

Unable to tear herself away from the window, Elizabeth looked out on the street outside, wondering at how the landscape appeared so very dull and drab that day. There was nothing different from the previous day; it was still warm, with the slightest hint of a breeze, yet it was overcast, lending to the gloom Elizabeth felt.

For what seemed like a hundredth time, Elizabeth sighed and continued her vigil. It was not as if she had anything which needed to be done. In fact, she was completely at her leisure, as her nieces and nephews were with the governess, attending to their morning lessons, her uncle, ensconced in his business with laughing assurances that he did not require her help. Her aunt was situated in the sitting-room behind her with a book and a smile, and though Elizabeth might have walked out that morning, she was afraid to go out lest she miss . . .

"Elizabeth, do step away from the window," said her aunt from behind. "Your insistence on looking out on the street this morning is quite unlike you."

"I am sorry to interrupt your activities, Aunt," said Elizabeth. She could not keep the hint of petulance from entering her voice, and she winced at it herself.

"Come here for a moment, Elizabeth," said her aunt, putting her book to the side.

Dutifully following her aunt's directive, though feeling little inclination for leaving the window, Elizabeth removed herself to the sofa. Still feeling a little sullen, she sat at some distance

"What is bothering you, Elizabeth?"

"Nothing," replied Elizabeth curtly.

"Nothing?" asked Mrs. Gardiner, watching Elizabeth in a pointed fashion. "So this uncharacteristic watching out the window, the frequent sighs I have heard all through the morning, the almost grieving dourness which has settled over your face—none of this is an indication of something bothering you?"

Elizabeth did not wish to talk of the matter, but it seemed her aunt was not about to allow her to leave without an explanation. Elizabeth thought to make up some story to appease Mrs. Gardiner, but she knew her aunt was perceptive enough to see through anything Elizabeth could invent.

"I am worried, Aunt," said Elizabeth at length, though unwillingly.

"Worried? About what?"

Glaring at her aunt, Elizabeth could only say: "Mr. Darcy, of course."

"And why would you worry about Mr. Darcy?"

Elizabeth threw her hands up in the air and stood, pacing about the room with restless agitation. "The season has grown late and the weather cold. Should I not worry for his safety?

"Besides, my father is liable to treat it all as some grand joke, my mother will exclaim over his wealth, and if he catches sight of Kitty and Lydia's behavior, I have no doubt he will return to Derbyshire and forget about me once and for all."

"And you think so little of your suitor's constancy that you would expect him to forget about you at the first hint of difficulty?"

"No, I do not," said Elizabeth, slowly enunciating her words in her pique. "But he is a man of sense, and any man of sense would hesitate before accepting connections which may embarrass him at every turn."

"Elizabeth, sit down!"

Though little inclined to obey her aunt, Elizabeth nonetheless sat rather inelegantly on the sofa, crossing her arms and staring at her aunt with defiance. Mrs. Gardiner only chuckled, further exacerbating Elizabeth's mood.

"You truly are being silly about this, Elizabeth. Let us take your concerns and dispense with them one at a time. Now, you know that your uncle and I have made this journey successfully a number of times in recent years, do you not?"

Grudgingly given though it was, Elizabeth nodded.

"Very well. Mr. Darcy is an experienced man and his carriage and horses are the best money can buy. I believe he has much less chance of running into difficulty than we ever did, and there truly has been little snow. You should cease to fret about this.

"Next, I must tell you that I believe you are doing your father a disservice."

Mrs. Gardiner glared at Elizabeth, silencing the petulant rebuttal which had been poised on the tip of her tongue.

"I know that you sometimes despair of your father, Elizabeth. But when has he ever given you cause to believe that he will be so cavalier with your future. Has he not always looked out for you in particular? His methods may not be common, but I do not think you doubt his esteem for you."

Elizabeth ducked her head. What her aunt said made sense, and she was ashamed of her conduct and her words.

"Finally, I do not think Mr. Darcy will have any congress with your mother and your sisters. He goes to speak to your father, and I imagine he will leave directly after."

"That does not ease my mind, Aunt," said Elizabeth. After her aunt had exposed her other worries for silliness, Elizabeth clung to the final one, certain this one was a legitimate concern. She had often wondered what would happen when Mr. Darcy met her mother. Would he be disgusted by her behavior? Would he decide that all the disadvantages of marrying her were made even worse by the behavior of certain members of her family? Surely any intelligent man would object on those grounds alone.

"Perhaps it does not, Elizabeth," said Mrs. Gardiner. "But I cannot think that Mr. Darcy would be frightened off by your sisters. If nothing else, Derbyshire is a great distance from Longbourn, is it not?"

In spite of herself, Elizabeth was forced to laugh. It was true.

Feeling her previous ill humor begin to fade, Elizabeth turned to her aunt with a grateful smile, saying: "Thank you for this, Aunt. I should not allow such things to bother me."

Mrs. Gardiner only directed a level look at Elizabeth. "Can you not imagine why such fears would beset you at such a time?

Frowning, Elizabeth said: "I cannot imagine to what you refer."

The serious look never wavered, and Elizabeth soon felt like a naughty child, caught engaging in mischief.

"I think if you examine your feelings, Elizabeth, you will find that perhaps Mr. Darcy is more important to your happiness than you thought. You have claimed that you do not love him yet, and maybe that is true, but I do not think you are as far from that depth of regard as you think."

And with that, Mrs. Gardiner once again picked up her book and began to read, leaving Elizabeth alone with her thoughts.

Travel was not something that Darcy had ever enjoyed. His tall frame, coupled with long legs, did not agree with the cramped confines of a carriage, and even though the carriage in which he road was large and spacious, he could never quite shake the impression of being constricted in the small space. This was the primary reason he was not in the best of moods, even though his mission had ultimately been a success. And his mood was only aggravated with what he found when he alighted from the carriage and entered the house.

As usual, Johnson was there to meet him, taking his outerwear, and commenting: "There is a lady sitting with Miss Darcy."

"Oh?" asked Darcy, thinking his aunt or one of his cousins had called on her. Darcy's mind was at Gracechurch Street, his next destination after he had refreshed himself from his travels. "Who is it?"

"A Miss Bingley, sir."

Darcy's head whipped around, his surprise quickly turning to ire, mirroring the slightly disapproving shade in his butler's expression.

"Miss Bingley?"

"Yes, sir." This time the censure in Johnson's voice was indisputable. "The young lady that visited Miss Darcy earlier in the week."

All thoughts of refreshing himself vanished in the face of the woman's audacity. With the situation with Pearce, Darcy had not had the opportunity to speak of Miss Bingley's behavior with her brother. Clearly that was a mistake.

"They are in the sitting-room, you say?"

"They are, sir. I believe that Mrs. Jenkinson is sitting with them at present."

Nodding, Darcy said: "I will join them directly." He paused and considered the matter, and then reversed the decision he had made the previous time Miss Bingley had come to his house. "In the future, should Miss Bingley present herself at the door, Georgiana is not at home to her."

A faint sense of satisfaction spread over his butler's face as he bowed and turned away with Darcy's winter accoutrements in hand.

A moment later, Darcy entered the sitting-room to the sight his butler had informed him of. Miss Bingley sat in close proximity to his sister on the large sofa in front of the fire, leaning over a book of some sort his sister held in her hand. Perhaps the lady did not realize it, but Georgiana was leaning away from her, while trying to appear like she had not moved. On a nearby chair, Mrs. Jenkinson sat watching the proceedings, the faint sense of disapproval which had existed on his butler's face clearly seen for anyone who cared to look on hers.

When Darcy entered the room, Georgiana looked at him and stood, a palpable sense of relief seeming to wash over her.

"William!" said she. "I am happy you have returned!"

Darcy did not miss the faint note of desperation in her voice, but before he could speak, the sound of Miss Bingley's dulcet tones assaulted his ears.

"Mr. Darcy, how wonderful it is to see you again, sir. I have been keeping your sister company in your absence."

Regarding her for a moment with annoyance, Darcy ultimately opted to ignore her in favor of accepting his sister's embrace.

"I could not rid myself of her, no matter how pointed my hints," said Georgiana in a whisper.

A smile settled on Darcy's face, and he looked at his sister with affection. However much confidence she had gained through her association with Miss Bennet, she still did not have it in her to behave in a fashion which could even remotely be construed as rude. For a woman as brazen and determined as Miss Bingley, she was easy prey.

"Have you completed your studies for the day?"

"No, William," replied she, seeming to understand the thrust of his question. "I believe Mrs. Jenkinson still wishes to conduct some language lessons."

"That I do, Mr. Darcy," said Mrs. Jenkinson. She had risen to her feet when Darcy entered and was now striding forward to join them, but the glare she directed at Miss Bingley as she passed could not be misinterpreted, least of all by the recipient. "We were prevented by . . . other matters."

"Very well. Perhaps you should see to those lessons now, so that the rest of your afternoon will be free."

"I shall, William." Georgiana turned to Miss Bingley and curtseyed, but she did not say anything in farewell, choosing instead to depart with Mrs. Jenkinson.

"Your sister is a wonderful girl, Mr. Darcy," said Miss Bingley, immediately turning to flattery, though she had to detect his annoyance with her. "She is so very accomplished. I was simply astonished by her maturity and intelligence. I dare say there are not half a dozen girls her equal in all of London.

"But truly, sir, you should perhaps consider replacing her companion with a more competent woman. Mrs. Jenkinson possesses neither the manners nor the knowledge to serve in such an exalted position. That your sister has turned out so well must be a testament to her character and not to any efforts that woman has made to improve her charge."

"Do you wish to apply for the position?"

Eyes wide as saucers, Miss Bingley stammered for a moment before her expression turned haughty and offended. "Of course not, sir! I have no need to seek out employment."

"I see. Then you are suggesting this due to the extensive experience you have in raising young girls of her class?"

"Well . . ."

"Of course not, Miss Bingley. After all, as a young debutante yourself, you would have no knowledge of raising a young girl to adulthood."

"Perhaps not," replied the woman, raising her chin in defiance, "but I have been educated at the finest seminary, and I am well aware of what is required of a young gentlewoman."

"You are?" asked Darcy, his voice laced with skepticism.

But Miss Bingley was not to be deterred. "I am well versed in all the proper behavior of members of our class, sir."

"That is astonishing, Miss Bingley, as you are not a member of *Georgiana`s* class."

Miss Bingley instantly turned a shade of red, partially, Darcy thought, from embarrassment and partially from affront. She attempted to stammer a reply, but Darcy cut her short.

"Let us speak frankly, Miss Bingley. You are not the daughter of a gentleman. Your father was a tradesman, and though by all accounts a good man, he was not a landowner. Your brother, much as I have come to enjoy his company, has not yet risen to that state. As such, you can have nothing to say about how the daughter of a gentleman is raised and educated, despite whatever education you have been blessed with.

"Furthermore, I have returned home twice this week to find that you have visited, despite the fact that my sister is not out, *and* without an invitation. Personally, I find your pretensions toward proper behavior laughable in light of this most *improper* behavior."

The woman quite clearly underestimated the power of her own allure, as she gazed at him with unconcealed astonishment. It was clear she had thought she could work her way into his life with nothing more than the power of her *education* and *superior manners*. It was all Darcy could do not to snort in disdain.

But what she apparently did not lack was courage, for as soon as he finished speaking, she plastered an insincere smile on her face.

"I apologize if my *friendship* with your sister appears to be . . . overeager, sir. I assure you that Georgiana voiced no objection to my presence."

"*Miss Darcy* is not in the habit of voicing objections to overbearing women who force their presence upon her. But this is not a surprise, given the fact that she has never had to deal with any such ladies before.

"Now, Miss Bingley, I believe it is time for you to return to your brother's townhouse. Please do not return, for my sister will not be receiving you, by my instruction."

Turning, Darcy moved toward the door, intending to call the butler to see her out, but his momentum was arrested when she spoke yet again.

"Again, I apologize if I seemed too eager, sir. But I truly must warn you against this friendship you have forwarded between Geo . . . Pardon me, between your *sister* and Miss Bennet. I have known her longer than you have, and I can definitively state that she in no way displays the kind of proper behavior I know you wish your sister to emulate."

"Miss Bingley," said Darcy, turning on her. She paled at the sight of his angered countenance, but her posture screamed her defiance. "I have, this very day, journeyed to Hertfordshire, and there, I obtained Mr. Bennet's permission for a courtship with Miss Bennet."

The woman's complexion turned chalk white at his words, but Darcy ignored her and continued speaking mercilessly. "She is the best woman of my acquaintance, and her manners are in no way lacking. In addition, she is a favorite of my sister and has the support of my family. Desist now. Even if I did not wish to marry Miss Bennet, I would not turn my attention upon you."

Then before Miss Bingley could muster a response, Darcy turned and opened the door, finding Johnson waiting patiently on the other side as he had expected.

"Johnson, Miss Bingley will now depart. Please escort her to the entrance hall and call her carriage."

"Of course, Mr. Darcy," said Johnson. He then held out Miss Bingley's pelisse, a clear indication he had been waiting for the opportunity to evict her. It was almost enough to cause laughter to break forth from Darcy.

Miss Bingley stepped forward, her head lowered to the floor. But as she passed him, Darcy caught the glitter of her eyes as they darted up at him, and he knew that her campaign to catch him was not at an end. Darcy also knew he would need to take care. She was the most dangerous form of fortune hunter—one who would stop at nothing to achieve her desires.

Chapter XVII

The day after Mr. Darcy had obtained her father's consent, Elizabeth, deciding she had been indoors long enough, decided to walk in the park. She had much on which to think, and a walk had always served as a means to allow her thoughts to flow.

Mrs. Gardiner, knowing of Elizabeth's proclivities, merely waved her off when she stated her intentions. As long as she was in the company of the footman provided by Mr. Darcy, Mrs. Gardiner knew she would not come to any harm. And thus with the man trailing a discrete distance behind her, Elizabeth set off, soon obtaining the comforting confines of the park, and continuing at a quick pace.

With her father's consent given, Elizabeth knew that her courtship would not remain a secret for long, if it was now at all. And if her mother knew of it, Elizabeth knew that it would not be long before she was summoned home. She was of two minds about the prospect. She missed Longbourn; that much was indisputable. But at the same time, she had no desire to endure her mother's officious attempts to direct the courtship, to instruct her on what she must do to secure the man, not to mention all the other ultimately useless advice she would dispense.

But Elizabeth knew that she could not ignore the summons when it came. Her father would also wish her to be home, if for no other reason than to have her back for a short season before she left him forever.

That thought, of course, led to thoughts of Mr. Darcy and the state of their courtship. By now Elizabeth knew enough of the man to know that should he propose, she could do nothing other than accept him. And as Mr. Darcy was a sober sort of man who would not enter into such a close relationship without intending to bring it to its logical resolution, she knew that she was already as good as engaged to him.

At one time, the thought would have filled her with indecision, not knowing if she felt enough for him to warrant such a step. But Elizabeth was filled with nothing more than peace. She would get on well with Mr. Darcy, she knew, and the members of his family with whom she was already close could be nothing more than a benefit as she became acclimated with her new position in his life. And as for Mr. Darcy himself . . .

Shivering, despite the warm layers in which she was wrapped, Elizabeth instinctively shied away from the thought. When he had come to her to formally ask for the courtship, his solicitude and the passion in his voice had reached out to her, spoken to her in a manner she had never before experienced. As a young maiden, she did not know exactly what passion between a husband and wife consisted of, but she was content not knowing for the nonce. The important part was that he appeared to hold her in considerable esteem. The thought of being bound to him for a lifetime could not be anything other than pleasurable.

Still, nothing was resolved just yet, and there were still hurdles to overcome. Her suitor had stopped briefly at the Gardiner townhouse to inform her of the results of his conference with her father. By all accounts, their discussion had been pleasant, and the required consent had been given with little protest. Elizabeth had been heartened at his story of her father's words, as it showed that her concerns had been silly, just as Mrs. Gardiner had pointed out.

On the other hand, other than mentioning that he had caught sight of her sisters in a window, Darcy had said nothing of whether he had met her mother. Such an omission could mean two things: either he had not or he had chosen not to speak of it. Elizabeth could not decide which she preferred. The earlier he met her mother, the earlier he could become inured to her ways, if such a thing was even possible. If he had not yet met her, then he had spoken to her father and obtained his consent, all without any direct knowledge of his future mother-in-law's character. Elizabeth suspected the latter, and she was not anticipating their ultimate meeting with any—

"Miss Bennet! What a fortunate meeting this is!"

Startled from her thoughts, Elizabeth halted and looked up into the eyes of the man she had seen at Mr. Darcy's house only a few days previously.

"I had no notion I would meet you in this, of all, places," continued Mr. Wickham. "How do you do?"

The words of her intended ringing in her ears, Elizabeth thought to bypass the man without acknowledging his greeting. But her innate sense of politeness stopped her, and she could only curtsey, though in a very shallow manner.

"Mr. Wickham," said she, intending to greet him and then continue on her way as soon as may be. Unfortunately, Mr. Wickham was having none of that.

"I must confess I would have expected to see you near Mayfair, not in this far flung district. Are you visiting friends nearby?"

Elizabeth was instantly suspicious. Why would he have shown up here, of all places, if he had no notion of her being here? It all seemed so very contrived.

"You might say that, sir. I might wonder why you are found in a place like this yourself. I had not thought you to be one given over to excessive walking."

"Usually, I am not, unless the company is as lovely as what I find before me." Mr. Wickham turned a beaming smile on her, and she could see that he wielded it like a club, no doubt to charm young ladies and convince them of his sincerity. "Today I have been visiting with a friend who lives only a few streets over and thought to walk through this charming little park before returning to my lodgings."

"I see," said Elizabeth, not believing his story of a friend for a moment. "In that case, I shall allow you to return to your path, while I shall return to mine."

"Shall we not follow the path together?" asked Mr. Wickham, offering his arm. "I should love to become better acquainted with the lady who has seemingly captured Darcy's heart."

There was no way Elizabeth was about to accede to his suggestion, and she was about to say as much when her escort strode up.

"Wickham," said the man, his tone congenial, though with undertones of menace.

For his part, Mr. Wickham started at the words and turned a surprised look on the footman, instantly paling at the sight of him. It seemed that however he had happened upon her, he had not known of her escort.

"Thompson!" exclaimed Wickham, apparently striving for

equanimity. "Fancy meeting you in a place like this."

The faint smile the massive man directed at Wickham told Elizabeth that he was not fooled at all.

"I was about to walk with Miss Bennet," said Wickham. "Perhaps you may follow behind us to ensure propriety is met."

"Miss Bennet will not be walking anywhere with the likes of you, Wickham." This time there was no mistaking the threat inherent in the footman's tone. "Especially when Mr. Darcy has warned me particularly against you. Now be off with you!"

A faint sense of injury fell over Wickham's countenance, but he did not protest. "It seems it is not to be, Miss Bennet," said he, gallantly bowing over her hand. "I assure you that I have nothing more than friendship in mind, even though we have met by chance. But I shall detain you no longer."

And with that, Mr. Wickham tipped his hat and sauntered off, whistling a merry tune. Elizabeth watched him go, wondering at his motivations. He must know that Mr. Darcy had warned her against him, but he acted as if he was the best of friends with her suitor. Could he really think she would be charmed by nothing more than the force of his pretty smile and insincere flattery?

"That one shall come to a bad end," said Jack by her side, and she turned to look at him quizzically.

"I was not aware that you were acquainted with Mr. Wickham."

"I travel with Mr. Darcy, Miss Bennet, but my home is in Derbyshire. Anyone who has been at Pemberley for any length of time knows of Wickham, and his reputation there is not a good one. The stories of his exploits are infamous. You should be cautious of him."

"I am," replied Elizabeth simply. "I did not wish to talk to him, but it would be rude to ignore his greeting."

Jack fixed her with a pointed look she would not expect in a servant. Then again, he was obviously trusted implicitly by Mr. Darcy, which meant he was likely given a certain amount of leeway.

"A little rudeness when it pertains to Mr. Wickham is not an undesirable thing. As I said, Mr. Wickham has a very poor reputation at Pemberley and in the area, and he is known to stoop to seduction, cheating, lying, and all manner of debauchery. In fact, I am personally aware of a situation in which he attempted to seduce a young junior maid, even though the young woman did not welcome his addresses, if you catch my meaning."

In fact, Elizabeth caught Jack's meaning quite well indeed, and she wondered from the manner in which Jack's expression became stony if he had a personal interest in the matter he related. A chill passed through her; Mr. Darcy's insistence on seeing her protected was now seeming shrewd indeed. There was no telling what might have happened had Jack not been present, especially given Mr. Darcy's warning of how Mr. Wickham was angry with him at present.

"Thank you for this additional report," replied Elizabeth. "Mr. Darcy told me something of the man, but I had not thought him to be this bad."

Jack smiled. "Mr. Darcy possesses a gift for understatement, miss, and a penchant for speaking as a gentleman ought. I am not a gentleman, so I need not be quite so circumspect."

Laughing, Elizabeth said: "And yet you have spoken in a manner which leaves no mistaken interpretation, but was still suitable for a young woman's ears."

His smile becoming a wide grin, Jack said: "One cannot be in the company of the quality for as long as I have and not pick up some of the finer manners."

"I suppose not! I thank you for your care and attention, sir. I think the next time I see Mr. Wickham, I shall not acknowledge his greeting."

"That is undoubtedly for the best, miss."

With that, Elizabeth turned and began to walk back in the direction of the townhouse. She had walked far enough that day, and it was time to return home. But as she walked, she could not shake the sensation of eyes watching her, little likely though she knew Wickham was still in the area. Even so, it was still nothing more than Jack's solid presence which prevented her from scurrying back home or even breaking into a run.

When Darcy arrived at the Gardiner townhouse that morning, he was eager to see Miss Bennet again, though he had come to conduct some final piece of business with Gardiner and Bingley. He was surprised and disappointed to learn that she was out walking in the park, knowing that his business prevented him from joining her there. Mrs. Gardiner, apparently seeing his slightly forlorn look, smiled at him to let him know that Elizabeth was expected back before long.

"I believe she will have returned by the time your business with Mr. Gardiner and Mr. Bingley is complete, sir. I will ensure she is waiting for you when you emerge."

Grateful for the woman's insight, Darcy thanked her and was led to Gardiner's study. In truth, he wished to complete this business as soon as may be, as he desired to be in Miss Bennet's company as soon as possible.

"Darcy!" greeted Gardiner when Darcy stepped into the study.

"Bingley and I were just waiting for you. I believe we are ready to sign the final contract, if you will join us."

Agreeing, Darcy stepped into the room and greeted Bingley, who responded with his usual cheerfulness. Gardiner pulled the contract from a folder which had been sitting on his desk and distributed copies for them all to look over once more. Darcy perused it briefly, knowing his own solicitor had already looked the document over and pronounced it acceptable. All that was left to do was to sign multiple copies of it, which would be distributed to the solicitors of all involved.

"Shall we toast our new business arrangement, gentlemen?" said Gardiner, producing a bottle of port and three glasses.

"Here, here!" said Bingley enthusiastically. "I am happy we have been able to conclude this merger, Mr. Gardiner, though it was exhausting in the details."

Gardiner raised his glass, which the other two men mimicked, and took a sip of his drink. "And now you are free to follow your father's dream, Bingley. I hope you find a situation to your liking soon, for I have no doubt you will like being a landed gentleman very well indeed."

"I believe I shall, Mr. Gardiner. I have some information in that vein, but I should like to announce it in Miss Bennet's presence, if I might."

Though appearing a little confused at the man's words, Gardiner readily agreed. Darcy had to own to a little perplexity himself, but he refrained from questioning the man. In fact, now that he was here with Bingley, he had another matter he wished to canvass with him.

As soon as they finished their port, Darcy spoke. "Mr. Gardiner, if you would, could I have use of your study for a moment? I have a matter I wish to discuss with Bingley."

Though Gardiner was obviously curious about the reason for such a request, he did not inquire, instead contenting himself with a statement that Darcy was welcome to use his study as long as required, and then departing from the room. For his part, Bingley was visibly curious as to why Darcy would wish to speak with him.

"Yes, Mr. Darcy?" said Bingley, a hint of a question in his statement.

"There is no need to be formal, Bingley," replied Darcy. "I do wish to speak of something, but I do not believe it is a matter which will take us long to discuss."

"Very well," replied Bingley with a nod.

"It has to do with your younger sister, unfortunately. Were you aware that she has visited my sister twice in the past three days?"

Bingley's reaction was all the reply Darcy required, though he blurted: "Caroline has visited your townhouse?"

"She has," confirmed Darcy. "The first time was three days ago. I was not at home and did not hear of it until later when my sister told me. The second time was just yesterday, and this time I met her when I returned from Hertfordshire."

"I dare not hope she stated the reason for imposing upon you?" asked Bingley, though Darcy was certain he knew exactly what his sister's purpose was.

"Not in so many words. Forgive me for speaking in such a direct manner, but it was clear that she hoped my sister was a path for her to gain *my* esteem. She stayed for some time three days ago, but yesterday she was with my sister for several hours, and none of Georgiana's hints induced her to depart."

"I *am* sorry, Darcy," replied Bingley with a shake of his head. "Caroline is . . . Well, she believes it is her destiny to marry a man of high society, and several comments she has made in the past weeks suggest that she expects that man to be you. I have told her of your courtship with Miss Bennet, but she has refused to listen to me."

"That will not happen, Bingley. As you know, I have now obtained Mr. Bennet's consent for a formal courtship, and I fully expect the courtship will only end in an engagement."

Bingley smiled and extended his hand, which Darcy grasped gratefully. "You have my congratulations, Darcy. She is a wonderful girl. Had my tastes run in that direction, I might have tried my hand at courting her myself."

Though Darcy was curious as to Bingley's meaning, he decided to focus on the matter at hand.

"I have instructed my staff to deny Miss Bingley access to the house in the future, unless she is specifically invited. My sister is not yet out, and I would not have Miss Bingley intrude upon her when she should be concentrating on her studies."

"I understand, Darcy. I apologize on my sister's account. She is headstrong and determined, but she has no right to impose upon you in such a manner. I will speak with her, as it seems she needs to be controlled."

"Thank you, Bingley." Darcy paused, trying to decide how to say what he needed to say next, but without much success. There was no way to soften the blow of what needed to be said. "We are now business partners and I will not withdraw my support. But I must tell you, Bingley, that any notice you and your family receive from me in the future is dependent upon Miss Bingley's behavior. I will trust you to keep her in check."

"And I shall do it, Darcy," said Bingley. He turned a wry smile upon Darcy, saying: "I am not unaware of the great benefit our friendship will be in my attempts to be accepted in society. I am also aware that a friendship with you may raise Caroline's prospects and give her hope for a much better match than she ever had a right to expect before. Perhaps if I make her understand that fact, she will desist. If not, I always have an aunt in Scarborough who would appreciate the chance to try to reform her character."

Darcy laughed; for a young woman with Miss Bingley's ambitions, banishment to Scarborough would be a punishment of the severest kind. Darcy did not doubt the threat would assist in keeping her in check, though he doubted it would completely extinguish her hopes.

"Thank you, Bingley. I appreciate our friendship, and I would not wish for anything to come between us."

After only a few more minutes, the friends rose and left the study. For Darcy's part, he was eager to once again be in the presence of the lovely Miss Elizabeth Bennet. He had spent too much time away from her of late.

When Mr. Gardiner joined them in the sitting room, it was with the news that his merger with Mr. Bingley's business was now complete. The ladies made all the appropriate congratulatory comments, but in reality Elizabeth was disappointed that Mr. Darcy had not joined them as well. With ill-concealed impatience—which she was well aware was transparent to her aunt and uncle—Elizabeth waited for the other gentlemen to appear.

It was not long afterwards when Mr. Bingley and Mr. Darcy entered the sitting-room to the greetings of those waiting for them, and he came forward and greeted Elizabeth.

"Miss Bennet, you grow more enchanting every time I am admitted to your presence."

Then Mr. Darcy did something he had never done before—he bowed over her hand and bestowed a kiss on it. The sensation of his lips on her skin travelled up Elizabeth's arm and down her spine, and for a moment she thought she might actually swoon from the pleasure.

In an attempt to hide her reaction to his presence, Elizabeth welcomed Mr. Darcy and invited him to sit next to her, which he lost no time in doing. Their conversation was a little sparse, as Elizabeth thought they were both affected by such a momentous event. But it was not long before their attention was drawn to Mr. Bingley.

"I have an announcement to make, if you please," said he to Mr.

Gardiner.

"Certainly, Mr. Bingley. Be my guest."

"Thank you, Mr. Gardiner. Taking Miss Bennet's excellent advice," Mr. Bingley smiled at Elizabeth, "I have investigated the property she informed me abuts her father's estate. After consulting my solicitor and investigating the property, and finding it to be exactly suited to my needs and very close to town, I have decided to sign a lease on the property, and I am to take possession of it immediately. As such, I am now the lease holder on Netherfield Park in Hertfordshire."

"On *my* recommendation, sir?" asked Elizabeth with a laugh.

"You spoke to me of the property, Miss Bennet. Otherwise I might not have known of it. I believe it will be an early challenge of my abilities, and I am quite anticipating it, I assure you.

"In addition, I understand that the courtship between my new friend Darcy and Miss Bennet has now been formalized, has it not?"

"Yes, it has, Bingley," replied Mr. Darcy.

"In that case, I do not doubt it shall not be long before Miss Bennet returns to her home. As I have a large manor house at my disposal, I would like to extend an invitation to you, Darcy, to visit whenever convenient."

Mr. Darcy appeared surprised at this bit of civility, but he was also quick to accept. "Thank you, my friend. I would be happy to stay with you, and I do not doubt it shall be convenient for my continued ability to call upon Miss Bennet for the duration of our courtship."

"I shall be happy to have you stay with me." Then Bingley paused and laughed. "I will confess my motivations are not completely altruistic. As I will be new to managing an estate, and as you are accomplished and experienced, I hoped you would be willing to advise me while in residence."

A nod met the man's statement. "I would be happy to, Bingley. Based on the size of the estate, which from what I am hearing is substantial, I believe it should provide an adequate challenge for a first endeavor. I am thrilled to assist you."

"Thank you, Darcy! You have been a good friend, and I appreciate your assistance."

For a time until the gentleman needed to depart, they were treated to a dissertation on Mr. Bingley's excitement for his upcoming establishment as a landed gentleman and his expectations for the society of the area. Elizabeth told him laughingly of those he might meet, and though she thought he would actually be perfect for Jane, she did not make mention of her. She thought he would be better served by making her acquaintance and taking her measure himself, rather than for Elizabeth to fill his head with descriptions of her which might color his own opinions.

At length, however, Mr. Bingley was required to depart, and he did so with many exclamations of pleasure at the prospect of meeting with them again.

Once Mr. Bingley had departed, Elizabeth's manner turned serious, as she knew there was an important communication she needed to make to Mr. Darcy which would almost certainly displease him. Though she was reluctant to destroy his good mood, she knew it was better he learn of it sooner rather than later.

"Mr. Darcy," began Elizabeth, drawing his attention to her, "you should know that when I was walking in the park, I met with Mr. Wickham."

"Wickham?" asked Darcy, his countenance suddenly falling. "He importuned you in the park?"

"He stopped to talk to me briefly, sir. But Mr. Thompson was quick to run him off. I do not doubt I would not have so easily rid myself of him if Mr. Thompson had not been present."

By this time Darcy was scowling, but before he could say anything, Mr. Gardiner, who had been following their conversation, interjected.

"Who is this Mr. Wickham, sir?"

"He is a man who grew up at my estate. In fact, he is my father's godson, though he is himself the son of my father's old steward. Unfortunately, Mr. Wickham's character is vicious, and his lifestyle is dissipative. I broke ties with him not long after my father's death."

"I happened upon him when I visited Mr. Darcy's house," added Elizabeth. "I could see that he was quite charming, but something in his manner warned me, and Mr. Darcy told me the truth. I was surprised to see him today."

"Do you think it happened by chance?" asked Mr. Gardiner.

"I highly doubt it, sir," said Mr. Darcy. Clearly he was only keeping his temper by the force of his will, when he most certainly would prefer to go and find Wickham himself to express his displeasure. "Though he did not observe Miss Bennet and me together long, I have no doubt he guessed the nature of our relationship. The day he met Miss Bennet, I denied another request for money, leaving him quite angry with me. It is entirely possible that he wishes to revenge himself upon me through Miss Bennet."

"Then there is some danger to Lizzy?" asked Mrs. Gardiner. She had grasped Elizabeth's hand and was holding it protectively.

"As long as she has Jack with her, she will be protected, Mrs. Gardiner." Mr. Darcy laughed, though there was a mirthless quality to it. "Wickham is quite afraid of Jack. He used to enjoy taunting Jack with the favored position he enjoyed with respect to my father. Jack took exception to it and thrashed Wickham soundly, and ever since, Wickham has avoided him. And then there was the matter of Wickham's inappropriate advances to one of the Pemberley maids."

Mr. Darcy turned and smiled at Elizabeth. "I should imagine that had you not been present, Wickham would have found himself sporting many more bruises at the very least. Wickham left Pemberley after that incident and did not return for some time, and then it was only to see my father and apply his charm. More than once, he narrowly escaped Jack's form of justice."

Wondering whether she would bring the matter up with Mr. Darcy, Elizabeth decided it was likely these peoples' concerns would soon be her own, so she mustered her courage.

"Does Jack have some interest in the young lady, Mr. Darcy?"

Nodding, Mr. Darcy said: "At the time she was a pretty girl, yet still young. Some years have passed since then, and he has recently proposed to her and she has accepted. They are to be married in the spring. That is quite perceptive of you."

Shrugging, Elizabeth said: "Something in his manner alerted me to his interest when he was speaking of the matter."

By the look in his eyes, Darcy had already turned to the problem of Mr. Wickham, and after a few moments, he turned back to the three waiting for him to speak.

"It has become clear that I cannot allow Wickham to continue in such a manner. I have tried to ignore his existence, but I now see that leaves him free to continue his depredations on unsuspecting society."

"You must not take this man's behavior on yourself, Mr. Darcy."

Mr. Darcy sighed. "I do not take the blame for his behavior. But he is what he is today, in part, because my father was blind to his character and would not hear anything against him. That makes him my family's responsibility. Without his gentleman's education and his upbringing at Pemberley, I doubt he would be able to pass himself off as a gentleman so effectively. It is high time I did something to rein him in."

A smile turned up the corner of Mr. Darcy's lips, and he turned to Elizabeth. "My cousin Fitzwilliam has been advocating doing something to curb Wickham's excesses for years. Fitzwilliam does not like him at all and would join in his chastisement without hesitation. I am certain I can convince him to assist in trying to find Wickham. Once we have found him, we can decide what we should do. I hold many receipts of Wickham's debts, enough to see him in debtors' prison for many years. While I have been reluctant to take such a step, I shall do so if it means your safety."

"Perhaps sending him away from England would also suffice," said Mr. Gardiner. "It seems that at the very least he should be forced to account for his deeds over the years."

A short curt nod was Darcy's response. "In that case, I should depart so as to arrange for some men to track him down."

"You will return for dinner with your sister, will you not, Mr. Darcy?" asked Mrs. Gardiner.

"Of course, madam," replied Darcy, and with that, he rose to leave.

Elizabeth walked him to the door to say her farewells, though she would be seeing him again in a few short hours. When they had reached the vestibule, he turned and directed a serious look at her.

"I will not allow Wickham to follow through with whatever devilry he has planned, Miss Bennet. He will be brought to heel."

"Thank you, Mr. Darcy. But I am not concerned about Mr. Wickham. I know you will deal with him."

Almost of its own volition, Mr. Darcy's hand rose to caress her cheek. "Thank you for your confidence, Miss Bennet."

For some time after Mr. Darcy left, Elizabeth's hand kept returning to the cheek he had touched. She almost fancied she could still feel it there.

Chapter XVIII

It was not many days later when the expected letter came, and all Elizabeth could do was shake her head with rueful annoyance at how accurately she had predicted her mother's actions. Two full sheets of paper, written on both sides, had barely been enough to contain all of Mrs. Bennet's paroxysms of delight at the prospect of a daughter being courted, and those words were interspersed with instructions that she soon return home along with her beau so they could be properly introduced to the neighborhood. Of course, she would need to return to London to shop once the engagement was made official, but that could wait in favor of more practical concerns.

It seemed that she was now her mother's undisputed favorite child, as if Mrs. Bennet had not been decrying her as the most disobedient child who had ever lived for the past four months complete. How long that would last was a matter of argument, but Elizabeth could not imagine it would be above a month. Once they disagreed about the amount of lace on Elizabeth's wedding gown, she had no doubt her mother would once again be at odds with her.

On her aunt's advice, Elizabeth replied to her mother's missive with alacrity, promising to consult with Mr. Darcy and determine when they would heed the summons.

"That is the best way to handle her," said Mrs. Gardiner laughingly when she made the suggestion. "Your mother would insist upon your returning home at once, but she will not risk losing your young man by disagreeing over a return date he chose."

Elizabeth had to confess her aunt was correct. Soon, she had composed the short letter and dispatched it to Longbourn.

The next day Mr. Darcy arrived for a visit, and he suggested they walk to the park. Readily agreeing, Elizabeth donned her outerwear and, placing her hand on his arm, allowed herself to be guided from the house. It was not long, however, before she noted the presence of another and turned a questioning gaze on her suitor.

"Am I really that fearsome, Mr. Darcy, that you must have Mr. Thompson along to protect you from me?"

A laugh was Mr. Darcy's response. "Completely fearsome, madam. In fact, I should wish for ten such men to protect my virtue."

They chuckled together for a moment before Mr. Darcy turned serious. "In fact, it seems prudent to have a protector of Jack's acumen accompany us. Wickham has not yet been caught, and though I doubt he would be brave enough to attempt something when I am present, I think it wise to take care."

Elizabeth nodded. "There is no sign of Mr. Wickham?"

In evident disgust, Mr. Darcy shook his head. "Wherever he is, he has concealed himself well. He is quite at home in the seedy areas of London, which must explain his success in eluding my men.

"But it is only a matter of time. He cannot remain hidden forever."

They entered the park and meandered for some time, speaking of inconsequential things. When the matter of her imminent departure for home was broached, Elizabeth told Mr. Darcy something of her mother's language in writing her letter. But though she was a little concerned about his reaction to such ridiculousness, he said nothing of the anecdotes she related. Instead, he focused on the question of when she would return.

"What is your opinion, Miss Bennet?" he asked when they had spoken of the matter for some minutes.

"My opinion is that I would not wish to return to Hertfordshire at all," blurted Elizabeth before she had a chance to think. A blush spread over her face as she realized what she had said, but Mr. Darcy only smiled, seeming to understand the reason for her words.

"I think that is not an option, Miss Bennet," replied he in a gentle tone.

"I am aware of that, Mr. Darcy, much though I wish it were."

"Then what would be best for your comfort? Surely a delay of a few days would be acceptable."

Elizabeth laughed, and when he looked at her askance, she related to him what her aunt had said, prompting him to join her in laughter.

"I believe that next week would be acceptable, Mr. Darcy," said Elizabeth when their mirth had run its course. "It is near enough that she will not dispute, while still early enough before Christmas that I may join in the celebrations." Elizabeth turned a sly grin on her companion. "And perhaps more importantly, early enough for my mother to display us before the entire neighborhood to her heart's content."

As Elizabeth expected, a grimace came over Darcy's countenance, but he nodded once, though a little curtly. Of course he would be aware that he would need to be introduced to all the neighborhood and her friends, though she did not doubt he would be ill at ease the entire time.

"Then shall we plan to return you to Longbourn on Tuesday? I shall send you in my carriage with a maid and Jack Thompson for your journey. I believe Bingley means to arrive at Netherfield on Friday. I shall travel to Longbourn with him."

"In the company of the estimable Miss Bingley, sir?" asked Elizabeth. Darcy had previously informed her of Miss Bingley's pretensions, and as she was acquainted with the woman and had understood her character herself, Elizabeth had only shaken her head at such willful blindness.

"I believe that five will be far too many for my carriage," replied Mr. Darcy, a twinkle in his eye. "Bingley and I shall travel in my carriage, while Miss Bingley shall follow in her brother's carriage, with Mr. and Mrs. Hurst as company."

Elizabeth laughed. "I do wonder how you shall be able to affect such arrangements, however. I do not doubt Miss Bingley will make a spectacle of how she would much rather travel in your conveyance."

"It is quite simple, my dear," said Mr. Darcy, "Bingley and I shall be departing an hour before his sisters and brother-in-law are scheduled to depart. Bingley is counting on his sister's desire to make an entrance keeping her from noting that we are ready to depart. In fact, I am certain the Bingley carriage will depart late for Hertfordshire, as I cannot but suppose she will wish to show me her superiority by being fashionably late."

"Well played, sir!" cried Elizabeth with a delighted laugh.

They walked on for several more minutes when Mr. Darcy commented: "Miss Bingley is to keep house for her brother in Hertfordshire."

"Would not the choice of his other, more experienced sister be more prudent?"

Mr. Darcy shrugged. "Perhaps. I believe Bingley wishes for his sister to gain some experience. I do not doubt he is hoping she will find a husband next season."

"I hope for his sake she does."

The days progressed and Elizabeth prepared for her departure with mixed emotions. She had become comfortable in London, though she was aware that was in no small part because of the man who had appeared out of nowhere to court her. But she loved her aunt and uncle and had enjoyed her time here with them. She was doubly appreciative of their willingness to accept her into their home and provide their love and support when she most needed it.

"You are very welcome, Lizzy," said Mr. Gardiner when she gave him her thanks. "We have been happy to have you here with us. It has been a pleasure to see you grow and mature these past months."

Elizabeth cocked her head to the side. "Have I really changed that much?"

"Of course you have, dear," replied Mrs. Gardiner. "When you came to us, you were a fearful young girl, desperate to avoid what you knew would be a most unhappy marriage. You are leaving us now as a poised and confident young woman."

"And it is without dispute because of your association with a certain young man," added her uncle. He favored her with an affectionate smile, taking in Elizabeth's blush as he said: "I also have no doubt that your feelings for that certain young man have progressed to the point where we shall soon be receiving word of an engagement."

Elizabeth chose not to respond to that statement, though privately she thought he was likely correct.

On the day before Elizabeth was to return to Hertfordshire, she visited Darcy house for the final time before her departure to take her leave of Georgiana. She had already seen Charity and her husband one more time, and the two women had promised they would meet again in the near future. Major Fitzwilliam would come just before Christmas, and Georgiana would not come until the major arrived himself. The last time Elizabeth spoke with her, Georgiana had been feeling the sting of their imminent separation, short though the duration would be.

When she arrived at Darcy house, she was met at the door by Mr. Darcy, as was his wont, but rather than smile at her appearance, he appeared to be a little worried. She soon discovered the reason for his disquiet.

"Miss Bennet. Thank you for coming today, but I am afraid I have a bit of a surprise for you. My aunt, Lady Catherine de Bourgh, is visiting from Kent, and she particularly desires to make your acquaintance."

"Oh," replied Elizabeth, unable to summon anything more.

She had heard little of Lady Catherine, other than her name, the fact that she was Mr. Darcy's mother's sister, and that she had lost her daughter to a long illness some years earlier. And though no one had made any specific statements on the matter, Elizabeth thought she had detected some mention of the woman's domineering manner and haughty ways, though they had been muted by her daughter's untimely death.

Offering his arm, Mr. Darcy led them into the house where the butler was waiting for Elizabeth's pelisse. She offered them up with a smile, though inside, her belly felt like a mass of butterflies.

"Courage, Miss Bennet," said Mr. Darcy.

Elizabeth looked up to see him watching her, an earnest sort of reassurance written on his brow.

"Lady Catherine is dictatorial, but she is also fair and can be impressed. As long as you hold onto your courage and show her you will not be intimidated, she will respect you." Mr. Darcy reached out to grasp her hand, and he gave it a gentle squeeze. "As for your other qualities, I cannot imagine she will not be impressed with your liveliness and your intelligence. She will approve of you, though she will likely persist in offering instructions."

Elizabeth raised an eyebrow in an attempt to show that she was little affected, and in truth, Mr. Darcy's words had helped calm her a little. "So I should expect her to be like my mother, offering advice that is at times nonsensical and always embarrassing."

Shaking his head, Mr. Darcy grinned and said: "Though her behavior can be a trial at times, my aunt is quite intelligent, and her advice is often good. The reason it annoys her family so much is because she offers it in a manner which brooks no disagreement and she expects to be obeyed."

"Then I shall keep my opinion to myself and only ignore her advice when she is not present."

"Good girl," said Darcy with another squeeze of her hand. Then he offered his arm to her and led her into the sitting-room.

It appeared to Elizabeth as soon as she entered the room that everything she had been told of Lady Catherine was nothing more than the truth, and indeed, it appeared to have been muted to a certain extent. She was seated on a chair, situated at the end of two long sofas, and had the chair only been a little higher in the back, it might have appeared to be a throne. The woman sat erect and rigid in it as she surveyed her domain, and she peered at Elizabeth as she entered, giving the impression of inspecting a horse at the market.

She was quite tall, likely standing at least a hand taller than Elizabeth. She was likely at least fifty years of age, and her hair consisted of more gray than black, though Elizabeth suspected it had been quite dark in her youth. Her face was a little long and lined, but around her eyes and in her strong chin, Elizabeth thought she saw in the lady's face a measure of beauty which would have been striking when she had been a girl. She was dressed in fine fabrics in a style which might be too ostentatious for a visit to a sitting room, especially with family.

But as Elizabeth approached the lady and began to feel the force of her scrutiny, she thought she saw something else in the woman's demeanor. Lady Catherine, for all her larger than life presence and haughty manner, was tired, as if she had run a great distance and had done so every day of her life. The death of the lady's daughter had obviously taken its toll on her and left her a lonely old woman, who was isolated due to her own choice. Elizabeth's heart went out to her, though she hid her reaction, knowing the lady would not appreciate pity.

"Aunt Catherine," said Mr. Darcy as they approached, "I would like to introduce the young lady I am courting, if you please."

The lady said nothing in response, only gesturing for Mr. Darcy to get on with it. He did so with promptness and Elizabeth curtseyed as required. Lady Catherine only watched her, eyes taking in Elizabeth's entire person, measuring and judging, if Elizabeth was to guess.

"So you are Miss Elizabeth Bennet, are you?" said Lady Catherine with an abruptness which took Elizabeth by surprise.

"I am, your ladyship," replied Elizabeth, not knowing what else to say.

Lady Catherine sniffed and continued her examination. "You are very small, are you not? Have you reached your full growth yet?"

"I cannot say, your ladyship. My sisters are all taller than I, but I have never found any reason to lament my lack of height."

A snort sounded to the side, and Lady Catherine looked over at Charity, who had managed to keep any other reaction silent, though her eyes danced with merriment.

"You should wear a shawl, Charity. You would not wish to come down with a cold."

"Yes, Aunt," said Charity, though her amusement did not alter a jot.

"You appear to have a hint of impertinence in your manners, Miss

Bennet. That is quite unusual for one as young as you." Lady Catherine paused and looked Elizabeth in the eye. "In fact, you appear to be full young indeed. May I ask your age?"

"I am not yet eighteen, Lady Catherine."

An elegant eyebrow rose at Elizabeth's response. "And have you been prepared to manage a house the size of my nephew's?"

"I have been taught to manage a household, yes," said Elizabeth. "I do not believe my education in that respect has been deficient."

"Seventeen is a young age to become a wife, especially to a man of my nephew's standing." Lady Catherine looked up at Mr. Darcy. "Did you think of such a thing when you requested a courtship, Nephew?"

"To me, Miss Bennet's age is not a consideration, Lady Catherine. I entered into this arrangement because I esteem Miss Bennet and because I have come to believe that she will be the perfect mistress of my homes and mother to my children. I do not believe that any other consideration should concern me."

"I am quite impressed with Miss Bennet's capabilities, Aunt," said Charity. On her other side, Georgiana, though obviously quite petrified of her aunt and unable to say anything herself, nodded her head vigorously. "I believe William has made a wonderful choice."

"Yes, I can see you are quite close to Miss Bennet, Charity," replied Lady Catherine.

The woman paused and scrutinized Elizabeth again, but this time there seemed to be a hint of respect in her manner, or at least that was what Elizabeth thought. Though she was still annoyed by the woman's dictatorial manners, she was hopeful she still might garner her approval.

"I wish to speak with Miss Bennet alone," announced Lady Catherine after a moment. "You will all leave us and give us a little privacy."

"Lady Catherine, I am not certain—"

"What, do you fear I shall haul your Miss Bennet over the carpet?" asked Lady Catherine, looking up at Darcy with displeasure. "You have no need to concern yourself. I wish to come to know Miss Bennet without all of you watching us as if you expect me to beat her about the shoulders with my cane. There is nothing untoward in my request."

Though Mr. Darcy appeared to be unconvinced, he ultimately acquiesced. The three relatives left the room without further comment, though Charity stepped up to Elizabeth, grasping her hand and grazing her cheek with a soft kiss. Then Elizabeth was left alone with their aunt, and she stood uncertainly, wondering what she should do.

"Oh, do sit down, Miss Bennet," said Lady Catherine with a sigh. "I do not wish to be left with a pain in my neck from looking up at you."

Elizabeth did as she was asked, perching near Lady Catherine's chair on the edge of the sofa, back erect and posture attentive. Lady Catherine watched her as she did this, again, a hint of approval appearing in her eyes.

"Miss Bennet," began Lady Catherine, "you can be at no loss to understand the reason for my desire to speak with you in private. I am certain your own heart, your conscience must tell you why I would wish to speak with you."

"I believe I do understand, Lady Catherine," said Elizabeth cautiously. "I am ready to answer any questions you might have of me."

Lady Catherine peered at Elizabeth for a moment before slowly nodding. "You appear to understand that I am not to be trifled with, Miss Bennet, and your deference for my superior rank is pleasing.

"The first thing you must know is that you are not what I—or indeed my brother, the earl—would have expected for my nephew. I will concede that I do not know much of your background, but I can guess based on some little information I have received through letters from my nieces. I wish to know all, so I will pose some questions for you, and you will answer them."

"Of course, Lady Catherine," replied Elizabeth. "I am happy to divulge any information which would help set your mind at ease."

A huff escaped the lady's lips and she said: "Whether my mind will be put at ease is still in question. Now, the most important thing is your father. He is a gentleman, is he not?"

"He is, your ladyship."

"And the size and location of his estate?"

What followed was an exhaustive inquisition about Elizabeth, her family, her connections, her life, her upbringing, and every other detail the lady could pull from her. She was clever and intuitive, seeing any hesitation in Elizabeth's manner, and extracting everything Elizabeth could provide with exactness and determination. Even if Elizabeth had been inclined to attempt to obfuscate, she knew that she would not have been successful, as the woman seemed to possess an uncanny ability to know when Elizabeth was not being so forthright as she wished. It was a taxing, and even an exhausting, ordeal, and Elizabeth felt like she was laid bare for Lady Catherine to see once the questioning had been completed.

When Lady Catherine had learned all she wished, she sat back in her chair and rubbed her temples with one hand. "My initial impression was indeed correct, child. You are most certainly not what we had all expected in my nephew's future wife, and I do not doubt you will face censure and criticism because of it." Lady Catherine turned a hawk-like eye on Elizabeth. "Are you prepared to face such contempt at the hands of society?"

Choosing her words carefully, Elizabeth replied: "I cannot imagine I would allow any scorn to affect me, and I am certain it would not affect Mr. Darcy's opinion of me. I have also been assured that only the most foolish will make open statements about me, due to Mr. Darcy's influence. I do not care for the approbation of those wholly unconnected with me, Lady Catherine. What concerns me is my family party, and I am confident in their love and support."

Lady Catherine nodded her head slowly. "You are very well spoken for one so young, Miss Bennet. That is a trait that will serve you well in society."

The lady watched Elizabeth for several more moments, seemingly deep in thought and Elizabeth was by now certain that whatever she had intended by this tête-à-tête, she did not appear hostile. It allowed Elizabeth the courage to sit and wait for the lady's judgment.

"I believe you will do, Miss Bennet," said Lady Catherine at length, "though you may have a difficult time convincing my brother. You have not fortune or connections to recommend you, but I believe you will be a passable mistress of Pemberley, with a little training and assistance.

"Furthermore," continued the lady, peering at Elizabeth as she spoke, "I saw the way my nephew looked at you when he escorted you in and his reluctance to leave you to my tender mercies. The fact that he esteems you to such an extent speaks well to your character, as did your responses to my questions. I believe I can support you in your future role as Mrs. Darcy."

"Thank you, Lady Catherine," replied Elizabeth. She had not thought to receive such a quick endorsement. "I shall strive to uphold my position in Mr. Darcy's home, in the event that he should decide he wishes to propose."

"I believe it is almost a certainty," said Lady Catherine, her eyes softening and her countenance relaxing to the point where she almost smiled. "My nephew is not one to do things by half measures. The fact that he thought enough of you to request a courtship means that he will almost certainly offer for you.

"I would never attempt to persuade him." Lady Catherine appeared introspective. "He is very much his father's son, and I knew as soon as I heard that he was calling on you that he would not be moved from his course. He listens to me when I offer my advice, but I have always understood the decision would be his own."

"He *is* a decisive man," said Elizabeth.

"Yes." Lady Catherine's mood suddenly turned imperious, and she directed a stern look at Elizabeth. "There is one more reason why I wish you to be successful in your role. You see, had my daughter lived, *she* would be assuming the position you will now occupy."

Elizabeth looked at the woman with astonishment. "Your daughter was intended for Mr. Darcy?"

A short but imperious nod was the lady's answer. "She was. It was the favorite wish of my sister and myself. We had planned the union from the time my daughter was born. Darcy knew about it, and though it was not made official or legally binding, I have no doubt he would have done his duty and married her if it had been possible

"I did not know."

"Of course you did not, Miss Bennet." Lady Catherine directed an even sterner glare at Elizabeth, which seemed to suggest she thought her deficient, but she soon relented. "I am certain Darcy would not wish to talk of it. You see, Anne, Darcy, Fitzwilliam, and Charity, as the younger cousins, were all quite close as children. There was some talk of betrothing Anne to Fitzwilliam and Darcy to Charity, but my brother would have none of it, as he intended to see them wed to further his political ambitions."

An indelicate snort indicated Lady Catherine's opinion of such a notion. "It has done him little good in the end. His elder children married most advantageously, but Fitzwilliam defied him to enter the army, and Charity defied him by marrying naught but a gentleman. She is happy in her union, so he tolerates it, but I am well aware that he aspired to the same sort of match his elder daughter made.

"And as for Anne . . ."

Lady Catherine fell silent as some great emotion welled up within her. Elizabeth did not know which bearer of the name she was thinking of—and strongly suspected that she was, in fact, thinking of both—but her heart went out to the lady. Her imperious manners and forthright ways could easily lead one to believe that she was all thistles and thorns and did not possess a heart. Lady Catherine felt her losses keenly, though Elizabeth knew for a fact the loss of her sister had been many years in the past.

At length Lady Catherine mastered her emotion enough to say: "My sister and I were very close, Miss Bennet; as close as sisters could be. I promised I would watch over her children when she was gone, and I have done my best to adhere to that promise. My daughter . . . My daughter was always sickly, even as a child, and though I hoped and prayed she would be spared and planned for her marriage to her cousin as per my agreement with my sister, it was not to be. Anne faded a little more each year until she finally left me three years ago. My life has been empty since."

Moved to compassion, Elizabeth leaned forward and placed a hand on the lady's arm. "I have a sister I love more than life. I could not imagine losing her. And I hope to never experience the pain of losing a child."

To Elizabeth's surprise, Lady Catherine moved her arm and caught Elizabeth's hand, holding onto it tightly, as if it was her only lifeline in the midst of a maelstrom. "I hope you never do, my dear. It is a pain I would not wish anyone to have to bear, though it is more common in our world than it ought to be."

The lady fell silent for a moment, before a light smile fell over her face. "Perhaps it is better this way. We all did our best to make sure that what years my daughter had were spent in happiness, but her health was such that she would not have been able to bear the burden of being the mistress of all Darcy has. I believe you will be more than capable in that regard."

She then let out a little laugh and said: "And though my brother knows it not, I have thwarted his designs with respect to Fitzwilliam."

Curious, Elizabeth asked: "Designs?"

Lady Catherine shook her head. "Lord Matlock is one who is proud of his position, and it has given him an elevated sense of his own importance. He does not like to be gainsaid, and when his second son not only entered the army against his wishes, but also spurned my brother's choice for his wife, he cut the major off from his inheritance. While I do not doubt he will eventually be made to relent, Fitzwilliam does not require it.

"You see, my Anne was the last scion of the de Bourgh line—with her death, the line has ended. And as Sir Lewis, my late husband, left the estate to me to pass onto our daughter when I deemed fit, the choice is mine to leave it to whomever I wish. I have chosen the earl's second son—the change in my will has already been enacted. Therefore, though my brother and his son do not know it yet, Fitzwilliam shall inherit Rosings Park after my death." Lady Catherine paused, as if in deep thought. "In fact, I may pass it off to him much sooner than I had originally intended. I am no longer young, and I am tired. I do not wish to bother myself with all the details of managing the estate much longer."

"Then I am happy for the major," said Elizabeth. "He is a good man, and I know he will be a wonderful steward of the land in your stead."

"Please do not say anything to anyone," admonished Lady Catherine. "I have not told anyone, and I would rather it remained a surprise."

Elizabeth readily agreed to keep her secret. "I also wish to tell you, Lady Catherine, that if you wish it, I believe Fitzwilliam and I would be happy to have you live with us. Your daughter may no longer be of this world, but I believe any children with which we are blessed would be doubly blessed to have you as a dear aunt."

A smile graced Lady Catherine's face, and she reached out to touch Elizabeth on the cheek. "You are so young, my dear, and so blessed with courage, determination, and optimism. I believe it would do me a world of good to have a measure of those qualities in my life. I may just accept your offer.

"But the important point at present is that you seem to have accepted the inevitable." Elizabeth blushed and Lady Catherine laughed. "Just remember what I have told you. I have no doubt my nephew will offer for you before the end of the year."

Though embarrassed, Elizabeth nodded. She rather thought she could not help but love her new aunt, for all her eccentricities.

The longer Miss Bennet stayed in the room with Lady Catherine, the more nervous Darcy became. He had always been aware of the status of Miss Bennet's position in society, and he knew that the elder members of the family would consider her to be unsuitable. His uncle's disapprobation was not in question, but Darcy thought that he would be able to persuade his aunt. As she had not emerged from Rosings after her daughter's death, he had thought the matter could be presented to her as a fait accompli.

But it seemed that the correspondence between Lady Catherine and not only Charity, but Georgiana as well, was much more extensive than he had thought. Both had apparently spoken of Miss Bennet and his courtship in their letters, prompting Lady Catherine's journey to London in order to meet the woman he had chosen. Darcy could not help but suppose that her other motive was to make certain that she was acceptable to be the future Mrs. Darcy. She would undoubtedly protest strenuously if he chose anyone she did not approve of to take the place her daughter should have had.

"William, please stop your pacing," said Charity. "You are beginning to make me dizzy."

Darcy paused in mid-stride; in truth, he had not even consciously realized that he had risen from his chair.

"Aunt Catherine is ready to be pleased with your Miss Bennet, and I am sure Elizabeth is up to the task of charming our cantankerous aunt."

"How can you be certain?" asked Darcy.

"Because I know my aunt's ways," replied Charity in a pointed fashion. "If Lady Catherine had been disposed to disapprove of her, she would have descended on us as an avenging angel. In fact, I do not doubt she would have sought Miss Bennet out at her uncle's house before even confronting us."

Darcy had not considered it in that manner, and he was forced to concede that his cousin was correct. And he had every confidence in Miss Bennet; her integrity, intelligence, liveliness, and all the other myriad virtues she possessed could not fail to garner his aunt's support. Lady Catherine, though authoritative and exacting, respected those of Miss Bennet's kind.

The door to the room in which they were sitting opened at that moment, and Mrs. Mayberry entered. "Lady Catherine has requested your presence again, Mr. Darcy."

Without prior thought, Darcy jumped to his feet and began to stride from the room, the sound of his cousin's hearty laughter mixed with that of his sister trailing along behind him. Darcy did not care; he only wished to see what had come of the long conference.

When he entered the room, Darcy stopped in surprise. Lady Catherine and Miss Bennet were sitting close together speaking animatedly, and Lady Catherine was actually laughing at something the younger woman had said. A tea service had been delivered in the interim, and both ladies had a cup at hand, the steaming liquid a testament to the fact that it had only just been delivered.

"Lady Catherine?" said Darcy, feeling as if his mind had suddenly ground to a halt.

"Come, William," said Charity as she stepped past him.

"I see Miss Bennet has worked her magic upon you too, Aunt," said Charity as she approached the two ladies.

A scowl appeared on Lady Catherine's face, but it was quickly clear that she was not displeased.

"We have been speaking and coming to know each other. Though I would not harm you by suggesting that you would be anything other than exacting when choosing a wife, I must own that I was concerned you would choose an unsuitable woman, if for nothing else than to assuage your loneliness.

"But it appears you have made a wise choice after all." Lady Catherine turned to Miss Bennet, and her visage softened a little.

"Though it will come as no shock for you to hear me say that her situation is not precisely desirable, I can find little fault with her manners or her person. I dare say that she is eminently suitable to become the mistress of Pemberley. I salute you for your choice, Darcy.

"Of course, she will require extensive training before she will be fully capable," continued Lady Catherine in an almost offhand tone. "But that may be accomplished once you are married. Since you are so close to Charity, I assume she will be quite willing to assist, as will I."

"It would be my pleasure," said Charity, while at the same time Miss Bennet said, "I thank you, Lady Catherine. I would be happy if you would share your extensive experience with me."

Wondering how such a thing could possibly have come about, Darcy could not even begin to respond. At length, his aunt noticed his uncertainty, and she looked up at him, pointing with one imperious gesture, and saying: "Do not stand there as if you are a mute, Darcy. Join us, or go to your study and concentrate on your work. Surely you must have something to do."

Faced with such a demand, and noting how Miss Bennet and Charity were barely successful in holding back their laughter, Darcy did the only thing he could: he sat down next to his sister.

The visit continued for some little time, and Darcy gradually regained his equilibrium. It seemed like his aunt had interrogated Miss Bennet and found her acceptable, though Darcy would have thought she would put up more resistance to his plans. Apparently she had mellowed since Anne had passed away.

When the time for Miss Bennet's departure arrived, she stood to leave, but before she left, two incidents occurred which utterly charmed Darcy and increased his regard for her tenfold.

As she was taking leave of them all, she approached Lady Catherine and dipped in a low curtsy, before she bent over to kiss the lady's cheek, pulling back and saying: "I was happy to make your acquaintance, Lady Catherine. I shall anticipate our next meeting and hope it shall be soon."

Darcy was surprised when Lady Catherine actually smiled and said: "I believe I shall be counting the hours myself, Miss Bennet."

Miss Bennet then excused herself, and with Darcy and Georgiana as escorts, she made her way through the house. As they walked, he could hear Georgiana speaking with her, lamenting the distance which would spring up between them with Miss Bennet's departure.

"Oh, Elizabeth, I shall miss you dreadfully! How shall I ever wait until we are reunited?"

Miss Bennet embraced Georgiana to her and said in a low voice he did not think she meant for him to overhear: "But we shall meet again very soon. Your brother is courting me, and as such, I cannot imagine our separation shall be of a short duration. Are you not to come to Hertfordshire for Christmas?"

"I believe so," said Georgiana. Her eyes darted to Darcy, and she seemed to note his close proximity with satisfaction. "Will you marry my brother, Elizabeth?"

Darcy could not help himself as he leaned in to hear what Miss Bennet had to say. He was not disappointed.

"I cannot say for certain, Georgiana. He has not yet asked me."

"But he will, Elizabeth. I do hope you will say yes. Surely you esteem my brother greatly."

"I do, Georgiana. I cannot imagine not esteeming him. He is the best man of my acquaintance."

A warmth spread through Darcy, and he looked on the woman he was courting with tenderness and affection. He was certain she had not been coy and had not even known that he was listening into their conversation when she spoke. The complete lack of artlessness in her manner and the way she had fit in with members of his family without trying spoke to his regard for her and raised her ever higher in his estimation. Though this separation would be of a short duration, Darcy was already anticipating the opportunity to be in her company again.

They reached the outer doors and with many tears and exclamations of their desire to be reunited, Elizabeth and Georgiana separated. And Darcy, taking Miss Bennet's hand in his own, escorted her the final few steps to the carriage. When she turned to him as she was about to depart, she regarded him with fondness, mixed with anticipation.

"I shall be in Hertfordshire on Friday, Miss Bennet. I can hardly wait to see you there."

Her eyes widened slightly, but Miss Bennet was quick to respond: "I am all anticipation myself, Mr. Darcy. The sooner you come, the happier I shall be."

"Then I shall come as soon as possible."

Darcy bowed and kissed her hand, and then helped her into the waiting carriage, giving the order for its departure, and he stood there watching it as it rolled down the street, contemplating its occupant far after it had passed out of sight.

Chapter XIX

Elizabeth's return home was everything she had imagined, both the pleasurable and the vexing. She had missed Jane and her father very much, and her arrival was met with tears, embraces, and statements of happiness at her return. The younger girls were also happy to see her, though their greetings were not so joyous as Jane's, and they were soon exclaiming with delight over the few trinkets she had purchased for them.

However, Mrs. Bennet's cries of delight upon seeing her were beyond even what Elizabeth had expected, and Kitty and Lydia were quick to argue who had received the prettier scarf and to fight between themselves in loud voices. The fact that her father only watched their behavior with amusement was no balm to Elizabeth's bruised feelings. When compared with the quiet, gentle nature Georgiana possessed, and the witty and lively, though ever proper nature of Charity, not to mention her aunt and uncle's sophisticated propriety, it was jarring to once again be in the presence of her silly sisters and mother.

When she had refreshed herself from her travels, Elizabeth dutifully joined her family in the parlor, expecting to be interrogated concerning her time in London and Mr. Darcy, more particularly. And she was not disappointed.

"Now, Lizzy," said Mrs. Bennet, accosting her as soon as she entered the room, "you must tell me everything about this man who is courting you. I shall not rest until I know it all!"

And with that the questioning began, and Elizabeth, who had never possessed a high opinion of her mother's intelligence, was surprised at how Mrs. Bennet's inquisition was in every way as effective as Lady Catherine's had been. Elizabeth kept the story of how she had met Mr. Darcy vague, as she did not think he wished to have such a story bandied about for all to hear, but Mrs. Bennet managed to learn much about Mr. Darcy's situation in life, his family connections, and his person, all of which served to stir her mother up into ever greater exclamations of delight. The young girl who left her home in disgrace, a victim of her mother's constant vilification, had now returned as the best of daughters, clever and wise to have refused the man of lesser standing in favor of the greater. It was all Elizabeth could do not to grind her teeth in frustration.

"I shall go distracted!" cried Mrs. Bennet when she had learned all she desired. "I could never have imagined that you would attract such a man to you when I sent you to London!"

"Nor could I," murmured Elizabeth.

"Oh, but he shall be coming here, shall he not?"

"By the end of the week, Mama," replied Elizabeth. "His cousin, Major Fitzwilliam, will also come in time for Christmas, bringing his sister Georgiana with him."

"So many great people coming to Longbourn!"

"They will stay at Netherfield with Mr. Bingley, though I expect we shall see them at Longbourn frequently."

This, of course, brought out a whole new line of questioning, for though the district had previously heard of Mr. Bingley's intention to lease the estate, details on his person were scarce.

"Mr. Bingley indeed!" exclaimed Mrs. Bennet when Elizabeth had finished speaking. "That sounds very well indeed. Perhaps he will do for our Mary."

"I believe Mary is as yet too young, Mrs. Bennet," said Mr. Bennet.

Though Mrs. Bennet looked long and hard at Mary, she was forced to agree. "Then we shall simply need to ensure Mr. Bingley stays in the area long enough for Mary or one of the younger girls to catch him."

"And here I thought you would be eager to throw Jane in Mr. Bingley's path," said Mr. Bennet, his sardonic amusement flowing out in his tone.

"Oh, stuff and nonsense!" exclaimed Mrs. Bennet. "If Lizzy has managed to capture herself a rich man of society, I am certain that Jane can to no worse than to marry a peer. A baron, or even an earl, should be her goal now!"

"I should be happy with a man who loves me," said Jane in her typical quiet voice.

Mrs. Bennet just ignored her, as was her wont when she was interested in a subject. "What about Mr. Darcy's cousin, the viscount? Perhaps he would do."

"Mr. Darcy's cousin is already married, Mama," said Elizabeth.

"That is unfortunate, but I am certain Mr. Darcy must have many friends in the upper echelons of society. He must be well able to throw all my girls in the paths of other rich men!"

Privately, from everything Elizabeth had heard of the viscount, it was just as well that he was already attached. And as for the rest of her mother's exclamations, Elizabeth was well aware that Mr. Darcy was not fond of most society, but she would not elucidate her mother on the true nature of the situation. It would do no good, as Elizabeth was certain Mrs. Bennet would not listen anyway.

"But that is something we must discuss for another time. At present, we should begin preparations for your wedding. I would die of shame if the marriage, your dress and trousseau, and the wedding breakfast, were not worthy of a man of Mr. Darcy's prominence. Do you think his uncle will attend?"

"Mama!" exclaimed Elizabeth. "I have not 'secured' Mr. Darcy, and I am not engaged. We are still only courting at present."

Mrs. Bennet, however, would not be denied. "A courtship is as good as an engagement, Lizzy. A man of Mr. Darcy's standing would not be paying such attention to you if he did not mean it to lead to marriage."

And nothing Elizabeth said made any difference to Mrs. Bennet. She prattled on about foods for the wedding breakfast, lace, dresses, earls and viscounts, and anything else which entered her mind, and within half an hour, Elizabeth was longing for the calm quietude of the Gardiner townhouse, not to mention Mr. Darcy's house.

He is an excellent suitor, mused Elizabeth as her mother continued to speak. *In fact, it might be worth it to accept him if he proposes, if only to get away from mama.*

The thought almost caused Elizabeth to giggle, but she stifled it, knowing her mother would ask her why she laughed. It was with these thoughts she passed the bulk of the time that afternoon, as her mother seemed to be indefatigable. And if her sisters noted her preoccupation, none of them seemed eager to comment on it.

* * *

The days between Elizabeth's return and Mr. Darcy's arrival were a trial for Elizabeth's patience in more than one way. Her mother's effusions on the subject of Elizabeth's courtship were inexhaustible, and Elizabeth did not know if she stopped speaking on the subject for five minutes complete except when she was sleeping. Elizabeth envisioned many battles to come, as her tastes were different from her mother's, and Elizabeth knew her mother would try to force her wishes on her. But Elizabeth was not of a humor to allow it, though she kept her own council for the time being.

When Mrs. Bennet was not speaking of Mr. Darcy and his ten thousand a year and how he had been as intelligent as to single Elizabeth out for his particular attentions, she was fretting at the separation, worried that Mr. Darcy would lose interest in her. Furthermore, she lamented, Elizabeth was wild and her interests far from ladylike, and she would undoubtedly drive him away with her impertinent ways and undisciplined behavior. It was all Elizabeth could do not to gnash her teeth in frustration.

The situation finally came to a head the day before Darcy's arrival in Hertfordshire, and though it resulted in her mother being offended, at least it bought her some relief from her mother's continual chatter.

It happened as they were in the sitting-room, with Elizabeth working on some embroidery. As was her wont, Elizabeth had managed to think of other matters, and she had only heard one word in three her mother had spoken.

"Oh, no, this shall never do! Lizzy shall never be able to induce this Mr. Darcy to marry her, I am absolutely certain! I know she could never attract a man's interest like you can, Jane."

Elizabeth watched as Jane darted a quick glance at her, clearly hoping she had not heard, and then tried to talk some sense to her mother. "I am certain you are wrong, Mother. Lizzy is lively and happy, and I dare say any man would be lucky to marry her."

"But she has not the fashionable manners, Jane. She is wild and impertinent, and I am certain she will chase him away! Oh, whatever shall we do?"

At that point, it sounded to Elizabeth like her mother was spouting her usual lamentations, and as it was something she had heard her entire life, she had largely become inured to it. She was about to sink into her own thoughts once again, when her mother said something which ignited the flames of her anger, which had been simmering since she had returned home.

"No, Jane, it simply will not do. It is far too important for our family to ensure this man is secured as soon as may be, and I am certain Lizzy shall not be able to do it properly. Therefore, when this Mr. Darcy arrives, we must direct him toward you. For what man can resist you? You are so beautiful and calm and sweet-tempered that I am certain you cannot fail to attract his attention and make him love you without trying."

"But, Mama!" cried Jane. "I am certain Lizzy—"

"No, no, she cannot. Lizzy shall simply need to accept Mr. Pearce, for if she does not, I am certain she shall never marry."

"Mother!" exclaimed Elizabeth jumping to her feet in indignation.

Mrs. Bennet started, apparently thinking that she was speaking quietly enough that Elizabeth would not hear her; she had never been able to judge the volume of her voice, which was part of the reason she was so often an embarrassment.

"*Do not ever* speak of such a thing again! How can you think that people will be manipulated according to your designs? I never thought you could be this senseless!"

"I am certain I am correct!" cried her mother in response. "You had best marry Mr. Pearce and leave Jane to this Mr. Darcy. Otherwise we shall lose them both."

"That is enough!"

Elizabeth locked eyes with her mother, and whatever Mrs. Bennet saw there, she blanched and did not speak, though her posture screamed defiance. Elizabeth, now incensed beyond all measure, stalked toward her mother, fists clenching and unclenching in a vain attempt to relieve the fury which had overtaken her.

"With such talk as this, you will succeed in nothing more than driving Mr. Darcy away from me forever, and if you do such a thing, I shall never forgive you."

"Why can you not just marry Mr. Pearce as you should?" asked her mother in a plaintive whine. "Why can you not simply accept your fate?"

"Because he is a reprehensible man with whom I would be miserable. Mr. Darcy—Mr. Darcy is a good man, reticent, yes, but he is in possession of the highest of intelligence and manners, and a display like this one would drive him away, despite whatever regard he possesses for me. *Never* suggest such a thing in my hearing again!"

Mrs. Bennet turned to Mr. Bennet and, in a voice which approached a shriek, said: "Will you allow your daughter to speak in such a manner to me?"

"I shall when you speak such nonsense, Mrs. Bennet," replied Mr. Bennet. In the midst of her anger, Elizabeth looked at her father, noting that he was watching his wife with a seriousness which was usually not present, and when he spoke, she could tell he was in earnest. "Much though you might wish to order the world to your own dictates, people will not be pushed according to your whims. You should be thankful that our Lizzy is vibrant enough to have attracted the attention of such a man.

"But, Mr. Bennet—"

"No, Mrs. Bennet," replied her husband, quietly but firmly. "When I spoke to Mr. Darcy, I saw no sign that he was anything other than completely devoted to Lizzy. I have no doubt that he will eventually propose when he deems the time right, and given what I have seen of our Lizzy's behavior," Mr. Bennet directed an affectionate smile at Elizabeth, "I have no doubt he shall be accepted.

"Now, let us leave the subject, Mrs. Bennet," said Mr. Bennet when his wife would have protested further. "I believe all will turn out as it should, if we only allow the young people to sort it out themselves."

It was rare that Mr. Bennet put a stop to his wife's behavior, and rarer yet that he would do so without some sort of statement he knew she would not quite understand, which was designed to vex her. Clearly Mrs. Bennet did not know what to make of her husband's words, but she nodded hesitantly, and the matter was allowed to drop.

For her part, Elizabeth was near tears and did not think she could bear another moment in her mother's company. She was saved by her father, who invited her to his bookroom.

"Hopefully that will silence your mother for the present," said Mr. Bennet when Elizabeth was seated across the desk from him. "I dare not hope that she will discontinue her constant flutterings concerning your wedding breakfast, trousseau, and all the other myriad details she believes need attending to, but perhaps in this we should allow her to speak as she pleases."

"She may do whatever she likes as long as she does not chase Mr. Darcy away with her behavior."

Mr. Bennet directed a level look at Elizabeth. "She is correct in that you should not be speaking of your mother in such a fashion, Lizzy, whatever the provocation."

Coloring, Elizabeth murmured a quiet apology, which seemed to appease her father, for he only nodded. He was silent for a moment, considering something, and Elizabeth, after being subject to her mother's assault for the previous two days, was quite content with the peace. She was, therefore, surprised when he once again spoke.

"I had hoped that this Mr. Darcy might be overstating the affection between you, but I am now certain that you greatly esteem this man." Mr. Bennet sighed a little sadly. "It seems I shall be losing you much sooner than I ever imagined myself ready."

"You do not begrudge me my happiness," said Elizabeth, not knowing quite what else to say.

Mr. Bennet chuckled. "No, indeed I do not, Lizzy. In fact, I am quite relieved that you have found a man you can love, and one who will care for you as you deserve to be cared for." The chuckle turned into a sigh, and Mr. Bennet said: "I am merely thinking of how empty and dull it will be at Longbourn when you leave it forever. With my most sensible daughter leaving for her own house, I dare say it will not be long before your sister Jane finds herself the object of some other young man.

"With you both gone, I do not doubt that I shall be left in the house with naught but your silly sisters and my silly wife for company, and words of sense shall be few and far in between."

"Oh, Papa," said Elizabeth in an admonishing tone.

"I know, Lizzy," said Mr. Bennet, waving off her censure. "I love your sisters, Lizzy, but their behavior is a trial at times, which even you must own yourself."

"It is, Father," said Elizabeth, "but perhaps if you took them in hand, their behavior might be amended. Kitty is bound to follow wherever she is led, and Lydia is intelligent enough that perhaps she might be brought to see the benefit of a more proper decorum."

"I suppose you are right," mused Mr. Bennet. "I shudder to think of what she might become if she is allowed to come out while still behaving in this manner." Mr. Bennet favored Elizabeth with a wan smile. "I know sometimes it seems as if I have no care for the reputation and credit of our family, but we have been respected in the community for many years, and I would not have that thrown away."

"Then please take her and Kitty in hand. They are not so old or set in their ways that they are beyond the reach of amendment."

"I shall miss you, Lizzy. You truly are the brightest of my daughters, and our home shall be dimmer without you present."

Embarrassed, and yet at the same time pleased, Elizabeth smiled at her father. She had always known of his regard, though she had not quite thought that he would mourn her going to such an extent. Casting about for something to say, Elizabeth latched onto an idea she thought her father would find agreeable indeed.

"I believe you are not considering the benefits of a connection to Mr. Darcy, Papa."

Interest piqued, Mr. Bennet looked at her with amusement. "Oh?"

"I do not believe I have told you of Mr. Darcy's library, and apparently what I have seen in London is nothing compared to what exists at Mr. Darcy's estate in Derbyshire."

Leaning forward with a half-smile on his face, Mr. Bennet indicated for Elizabeth to continue: "Tell me more."

And thus an agreeable time was spent with father and daughter discussing the wonders of Mr. Darcy's fabled library at Pemberley, and though neither had ever seen it, they allowed their fancies free rein. With the light appearing in his eyes at the description of so much wealth of knowledge, Elizabeth was certain her father would be a frequent visitor when she married. In fact, she wondered whether he would even bother to inform them of his coming.

It was later that morning and Elizabeth was back in the sitting-room with her mother and sisters when a most unwelcome visitor arrived at the estate. The door chime sounded and the five ladies looked up from whatever they were doing. Thinking it was Charlotte—Elizabeth had only spoken with her friend once after her return to Hertfordshire—Elizabeth rose to meet her friend with pleasure. It was with no little shock that Mrs. Hill entered the room with a visibly angry Winston Pearce trailing behind her."

Elizabeth blanched, looking up at the man who had pursued her so relentlessly all these months, and Mr. Pearce's eyes bored into her, daring her to object to his presence. Hill was apparently not insensible to the sudden tension in the room, but Elizabeth belatedly realized she had not been given any instructions to deny the man entry and had thus led him in.

"Mr. Winston Pearce to see Miss Elizabeth," said the housekeeper, though in a tone laced with uncertainty.

"Mr. Pearce!" cried Mrs. Bennet, rising to her feet. She directed a nervous glance at Elizabeth. "You are quite welcome, sir."

A scathing glance at the Bennet matron caused her to step back. "I am, madam? After you have all so grievously used me and attempted to give what is rightfully mine to another, I am surprised you can stand there and call me welcome."

"Hill, please summon Mr. Bennet," said Elizabeth, ignoring the man. Given the seeming state of his feelings, Elizabeth thought that Mr. Pearce would not be put off by a gaggle of women he considered to be his inferiors.

Mrs. Hill curtseyed and departed from the room. Mr. Pearce only watched her with contempt before turning his attention back to

Elizabeth. For her part, Elizabeth moved away from him, refusing to even look in his direction.

"I might wonder why my generous offer of marriage has thus been thrown to the ground, to be trodden on by all of your silly family. Am I not able to give you enough, Miss Bennet? Is this other man so well endowed with worldly possessions that you spurn me in order to draw him into your web?"

"I have nothing to say to you, Mr. Pearce."

Hearing the rustling of his clothes, Elizabeth though the man was moving toward her, and she stepped behind a sofa to face him. His face was red and his fists clenched in rage. By her side, Jane stepped forward, intent upon putting herself between Elizabeth and her antagonist, and Elizabeth felt a rush of affection for her dearest and bravest sister. A glance about the room showed Kitty and Lydia watching with astonishment from where they had been poring over a fashion magazine, while Mary only watched the man with pursed lips of censure. For her part, Mrs. Bennet was watching him, astonishment writ upon her brow; it was clear she had not quite understood what kind of man he was.

"You *shall* have something to say to me. An explanation at the very least."

"What need have you for an explanation?" retorted Elizabeth as she raked her scathing glare at him. "Did I not refuse you from the very first and refuse to entertain any repetition of your ill-fated offer? And did you not persist in the face of my repeated rejections? What more do you need?"

"I must assume then that you are deficient."

"The only deficiency is yours, Mr. Pearce. I might wonder why a man possesses so little sense that he will continue to chase a woman who has repeatedly claimed to detest the very sight of him. I cannot make you out, sir. I am certain there are many young ladies who would be quite happy to marry for nothing more than pecuniary reasons. Why not pursue one of them?"

Pearce, however, only turned a derisive glare on Mrs. Bennet. "And what of you, madam? Did you not promise me repeatedly that your daughter would marry me? Did you not say, 'my Lizzy shall be brought to see reason'?"

Mrs. Bennet stammered and was not quite able to say anything. But Elizabeth was infuriated on her mother's behalf.

"Speak not so to my mother! You are the last man in the world I could ever be prevailed upon to marry, and it would not matter what my mother said."

At that moment several things happened at once. Mr. Bennet entered into the room followed by Jack Thompson—who had come to Longbourn with Elizabeth at Mr. Darcy's insistence—saying: "What is the meaning of this?" Mr. Pearce was already moving, however; he lunged forward, attempting to capture Elizabeth's arm, but Elizabeth, sensing he was becoming angry enough to accost her, deftly moved out of the way. Mrs. Bennet screamed at the sudden violence, and Jane moved in front of Elizabeth and confronted Mr. Pearce.

"You shall not touch my sister!"

Jack surged forward and caught Pearce by the arms, and soon Mr. Hill had joined them. Between the three of them, they manhandled Pearce from the room, though to Elizabeth's eyes, Jack required little help, Mr. Bennet exclaiming: "Enough of this!"

Pearce continued to struggle and swear, but they forced him from the room. Through the open door, Mr. Bennet's voice could be heard to say: "You will leave and never return. You are not welcome back at Longbourn."

In the sitting-room, Elizabeth allowed herself to be coaxed into Jane's embrace, and she was surprised to find that she was shaking, though whether it was fear, indignation, or fury, she could not quite determine for herself.

"Lizzy, are you well?"

"I believe I am well, Jane."

On the other side of the room, Mrs. Bennet shrieked and fell into her chair, calling for Mrs. Hill to bring her smelling salts, while Kitty and Lydia were clutching each other in fear, their eyes wide and disbelieving. Mary had risen and was patting Elizabeth awkwardly on the back, saying: "It is well, Lizzy. Papa made that horrible man leave."

Soon matters were put to rights. Mrs. Hill calmed Mrs. Bennet with an efficiency born of much practice, and while Mrs. Bennet continued to moan about the disgusting conduct of the man, the room began to settle. Elizabeth and Jane approached their youngest sisters and spoke to them in calm and comforting voices.

"I am happy you were not made to marry that man, Lizzy," said Lydia, making a face. "To think that a gentleman could behave in such a manner."

"Gentleman possess status, Lydia, but that does not guarantee good behavior. Some gentlemen are *not* good men."

"How can I ever know whether a man is a good one?" fretted Kitty.

"It can be difficult, Kitty," replied Jane. "You must learn a little discernment. You can know a man by his works and his reputation, though that is not without risk, of course."

Mr. Bennet reentered the room at that moment and, taking stock of the situation, called Mrs. Hill to him; Jane left Elizabeth's side to go to her mother in Hill's absence.

"Please bring a pot of tea, Mrs. Hill. I believe the ladies require a little fortification after that bit of excitement."

Hill curtseyed and departed the room, leaving Mr. Bennet to approach Elizabeth. He caught her hands in his and looked at her closely.

"Are you well, Lizzy?"

"I am, Papa. He was not able to lay a hand on me, and Jane stepped in front of me to prevent a second attempt."

Chuckling, Mr. Bennet turned to his eldest and winked at her. "I had not known our Jane was such an intrepid young lady. Well done, Jane!"

While Jane instantly blushed at her father's praise, Lydia was able to find her voice. "Any of us would do it for Lizzy!" She seemed to have recovered her previous confidence and sense of invincibility and was watching Elizabeth with determination.

"I dare say you would, Liddy, my dear," said Mr. Bennet with fond affection at his youngest. "However, I believe we shall need to let Lizzy's bodyguard take care of the blackguard."

Mr. Bennet turned to Elizabeth with a grin designed to dispel the attention in the room and said: "That mountain of a man Mr. Darcy sent back with you is quite the sight to be seen. When Pearce attempted to strike him to free himself, he simply picked Pearce up by the scruff of the neck and deposited him in the dust of the driveway. I thought Pearce would faint with fear when Jack stuck his face inches from Pearce's and told him it would go ill for him if he ever returned."

Elizabeth laughed. "I think Jack could intimidate a brick wall if he so chose."

"He might be harder than a brick wall, Lizzy."

The whole family laughed at their ridiculous banter, except for Mrs. Bennet, who regarded them all as if they were bereft of their senses.

"How can you all carry on so at a time like this?" was her shrill cry. "Who could have predicted Mr. Pearce, who possesses every advantage, could be such a villain? My nerves are quite overset!"

"Do you understand what kind of man he is now, Mama?" asked Elizabeth, plaintively hoping her mother could finally be induced to desist lamenting about the man.

It was almost comical the way Mrs. Bennet's head nodded fervently.

"I do, Lizzy. I would never allow any of my girls to be married to him. Oh, to be at the mercy of such a man! I cannot even think of it without abhorrence."

Mr. Bennet shook his head, his amusement with his wife back in place. "I am happy to hear it, my dear, for I have instructed Mr. Hill and the footmen that Pearce should be run off if he ever shows his face here again.

"Thank you, Papa," said Elizabeth, thankful that this chapter of her life had finally been brought to a close.

The family settled in with the tea service which was soon brought for their consumption, and it was not long before spirits were restored and they were once again talking and laughing. Mr. Bennet soon excused himself and returned to his rooms when the chatter became too much, and more particularly, when Mrs. Bennet began to once again plan in a loud voice what tasks she needed to complete for Elizabeth's ultimate wedding, and all of Elizabeth's protestations and Jane's words of sense on the matter did not deter her.

Even though Elizabeth would now be free of her mother's comments on the matter of Mr. Pearce—for he was now the most disagreeable man of her acquaintance—she reflected that some things would not change. Mr. Darcy's prompt arrival on the morrow was now Elizabeth's firmest hope, for at least she would be able to escape some of the tumult with her suitor!

Chapter XX

Before Darcy could leave London to reunite with Miss Elizabeth Bennet, there was an unpleasant duty which he needed to attend to, and the day before his departure was the date he chose. This would accomplish two desirable objectives in Darcy's mind: it would delay the agony until the last possible moment, and it would allow him to escape to Hertfordshire and avoid the harangues he would almost certainly be subjected to if he was close at hand.

As Darcy stood before his uncle and aunt that day, he was forced to reflect that Hugh Fitzwilliam was not a *bad* man by any means. In fact, he was a very good master of his estate and he was fair and honest in all his dealings. It was true that the viscount tended to be a bit of a spendthrift and somewhat of a gamester, but though Darcy despised that lifestyle, the man seemed to know when enough was enough. The earl himself had never engaged in such behavior, even as a young man, and he was also free of the other vice so common to men of his station—he did not keep a mistress and had remained faithful to his wife through all the years of his marriage.

But he could be infuriatingly inflexible at times, and more times than Darcy could count, he and the countess had tried to match Darcy with some insipid peer's daughter in order to better the family position. He would not take kindly to Miss Bennet's background, and Darcy did not think he would be able to induce the man to relent, though he would certainly not wish to publish a break in the family over the matter. In addition, though Darcy did not think his uncle would publicly shun Miss Bennet for that same reason, he also could not imagine the earl ever paying her much attention.

Darcy was happy for the support of his relations who knew Miss Bennet. Charity was present with her husband, as was Fitzwilliam, though the two elder children were not there. It had come as a shock to Darcy that Lady Catherine had also elected to stay in London for a few days to support Darcy when he told the earl. The only one of his family who was not present was Georgiana, as Darcy did not wish to expose her to her uncle's displeasure.

"Well, Darcy," said the earl, his voice a deep rumble, "I understand you have something to inform us of."

"I do, Uncle. In fact, I have the best of news. I have entered into a courtship with a young lady."

"A courtship?" The earl leaned forward and regarded Darcy with a frown. "I have heard nothing of any rumors of a courtship. I would have expected such news as you finally deigning to show some interest in a woman to be in all the society papers."

"It has not been published because I have exercised caution, Uncle. I have no desire for my private life to be bandied about in such a fashion."

"I am well aware of your desire for privacy," said the earl with a grunt. "But not everyone is as circumspect as you are. The young lady should have been crowing about it to all her friends, which would have led it to be on the tongue of anyone in society."

"I believe I have managed to find a lady unlike most of those debutantes."

"*That* is an understatement," said Charity, laughing no doubt at the way Darcy was still dancing about the subject.

"Well, then, out with it," said the earl. "Who is this young lady of whom Charity speaks in so glib a fashion?"

"Her name is Miss Elizabeth Bennet."

"Bennet?" asked the earl. "I know of no Bennets in society. Where is she from?"

"Her father's estate is in Hertfordshire, near the town of Meryton."

"Is Meryton that little market town we sometimes pass through on our way to Derbyshire?"

"Aye, it is," said Fitzwilliam. Darcy thought his cousin was about to laugh aloud at his enjoyment of the situation, but he kept his composure, though the amused twinkling in his eye told Darcy that he was entertained immensely.

The earl turned a shrewd eye on Darcy. "I think you had best explain yourself, Darcy. I smell a hint of obfuscation in your manner, which suggests that I will not approve."

"You might not, Uncle, but I will not be moved from my purpose."

Studying Darcy intently, the earl sat back and let out a sigh. "When have you ever been moved from your purpose, Darcy? Your young woman is at the very least the daughter of a gentleman by your own admission. As long as you are not marrying a servant girl, she must have some measure of acceptability about her."

"To me, she is quite acceptable, sir."

And with that, Darcy began to explain how he had come to know Miss Bennet—edited, of course. He spoke of the situation of family, noting how he knew she was not a fortune hunter. Charity and Fitzwilliam both spoke on Miss Bennet's suitability, though Lady Catherine remained silent for the present. And Darcy followed up with another statement to the effect that when the time was right, he would ask Miss Bennet to marry him, regardless what any of the family or society thought.

By the end of the recitation, the earl was frowning and rubbing his temples in exasperation, while the countess appeared to have been assaulted by some particularly foul odor. It was nothing Darcy had not expected.

"Ties to trade, Darcy? Are you out of your mind to be paying attention to such an unsuitable girl?"

"I care not for her connections, Uncle," said Darcy. "If having her for a wife means I will be forced to accept her relations as my own, I will gladly accept them. Mr. and Mrs. Gardiner are exceptional people, and you would never know his profession by their behavior."

"As I recall, your erstwhile companion Wickham possessed pretty manners of his own. That does not make him an estimable character."

Mention of George Wickham set a scowl to Darcy's face. Not only had the man eluded the men Darcy had hired to discover him, but Darcy was certain he would attempt something, likely with Miss Bennet.

"Nor does the fact that the Duke of Worchester is a slave to the gaming tables and a rake as well, mean that his character is any more estimable."

"That is not what I meant," snapped the earl.

"I know precisely what you meant, sir. The Gardiners, regardless of their position in life, are two of the most decent and admirable people I have ever met. It will be no hardship to share a connection with them."

"Does your lady even know how to behave properly?" asked Lady Matlock, with a derisive sniff. "With such examples to be had, I cannot imagine she will fit into our society."

"Miss Bennet's behavior is impeccable," said Charity. "I have the highest opinion of her, and Georgiana quite adores her."

"And that is another thing," said the earl. "What of Georgiana's prospects? Marrying beneath yourself will almost certainly damage them."

"I would not wish to part with my sister to someone who would reject her on such frivolous grounds regardless," said Darcy, glaring at his uncle pointedly. "If a man cannot appreciate Georgiana for herself, then he had best move along, as I would not grant consent."

The earl through his hands up in frustration. "Catherine, what of you? You have sat there this whole time, watching with a more than your usual insolence. Have you nothing to say on this matter? Did you not wish for Darcy to marry your daughter?"

Lady Catherine's eyes narrowed, and she looked at her brother with all her considerable displeasure. "My daughter is no longer of this world, Hugh. I would ask that you remember that fact."

"I know that!" snapped Lord Matlock. "I am merely pointing out that you once harbored such designs for your daughter, and since that is no longer possible, I would have expected you to wish for something more substantial for Darcy's future bride."

"You are assuming I do not."

Darcy caught Lady Catherine's eye and regarded her with a question in his gaze. The woman only smiled back at him, clearly attempting to put him at ease.

"I merely understand that Darcy is well within his rights to marry where he chooses, since he is beholden to no one. Make no mistake, Hugh, he does not require our permission, nor has he asked for it. As such, I merely choose to support him in his choice."

"And what is your impression of this young woman?"

"She is full young yet," said Lady Catherine, her manner becoming introspective. "But as she is intelligent and lively, I do not doubt that age and experience will allow her fill the role adequately. She is happy and friendly, and she gets on with Georgiana very well indeed. Though there is a hint of impertinence in her manner, it is not improper, and I believe, at least in Darcy's case, it only adds to her charms.

"In fact, once I was able to speak with her and determine her situation, upbringing, her innate goodness, and her capabilities, I was forced to acknowledge that Darcy has indeed made a fine choice. She is not of our circle, and she does not possess the connections I would wish for, but of her person there is little to censure. She will do well, I think, with Charity's help along with my own."

"I might wonder why I am only hearing about this woman now," said Uncle Hugh, spearing Darcy with an annoyed look. "It seems like you have arranged for this young woman to meet every member of the family you thought would approve of her."

"I do not deny that, Uncle," said Darcy. "I wished to supply Miss Bennet a welcoming atmosphere for our courting, and I knew you and Lady Susan, as well as your two eldest, would not approve of her."

"And you are set on this course?"

"I am."

Earl Matlock waved his hand, and though Darcy knew he was no happier about the matter than he had been before, he now exuded nothing more than resigned acceptance.

"Very well, Darcy. You know your own mind, and I do not doubt that any attempt to convince you will be met with failure. If you must have this young woman, then you shall have her. I will trust that she will not embarrass the family."

"As I said, Hugh," replied Aunt Catherine, "I have no doubt that she can behave properly in all occasions. I will assist her to become used to her new situation."

A grunt was all the answer Lady Catherine was to receive. Feeling the matter was resolved, Darcy bowed and was about to depart when Lady Matlock spoke up.

"Will you bring this young woman around to meet us, Darcy?"

"I have no wish to know her," said the earl in a tone brooking no opposition. "At least for the present. We shall be obliged to meet her eventually, but it would be best if you allowed us to become used to the idea first."

Lady Matlock only rolled her eyes. "You are not thinking of practicalities, Hugh. This young woman will be connected to us, and if you do not wish for there to be whispers of a breach in the family, we need to act to dispel such rumors before they exist."

"What do you suggest?" asked the earl, though it was clear he was still discontented.

"Nothing onerous. We should meet her, even if we are not to attend the wedding." Lady Susan paused and looked at her children and Lady Catherine. "Can I assume you shall all be attending the wedding?"

"I shall be standing up with Darcy," said Fitzwilliam.

At the same time, Charity nodded. "We have not discussed the matter, but as I approve of Miss Bennet and Gerald also likes her, I think it would be prudent to add our support."

Lady Catherine did not respond immediately. Darcy, knowing what she was feeling, moved to assure her of his understanding of her situation.

"You do not need to attend, Lady Catherine. I understand it will be difficult."

To his surprise, Lady Catherine only shook her head. "Though it *is* still painful, Darcy, Anne's death *was* more than three years ago. I still mourn my daughter, but I think in some ways it would almost be cathartic for me to attend. It would also send a greater message to society if I, as the mother of the woman you were to marry, were in attendance."

"I agree," said Lady Susan. "I think that Hugh will insist on our not attending." The earl nodded vigorously, "but the fact that three members of our family will be there should send enough of a message. I believe it would also be prudent for me to act as her sponsor for her curtsey before the queen."

Rarely had Darcy been so surprised in his life. His aunt, though intelligent, was not one of his favorite people, for the simple fact that she tended to consider society above all other things. He had thought she would be vehemently opposed to even making Miss Bennet's acquaintance, let alone sponsoring her in society. Clearly the other members of her family were as shocked as was Darcy himself.

"I do not think we need to show such attention to such an inferior young woman," said earl Matlock in a stiff tone.

Darcy, though angered at the man's reference to Miss Bennet's inferiority, held his tongue.

"That is because you are not considering the situation properly," replied Lady Susan, calmly deflecting her husband's displeasure. "You may speak to her as little or as much as you like, but to ensure that she is accepted by as much of society as will accept her, we must present a united front. That means she must be introduced to us, she must have her curtsey before the queen, and she should receive an Almack's voucher, which is something I can influence, so long as she is not completely unsuitable. And for all this to have the maximum effect, I must be the one to sponsor her, though if Catherine joined me, that would also be beneficial."

"I agree," said Lady Catherine. "I approve of the girl, so it will be no hardship for me to provide my endorsement."

Out of the corner of his eye, Darcy saw his cousins sharing an amused grin, and he immediately understood. As Lady Susan was an intimate of the ladies who controlled Almack's, she would wish for Miss Bennet to prove herself worthy and was doing everything in her power to ensure that eventuality. In essence, she was making the best of the situation and protecting her own reputation and position in the bargain.

"Do as you will," replied the earl, though it was clear he was still not happy. "I will accept the girl, though I warn that you should not expect more from me. But by all means, ensure her debut is a success and that she does not embarrass us. I think I do not need to inform you all that Rachel and James will undoubtedly be much colder toward her."

"As long as they are respectful, it does not signify," said Darcy firmly. "Disrespect I will not tolerate."

"You may be assured of that, at the very least, Darcy," said Lady Susan, her tone and expression firm. "I have raised them to be respectful of all, regardless of station. I will speak with them and make certain they understand your strictures."

Darcy nodded. Within moments, the discussion ended and Darcy took his leave. In all honesty, the discussion had proceeded much better than he would have thought he had the right to hope for. That Lady Susan would actually sponsor Miss Bennet was a boon he had not thought would be possible to obtain, though her reasons—at least from her point of view—were understandable. They would result in Miss Bennet's entrance into society being accomplished in an easier manner, which Darcy could only welcome.

The next day Darcy left for Hertfordshire in the company of the Bingleys, and though he had hoped to depart with Bingley as they had intended, Mr. Hurst and his wife decided not to accompany them as they had originally planned due to some indisposition of Mrs. Hurst.

"I apologize, Darcy," said Bingley when Darcy arrived at Bingley's townhouse to retrieve man, "but I cannot leave Caroline to travel by herself in my coach. I know this is not what you wished, but unless I forbid her from coming, I do not see any other choice."

"Do not concern yourself, Bingley," said Darcy, though he wished to do anything other than travel in a small space with Caroline Bingley. "I fully understand."

Though he might have expected Miss Bingley to wish to make a grand entrance—and somehow such a desire usually coincided with being late, in Darcy's experience—she actually came down only minutes before Darcy had initially intended to depart. The exasperated looks she directed at her brother led Darcy to believe he had presented her with an ultimatum and would likely have left her behind had she not arrived as planned.

"So good of you to join us, Caroline," said Bingley upon espying his sister. "We were about to depart, thinking that you had changed your mind about accompanying us."

Miss Bingley's eyes darted to Darcy, but she contented herself with a sniff and curtly spoke: "Of course, I wish to accompany you, Charles. Otherwise, you would have no hostess."

"Indeed," replied Bingley. "Now, if you will board the carriage, we shall be on our way."

The three travelers were soon in the carriage, which made its way through the busy London streets, followed by the Bingley carriage carrying the rest of their luggage and the servants. The morning was cold and clear, and the travelers huddled under blankets, warm bricks by their feet to help ward off the chill. Darcy's carriage driver, a man of many years' experience, deftly directed the carriage through the narrow streets, and they were soon beyond the borders of the great city on their way to Hertfordshire.

But what might have otherwise been a pleasant journey was ruined by Miss Bingley, as she seemed to believe it necessary to speak the entire distance. She spoke of many things: her experiences traveling, how she despised winter, what she would do to make her brother's estate habitable in the wilderness, and just about anything else which crossed her mind. Darcy might almost have thought Aunt Catherine was sitting across from him, for she spoke at great length and rarely required a response.

Darcy bore it with patience, choosing the simple expedient of ignoring her, while trying to appear as if he was listening. He thought she was attempting to impress him with the breadth of her knowledge and skills, for much of what she said carried a hint of self-aggrandizement. Darcy, however, did not hear one word in ten, for he was often engaged in watching the surrounding countryside or in pleasant recollections about Miss Bennet.

For his part, Bingley seemed to be exasperated by his sister's behavior, and he tried several times to halt her constant words. Miss Bingley, however, merely listened to him when he spoke and then continued on, often without even breaking her train of thought.

It was about two hours into their journey when it changed for the better. They had stopped at an inn to refresh themselves, and when they had once again embarked, Miss Bingley set off on her unending commentary yet again. But this time her remarks were more pointed, and it was not long before it was obvious that she was attempting to disparage Miss Bennet.

"I shall do what I can to improve the house, Charles," said she, after enumerating the disadvantages she expected to see upon their arrival. "Unfortunately, I do not know what can be done when I expect the entire area to be no less than savage. I cannot imagine why you took the lease on such an unsuitable estate in the first place."

"How is it unsuitable?" asked Bingley, clearly annoyed by his sister's harping. "Perhaps you should wait until we arrive before you pass judgment. It is a good house, and the terms are favorable."

Miss Bingley sniffed. "I suppose such a situation is to be desired, and perhaps the house will be passable after all. Still, it will need to be improved upon, I am absolutely certain."

"I doubt I can be induced to make many changes at all, Caroline," said Bingley. "It would not do to make substantial changes, only to decide in the end not to purchase."

"But, Charles," said Miss Bingley with a horrified gasp, "you must make changes. We . . . we must do what we can to make our guests' stays as comfortable as possible."

Forced to turn away in disgust, Darcy considered the woman's desire to present herself as an attractive option as a wife. She was inferior to Miss Bennet in so many ways that Darcy could not even recite them all. It was fortunate for Miss Bingley that he was too much the gentleman to relate those reasons directly to her.

"And yet I am unmoved," said Bingley. "As I said, I have toured the house, and it is in need of little updating, not that I would agree to such expenditures anyway. I am certain Darcy will be comfortable in his room, even if the wallpaper is two years out of date."

"You need not concern yourself for me, Miss Bingley," said Darcy, feeling it incumbent upon himself to support his friend. "From everything your brother has said of Netherfield, I believe it is a very good property for him, and he only speaks sense about not updating the interior."

Miss Bingley huffed at their united front against her, but she said nothing further on the subject. Instead, she turned her attention—and the razor edge of her tongue—on the inhabitants she had never met.

"If you insist, Charles. I suppose it will be lost on the savages of such a town regardless. I doubt any of them would understand true elegance, as I am completely certain none of them have any taste whatsoever."

"And I will restate," said Bingley. "It might be best to wait until you are introduced to make any judgments upon our new neighbors."

"On this matter I am absolutely certain. After all we have already had an . . . example of what to expect from those of the area, and I am certain it is an accurate portrait. I expect nothing less from the society as a whole."

Knowing exactly to whom she was referring, Darcy was ready to deliver a stinging set down to the woman, but Bingley spoke first.

"That is enough, Caroline!"

Blushing at being called to order, Miss Bingley nevertheless glared back at her brother, assaulting him with a mulish scowl. To say it had no effect on Bingley was an understatement.

"Do not speak about that which you have no knowledge. And remember, the one member of Meryton society whose likeness we have already taken has shown impeccable manners, and I am very fond of her. Furthermore, you should remember that she was born to a gentleman and was raised to that society, while we have only recently risen to it."

Though coloring with fury, Miss Bingley was nevertheless induced to be silent by her brother's implacable glare. She huffed again and turned her attention to the window, sulking for the rest of the journey. Needless to say, it was the most pleasant two hours Darcy had ever spent in the woman's company.

Chapter XXI

It was in the afternoon of the day of Mr. Darcy and Mr. Bingley's arrival from London that the gentlemen came to Longbourn, and though Elizabeth still considered the matter of Mr. Darcy being introduced to her mother with some trepidation, she was happy to see him nonetheless.

Upon being escorted into the room by Mrs. Hill, Mr. Darcy approached Elizabeth, who had risen to greet him, and he bowed over her hand, kissing it in a fashion which left her with butterflies fluttering in her midsection. When he rose, the smile he bestowed upon her told Elizabeth that he was as happy to see her as she was to see him. The knowledge put her a little more at ease.

"Miss Bennet," said Mr. Darcy, "it seems like an age since I last saw you. How do you do?"

"I do very well, Mr. Darcy," said Elizabeth. "But I must warn you, sir, that here I am merely 'Miss Elizabeth.' My sister claims the title 'Miss Bennet.'"

"That will not do at all," said Mr. Darcy, a twinkle in his eye showing his pleasure. "I have become accustomed to referring to you as 'Miss Bennet,' and I am not sure I will remember the change."

"Teasing man!" said Elizabeth, laughing a little at his silliness. "I am afraid there is nothing to be done. You would not wish to disrespect my sister, would you?"

"No, indeed not." Mr. Darcy paused, making a great show of thinking the matter over. "I suppose I can be induced to call you 'Miss Elizabeth,' if that is what is required. However, I believe that on the whole, I would prefer to simply call you 'Elizabeth.'"

Feeling bashful, Elizabeth nevertheless looked at him boldly, saying: "I do not believe that is completely proper, sir. We are not engaged."

"Yet," said Mr. Darcy, his earnest gaze fixed upon her. "But on this I will not insist, though I would appreciate it when we are alone."

"That would be acceptable, sir."

Mr. Darcy gazed at her, expectation in his manner. "Shall you not also call me 'William?'?"

Elizabeth nodded. "But only when we are alone."

"Thank you."

"Elizabeth!" exclaimed Mrs. Bennet in that moment. "Shall you not introduce your suitor to the rest of the family?"

The manic quality of Mrs. Bennet's tone alerted Elizabeth to the fact that she had overheard some of Elizabeth's conversation with Mr. Darcy, though Elizabeth thought she likely had not heard the last few comments, as they had been speaking quietly. Mr. Bingley was standing awkwardly behind Mr. Darcy, waiting for introductions, and a glance in Mr. Darcy's—*William's*—direction revealed his amusement at the situation.

"Of course, Mama," said Elizabeth, and she proceeded to present each of those not known to one another.

That task accomplished, the company sat down, and Mrs. Bennet sent for tea. It soon became clear to Elizabeth that Mrs. Bennet was in awe of her suitor, for other than a few words of welcome, she was uncharacteristically silent for much of the first few minutes after the gentleman's arrival. That did not stop the rest of the company from being animated in conversation, but as Kitty and Lydia were largely occupied by giggling together in a corner in quiet voices, Elizabeth was content that her family was on reasonably good behavior that day.

"I trust your return home has been everything you anticipated, Miss Elizabeth?"

Elizabeth turned from her contemplation of the room, noting with amusement how William had used her title instead of only her name. "It has been . . . interesting," replied Elizabeth, thinking of the happiness at once again being with her family, tempered by her mother's improper statements and the situation with Pearce.

That last thought brought a grimace to Elizabeth's face, which she was not quite successful in suppressing. She was not surprised when William noticed it, perceptive as he was.

"Has it been a trial?" asked he, lowering his voice so they could speak more privately.

"In some ways, Mr. Darcy. I missed my family, and I wished to see them again, but there have been times when I longed to be back in London."

"I understand, Miss Elizabeth. There were times when I wished we were together without the influence of any others. In fact . . ."

William's voice trailed off and this time it was his turn to grimace.

"Yes, sir?" asked Elizabeth. In a tone filled with humor, she continued: "Can I assume from your frown that you told your uncle about our courtship?"

"Indeed, I have, Miss Elizabeth," said William with a sigh. "I will not attempt to claim he was happy to hear the news, but to be honest, the revelation turned out to be more of a success than I had thought possible."

"How so?" asked Elizabeth, intrigued.

William shared the story of his uncle's reaction, along with the surprising offer by his aunt to sponsor her in society. This, along with Lady Catherine's own support, was obviously a boon which he had never expected to receive.

"I believe I shall endeavor to interpret it as a good omen," said Elizabeth. "Perhaps my introduction to your society would be smoother than we had hoped for."

"If society has any sense at all, they will accept you for what you are—a lovely, vibrant young woman."

Elizabeth blushed at the praise, but she was able to direct a smile at her suitor in thanks. Their conversation continued for some minutes, speaking of smaller doings they had undertaken in the past several days, until a chance remark brought Mr. Pearce's visit to William's attention. Elizabeth had meant to inform him, but she had thought to do it in a more circumspect fashion. William was clearly angered by the man's continued presumption.

"Your father has barred him from the estate?"

"He has," said Elizabeth. "I do not doubt that we have seen the last of Mr. Pearce at Longbourn, though I expect he will show up at other functions of the neighborhood. In fact, there is an assembly early next week at which I expect we shall see him."

A scowl came over her suitor's face. "I believe I shall be required to speak with this Pearce fellow. He seems unable to understand the reality of the situation."

"Oh, Mr. Darcy," said Elizabeth, laying a hand on his arm, "I am not afraid of Winston Pearce. I do not go out without Jack's escort, and since Pearce is barred from Longbourn, I believe there is little danger."

"That may be," said William, "but I cannot allow him to continue to importune you. The man is obsessed, and he must be induced to let go of this obsession."

Knowing there was little she could do concerning the matter, Elizabeth conceded William's right to confront the man, but she elicited a promise from him to wait until the assembly—she did not think it would be wise for him to approach Pearce at his estate, especially when he was angry.

They continued to speak of other things for the next several minutes, and Elizabeth could only reflect with happiness that their previous camaraderie seemed to have been little diminished by their separation. William was as attentive a suitor as he had ever been, and Elizabeth was able to speak to him with their former ease. With her family seemingly on their best behavior, she found that she had nothing to repine.

Unfortunately, and perhaps not unforeseen, such complacency was not to last, as the longer the company continued in the sitting-room, the more vocal Mrs. Bennet became. The first indication Elizabeth heard of her mother's growing volubility only flitted along the edges of her consciousness, and as she and Darcy were engaged in close conversation, she paid it no mind. However, it was not long before Elizabeth was forced from her conversation in favor of listening in growing horror as her mother's comments became more outrageous.

"Oh, Mr. Bingley, we are very glad to make your acquaintance! It is very fortunate indeed that you have taken the lease at Netherfield. I am sure you and Mr. Darcy will add much elegance to the gatherings of the area."

"My sister is also come to stay with us," said Mr. Bingley. "She was fatigued from traveling, but I am hoping to be able to introduce you as soon as may be."

"We would be quite happy to make her acquaintance!"

Having said this, Elizabeth, though vexed with her mother's loud exclamations, could not help but notice that Mr. Bingley, as soon as he finished speaking with Mrs. Bennet, turned his attention back to Jane, beside whom he was sitting. Elizabeth watched with a critical eye as their conversation, though quiet, focused entirely on each other, also noting Mr. Bingley's happy countenance and Jane's more modest one. The light in her eyes, however, told Elizabeth that her sister was not averse to the man's presence. A contented smile settled over her face as she watched them.

"What amuses you, Miss Elizabeth?" asked Mr. Darcy.

Elizabeth turned back to him and indicated her sister. "I have long suspected that Mr. Bingley and Jane would be well suited should they ever meet. What I am seeing seems to bear that out."

While Darcy's eyes flicked to the two Elizabeth had indicated, his attention was soon fixed again on Elizabeth. "Then I am happy for them. But I believe I will leave them to it, as I have a much more pleasurable lady to contemplate."

Blushing, Elizabeth thanked him with as much composure as she possessed and, in a voice almost firm, indicated her own happiness to be the subject of his attentions. And so they might have continued, had her mother's voice not interrupted them.

"See, Lydia!" cried Mrs. Bennet to her youngest, who was by no means close to her. "I knew that Lizzy's courtship with Mr. Darcy would throw you all in the path of other wealthy men. It is already happening!"

Her unsubtle allusion was in no way difficult for anyone in the room to understand, and though Lydia—mercifully—only giggled with Kitty, Mr. Bingley, though still cheerful, was taken aback by her comment.

"Actually, Mrs. Bennet, I am you brother's business partner, and I have only known Darcy for less than a month."

"And we are happy to have you, sir! Your coming with Mr. Darcy gives us the greatest of pleasure!"

Her smug leer in the direction of her eldest left nothing to the imagination as to what her expectation consisted of. Mr. Bingley, however, in the manner of a truly well-bred man, only ignored her words, choosing to focus back on Jane instead. And for her part, though Jane's cheeks were rosy, she happily immersed herself once again in conversation with Mr. Bingley.

As the visit ended and the gentlemen rose to leave, Mrs. Bennet stood up with them and invited them to dinner the following day. "For having just arrived yourselves, it must be difficult to put the house in order enough to have things the way you wish them. If you would allow it, we would be happy to take this burden from you for one night at least."

The invitation was quite generous, but Elizabeth knew without a doubt her mother's primary goal with it was to ensure her daughters stayed firmly within the sights of their suitors. Elizabeth also had no doubt that Mrs. Bennet already considered Mr. Bingley to be Jane's suitor.

"I believe we can accept, Mrs. Bennet," said William, speaking for them both. "As we have just arrived, I am sure we have no other engagements."

"Wonderful!" exclaimed Mrs. Bennet. "I can promise you at least three courses, as Longbourn's cook is quite the most gifted of any in the area. I cannot wait to see you both again."

It was a few moments before the gentlemen were able to extricate themselves from Mrs. Bennet's continued effusions on the subject in order to leave. But before they were able to escape, Mrs. Bennet commanded her two eldest daughters to see the gentlemen to the door.

Cheeks burning with shame, Elizabeth led William back to the entrance, wondering if he would ever wish to return, given her mother's behavior. He said nothing during the short walk and Elizabeth did not dare to look at him. The only words they exchanged were the words of farewell when William left, along with a kiss to her hand, as had become his custom. Elizabeth watched him go, wondering what he was thinking. She could readily imagine.

If Elizabeth had been able to see into Darcy's thoughts at that very moment, she would have found, in some ways, thoughts very like what she would have expected.

Darcy had hardly been insulated from poor behavior. There were many among society who did not possess impeccable manners, and though Darcy would readily confess to being biased, it seemed like improper matchmaking mamas were rife in society. It was not unusual for a woman to throw her offspring at him in hopes that he would take a liking to them, and more than once he had been the target of attempted compromise.

But even considering all this, one thing he had never before witnessed was a woman who was as overtly improper as Mrs. Bennet. Elizabeth had prepared him for the meeting with her mother, but the scope of the woman's behavior was so far beyond what he had expected to find.

But contrary to what Elizabeth feared, there was no thought or inclination on Darcy's part to end his courtship with her. Had the thought actually occurred to Darcy, he would have put such a notion aside in an instant. Whatever her mother was, Elizabeth was a gem of the first order, and Darcy could not imagine being released from his obligation. It was not even a duty any longer—he was becoming convinced that she was the only woman in the world who could make him happy, and he was not foolish enough to give that up.

But her mother was an embarrassment who would reflect poorly on them in society should her behavior ever be witnessed, and, as such,

Darcy was considering what might be done to distance themselves from the Bennets. The eldest daughter was acceptable, if reticent, and though Darcy was not impressed with the way the man had avoided his duty with respect to his family, Mr. Bennet's behavior was adequate as well. Miss Mary, the third child, was quiet, and Darcy did not have an opinion of her, though he supposed next to the mother's behavior that was a good sign. The two youngest, though, would need much refinement before they would be ready to be seen in London society, and given the woman already had grown children of her own, Darcy did not think there was much hope for the Bennet matron. Avoidance in any situation in which they might be seen together in society seemed to be the best option, else the woman would undoubtedly draw attention, which would reflect on the Darcys and, by extension, the Fitzwilliams.

"I say, Darcy," said Bingley, pulling Darcy from his thoughts. "That was a pleasant half hour, was it not?"

"Indeed it was," said Darcy, thinking that the time he had spent in conversation with Elizabeth had certainly been pleasant.

"I dare say I have rarely met pleasanter people. And though Miss Elizabeth had spoken to me before about her eldest sister, I must say that the reality is far beyond anything I had expected. The woman is a veritable angel!"

Startled by the man's sudden declaration, Darcy peered at Bingley, wondering at his seeming infatuation with the eldest Miss Bennet, and after nothing more than a single meeting, no less!

"She *is* very beautiful," said Darcy, attempting to prompt a response from Bingley.

"She is!" exclaimed Bingley. "I cannot imagine a more beautiful or a more graceful girl!" Bingley stopped a little, and he looked at Darcy a little hesitantly. "I believe I mentioned that I had considered pursuing Miss Elizabeth."

Darcy nodded, and Bingley continued: "I am now happy that I did not do so, as I find her sister much more to my taste, though Miss Elizabeth is a wonderful girl, of course."

Frowning, Darcy took in his new friend's slightly dreamy smile and the fact that his eyes were unfocused, seemingly back at Longbourn with his angel.

"She seems to be everything lovely, but you have only met her once."

Bingley laughed. "And did not you approach a young woman you had never before met to learn of her and ultimately propose a courtship with her?"

Laughing, Darcy was forced to acknowledge the hit.

"Do not worry, Darcy," said Bingley. "You may save the elder brother speech; I am impressed with Miss Bennet, but I know I need to come to know her better before I can determine whether I want more. I shall not act precipitously."

"See that you do not," replied Darcy sternly, though Bingley's laugh suggested the man had seen through his stern persona. "The woman will become my sister before long, and I would not wish to call you out."

Again Bingley laughed. "I think you have revealed more of your intentions than you might have wished."

"Did you doubt me?"

"No, my friend, I did not. I believe I have enough of your measure by now to know that you are committed to Miss Elizabeth. And a good choice, I say!"

"Thank you, Bingley."

The gleam in Bingley's eye told Darcy his friend was amused about something, and his next words confirmed that fact. "Now all we need to do is make certain your *other* suitor does not intrude upon your courtship!"

At Darcy's grimace, his friend laughed louder and harder.

"If she becomes a nuisance, please make me aware of it," said Bingley after his laughter had settled. "I have the option of returning her to London if necessary."

"I would not wish to be the reason your sister is banished."

"I do not think you would be the reason, Darcy." All levity was gone from Bingley's countenance. "I love Caroline, Darcy, but she has developed some unlikely aspirations for her future, and I cannot ignore her behavior. I have told her to cease importuning you and your sister, but she is headstrong, and I doubt her ambitions are at an end."

"I never believed they were for a moment, Bingley," said Darcy quietly.

Soon they had arrived at Netherfield and the gentlemen debarked from the carriage and went to their own rooms to refresh themselves. Darcy seized on the opportunity to stay in his rooms and write a few letters before his presence was required at dinner.

When he gathered with his host and hostess that evening, Darcy was reminded of just why his friend had made those comments about his sister. It was past the dinner hour when Miss Bingley finally breezed into the sitting-room.

"I believe it is time to test whether the cook on this estate is adequate."

"The time was actually fifteen minutes past," said Charles, looking at his sister pointedly. "Let us go in now."

"Of course, Charles," said Miss Bingley with blithe unconcern.

She then turned to Darcy, looking at him with expectation in her eyes, knowing she had a captive audience, and it would be his duty to escort her into the room.

He was saved by Bingley, however, who approached his sister and said: "Come, Caroline. I shall escort you into the room."

The woman looked at her brother with barely concealed annoyance, but she relented and put her hand on his arm, allowing herself to be led into the dining room. Bingley led them to the smaller dining room where the table had been modified to allow for a small party. There, Bingley sat his sister at the foot of the table, while he sat at the other end, allowing Darcy to take the seat in the middle. The dinner started off quietly enough, as the diners concentrated on the food which had been placed in front of them. Contrary to Miss Bingley's assertions, Darcy could not find anything wrong with the fare—it appeared Netherfield's cook had some skill.

"I understand you visited the Bennet estate today," said Miss Bingley, breaking the silence. "I suppose it was as charming as Miss Bennet herself?"

"In fact, I found it quite charming," said Bingley, clearly understanding the undertone in his sister's words. "Inasmuch as I am qualified to speak of such things, I thought the estate was agreeable and the inhabitants everything obliging. What say you, Darcy?"

"Longbourn is well maintained and prosperous indeed," replied Darcy. "I could detect no deficiency."

"I believe you would like some of those in residence very well indeed, Caroline," continued Bingley. "Miss Bennet, the eldest sister, is a lovely young woman."

Miss Bingley's eyes darted to Bingley at that statement, and Darcy could not help but wonder the reason for it. Whatever it meant, her eyes narrowed, and she seemed to be considering saying something further. In the end, she contented herself with sniffing in disdain.

"A young woman you find beautiful. I suppose I should not be surprised."

Coloring slightly, Bingley looked back at his sister, glaring at her and daring her to say anything further, unless Darcy missed his guess. Miss Bingley instead continued to eat her soup, seemingly unaware of her brother's scrutiny.

"Then it is well there is someone who seems to possess a hint of gentility. I cannot imagine we will find much in this backwater part of the kingdom."

Darcy could hardly suppress his urge to sigh. It would be a long stay at this estate, he was certain. For a moment he wondered if he should accept Bingley's offer to have his sister returned to London. Netherfield would be nigh intolerable with her in residence.

But he said nothing. It was not as if Darcy had never been required to put up with the attentions of a determined young woman before. Of course, such determined young women had never had him as a guest in a house which they presided over as mistress.

The days passed and early the next week Elizabeth prepared for the assembly to be held that evening, thinking of the days since William's arrival in Meryton. Though she had wondered if he would withdraw his attentions—and fervently hoped he would not—she had recently begun to breathe a little easier. Though it was clear that he sometimes found Mrs. Bennet's company to be a trial, he seemed to be ignoring her. And as Elizabeth could not but own to her own opinion of her mother's behavior, it was something she could live with easily.

They met in several forums in those days; the gentlemen visited Longbourn nearly every day—once in the company of Miss Bingley, though the woman stayed away every other time—and they met at church on Sunday. Even the dinner at Longbourn the day after their arrival passed by with very little incident. Elizabeth could not repine their interactions, and she thought their courtship was proceeding well.

The assembly would be a different kind of test. Elizabeth had always known that William was not comfortable in company with those with whom he was not well acquainted. The assembly that evening would be well attended, in no small part due to Mrs. Bennet's crowing about Elizabeth catching such an important man. William, as a gentleman, would be expected to perform his duty and dance with the young women of the neighborhood. Elizabeth could barely wait to dance with her suitor, as she had never before had the opportunity.

When the Bennet party arrived at the assembly hall, Elizabeth quickly determined that the Netherfield party had not yet arrived. She spent the time waiting for his arrival, speaking with those of the area she still had not met since her return. Before long, she found herself in Charlotte's company, and they stood talking for some time

"I have to hand it to you, Eliza," said Charlotte. Elizabeth could feel the force of her friend's mirth as she spoke. "You were banished from your home when you refused to marry an eligible suitor, but then you return in triumph not four months later, a new suitor of greater consequence in tow. I cannot think of anyone else of my acquaintance who might have accomplished such a feat!"

Elizabeth blushed and looked at her friend with exasperation. "I did not plan it that way, Charlotte!" protested she.

"I know," was Charlotte's smug reply. "That is what makes it so much more impressive. Can I assume that you are happy with Mr. Darcy as a suitor?"

Feeling suddenly bashful, Elizabeth directed a shy smile at her friend. "I cannot imagine I could be happier, Charlotte. Mr. Darcy is everything a suitor ought to be."

"And, by all accounts, he is quite wealthy too," said Charlotte, directing a grin at her friend."

"Charlotte! You know that is the least important category."

"Oh, I am not certain of that, Elizabeth. After all, if you wed a man with nothing, you would have nothing. Great wealth is perhaps not a requirement, but you must take some thought for the man's prospects so you may be able to raise your family without fear."

Forced to confess her friend was right, Elizabeth nevertheless said: "Yes, Mr. Darcy is wealthy, and I am happy for that fact. But his character is above reproach, and I know that should I marry him, he shall always uphold his duties—I shall never be required to worry on that score.

"Furthermore, I believe that he will only propose if he is convinced of his love for me and mine for him. In my estimation, that is far more important than all the diamonds in the world."

"I dare say that for your disposition, that is quite correct," said Charlotte, looking at Elizabeth with happiness. "Personally, I would be happy with a man of good character who would provide for me."

"A man of good character could not help but love you, Charlotte," said Elizabeth.

"Perhaps," said Charlotte with a coy smile.

Before their conversation could proceed any further, a young man, approximately Mr. Darcy's age, approached and bowed before the ladies. "Miss Lucas," said he, "may I request an introduction to this young lady?"

"Of course, Mr. Grady."

Charlotte performed the duty and the three fell into conversation. Elizabeth could immediately see that Mr. Grady paid far more attention to Charlotte than to Elizabeth, and Elizabeth had the delight of seeing her friend blush. Clearly this was gossip of which she had not been apprised, for Charlotte had not spoken of him when they had met since Elizabeth's return.

Feeling lighter than she could remember, Elizabeth soon excused herself—noting that the other two hardly noticed her departure—and went in search of her elder sister. It was then she noticed that the Netherfield party had arrived.

Miss Bingley—to whom Elizabeth felt she must attribute the party's lateness—stood by the door looking out on all and sundry with barely concealed contempt. The gentlemen, however, had moved into the room, Mr. Bingley heading directly toward Jane, Elizabeth noted, while Mr. Darcy had caught sight of Elizabeth and was even now approaching her.

He stepped up to her and greeted her as was his wont, his smiling face showing his pleasure at their meeting.

"Miss Bennet, might I say that you are enchanting tonight?"

"You certainly might, sir," said Elizabeth, "though with my sister in attendance, I wonder if you require spectacles."

His gaze never wavering, William once again raised her hand to his lips, looking at her intently all the time. "I find I must disagree with you. Your sister is a beautiful woman, it is true, but I must confess that in my opinion, she does not hold a candle to you. You are positively radiant, and I shall not hear anything to the contrary."

Blushing, Elizabeth thanked him for his words, knowing that he meant every one of them. But as the conversation was uncomfortable, Elizabeth directed it to other subjects.

"I believe you have arrived just in time, sir. The first dance shall begin within the next few moments."

William scowled. "It was, as I am certain you already apprehend, due to Miss Bingley that we are late. I would rather have been here fifteen minutes ago. I do not doubt she wished to deny me the pleasure of the first dance with you."

"Then I would have had to sit it out, sir," said Elizabeth with an impish smile. "For I have not been asked by another, though I was certain I would have had to turn down several offers by now."

"I do not find that to be a surprise at all. You are known to be courting, and anyone who has seen us must understand how besotted I am. That is almost certainly why you have not received any solicitations."

"How did you finally manage to induce Miss Bingley to allow your presence before the first dance?" asked Elizabeth, her voice a little strained yet again.

"Bingley took the simple expedient of informing her maid that we would leave if she was not down directly. It seems she would prefer to be here, most likely to watch us and spin her webs, than miss the evening altogether, though she has termed it a 'tedious affair' more than once."

Elizabeth laughed. "Well played, sir! I can well imagine how she scurried down the stairs when presented with Mr. Bingley's ultimatum."

William's smile was positively feral. "It *was* amusing, Miss Bennet. Though perhaps I should not laugh at the lady, she is eminently deserving."

The musicians began playing the opening bars of the first dance at that moment, and William gestured to the floor, taking Elizabeth's hand and leading her there. Within moments, the dance started and they began the steps.

For a man who claimed he was not at all inclined to dance, William was light on his feet and possessed all the skills worthy of being called accomplished at it. When they came together, he held her hand lightly in his grasp, yet gently cradled it, and when they separated, his glances in her direction told Elizabeth that he wished for nothing more than to once again be taking her hand. It was the most enjoyable half hour Elizabeth had ever spent on the dance floor.

Their conversation, when their proximity in the dance allowed, was lively and carefree, with very little of substance said. But for all that, it was engaging, and Elizabeth was happy they were so comfortable in each other's company.

At one point in the second set, she happened to look over at the side of the dance floor to see Miss Bingley spearing her with an angry glare, her envy telling Elizabeth the woman wished to be in her position. But then the woman's angry gaze shifted to another part of the floor, and she noted the woman's scrutiny of Jane, where she was dancing with Mr. Bingley. The very sight caused Elizabeth to laugh with delight—it seemed the woman had detected Mr. Bingley's interest in Jane, which Elizabeth had known of since their first meeting.

At length, the dance ended, and William escorted Elizabeth to the side of the dance floor. There she noticed Mary, who was sitting to the side not far from her mother. Knowing she usually had little opportunity to dance, Elizabeth turned to her companion and arched an eyebrow at him.

"Are you determined to make a good impression on the company tonight, Mr. Darcy?"

A slight smile graced his face. "I would suspend no pleasure of yours, Miss Bennet. Though I am not the most sociable of men, as you well know, I am more than happy to pay the required deference to your friends."

"I am engaged to dance the second with Mr. Lucas, who is my good friend's brother. Would you be so good as to ask my sister Mary to dance?" Elizabeth leaned in a little closer, and in a tone which she was certain would not be overheard, said: "She is often forced to sit out, in part due to her own reticent personality, but also because she is not perceived to be as pretty as her sisters."

William's eyes moved to where Mary was sitting, and he studied her for a moment. "Though you are well aware that I cannot consider her to be your equal, I can find no criticism for your sister's appearance. Her hair is perhaps styled in a severe style, but she seems to be a pretty sort of girl."

Elizabeth sighed. "If only she would understand that. My . . . My mother's words on the subject do not help, and like I said, Mary is not truly interested in the dance, though I believe she could enjoy herself more if she had the chance."

"Shall we change her fortunes for this evening?" asked William, looking at her with what could only be deemed determination. "I, too, do not take much pleasure in a dance, so perhaps we shall have something to discuss."

A laugh escaped Elizabeth's lips. "I wish for her to *enjoy* herself, William, not speak about a mutual distaste for the activity."

"I shall not dissuade her, Miss Bennet," said William. "I shall do my best to be an agreeable partner and allow only a few words of censure for such a tedious activity to escape my lips."

Laughing again, Elizabeth was forced to separate from him at that moment, as Samuel Lucas appeared to claim his set. But Elizabeth had the pleasure of seeing William approach Mary and request her hand, and unless she was very much mistaken, Mr. Bingley solicited her hand for the third set. Though Mary's response was hesitant, it was clear she was at least a little flattered to be asked by two such handsome men. Elizabeth was well enough content.

Thus began Elizabeth's night, and it was a most pleasurable night indeed. Being a social creature, Elizabeth enjoyed her succession of partners and dances, and most of those with whom she danced she had known all of her life. She was even asked to dance with Mr. Grady, and though the focus of his conversation was Charlotte, Elizabeth was well entertained relating some anecdotes of her friend's childhood. She finished that set full of hope for her friend's future. Charlotte had reached the age where she feared that she would never marry, and Elizabeth was happy that there was some man in the world who could see for himself just what a gem her friend was.

When the evening had progressed until it was quite late, Elizabeth found herself standing by the dance floor, watching the dancers as they moved through the forms. She had sat out that dance due to the scarcity of young men, which was actually no hardship, as it allowed her to rest her feet. She was happy with William's efforts to perform his duties—he had not danced every set by any means, but he had danced with both of her sisters, Charlotte, Miss Bingley, and one or two other ladies of the area. He was dancing with Charlotte at present, and she had no doubt that he would soon join her once his duty was complete.

"Miss Elizabeth Bennet."

The sound of her name startled Elizabeth, and she turned her head to see the implacable glare of Mr. Winston Pearce boring through her. She had not seen the man at all that evening, and she had begun to believe that he had decided not to attend. Wherever he had been hiding, he was here now, though Elizabeth was little inclined to speak to him.

"Mr. Pearce," replied she, with stiffness of manner and haughtiness of tone.

Her erstwhile and unwelcome suitor favored her with a slight smile at her response. "You seem to be taking on the characteristics of a woman of high society, my dear. It seems you truly were aiming for a much higher match than what I could provide for you."

"You think that, sir," said Elizabeth "if it gives you comfort. If you tell it to yourself enough, you might even begin to believe it."

"You are uniformly charming, my dear."

"Am I?" asked Elizabeth with feigned amazement. "It must be a talent I possess, for I was not intending to be charming. And I would ask you to desist from calling me 'my dear.' I am not *your* anything."

"Perhaps," said Mr. Pearce, clearly unmoved by her disdain. "At present, however, I wish to be your partner for a dance. Surely your next set is open."

"Why would I wish to dance with you, of all people?"

"Because I know you like to dance, and if you do not, you must sit out the rest of the evening."

"It would be better to sit out than to be forced to dance with you."

A little exasperation began to show through his carefully maintained façade. "Can you not be polite, Miss Bennet? *I* am the rejected suitor. Come, I am assured that you are not engaged for the next set."

"She *is* engaged for the next set."

Elizabeth had been so focused on Mr. Pearce that she had not even seen William's approach. She turned with surprise, noting his displeasure in the set of his jaw and his narrowed eyes.

"And who might you be, sir?" asked Mr. Pearce, though Elizabeth was certain he already knew exactly who William was.

"Fitzwilliam Darcy," replied William, though he offered nary a hint of a bow to the other man. "Given you are accosting the woman I am courting, I must assume your name to be Pearce."

"It seems your *suitor* has the advantage of me, my dear," said Mr. Pearce, turning back to Elizabeth. "Given what I know of your portion and your family, I might wonder what allurements you employed in an effort to avoid my proposal."

William's visage darkened in affront, but before he could reply, Mr. Pearce continued: "Come, Miss Bennet, I have asked for nothing more than a dance. Call it a taste of what I have been denied, if you will."

"I will not allow it," declared William, and he stepped forward and looked Mr. Pearce directly in the eye. The relative disparity in height alone suggested that Mr. Pearce would be intimidated, but if he was, he gave no indication of it.

"Given the way you have behaved, I will not allow Elizabeth to dance with you."

Mr. Pearce raised an eyebrow at William. "Are you her owner, sir?"

"No, but I shall soon be her fiancé. If you would prefer, I can have Mr. Bennet second my stricture, little though I think it necessary.

"Furthermore, *sir,* if you so much as breathe such words of disparagement concerning Miss Bennet's character again, I shall call you out. Stay away from her."

A chuckle was Mr. Pearce's response. "All I see before me is a young pup who thinks he can intimidate me and claim the woman I had already singled out."

"You may believe what you wish to believe. But do not come near to Miss Bennet again. I will most assuredly make certain you regret it if you do so."

And with that, William turned away from Mr. Pearce and, gathering Elizabeth's hand, led her away from her tormentor. As they were walking, Elizabeth noted they had drawn a crowd. Mr. Pearce seemed to realize it too, given his scowl at those who were looking and whispering. He turned and left the room, and Elizabeth hoped the man had left the hall altogether.

"That was perhaps a little high-handed, sir," said Elizabeth. Her feelings were complex—on the one hand, she was a little annoyed that he had taken the confrontation into his own hands, when she had been handling the man herself. On the other hand, she was thrilled that she would have a protector. She need never worry about being imposed upon by the Pearces of the world.

"I suppose you might consider it to be so," replied William, not at all appearing contrite for his actions. "But I will not allow that man to continue to impose upon you when it is in my power to prevent it."

Elizabeth smiled, amused that William's words were such an echo of her own thoughts.

"As long as you remember that I am no helpless female, running to hide behind a man at the first sign of trouble, we shall get on famously, sir."

Her words brought a hint of levity to their conversation, and William looked on her with affection. "I am sure I do not consider you to be such a female, Miss Bennet. I shall surely endeavor to recall your intrepidity of character, lest your sharp tongue be turned upon me."

Elizabeth laughed gaily.

As the night progressed, Darcy began to feel more at ease, not least of all as Pearce seemed to have taken the hint and departed from the assembly hall. Darcy was not certain that was the case, but as he did not see the man again, he was content. Even ignoring the charges which Elizabeth had leveled at the man, Darcy, on his first meeting, felt Pearce to be somewhat ill-favored and far prouder than he had any right to be. Darcy hoped rather than believed that he would desist in his doomed attentions.

Another issue soon intruded upon Darcy's notice, however, and it was not long before he began to witness it with some concern. Darcy had no great opinion of Mrs. Bennet, not only because she was a silly woman, but also because he had seen her speak criticisms and other such nonsense about Elizabeth. Why Mr. Bennet would merely watch her, as if she was the side show at some circus, was beyond Darcy. That evening Mrs. Bennet seemed to over imbibe in the punch which was served on a side table, and the longer the evening became, the sillier she became, *and* the less inhibited. Before long, she was speaking with her cronies in a loud voice, completely insensible to how her words were embarrassing her daughters.

"My eldest girls shall marry men of good fortune," slurred she after the last set came to an end, an almost empty glass of punch held, forgotten in one hand. "My worries about how I shall keep myself after Mr. Bennet passes are at an end!"

"As of yet no engagement has been announced," said one of the other ladies, sniffing in what Darcy thought to be envious disdain. "Perhaps you should not count the chickens which have not yet hatched."

"Can you not see them?" demanded Mrs. Bennet, turning to glare at the woman who had questioned her. "Mr. Bingley looks on my Jane as a heavenly being who has descended from on high."

"They have only just met," said another woman. "Surely you cannot be counting on the match already."

"I tell you there will be wedding bells before long. I never doubted for an instant that he would be able to resist her charms."

"What of Mr. Darcy?" asked Lady Lucas—she was the one matron in the room to whom he had been introduced and actually remembered. "By all accounts he is much higher in consequence than Mr. Bingley."

"Oh, Lady Lucas!" gushed Mrs. Bennet. "I never would have suspected Lizzy could have attracted such a man, though I am very happy she has. He has ten thousand a year if he has a farthing. Theirs will be a great match and very advantageous indeed. My only concern is that Lizzy is dragging her heels. I am sure if Jane had been the first to meet Mr. Darcy, she would have him in love with her already and would have induced him to propose by now."

"I do not think I can agree with you, Mrs. Bennet," said another woman. "The way Mr. Darcy looks at Elizabeth . . . I only my husband would look at me that way, even when I was young!"

"Oh, it does not matter! I care not if he waits another six months to propose, as long as he eventually does. Then he can introduce my other girls to his wealthy friends. Once they are all married, I may rest myself—it is not easy marrying five daughters off, you know."

By the time the woman had spoken about her five daughters, Darcy was incensed. The implied insult to Elizabeth, the expectation that he would introduce such an uncouth woman to his acquaintances, the fact that she was as selfish and senseless a woman as he had ever met—these were all enough to make Darcy pledge to never return to Hertfordshire again! And Elizabeth, walking with her hand on his arm, her face as red as a ripe tomato, would undoubtedly be relieved never to lay eyes on the woman again too!

"Oh, there they are!" exclaimed Mrs. Bennet when she caught sight of them. "Mr. Darcy, have you made the acquaintance of all the ladies of the neighborhood? I shall be happy to introduce you!"

Darcy looked at the woman, barely able to hide his disgust, and he nodded, though very shallowly, in her direction and led Elizabeth off toward the vestibule so that they might gather their coats. Truly, the woman was far too much to bear!

As they walked away, Darcy could hear the women carrying on behind them, particularly Mrs. Bennet's loudly spoken, "Well, I never!"

"It serves you right, Maggie. I would not wonder why the man did not wish to speak with you, the way you were carrying on."

When they reached the coat room, Darcy looked around for Elizabeth's pelisse and was surprised when she wrenched her hand from his arm and stood staring at him, foot tapping on the floor, her eyes almost impaling him with her displeasure.

"Just what was that, Mr. Darcy?"

"What was what?" asked Mr. Darcy, confused as to her meaning.

"The fact that you stopped just short of cutting my mother, of course!"

"I did what any other gentleman would do when faced by such ridiculous statements," said Darcy stiffly. "I refrained from responding to such nonsense."

If anything, Elizabeth's glare became even more heated. "It seemed much more like the cut direct to me. How could you presume to treat her that way?"

Darcy was confused, but the emotion was rapidly turning to anger. "How could your mother presume to speak of me—of you!—in such a manner? Were you not embarrassed by her words?"

"Of course I was!" cried Elizabeth. Tears of frustration were starting to leak from the corners of her eyes. "Trust me, sir, I am well aware of my mother's excesses. I have had to live with them for many years now.

"But regardless of what she says, she does not deserve to be cut in such a manner. She loves her daughters and wishes the best for them, despite her inelegant way of showing it."

"And that inelegance is precisely what offends me," said Darcy, his own voice rising in response to hers. "After we are wed, I cannot imagine spending much time in Hertfordshire. The further we are from your mother, the better."

As soon as the words left his mouth, Darcy knew that he should not have said them, and the ashen pallor of Elizabeth's face testified to that fact.

"You would deny me my family?" asked she, her voice trembling a little with emotion.

"Would you wish to continue to see them?" demanded Darcy, the words spilling out without heed or forethought. "Your mother will bring us nothing but censure and embarrassment if she is ever seen in London, and I am sure you already apprehend this. At the least, we should see them infrequently, and never in town where anyone else can witness your mother's behavior."

Elizabeth seemed almost mute for a moment, her wide open eyes betraying her shock. When she finally spoke, he thought she might actually burst into tears.

"As I said before, I am well aware of my mother's character, sir. But regardless of her thoughtlessness, Kitty and Lydia's silliness, my father's distance, or any other deficiency you feel obliged to point out, I love them. They are my family. I cannot imagine marrying a man who would deny me my family."

"I said nothing of the sort," retorted Darcy.

"You did not? I sounded like it to me."

"If I did, it was said for the best. If you wish to make your entrance into London society all that much more difficult, then by all means, invite your mother to host our first ball. I am certain she, along with your giggling sisters, will be successful in drawing all eyes to their antics the instant they enter a ballroom."

There was a brief pause while Elizabeth looked at him, her eyes shining with tears.

"There is as of yet no guarantee that I shall ever *have* a London debut, sir." Her words were cold and distant. "Now, if you will excuse me, I believe it is time for me to return home with my *family*."

She turned and walked away from him, her pelisse forgotten. Darcy watched her go, wondering how it had all unraveled so quickly. In fact, he was not even certain exactly what had happened.

"Very well done, Mr. Darcy," a voice whispered in his ear.

Anger erupted in Darcy's breast, and he turned and looked at Miss Bingley, who had stepped close in behind him. The woman started and actually retreated at the look in his eyes.

"I am afraid I have not the pleasure of understanding you."

Miss Bingley plucked up the courage and said: "I knew you would eventually see through that artful adventuress. Now all we need to do is remove my brother from the clutches of her sister and return to London where we belong."

"I do not *belong* in London," said Darcy, stepping forward and towering over her. "And I have no intention of removing your brother from *anyone's* clutches. I suggest you do not try my patience, Miss Bingley."

And with that, Darcy turned away from her and gathered his great coat, stepping out into the cool December air.

Chapter XXII

The very last thing Darcy wished to do that evening was to listen to Bingley wax eloquently on the subject of Miss Bennet, the charms of his dance partners, or the pleasant nature of the neighborhood and how it all suited him. Unfortunately, that was to be his lot from the time they left the assembly hall to the moment the carriage pulled up in front of Netherfield's front door. Darcy had not the heart to attempt to quiet his voluble friend, as Bingley had truly made a favorable impression on the populace that evening and, more specifically, on his own Miss Bennet.

As for Miss Bingley, the woman was mercifully silent the entire way. It seemed like Darcy's set down in the vestibule of the assembly hall had opened her eyes to more than just the fact that he was courting Miss Bennet, and he thought she was now reconsidering her quest to turn his head in her direction. Hopefully, she now knew he did not think highly of her and would never offer for her.

At length, they arrived at Netherfield, and Darcy was happy to see Miss Bingley immediately enter the house and retire to her rooms for the evening.

"Would you like a nightcap, Darcy?" asked Bingley once they had gained the entry hall.

"I thank you, no," said Darcy. "I would much prefer to seek my bed."

"Ah, I fully understand," said Bingley, slapping Darcy on the back. "And I must agree with you. What better ending to the night than to surrender to dreams of your Miss Bennet!"

And with a final grin, Bingley turned and made his way up the stairs, with Darcy following along behind, albeit more slowly. Perhaps he should be grateful that his altercation with Elizabeth seemed to have gone unnoticed and there would be no gossip. Of course, Bingley's focus on Miss Bennet was such that the man likely would not have noticed if Napoleon and his entire army had passed through the assembly hall. Darcy made a mental note to remind himself to warn Miss Bingley; it would not do for her to spread rumors in the hope of forcing Darcy apart from Elizabeth.

Once he reached the confines of his room, Darcy stopped and took in his surroundings, noting the fine furniture, the wallpaper, the bed situated in the center against the far wall. It was nothing to his bedchamber in Pemberley, but the estate was a good one, as he had told Bingley after his arrival. It would do him well, though Darcy thought he might advise against buying it, if he was serious about pursuing Miss Bennet as a wife.

All at once the annoyance from earlier came crashing down on Darcy, and he threw himself into a nearby armchair in his pique. He loosened the cravat around his neck with an altogether violent motion and flung the cloth down on the floor, unbuttoning his jacket and his shirt at the same time. Darcy was grateful he had dismissed his valet for the evening before he had left for the assembly—not only did he not wish for an audience to see the extent of his anger, but he would not wish the man to see what had become of the clothes Darcy had removed with such aggression. He was rather fastidious, in many ways much like his master.

Darcy brooded. Was it not the mark of a gentleman to ignore the ridiculous and not react to those who were making a spectacle of themselves? And how could she possibly call him out for his behavior, she who possessed nothing and was about to receive everything from him? Did she not understand this, or was her independence and fortitude merely a mask for a shrewish character? Perhaps it was best that he learned of this now, rather than when he reached the point of no return and proposed to her.

He could not make her out at all; that was the salient point. He had seen her reaction to her mother's behavior more than once since arriving in Hertfordshire. He would have thought she would be eager to remove herself from her improper relations and into his more exalted sphere.

Was that not what all women wished for?

As soon as the notion occurred to Darcy, he dismissed it. Was he not attracted to Miss Elizabeth Bennet because she was different? Had not the entire reason he knew her at all been because she showed herself to be different before he had ever met her? Surely it was so; otherwise, he would merely have disdained her and walked away that day in the park, rather than berating himself for a week for his inability to open his mouth and returning day after day, hoping to catch a glimpse of her.

Furthermore, Darcy thought of his own relations, who were far from perfect. Lady Catherine, who thought nothing of directing those within the realm of her influence, Uncle Hugh, who looked down on all and sundry, Lady Susan who cared for nothing but improving her social consequence, not to even mention his cousins and their arrogant ways, or several more distant relations with whom he would not wish to associate at all. They were, most of them, good people, but their behavior was often embarrassing. Was Mrs. Bennet any worse?

His thoughts turned to Elizabeth and how she had castigated him in her righteous fury, eyes flashing with fire, her face a mask of fury. In that moment, little though he had wished to acknowledge the fact, he had found her to be incredibly beautiful, and he now belatedly realized that he had seen that look before—when speaking with Caroline Bingley at times, and tonight when she had been speaking with Mr. Pearce, were both examples which came readily to mind. And Darcy realized that he appreciated that about her; he found her to be practically irresistible when she was in the midst of some great emotion. He imagined that he would lose many arguments with her for this simple fact. Heaven help him if she ever became aware of her power!

She was the bravest, most impressive young woman of Darcy's acquaintance. She was willing to brave her mother's displeasure in order to avoid marrying a man she could not respect. Furthermore, he realized with a start, she was willing to refuse Darcy himself if he could not show respect to her mother, a woman who barely showed any respect to Elizabeth herself. And what would a cessation of his attentions result in for her? Likely the renewed and increasingly shrill demands for her to marry Pearce, little though he believed Elizabeth would ever submit.

No, Darcy could not do that to her. He could not leave her to her mother's mercy, could not leave her to Pearce's. Though he had not consciously known it before that moment, Darcy now knew that he was in love with her, that she irretrievably held his heart in her dainty, gentle hands, and that there was no backing out for him now. He would forever be hers.

The question was did she feel the same way about him. A moment's thought on the subject brought a feeling of warmth to Darcy's breast, unlike any he had known before. Though it was painful to think of their argument, he was convinced she could not have responded with such passion if she did not love him. He was certain of it.

Darcy knew just what to do.

When William arrived at Longbourn the day after the assembly, Elizabeth was surprised, not only for his request for a private audience, but also for the fact that he had come to Longbourn at all.

Upon arriving home the previous evening, Elizabeth had excused herself to her bedchamber, only to spend the night alternately furious for him for his insensitive actions and words and weeping for what she thought she had lost. He was the best man of her acquaintance; why had she reacted so strongly to his curt dismissal of her mother, when her father had done worse over the course of their marriage?

In her heart of hearts, Elizabeth knew exactly why, though she shied away from the thought. He might have deserved it, but Elizabeth was soon sufficiently master of herself to know she should have handled the matter with more understanding and earnest discussion, rather than acrimonious recriminations.

"May I have a moment with you, Miss Elizabeth?"

Those words so startled Elizabeth that for a moment she knew not how to respond. She was tempted to deny him, to make him understand without misunderstanding how he had hurt her. But William was so earnest, so *honest*, that Elizabeth found she could deny him nothing. It was well her mother still had not descended from her rooms that morning, due to a delicate constitution brought about by drinking too much punch, or Elizabeth would not have had a choice at all.

Assenting, Elizabeth proposed they walk in the back gardens, for the day was fine. William agreed without hesitation. Within moments, Elizabeth was dressed for the weather, and they were once again walking behind the manor house.

If Elizabeth thought that William would immediately start speaking, she was disappointed, for the man's reticence was frustrating; he did not appear to be eager to break the silence. For the briefest of moments, Elizabeth was almost inclined to be angry with him, for it seemed as if he simply intended to forget about their argument. Mastering her pique, however, Elizabeth determined to hold tight to her patience and allow him to speak in his own good time.

As they walked, Elizabeth attempted to watch William in as

surreptitious a manner as possible, trying to assess his state of mind. He appeared to be serious and introspective, but that was nothing out of the ordinary for William. She thought several times that he was about to speak, but he did not, though whether it was because he did not know what to say or for some other reason, she could not fathom.

They had completed the circuit of Longbourn's wilderness and arrived back by the side of the house when William finally spoke.

"I am curious, Elizabeth," said he, "about your reaction to what happened last night. I will readily concede that ignoring your mother was rude, but I cannot help but think there was something else behind your reaction."

Elizabeth watched William closely and though his manner was as serious as ever, he seemed to possess a hint of . . . Well, Elizabeth could not quite determine what it was, though anticipation or even expectation passed through her mind. The fact that he did not attempt to simply push their argument aside or explain his behavior away indicated his good intentions and prompted Elizabeth to respond.

"I would not wish to be treated in such a manner myself."

A frown settled over William's countenance. "Have I ever given you any indication that I would treat you with anything other than the utmost respect?"

"No, you have not. But I do not believe my father had given my mother any clues as to what her married life would be when they were courting either."

"So, you fear that our marriage will become like your mother's?"

A little embarrassed, Elizabeth turned away, only to have William reach out and touch her chin, turning her head back to face him with gentle pressure. He was watching her, a hint of understanding now evident in the way he watched her, not to mention, Elizabeth thought, a measure of compassion. It caused a dam inside Elizabeth to break, allowing her to sag a little and respond to his question.

"I have not had a happy example of marriage in the home in which I was raised. You have seen something of how my father treats my mother, so you must know that he holds her in barely concealed contempt."

"But you do not think that I would treat you the same way!" exclaimed William. "Whatever else was to pass between us, I would hope you would never suspect me of such a thing."

"I do not know what to think. I would hope not, especially given what I know of your character and how you have conducted yourself. I would think that what lies between us—" Elizabeth could not continue for the emotion which was building up in her breast and for a moment she was forced to silence, fighting off the feelings for this man, which were warring with her desire for respect.

"I am much more intelligent than my mother," said Elizabeth at last, grateful for the way he had waited for her to find her voice. "I will not misapprehend any cutting remarks you choose to make. I think for me it is so much more important to have all the things I desire in a marriage, as it will be a misery without them."

"But it is entirely for your intelligence that I was drawn to you," exclaimed William. "I could not hold you in contempt for those things your father holds against your mother. It is in every way unfathomable."

"And I thank you for it, sir," said Elizabeth. "But there are other things you can hold against me if you so choose. My lowly origins, my ties to trade, my lack of a fortune to boost your family coffers; all of these things you have chosen to ignore at present. But what if you come to regret your choice? It would be difficult for us both to live in such circumstances."

William's eyes softened, and he reached out to capture one of her gloved hands, holding it between his own, his grip gentle. He regarded her with compassion which Elizabeth thought would be her undoing, and though he did not say anything immediately, Elizabeth thought he now understood her better.

"And by ignoring your mother's words, you thought you saw a vision of your own future?"

Elizabeth blushed and looked down. "It *did* upset me, sir, but I am aware of the fact that I overreacted. We should have spoken of it in a rational manner, rather than with acrimony. I am at times embarrassed by my family's conduct, but I would not wish to be forever estranged from them."

"That is where I made my greatest mistake, I suppose," said William, a hint of rueful regret entering his tone. "I was not intending to deny you your family. In that moment, your mother's behavior annoyed me to the extent that I spoke without thinking.

"Elizabeth, my love," continued William, and Elizabeth looked up, startled, peering into his eyes, "I cannot promise anything concerning the future. For all I know, Pemberley could fail tomorrow, and I would have nothing to offer you but the meanest hovel."

"Oh?" asked Elizabeth lightly. "Is there something I should know now, sir?"

William grinned. "I think the eventuality is remote, though I cannot say it does not exist. What I am trying to say is that I cannot tell you how the years of marriage will change us or what trials we will face. But I hope that I can promise you my respect and to always allow that respect color our interactions."

The only thing Elizabeth could do was nod and say: "And I believe it of you, sir. I responded in a way which was wholly inappropriate, and for that I apologize."

"Do not apologize for demanding respect. It is your due."

Smiling, Elizabeth thought to suggest they return to house when William did something completely unexpected. He led her to a nearby bench, and there, he knelt down on one knee, holding her hand between his own and watching her earnestly.

"We have managed to make our way past our first disagreement, Elizabeth, and I am grateful for that. But I find that I can no longer wait and put off that which will give us the greatest of happiness. You are still yet full young, and I am aware of your youth and inexperience. Yet for all that, you are the most confident, intelligent, articulate, and erudite young woman I have ever had the good fortune to meet. You possess a poise far beyond your years and far beyond that most other young women could only imagine they possess. I have marveled at your ability to bring out the best in my shy sister and how you charm everyone with whom you come into contact. You are truly an exceptional woman, and I now know that I love you unreservedly. I would be fortunate indeed if you will consent to marry me."

Speechless, Elizabeth could only stare back at the man who had just proposed to her. She thought he must be uncomfortable waiting for her answer, but in that moment, she could only watch him, wondering what she could possibly say to such a heartfelt declaration.

And then there was only one thing she could do. Elizabeth had already known she loved him—to do anything other than accept him was impossible.

On impulse, Elizabeth pushed herself off the bench and flung her arms around the man who would be her husband, putting herself as close to him as she could possibly manage. She heard a slight grunt as she impacted into him, but his response was to put his own arms around her and hold her tightly.

"So, may I take your response as acceptance?" said Mr. Darcy, the nearness of his voice, his breath tickling her ear.

"You may," said Elizabeth, pressing her head into his chest.

A laugh bubbled up from the depths of his breast, and it was not long before Elizabeth found herself laughing along with him.

* * *

Having obtained his heart's desire, Darcy's first mission was to secure Mr. Bennet's permission for their engagement, something he determined to do as soon as may be. Elizabeth was reluctant to part from him, and Darcy was forced to confess that he was less than eager to be parted from her. They quickly regained their previous and proper positions, and a look around the park suggested that they had been unobserved, for which he was grateful. Her ardent reaction to his proposal boded well for their marriage—Darcy had always known she was a passionate woman, but the confirmation was welcome—but it would not do to be called out by her father for any supposed liberties.

When Darcy at last left Elizabeth and went in to face her father, it was with reluctance, but also with an insistence that the final hurdle to their ultimate marriage be set aside as soon as may be. It was thus only a few moments later when Darcy found himself sitting in a chair across from her father. The man's demeanor did not boost his confidence, but since Miss Elizabeth had given her consent, Darcy thought her father would not likely refuse his.

"I am surprised to see you in my study so soon, Mr. Darcy," said Mr. Bennet. "It has only been a matter of two weeks since the last time you were here, and from what I understand, you exchanged words last night."

Shocked, as he had thought it had gone entirely without notice—except for Miss Bingley, whom he had warned that morning to never speak of the matter—Darcy asked: "We did, though I am not certain how you are aware, sir."

"I have my sources," said Mr. Bennet. A mysterious smile settled over his face, and Darcy, looking at the man, was forced to chuckle. Mr. Bennet truly was an interesting man, and Darcy did not think it would be any hardship to have him as a father-in-law.

"Very well," said Darcy, "but I assure you the difficulty of which you speak now no longer exists. Miss Elizabeth and I have spoken on the matter, and we have put it behind us. We have both promised to behave better in the future. This morning I have proposed to your daughter and received her consent. Now I would like yours and to obtain your blessing."

The conversation continued from there, and to Darcy's amusement, it was largely a repeat of that he had just had with Elizabeth that morning. It seemed like Mr. Bennet, though he appeared to be an indifferent parent, truly knew his daughter well. It was also clear that his esteem for Elizabeth was deeper than for almost any other person.

"In that case, Mr. Darcy," said Mr. Bennet, leaning back in his chair, "then I have nothing more to say. It is the hope of any man to have his daughter cared for when she leaves his home for that of another, and I do not doubt you are up to the task. The only question is whether you will be able to keep up with my Lizzy."

"I shall be happy to make the attempt, Mr. Bennet. She is about the most intelligent woman of my acquaintance. It shall be a joy to endeavor to match wits with her."

"Well said, sir! It is clear that Lizzy has chosen well. Now have you any thoughts as to when this blessed event will take place?"

"I have not yet spoken with Miss Elizabeth about it, sir. I have no particular desire for a long engagement, but I will defer to her opinion on the matter."

Mr. Bennet laughed. "I think you will make an excellent husband, Mr. Darcy! There is no greater skill than knowing when to simply allow the ladies to have their own way."

The two men laughed together for some moments, and Darcy was thinking about how often he imagined Elizabeth would have her own way. All she would need to do was to turn those beseeching eyes on him, and he would no doubt give her whatever she wanted.

"But if I may offer you some advice on your wedding date," continued Mr. Bennet, "it would be to take a stand and not allow any dissent to the contrary. You are aware of my wife's character, and I suspect you apprehend that she will wish to have a grand celebration. If you allow her, she will make the decision on the date, and it shall not be for some time, allowing her to prepare the most elaborate festivity this town has ever seen."

Once again Mr. Bennet laughed when Darcy grimaced, and they spent some moments speaking of the matter further, finally deciding—with Elizabeth's concurrence, Darcy insisted—on the first week in March, which would constitute a three month engagement. It would be long enough that society would think nothing of it when it was announced and yet short enough for Darcy's sanity. Mrs. Bennet would be a trial over the course of those three months, but Darcy was determined to bear her effusions with perfect grace, for Elizabeth, if nothing else.

The date decided on, Darcy paused, wishing to speak of another matter with his future father-in-law. Mr. Bennet regarded him with curiosity, and when he asked Darcy if there was something else he wished to discuss, Darcy could only oblige him.

"There is something else, Mr. Bennet. It is a delicate matter, however, and I would not wish to cause offense."

The curiosity writ upon Mr. Bennet's brow grew apace, and he motioned for Darcy to continue.

"I have been thinking of your youngest daughters, Mr. Bennet," said Darcy, speaking slowly while he tried to find the right words. "I wonder if you have given any thought to their provision."

A smile settled over Mr. Bennet's face, and he sat back. "I imagine they will manage just as well as their elder sisters. Lizzy seems to have done quite well for herself, and Jane has managed to attract your friend, assuming he is all he seems."

"I cannot truly answer for Bingley," said Darcy, "as I have not known him for long. I believe he is sincere, however, and I believe I have enough of a measure of his character to know that he would never toy with your daughter's affections.

"But as for your youngest daughters, if you will excuse my saying so, I do not think leaving them to their own devices will be for their best interests."

"Oh?" asked Mr. Bennet. Darcy had the distinct impression that Mr. Bennet was more amused than offended at present, giving Darcy the courage to proceed.

"I have been thinking of sending Georgiana to school, as she is of age. I believe Miss Catherine and Miss Lydia are also of age now and would also benefit from the experience."

Mr. Bennet watched Darcy, giving no hint of his thoughts at Darcy's suggestion. He did drum his fingers on his desk, which Darcy found jarring enough, without the man's silence to compound the problem.

"I take it you do not appreciate the behavior of my youngest daughters."

The statement caught Darcy by surprise, but he was quickly able to agree with the man's statement. There was no point in obfuscation; Mr. Bennet was an intelligent man—Darcy was not surprised he was quickly able to see what Darcy had not explicitly stated.

"Their manners . . ." Darcy paused, wrestling with how to say what he knew needed to be said. But soon Darcy knew it to be a hopeless business, and he fixed his gaze on Mr. Bennet, saying: "Your daughters do not possess fashionable manners, sir. Given what Miss Elizabeth has told me, it seems like she and your eldest were given the benefit of instruction from their aunt and uncle, which largely ceased when the Gardiners' own children arrived."

"And you believe my youngest will not be well received."

It was a statement, and Darcy could only nod in agreement. "I *know* they will not be well received, sir. You have some familiarity with

London society, so you must apprehend that young ladies—newcomers—who do not possess the most excellent of manners, will not be accepted."

"Unless, of course, they possess a handsome dowry."

Mr. Bennet's tone was sardonic, and Darcy could only agree with him. "It is what it is, Mr. Bennet. With a bit of schooling, your daughters might be able to make good matches—simply being connected to the Darcy and Fitzwilliam families will be an attraction in their favor, and I would be willing to assist as well."

Mr. Bennet seemed to understand the thrust of Darcy's words, though he did not comment further. Darcy said nothing more, deciding it was a matter which could be discussed another time.

"This is why I dislike London society so much," replied Bennet with a grunt. "A duke's daughter might escape with little damage to her reputation regardless of her behavior, simply because she belongs to a prominent family."

"I have as little liking for it as you do, Mr. Bennet. Still, it is a facet of our society. I merely propose that we give your daughters every advantage."

"Very well, Mr. Darcy. There is sense in what you say. I believe my wife will be little disposed to send her favorite to school, but if I insist—and perhaps more importantly, if we give her to believe it will help them marry—she will be won over."

"Excellent! I shall ask my aunt for a list of suitable schools. You can choose the appropriate establishment based on need and budget."

Mr. Bennet merely waved his hand. "If Lydia and Kitty are gone from my home, I save on their upkeep, and with Lizzy leaving, and Jane soon to follow, the expense will be manageable."

"Very well, Mr. Bennet.

The two men shook hands to seal their agreement, and Darcy promised to have the documents for his engagement to Miss Elizabeth made up and submitted for his approval as soon as possible. Then they departed from the room to return to the sitting-room and announce the engagement. Darcy followed Mr. Bennet, eager to once again be in the company of his beloved.

Chapter XXIII

In the sitting room with her mother and sisters, Elizabeth felt as nervous as she ever had in her life. Always a little contemptuous of her mother's predilection for nerves and never feeling quite that way herself before, Elizabeth almost thought she could empathize with her mother at that moment. Once consent was given and it was announced, there would be no return. Elizabeth would be irrevocably tied to William for the rest of her life. What had been a romantic proposal which any woman would be happy to receive had suddenly turned into a serious matter which would affect her life profoundly. What intelligent young woman would not be nervous?

"What has become of Mr. Darcy, Lizzy?" asked Mrs. Bennet for about the fourth time.

Elizabeth sighed. She had not made mention of what her suitor was doing for fear of her mother's effusions on the subject. She wished now that she had asked him to return to Netherfield so she could take upon herself the first exclamations of delight which her mother would certainly release. Given his censure the previous evening, Elizabeth did not wish to give him any further reason to despise Mrs. Bennet, though she knew his resolve to respect her mother was given with the best of intentions.

"I believe he shall be joining us in a moment, Mama," said Elizabeth, feeling she could no longer delay answering."

"They were outside in each other's company for some time," chimed in Lydia from a corner where she sat with Kitty. "Perhaps he has made her an offer and is seeking consent from our father."

Glaring at her sister, Elizabeth could not quite hide the wince when her mother cried: "Is it so, Lizzy?"

Fortunately she was saved from answering when the door opened and Mr. Bennet stepped in, followed closely by Mr. Darcy, thereby ending her misery. If only it would not bring another form of misery, almost guaranteed to be much more mortifying and long lasting.

"Mrs. Bennet," said her father as he stepped toward her chair.

"Yes, Mr. Bennet?" asked she, and Elizabeth saw she was almost quivering with delight, certain she knew what was about to be announced.

"As you are probably already aware, Mr. Darcy and I have been conferring in my bookroom, and we have come to some conclusions regarding some of your daughters."

"Conclusions?" asked Mrs. Bennet, clearly mystified and not a little disappointed at her husband's words.

"Yes, my dear. You see, Mr. Darcy and I have agreed that it would be best if Kitty and Lydia are sent to school."

"School!" screeched Mrs. Bennet. "Whatever for?"

"To prepare them, of course. They shall be old enough to enter society before long, and we wish them to attract suitors as their sisters have done, do we not?"

"And why can they simply not do as Jane and Lizzy have done?" demanded Mrs. Bennet.

"Because they have not had the benefits that our eldest daughters have had." Mr. Bennet turned to the youngest girls, saying: "What do you think of the matter? Would you like to attend school?"

Kitty's answer was hesitant, but she readily spoke up. "I have no objection, Papa."

"It does not signify," said Lydia, "for I am still three years away from my debut. It matters little if I spend it here or in some school, though I am not certain I shall enjoy lessons."

Elizabeth was actually surprised Lydia did not decry the very notion of attending school and gratified that it might not be so difficult as she feared for her sister to learn some proper manners.

"Excellent!" said Mr. Bennet, rubbing his hands together. "Mr. Darcy has promised me a list of suitable establishments. We can make a choice based on your interests and the associated costs." Mr. Bennet looked at his youngest daughters fondly. "I am happy you are both open to the idea. I dare say that with the exalted company you will keep when you return, those lessons will be invaluable."

At first Elizabeth thought her mother was about to protest, but she seemed to catch the last part of her husband's statement.

"What exalted company?" demanded Mrs. Bennet.

"Oh, nothing really," replied Mr. Bennet, sounding almost bored. "Mr. Darcy has made our Lizzy an offer, and I have given my consent. I am certain his friends will find your other daughters enchanting, once they have learned to act in a way which befits young gentlewomen."

The stupefaction on Mrs. Bennet's face was almost comical, and she did not appear to grasp what her husband had told her. The other girls, however, caught his gist quickly, and with several cries Elizabeth's sisters congregated around her, their voices raised in congratulations.

"Oh, Lizzy!" exclaimed Jane, her best friend and confidante. "I am so happy for you! I knew Mr. Darcy could not possibly resist your charms."

"Apparently you were correct, Miss Bennet," said Mr. Darcy. While the girls were milling around her, William had approached and now stood watching the celebration, his pleasure evident in his countenance. "I am happy you had such faith in my constancy."

"What fun you shall have in London!" added Lydia. "The balls and parties, dinners, teas. I can hardly wait until my coming out so I can attend!"

"Shall we receive invitations to attend the events of the season?" asked Kitty.

"There are other events to anticipate than simply balls," said Mary, with a sniff. "I should like to attend plays and museums rather than waste all my time at balls."

"Girls!" exclaimed Elizabeth, laughing with her sisters. "I think there will be more than enough amusement to go around." Elizabeth attempted a stern look at her youngest sisters. "But you must pay attention to your lessons and learn the proper deportment."

"If it means balls and parties, I shall do my best," said Lydia, with Kitty nodding her head vigorously in counterpoint.

"I must own that I share your view of the matter, Miss Mary," said William, smiling at Elizabeth's younger sister. "Balls only have limited appeal, but I appreciate the theater. I am certain your sister would also enjoy such amusements."

"I do, Mr. Darcy," replied Elizabeth, feeling a warmth growing in her breast at the thought of being married to this man.

"And what of Jane?" asked Lydia, looking at her sister with laughter evident in her eyes. "Shall she be joining you in London as the wife of Mr. Bingley?"

"Lydia!" exclaimed Jane, cheeks red with mortification. "I have only known Mr. Bingley for a matter of two weeks!"

"I do not claim to know Mr. Bingley's mind, Miss Lydia," said William, "but it is clear he likes your sister very well indeed. I believe it is best to leave them to their own devices."

"But it is so much more fun to help them along!"

They all laughed at such a statement, William the loudest of all. Elizabeth thought that somehow he was softened toward her sisters. Lydia and Kitty's exuberance was something which often caused Elizabeth to fear for their behavior when they came out, but they were not bad girls. In fact, with the right training, she thought they would be the belles of any ball.

"Mr. Bennet!" cried Mrs. Bennet into the tumult, her voice seeming a little more strident—and more strained—than usual. "Am I hearing you right? Mr. Darcy has proposed to our Elizabeth?"

"I thought I was quite clear on the matter, my dear," said Mr. Bennet, his tone was as bored as it had been before. "The matter was decided on this morning, and I have given my consent. You have achieved your heart's desire and now have a daughter engaged."

With a great cry, Mrs. Bennet shot up out of her chair and bolted to Elizabeth's side, exclaiming her happiness.

"How grand you shall be, Lizzy!" exclaimed she. "Such an advantageous marriage with such a great and important man. And he is so very handsome too! I never imagined such a match for any of my daughters!"

"I thank you, Mrs. Bennet," said William "In fact, I am quite enraptured with your daughter. She is the best woman of my acquaintance, and her beauty shall be the envy of London."

It took no great insight to deduce that Mrs. Bennet was puzzled by Mr. Darcy's words. In her mind, Jane had always been the most beautiful of her daughters. But she was not about to gainsay William, not with so much depending on the man marrying her daughter. Elizabeth could almost see her mother's thoughts as they moved through her mind—the engagement was not yet announced to the neighborhood at large, so he could still withdraw!

"I am happy to hear it, sir," was the only thing Mrs. Bennet said on the matter, before she turned her attention to other considerations. "Now that you are engaged, and just before Christmas, I think that a wedding planned for next summer would be the very thing. Perhaps close to Elizabeth's birthday would be best. The park can be decorated with the best of our roses and carnations, and we may have a celebration such as the neighborhood has never seen!"

Though Elizabeth watched her mother's growing excitement with horror, her attention was caught by the amused look which passed between her fiancé and her father, and she wondered at its meaning. She had expected that William would be annoyed by her mother's presumption, and yet he appeared to be laughing at some private joke with her father.

"I believe the wedding will take place sooner than that, Mrs. Bennet," said her father. "Mr. Darcy and I have already spoken on possible dates, and have decided on the beginning of March for Lizzy's nuptials."

"With Elizabeth's approval, of course," said Mr. Darcy. He approached her and took her hand. "March will give us plenty of time to announce the matter in a manner which will make it clear it has all been done properly and yet soon enough that I am content with the wait. But if you have any objections, please state them. I wish you to be comfortable with what we decide."

"*I* have objections!" cried Mrs. Bennet. "How can I possibly plan such a wedding in merely three months? I shall need six at the very least!"

"I am certain that you are capable of organizing a proper celebrations in three months," said Mr. Bennet. "And besides, it is Lizzy and Mr. Darcy's wedding. Should they not have the final decision?"

Mrs. Bennet appeared to have a retort ready on the tip of her tongue when William added: "Though perhaps I am speaking out of turn, I suspect Miss Elizabeth possesses the same expectations for our wedding as I. I am not a man who prefers grand gestures and elaborate revelry, Mrs. Bennet. I am cognizant of the fact that Miss Elizabeth will be the first of your daughters to marry and that you wish to celebrate accordingly. But I also believe we would prefer to have a simple ceremony and wedding breakfast in the company of friends and family."

"Mr. Darcy is correct, Mama," said Elizabeth, eager to have her own opinions heard. "I am quite happy to forego such an exhibition before all the neighborhood."

"But—" managed Mrs. Bennet before she was brought up short by the combined looks with which she was faced.

"You shall have your triumph, Mrs. Bennet," said William, compassion filling his voice. "But let us not wait too long. You would not wish for me to be required to wait to carry your enchanting daughter away to my estate in Derbyshire, would you?"

A slow smile tentatively spread across Mrs. Bennet's face, and while

Elizabeth would have thought such an expression would have been filled with cunning, and perhaps even a hint of avarice, it actually appeared to be genuine. It was rare, in Elizabeth's experience, to be witness to such pure emotion from her mother, not because she was filled with greed, but because her fears for the future more often than not trumped all other concerns.

"Very well, Mr. Darcy," replied Mrs. Bennet. "I shall plan a wedding according to your desires, and those of my daughter, of course. But you must allow me to display my heartfelt happiness to all our friends, and I cannot think that they would not wish to celebrate with us."

"Of course," said Mr. Darcy. "I believe it is cause for your daughter to be feted, so by all means, let us do so."

The matter settled, conversation related to the engagement continued for some time, and though Elizabeth did not have any time alone with her intended, still she was able to revel in the feelings which coursed through her.

It was much later in the day before Darcy was able to take his leave from Longbourn and depart, though he did not begrudge the time he had spent there. For all their deficiencies of behavior, Darcy had enjoyed himself. It was clear that the Bennets cared for one another as family, and though there were disagreements amongst them, that affection always shone through. He had almost forgotten what it felt like to be part of a family, for though the earl and his family were closely related, he had never thought his feelings when with them to consist of that which he would commonly associate with "family."

His arrival at Netherfield was quiet, and as Miss Bingley was not in evidence, Darcy was able to retire to his room in order to prepare for dinner in solitary reflection. For the most part, he spent his time reminiscing about Elizabeth, how she had looked, her surprised response to his proposal, and, most importantly, how she had responded to his declaration of love with one of her own. It was almost more than he had ever hoped for, and Darcy now could look forward to a life brightened by an intelligent and lively woman.

When the time for dinner arrived, Darcy descended, still caught up in thoughts of his beloved. Upon entering the sitting-room where his host and hostess were waiting, Darcy was unsurprised to be immediately accosted by the latter.

"Mr. Darcy, there you are!" exclaimed the woman, the hint of hysteria in her voice easily detected. "We cannot fathom where you have been all this time."

"On the contrary, Caroline," said Bingley, throwing his sister an amused smile, "I have known *exactly* where Darcy has been all day today. Had I not been caught up with some business which could not be put aside, I should have been with him all this time."

That Bingley had been detained all day had been a circumstance for which Darcy was actually happy, as he wished for Elizabeth to be the focus of all her family. Besides, if Bingley had come, it was possible Miss Bingley would have accompanied her brother; though she was not hesitant about showing her contempt for the Bennets, she had also shown no signs of abandoning her pursuit of him.

"In fact, I have been at Longbourn today," said Darcy, after he had greeted his hosts.

"It is admirable the notice with which you have favored the Bennets, Mr. Darcy. I cannot help but think your civility is wasted on such a family. Surely you do not need to extend such notice any longer."

Darcy regarded Miss Bingley for some moments, saying nothing, but noting with amusement the way she soon seemed uncomfortable with the scrutiny. She fidgeted with a handkerchief which she held in one hand, shifted her weight from side to side, and before long, she could not hold his gaze, though even when she looked away, her eyes still darted back to him with great frequency.

"I believe you are well aware of what draws me to Longbourn, Miss Bingley."

Miss Bingley feigned astonishment. "Truly? After your . . . disagreement last night, I thought your little . . . infatuation was at an end. For did not Miss Bennet display her lack of refinement and suitability? I had thought it to be a death knell for your dalliance with her."

Out of the corner of his eye, Darcy saw Bingley's cringe, but his shaken head told Darcy that he had spoken to his sister several times with no success. It was just as well, Darcy decided, as it was more than obvious that the woman would not desist without Darcy's direct declaration concerning his now acknowledged engagement.

"I will thank you not to refer to my relationship with Miss Bennet as a 'dalliance,' Miss Bingley. I assure you that I would never toy with a woman's affections in so cavalier a manner."

Miss Bingley colored and was only able to respond: "Of course, sir."

"In fact," continued Darcy, "the conversation to which you refer was nothing more than a minor disagreement which was quickly put to rights."

"How fortunate," mumbled Miss Bingley.

"But now that you have raised the subject," said Darcy, enjoying the impending set down far more than he ought, "I have the best of news to impart tonight. You see, I have, this very day, made an offer of marriage to Miss Bennet, and I have been accepted."

No two reactions could have been less alike. Bingley surged forward, offering his hand and exclaiming, "Well done, Darcy!" while Miss Bingley watched with horrified disbelief.

"Thank you, Bingley," replied Darcy, while accepting the offered hand. Darcy's attention, however, was fixed on Miss Bingley, for though she was pale and had not yet made any response, he did not think her objections were at an end.

"Mr. Darcy," said Miss Bingley, once she had gathered herself, "while I wish to be happy for you, I must tell you that I cannot but think you are making a mistake. I know you have felt a certain level of fascination for Miss Bennet, but you have not known her long enough to be truly acquainted with her character. I have known her for longer than you, and I have seen her in unguarded moments. She is not what you think she is."

"And *I* have known her for longer than *you*, Caroline," said Bingley, the displeasure in his voice clear, "and I can assure *you* that Miss Bennet is as genuine as she appears to be. I do not think Darcy could do better in choosing a wife than to choose Miss Bennet."

"And you are nothing more than a man infatuated by a pretty face," sneered Miss Bingley. "A few moments spent in the company of her family reveal the Bennets to be nothing more than fortune hunters of the worst kind. Marriage to her will bring nothing more than misery and embarrassment. Unless, of course, you believe that Mrs. Bennet will be a smashing success with the other members of your circle."

This last was said with contempt dripping from the woman's voice, and Darcy wondered at her. Miss Bingley's behavior often reminded Darcy of that of some members of the Fitzwilliam family, which was no less than astonishing for one of her social background.

"Miss Bingley," replied Darcy, "I would appreciate the immediate cessation of your attacks against my betrothed and her family."

"But, sir—" cried Miss Bingley.

Darcy, unable to support any further commentary from the woman, interrupted her, uncaring at present that it was ungentlemanly; was her behavior not unladylike?

"I believe it is time for you to be silent, Miss Bingley." The woman stared at him, but Darcy's returning glare soon caused her to drop her gaze in embarrassment. "I am required to be blunt, Miss Bingley. And I apologize to you," said Darcy, looking at Bingley, "for being so. It is inexcusable, I know, but it appears nothing less shall do."

Bingley only waved him off. "It appears to be so, Darcy. Say what you must."

Miss Bingley regarded Darcy with fear and loathing—though he suspected the last part was directed at Miss Bennet—but for once she exercised some measure of judgment and did not speak.

"By the time I met you, I was already courting Miss Bennet, Miss Bingley. Even if I had not already been courting her, you would never have been a candidate to become Mrs. Darcy."

"How can you say that?" demanded the woman. "I have the best education, an impressive array of accomplishments, not to mention the highest in fashion sense and the keenest knowledge of all the social graces. What does she have?" Miss Bingley's lip once again curled in contempt. "Unfashionable manners, nothing in the way of dowry, connections to the lower echelons of society, and neither face nor form which is in any way appealing. In all honesty, I cannot account for what she has to tempt you with."

"I shall not comment on the state of my affections for Miss Bennet," said Darcy.

"Which only proves them to be deficient, sir," exclaimed Miss Bingley. "I know not what hold she has on you, but it is clear she has somehow managed to draw you in."

"Then I shall tell you exactly what hold she has on me," replied Darcy in a quiet voice, which hid his rising annoyance. "It is love."

By this time, Darcy thought the woman's lip would be permanently locked in its sneer, which had only grown more pronounced the longer the conversation had continued. "I am surprised at you, sir. I had thought better of you than to suppose that you would throw your family heritage away on something so transitory and fleeting as *love*."

"Oh, and you would obviously prefer I would throw it all away on a woman who was not even born to a gentleman?"

The sound of Miss Bingley sucking in air in her outrage told Darcy that he had scored a significant hit against the woman's vanity. She appeared uncertain what to say next, so Darcy continued, wishing for the conversation to end.

"I apologize, Bingley, Miss Bingley, for stating this in such an abrupt manner, but it seems I have no choice. Miss Bingley, I know not in what manner you were raised, but I can tell you that I do not consider love to be fleeting and transitory. I consider it to be the foundation of a successful marriage. If you do not wish to marry for love, there should be many opportunities in society, for there are many who think as you do. I am not one of them.

"My parents were close as two people could be, and I would wish to emulate their example. Furthermore, I must tell you that if you think your accomplishments and attendance at an expensive school for girls will make your background disappear, you are mistaken. I will own that my uncle was not happy to hear of my engagement to Miss Bennet, as she has not been brought up in my level of society, but his reaction was mild in comparison to what it would have been if I had presented you as my future bride."

Darcy turned to Bingley, noting the man's faint smile of amusement at his sister, even while Miss Bingley was watching Darcy with horror.

"Again, I apologize for insulting you and your sister, Bingley. If you would prefer, I shall arrange to stay at the inn in Meryton if you cannot overlook the offense."

"Nonsense, Darcy," replied Bingley, his tone brooking no disagreement. "It appears my sister needed to hear what you said. For my part, I have never forgotten my origins, so I felt no affront at your words.

"Besides, I have the highest opinion of Miss Bennet, and I believe she will make you an excellent wife. Had you taken a liking to Caroline, I would have been happy to see you married to her. It has been clear to *me* that your affections were engaged with Miss Bennet from the start, so I knew it would not happen."

"Thank you, Bingley," said Darcy, eyeing Miss Bingley and wondering if objections would continue in the face of all she had heard in the past few minutes.

"I . . . I . . ." Miss Bingley apparently could not find any further words.

"Miss Bingley," said Darcy, looking on the woman with more compassion than he ever thought to feel for her, "I suggest you turn your attention on the other men of London. I believe Bingley mentioned you possess a fine dowry?"

"I was able to add to it with the additional funds obtained from the merger of my business with Mr. Gardiner's."

The scowl which appeared on Miss Bingley's spoke to her annoyance at being reminded of from where her dowry had originated, but she did not say anything.

"A large dowry may induce some men to ignore your origins, so long as you do not set your sights too high. Someone of Mr. Hurst's general level of society should be your focus."

"I shall not marry another Mr. Hurst!" cried Miss Bingley.

"Nor was I suggesting you do so, Miss Bingley," replied Darcy with calm complaisance. "But your best chance at marrying a gentleman is someone in a similar situation to that of your sister's husband."

Miss Bingley glared at him for a few moments, and Darcy almost wondered at there being no lightning shooting from her eyes. Darcy merely returned her gaze with indifference, eventually forcing a huff of exasperation from her.

"Charles, I believe I have a headache," said she, turning to her brother. "If you and Mr. Darcy will excuse me."

Then without waiting for a reply, Miss Bingley turned and swept from the room, leaving the two men watching her in bemused silence. She was audacious, Darcy had to give her that much, little chance though her ambitions had of ever being fulfilled. He hoped, at the very least, she would refrain from imposing on him any longer; surely she had enough self-respect to know when to refrain from making herself appear ridiculous.

"Do you suppose she will take the advice I gave her?" asked Darcy after a few moments.

"I hope so," replied Bingley. "But I would not make a wager on it."

Darcy turned to regard his friend again. "I do apologize for speaking to your sister so bluntly, Bingley. I did not think she would believe me if I softened my words."

"You did what I have attempted to do on a number of occasions," replied Bingley. "My sister has always been headstrong. Inducing her to listen to me is a difficult proposition. Hopefully she will believe you.

"Regardless, you have my congratulations." Bingley beamed a great smile. "I do esteem Miss Elizabeth Bennet very much indeed. Perhaps we shall be brothers before too much time has passed."

Bingley laughed when Darcy turned a stern eye on him. "I know I have not known Jane for long, but I am greatly attracted to her. We shall see if it will lead to anything."

There was nothing to be said; Bingley had already indicated his understanding of the situation, and as Darcy was not Miss Bennet's father, cautioning his friend once was as far as he was willing to go.

Besides, Darcy had a suspicion his friend was correct. Only time would tell.

Chapter XXIV

The next days and weeks were happy, spent with family and friends. With his engagement to William now acknowledged, Elizabeth found much happiness in the fact that they were now allowed a certain leeway which was not permitted before. There were walks in the garden, and some even further afield, and nooks and crannies to be explored which allowed for a few stolen kisses and heartfelt murmurs of devotion. Both William and Elizabeth possessed a firm sense of propriety, and they did not go any further than those simple pleasures, but the intimacies in which they did indulge told them both they wanted more than they were allowed at present. However, they were also both young and patient and knew this season of engagement would be one they would remember for the rest of their lives. There was no need to hurry.

As the Christmas season arrived, the number of engagements increased apace, and the couple found themselves to be the center of attention no matter where they went. Elizabeth was content with the attention, being at ease in social situations, and though William was often made uncomfortable, he endured it with fortitude, and even pleasure at times. She knew he would never claim to enjoy the attention, but the ability to be together constantly was a circumstance to be relished.

The Gardiners arrived for their customary visit during the Christmas season, and Darcy and Elizabeth were happy to see them, sensible that their unstinting support of Elizabeth and their gentle guidance were largely the means of bringing them together. William shook Mr. Gardiner's hand with great vigor and pleasure when they appeared, but Elizabeth almost bowled her aunt over in her eagerness to greet her and thank her for everything she had done.

"Engaged to be married!" exclaimed Mrs. Gardiner once she was able to pry Elizabeth's arms from around her. "I had not believed that Mr. Darcy would act in such a precipitate manner as to propose so quickly."

They all laughed, William most heartily of all. "I am afraid I simply could not resist your niece, Mrs. Gardiner!" said he, a grin affixed to his face.

"We are all fools in love, are we not, Darcy?" asked Mr. Gardiner.

"I cannot dispute that, sir."

"Well, I am glad to hear of it," continued Mrs. Gardiner. "I am very happy for you, Elizabeth. I believe you will be a happy woman."

Elizabeth paused and looked at Darcy. "I believe I will, Aunt," said she after a moment. "I believe I truly will be happy."

The Christmas season was festive and gay, and Elizabeth thought that William enjoyed himself as much as did Elizabeth herself. Georgiana arrived a few days before, and the two girls had a happy reunion, exclaiming their excitement at once again being in each other's company. When the time came for the formidable introduction to Elizabeth's family, Elizabeth could sense the younger girl's trepidation, but she faced it with fortitude, meeting Elizabeth's younger sisters, though shyly. She quickly became a favorite of Kitty and Lydia, in particular, and for the entire time of the holiday, the three girls could often be found together. Georgiana even induced the other two girls to take an interest in the pianoforte, her own enthusiasm for the activity serving to provide a push to the other girls. While the discordant noises her two younger sisters produced often produced cringes in the rest of the party, most of the company looked on them with indulgent affection.

One further development which came of the three girls' new friendship was an insistence that they would attend the same school. William, it appeared, had already chosen a school for his sister, and as it was one which catered to the higher echelons of society, it was not only populated with girls who thought highly of themselves, but it was also expensive. It was William who came up with a solution for the dilemma.

"If you would, Mr. Bennet," said William to Elizabeth and her father the night that the girls had made their wishes known, "I would be happy to make up the difference if you would prefer to send your daughters to the school Georgiana will attend. And I am sure a letter to the headmistress would result in an offer of a position to attend being extended to Miss Kitty and Miss Lydia."

Mr. Bennet frowned. "I would hate to be an imposition, Darcy. My girls will be fine going to a school more appropriate to my means."

"But it would not be an imposition. I have rarely seen my sister show this much animation with anyone, let alone someone she did not even know only days ago. It would be beneficial for her to go to school with some friends who would help her adapt and make friends with others."

"What of the difference in station?" asked Elizabeth.

Smiling at her, William raised Elizabeth's hand to his mouth and kissed it, sending delightful shivers down her spine. "I hope you will not think me proud, dearest, but the Darcy name carries much weight in society. Your sisters will be sought after due to their connection to my family, and if I let it be known that they are under my patronage, they will be accepted. Young girls may have their own thoughts on the matter, but I suspect that others will treat them well when they realize that Georgiana is such great friends with them. I do not foresee many difficulties."

Although Mr. Bennet protested further, eventually the matter was decided, and William sent a letter to the school to request positions for his future sisters-in-law. The school, which was located in nearby Bedfordshire, responded with alacrity, confirming the girls' enrollment.

If there was one blight on the joy of the season, it was Caroline Bingley. Mr. Bingley's other sister and her husband soon joined their relations for the Christmas season, and though Elizabeth did not come to know either very well, she found them both infinitely preferable to Miss Bingley's airs and her continued ill humor. The woman made no overt comments concerning William and Elizabeth's engagement, but it was clear she was still hoping for a miracle to occur to allow her to slide into Elizabeth's place. If she did not think it was so pathetic, Elizabeth might have been angry. As it was, she took no notice of the woman wherever possible.

Of Mr. Pearce they saw nothing. It seemed like he had finally given up his doomed pursuit, for he did not appear at any events of the area. Perhaps it was the gossip—the county was full of whispers concerning Elizabeth's refusal—or maybe it might have been the fact that many of the area were not hesitant to show their displeasure for the way he had behaved, but he chose to stay home during those days. Relieved to finally be free of the uncertainty, Elizabeth thought no more on him, allowing her interactions with the man to fade into the past.

When Christmas ended, the Gardiners once again returned to London to Mr. Gardiner's business, and Colonel Fitzwilliam also left as he was required to return to his regiment. Georgiana stayed at Netherfield, and she visited Longbourn daily. The two youngest Bennets were even induced to sit in with her lessons with her tutors, though there were less of those due to the season. In all, life settled to a routine, and planning for Elizabeth's upcoming wedding began in earnest.

This, of course, was both a source of pleasure and one of exasperation for Elizabeth. She was excited for the approaching of her nuptials, but her mother was in her element in such situations and was in a constant state of frenzy, deciding on fabrics, flowers, foods, and all manner of items she deemed necessary for the marriage of her first daughter to a man of great consequence. While the younger girls had their escape in their friendship with Georgiana, and Jane was often to be found with Mr. Bingley (Mrs. Bennet not wishing to interrupt that courtship, though it was still an unacknowledged one), Elizabeth and William often had no such escape.

One morning a few days after Christmas, Elizabeth rose early as was her wont, and after breaking her fast, she decided that a short walk around the boundaries of Longbourn was necessary for her to retain her equanimity. William still had not arrived that morning, and though she expected him, she knew that he would instantly guess where she was and walk out to look for her when he arrived, if she had not already returned by that time. She decided not to bother Mr. Thompson—she did not intend to go far, after all, and there was nothing in the vicinity to harm her.

The morning was fair but cold, and Elizabeth dressed warmly in woolen stockings and her heaviest pelisse. After exchanging a few words with Mrs. Hill, informing her of her plans, she slipped out the door and hurried to the paths leading toward the back of the property. Soon she was surrounded by the bare branches of the trees, marveling at the stark beauty of the frost-covered foliage. Here and there she caught hints of birdsong from those few species hardy enough to wait out the winter in the cold of Hertfordshire. She missed the chattering of squirrels and other small animals, knowing that they were sleeping the winter though, waiting for the rebirth of spring.

After she had walked for some little time, Elizabeth was halted by the sound of a footfall behind her, and though she knew it was early, she was happy that William had come so soon to see her. It spoke to his devotion.

"Good morning, William," said she, turning to greet him with a side smile.

And she was shocked when a hand went over her mouth, and she was wrestled to the ground, strong arms pinning hers to the side. Elizabeth attempted to struggle, twisting this way and that in an attempt to free herself from her assailant, but the man held her steadily. She attempted to bite his hand, but the hand came away for a moment, allowing her to draw breath to scream, when the rancid odor of an unclean cloth assaulted her nose and mouth as it was shoved in, none too gently.

"None of that, now," said a voice close to her ear, and she turned her head, catching a glimpse of the man who had assaulted her.

It was Mr. Wickham, leering at her with a self-congratulatory smirk affixed to his face. Her moment of paralysis allowed Wickham to loop a rope around her hands and before she knew what was happening, he had pulled it tightly enough that she was unable to wrest her hands from their bonds.

"Well, well, Miss Bennet," said Mr. Wickham in an almost conversational tone, "it seems like you have become very popular in a very short period of time. I cannot tell you how happy I am that you will be the means by which I will have my revenge on your paramour."

Elizabeth attempted to roll away from him and come to her feet, but Wickham pulled her back and quickly bound her feet, affixing a gag to her mouth so that she could not spit out the rag he had stuffed in.

"Now, shall we take a short trip? I am eager to bring you to your next abode and take my payment."

Hoisting her up on his shoulders, Wickham began to walk into the woods, all the while whistling a jaunty tune. Twisting this way and that, Elizabeth attempted to dislodge herself from his grip, but Wickham just laughed and grasped her closer.

"None of that," said Wickham, laughing at her attempts. His hand crept up her thigh and he patted her bottom familiarly, eliciting a gasp from Elizabeth. "Do not worry, my dear," said Wickham, "I believe you will still get everything you want. I would almost wish to have a go at you myself, but I had best not. You're far more valuable to me unsullied."

Soon they approached a horse which Wickham had tethered to a nearby tree. The animal whickered softly in greeting, and Elizabeth almost hated it for being so docile and obliging. Wickham hoisted her up onto the animal and then scrambled up behind, placing one hand on the reins and the other around her midsection. He shook the reins and urged the horse into a trot, chuckling as he did so.

"Now, settle in for a short trip, my dear. We do not have far to go."

As the horse took its first steps, Elizabeth felt the first tear trickling down her cheek for a life lost. Even if William managed to find her, he could not marry her now with her so compromised.

Upon arriving at Longbourn that day, Darcy instantly knew something was amiss. It was not unusual for Longbourn to be in uproar; its mistress was often able to induce that state by the force of her voice alone. But this morning was something different from what Darcy had ever heard before. It was more exasperated than desperate, for one thing, and Mrs. Bennet's nerves were nothing if not desperate

"Oh, Mr. Darcy!" exclaimed Mrs. Bennet when she caught sight of him. "I am afraid Elizabeth is not here to greet you. The girl left for a walk this morning, and she has not yet returned. It is just like her to walk at all hours and not take any thought for the feelings of others."

Darcy frowned. "She left for a walk? Where did she go?"

"I do not know!" cried the Bennet matron with exasperation. "She informed Mrs. Hill she would be walking about the grounds an hour ago, and she still has not returned. She no doubt decided to leave on one of her endless excursions and left for Oakham Mount, or some other such nonsense."

"It *is* quite cold today," said Darcy slowly. "Surely she would not have walked so far."

"That girl . . ." Mrs. Bennet paused and looked sidelong at him, and then continued in a more conciliatory tone. "That is to say, Lizzy is very fond of walks, sir."

"So I am aware, Mrs. Bennet," said Darcy, a trifle impatiently. He had no time for Mrs. Bennet's fear of annoying him this morning. "But she is also a sensible girl, and I do not believe she is prone to putting herself in jeopardy. Has Mr. Bennet been alerted to her absence?"

Mrs. Bennet shook her head, her eyes wide. Clearly she had not thought Elizabeth's absence to be anything other than her usual propensity to walk out.

"Please inform him and have him conduct a search of the grounds for your daughter. I shall ride toward Oakham mount and see if I can discover her."

Something in Darcy's voice or countenance must have induced the woman to believe that he was not only serious, but worried for her daughter. She curtseyed to him abruptly and turned toward Mr. Bennet's bookroom.

For his part, Darcy cast about the entrance hall, and he espied Mrs. Hill standing to the side, where she had been watching the proceedings.

"Mrs. Hill, did Miss Elizabeth mention where she would be walking this morning?"

"Only that she would be walking about the grounds, sir," said the housekeeper.

"And she did not take Jack Thompson with her?"

The woman shook her head. "Being so near to the house, I believe she did not think his presence to be warranted."

Darcy wavered in his purpose for a moment. If Elizabeth had told the housekeeper she was to walk about the grounds, he did not think that she would suddenly change her mind without informing anyone. At the very least, he would have thought she would inform Jack. But on the chance that she might have acted in such a manner, he determined that he could leave the search nearer home to Mr. Bennet while he rode out to try to discover her. It would not take long for him to cover the distance, and he would be back soon.

"Mrs. Hill, please send a note to Netherfield requesting Mr. Bingley's assistance. There is no need to alarm my friend or any of the residents there at present, but I would prefer Bingley be available to assist should it be necessary."

The woman nodded and departed, and Darcy lost no time in leaving the entrance hall, exiting out through the door. The groom was in the process of leading his horse away to the stables, but a word from Darcy halted him in his progress. Soon Darcy had mounted and was riding his horse away from the house at a canter.

It became apparent very quickly that he would not find Elizabeth unless she walked along the trail he followed or could be found at Oakham mount. The growth of trees was thick in the area immediately surrounding Longbourn, and there were undoubtedly a myriad of trails which passed through them. Darcy was unfamiliar with the land for the most part, though he was fortunate to have walked to Oakham Mount with Elizabeth one fine day not long before Christmas and knew the way.

The forest was almost preternaturally silent that morning, and nary could a sound be heard. Darcy's sense of unease only increased the further he rode, though what exactly worried him he could not say. It was almost as if the whole world was holding its collective breath.

It was not long before Darcy reached Oakham Mount, and a quick survey of the area revealed no sign of his fiancée. Though the hill was heavily forested to the north, it was clear on all the other sides, and Darcy stood on the summit for several moments, searching for any sign of his beloved. But nothing met his eyes. He searched the top of the hill for several moments, trying to find any trace that she had come this way, but though he had a passing familiarity with woodcraft, he was not able to find any evidence that she had been here.

Now quite alarmed, Darcy once again mounted his horse and turned the beast back toward Longbourn, this time at a much quicker pace. The animal, long confined to Bingley's stables with only infrequent trips to Longbourn for exercise, was apparently relieved to be given its head, and it snorted, its hooves pounding on the turf as it returned to Longbourn at a full run.

"There's a good fellow," whispered Darcy in its ear as it ran.

Within moments, Darcy reined up at Longbourn and vaulted from the saddle, striding toward the door. The door opened at his approach, and he entered the house to be greeted by the housekeeper. From the sitting-room Darcy could hear voices raised in what appeared to be lamentation. The mistress had apparently realized that her daughter was nowhere to be found.

"Mr. Bennet is waiting for you in the library," said Mrs. Hill.

Nodding, Darcy strode toward the bookroom and stepped inside, noting the fact that there were several men—a footman, a stable hand, Jack Thompson, and Mr. Hill, the butler, as he recalled—standing inside the room.

"There is no sign of Miss Elizabeth in the rear of the property, Mr. Bennet," the butler was saying as Darcy entered the room. "Of course, there is no new snow, so it is difficult to know what path she took or if she left the grounds."

"I could not find her at Oakham Mount," said Darcy shortly. "There was no sign of her from the summit either."

"She has been gone for almost two hours, sir," replied Mr. Bennet. "Though Lizzy can sometimes be single-minded when it comes to her walks, she rarely ranges so far in the winter."

Darcy scowled. "We must organize a search party. Can men from Lucas Lodge be spared?"

"David," said Mr. Bennet, looking to the stable hand, "ride to Lucas Lodge and ask for Sir William's help. We will meet here."

The man nodded and departed with haste.

"Did Mrs. Hill send word to Netherfield?"

"Indeed she did," said Bingley as he strode into the room. "But she shared very few details. What is the emergency?"

In short, clipped tones, Darcy informed Bingley of what had

happened. Within moments, Bingley had departed, pledging his own staff to assist in the search. Mr. Hill announced his intention to create a plan to search the area most effectively, and he left the room.

"I cannot imagine my Lizzy being so senseless, Mr. Darcy," said Bennet, his brow wrinkled in worry. "Her mother bemoans her penchant for walks, but though she walks, she has never been so reckless before."

"Do you think Pearce might have had something to do with her disappearance?"

Though surprised, Bennet shook his head in denial. "Surely he has given up. The man is immoral, but I do not believe him to be depraved."

"Perhaps," said Darcy.

"Son, I know you want to find her," said Bennet, looking at Darcy earnestly. "But we cannot accuse a man simply because of what has happened in the past. We have no choice but to search for her first. If we can find no hint of her, then we may begin to explore other possibilities."

Though he did not like it, Darcy was forced to agree with Bennet's assessment. Something told him, however, that the path to Elizabeth would ultimately lead to Pearce, and he requested paper and a pen and jotted a quick note off to his cousin. The footman was engaged to take the note to Meryton and engage an express rider to ride to London with the missive. Unless Darcy very much missed his guess, he suspected that his cousin's presence would be required before all was said and done.

Situated uncomfortably on the back of the horse as she was, Elizabeth found the journey to wherever Wickham was taking her to be uncomfortable in the extreme. Not only was she jostled about by the horse's gait, but Wickham talked incessantly, crowing about how he had finally managed to exact his revenge on Darcy for all the perceived insults he had suffered over the years.

"Soon I shall once again have all the money I desire," said Wickham with an amused cackle. "And when I do, perhaps I shall make sport of Darcy's heartache, without noting my involvement in the matter, of course. Darcy always considered himself to be smarter, superior to me." A snort indicated Wickham's feelings on the matter. "I have always been the superior, the more resourceful. I have had to be, curse Darcy. Had I received my due, I would have had no need to develop such talents. How ironic it is that the man's own actions which compelled me to develop my own skills will lead him to an end he never foresaw!"

Wickham was blessedly silent for some time, and Elizabeth thought he was lost in thought. Her position in front of him meant that she could not see his face, but she longed to slap the self-congratulation she imagined him displaying from his countenance.

"In fact, I can imagine that this loss might even break our dear Darcy," said Wickham after a few moments. "That is a delightful thought indeed. And should he never marry due to his heartbreak, it might leave me an opportunity. His sister is young and naïve—surely it would only be the work of a moment to convince her she is in love with me. If Darcy should suffer . . . an unfortunate accident, that would leave me in control of Pemberley, as I always should have been."

Shocked at such brazen and depraved scheming, Elizabeth twisted about to glare at Wickham, but the man simply laughed.

"I suggest you forget all about your dear Darcy, Miss Bennet. For it is doubtful you shall ever see him again."

Though still angered beyond all endurance, Elizabeth was forced to once again face forward. The path they were following had led them north from Longbourn, and it skirted Oakham Mount to the west, passing close to the prominence, and traveling alongside the woods which grew about the base of the hill to the north. They had continued on in this manner for some time before Wickham suddenly turned them into the woods themselves, using a small trail that Elizabeth might have missed had they simply gone past

For the next quarter of an hour, they weaved their way along the trail, making their way under branches and over protruding tree roots. The trail was overgrown in many places and had obviously not seen much use in recent years, so rough and uneven had it become. The woods were silent, feeling oppressive, and Elizabeth could almost feel them closing around her, suffocating and surrounding her.

At length they came upon a small, rude cabin, weathered and beaten down by the elements. It appeared to be a single room structure, constructed of logs from the wood in which it was situated, with a stone chimney rising from behind. There was no paint, or it had peeled and faded away long before, and perhaps most disquietingly, the windows, which might at one time have been covered by shutters, were now boarded up with wood which looked to be much newer than the rest of the building.

"Welcome to your new home," said Wickham as he reined in the horse before the cabin.

He dismounted and turned back, lifting Elizabeth down as if she weighed no more than a feather. He then strode into the cabin with his burden, depositing her on the rough floor.

"Now," said he, as he took out a wicked looking dagger, "this is to be your residence for some time now, or at least until Darcy gives up searching for you. There is no wood for a fire, as smoke can be seen, so you will not have that luxury. However, the house has been stocked with blankets which will keep you warm. I suggest you make use of them."

With the knife, Wickham cut the gag surrounding her head, enabling her to spit the cloth out of her mouth. She glared at him, noting with fury his amusement.

"How long do you mean to keep me here?"

"That is not for me to say, Miss Bennet," replied Wickham. "Someone will be along to feed you before long. Until then, I suggest you keep yourself warm with the blankets."

Saying that, Wickham sawed through the bonds on her wrists and directed a smug sort of smile at her. "I shall let you work the bonds on your legs by yourself. It would not do for you to try to escape, now, would it?"

Then chuckling to himself, Wickham removed himself from the hut, closing the door firmly behind him, the sound of a bar being thrown across the door the final lock to her cage.

It took Elizabeth several moments to work the ropes clear from her legs, and when she was able to stand again, she walked gingerly about, as much as the narrow confines of the room would allow, working the feeling back into her legs. A quick inspection of the interior revealed what she already knew; it was nothing more than one room, bare of any adornment, with a floor of rough planks and a pile of blankets in one corner. There were no implements of any kind, nothing that Elizabeth could use to try to free herself, not that she had expected to find anything. An experimental push at some of the boards in the windows revealed them to be firmly nailed to the wall, with little chance of Elizabeth's loosening them. And when she tried the door, she found it firmly bolted closed as she had expected.

Knowing it was important to stay warm, Elizabeth retrieved several blankets and hunkered down in them to wait. From Wickham's words it seemed like he was not the author of her present misery, and it did not take much thought to determine just who that might be. But she could do nothing at present, so she waited for the man to appear. It was not long before the heartbreaking nature of her situation, coupled with a sense of fatigue, lulled Elizabeth into a light sleep.

Chapter XXV

It was some time later when Elizabeth was jolted from her sleep by the scraping of the bar being removed from the outside of the door. What light was able to enter through the boarded windows gave no indication as to how long it had been since she had been left alone there, but she scrambled up, thinking in the panic of newly regained consciousness to dart out the door and attempt to escape.

The door opened too quickly, however, and before she had truly attained her bearings, the smirking visage of Mr. Winston Pearce appeared before her eyes as the man sauntered into the room.

"Miss Bennet," said the man, dropping into a courtly bow, his motions not concealing his insolent arrogance in the slightest. "I do hope you are enjoying your accommodations."

"Have you lost all your wits, Mr. Pearce?" demanded Elizabeth. "What can you possibly mean to accomplish by abducting me in this manner?"

"I mean to have what is mine, Miss Bennet."

"I am *not* yours, sir! By my count I have refused your offer more than half a dozen times. What kind of stupid arrogant man would want a woman who is so decidedly set against him?"

Pearce only smiled at her words. "I told you, Miss Bennet, I will have what I want, and what I want is you. No whelp from the north is about to take from me that which is mine."

"And my acceptance of *his* suit is of no matter? Or the fact that Mr. Darcy has already published it in the London newspapers? Are you insensible to the consequences of your actions?"

"It is of little matter," said Pearce with an airy wave of his hand. "Once we are wed, this Darcy fellow will have no choice but to accept it and look somewhere else for a bride. Perhaps your sister might do."

"You are mad, sir. I shall never go willingly with you, and you are senseless to think that Mr. Darcy will simply give me up."

"That is why you will stay here for the nonce. Once the furor over your disappearance has died down, we shall depart for Gretna Green, and no one will be the wiser. If necessary, I own a small property in the north of Scotland which will do nicely for you."

Almost blind with rage, Elizabeth moved forward, hand raised to slap the expression off the odious man's face, but he caught her hand in his iron grip and squeezed it painfully, forcing her back against the wall behind her with a violent thud. His expression as he regarded her was implacable, and she did not doubt that regardless of the state of his sanity, he would do exactly as he said and would hurt her if necessary. Her wrist already throbbed from the force of his grip.

"You would do well to remember that I am in control of you now, my dear. I have power over you, and if you do not do exactly as I say, it will go ill for you. You have already earned yourself substantial punishment for your recalcitrance. Your good behavior now will ease that punishment to a certain extent."

"I will never submit to you."

The only response Elizabeth was to receive was a sardonic laugh. The man released her wrist and strode away to the door, leaving Elizabeth to rub her arm, which was already showing signs of bruising.

"Here is a little food and water for you," said Pearce, dropping a sack on the floor. "I would suggest you do not let the water freeze, as you will not have anything to drink if you do. More will be brought at certain times during the day and night until we are ready to leave. You had best become accustomed to the thought of becoming my wife, Miss Bennet, as that is to be your fate."

And with those final words, Pearce turned and exited the cabin, closing the door and replacing the sturdy bar as he departed. Elizabeth was left alone in silence.

For a few moments, Elizabeth could do nothing but stand and stare at the closed door, wondering at the audacity and stupidity of the man she now knew to be her captor. How was she to possibly extract herself from this predicament?

And then reason asserted itself. William would be looking for her—this she did not doubt. But she could not count on him to free her from the cabin. She would need to do something to affect her release from her bonds. And to do that, she would need to be smart with the resources she possessed.

The sack contained a flagon of water, as Pearce had said, and she could already see chunks of ice forming inside due to the coldness of the ride from Pearce's estate to the cabin. In addition, there was a loaf of rough but filling bread and a block of cheese. Knowing that the only way she could keep them from freezing was with the heat of her own body, Elizabeth carried the meager items to her pile of blankets and placed them inside. Then she looked about the room, knowing that there would be nothing for her to use, and focused on the window. The boards were fastened tight, but Elizabeth thought that she might be able to force one loose if she worked at it. With nothing else to do she began to work on the boards, patiently attempting to remove them. It would take time. But time was one thing she appeared to have in abundance at present.

It was a miserable day of searching, not only due to the cold, but due to the fact that no trace of Darcy's beloved could be found. Together with men from Lucas Lodge and Netherfield, search parties inspected every square inch between the three estates, though the strands of woods and fields. There was nothing to be found. Even the inclusion of Sir William's dogs did nothing to assist in the search—Elizabeth had disappeared thoroughly, as if she had never even existed.

As the day wore on, Darcy's mood became blacker, and his thoughts turned to the man who had been at the center of Elizabeth's misery this past half year. If she had walked and fallen, or some other mishap had befallen her, Darcy did not doubt she would have been found. That no trace of her had been found suggested that there was some foulness at work here, and though it was possible it was the work of someone else, Darcy knew of no one else who would wish Elizabeth harm.

When the skies darkened to the point where there was not enough light to see, Darcy reluctantly turned his party back toward Longbourn. The cheery lights of the estate were a direct contrast to the moroseness which had settled into Darcy's heart. The woman he loved was missing, and he felt powerless to do anything about it.

Upon entering Mr. Bennet's study, Darcy was confronted with the sight of his cousin standing with Mr. Bennet, poring over a map of the area.

"Fitzwilliam," said Darcy, greeting his cousin with a shaken hand, "thank you for coming."

"Of course, Darcy. I am happy to help. I have brought several men from my regiment to assist in the search."

Nodding, Darcy slumped tiredly into a chair. "We have been able to find nothing. There is simply no trace of her."

"I also found nothing," said Bingley, as he entered the room behind Darcy. "We ranged west for several miles, and there was no sign of her."

"Elizabeth's usual haunts are to the east," said Mr. Bennet. "Between here, Netherfield, Lucas Lodge, north to Oakham Mount, and south as far as Meryton."

"But searching in usual places was also prudent," said Fitzwilliam. He regarded them all, a seriousness which was not normally present in the jovial man on display. "Can we safely say that she is not within a three mile radius of Longbourn?"

Darcy shrugged, feeling dejected. "Though there is a possibility the search parties have missed her, I think it likely she is not."

"Then it is possible she was abducted."

"I think at this point we had best *hope* she has been abducted," said Bennet. "If she is lying injured somewhere, she will likely not survive the night."

That ominous statement seemed to sink into the minds of all present, and silence reigned over the room for several minutes. In the distance, Darcy could hear some lament, knowing it was Mrs. Bennet exclaiming for her lost child. In that moment, Darcy felt more empathy for the woman than he had ever felt before.

"My mind keeps going back to the thought of Pearce," said Darcy, forcing such thoughts away. "I can think of no other who would wish her harm."

"Nor can I, Darcy," said Mr. Bennet. He sat down in his chair with a tired sigh. "But surely he would not be so lost as to abduct my daughter? How could he think he could even manage such a deed without fear of reprisal?"

"Obsession can make men do irrational things," said Bingley.

"Perhaps we should pay a visit to this man?" asked Colonel Fitzwilliam. "How far away is his estate?"

"Between four and five miles," said Mr. Bennet. "It is north, past Oakham Mount in the direction of Stevenage."

"More than enough time to go there today," said Colonel Fitzwilliam.

He turned and looked at Darcy, a question in his gaze. Darcy nodded and stood. "I believe you are correct, Fitzwilliam. It would be best to confront Pearce now."

Their course set, the gentlemen quit the room and made for the outside of the estate. Within a few moments, the horses had been brought to the front door, and they were ready to depart. But before they mounted, Fitzwilliam approached Darcy, and in a low tone, said:

"There is one other piece of news I bring from town, which I did not want to state in front of Mr. Bennet. It seems our friend Wickham has left London."

Darcy blinked, looking at his cousin oddly. "Wickham? I thought the men we hired had uncovered no trace of him?"

"They did not until yesterday morning. Though he still remains at large, there have been whispers that he was seen leaving London on the north road heading into Hertfordshire. I have men watching for his return—with any luck we will have him when he comes back."

Frowning, Darcy looked at his cousin, wondering what he was suggesting. "You do not believe Wickham has had something to do with Elizabeth's disappearance, do you?"

Fitzwilliam only shrugged. "I cannot say. But wherever Wickham is, trouble follows, and you know they he did not take kindly to your refusal to extend him more money. With your fiancée now missing, it is possible that he has taken her for revenge or, more likely, for ransom."

"Wickham has always been a bounder of the worst sort. A womanizer, a charlatan, a trickster, a gambler. But I have never known him to become involved in something so underhanded. He might be hanged for it, if his role was ever discovered."

"Do you think that will stop him?" asked Fitzwilliam. "Wickham tends to think of immediate rewards, rather than long term consequences. I do not know that he has taken Miss Elizabeth, but I would not be surprised if we received a ransom note in the next day or so."

There was nothing Darcy could say to that. It was clear that Fitzwilliam was correct, and Darcy realized that his opinion of his one-time friend was so low that it was easy to suppose he had become involved in the matter.

"Perhaps we bring Wickham's name up to Pearce, see if we can shake him up?"

Fitzwilliam unleashed a feral grin. "Now you're thinking like a soldier, Darcy. Even if he will reveal nothing, a man's reaction will often reveal much."

"Then let us get to it," said Darcy, and he swung up into his saddle. Within moments, Darcy, along with Fitzwilliam and Bingley, were cantering down Longbourn's drive, headed north.

The estate they arrived at was obviously a prosperous one. The building was well maintained and handsome, and to Darcy it indicated an estate approximately the size of the Bennets' Longbourn. However, he found it a little disquieting. The house was quiet, which he supposed was not unusual, since by all accounts Pearce was a bachelor and lived alone. But there was also a pervasive sense of . . . well, Darcy could not quite determine what it was. Not neglect, precisely, as everything seemed to be in good condition and maintained as it ought to be. But there was something about the place that he did not like, as if it hid some sort of secret concerning its proprietor.

When they dismounted in front of the door, it was several minutes before a stable hand appeared before them to see to their horses, and when the man did appear he was slovenly and curt, seeming to look upon them as if they were an imposition. Surely it was late and not a usual time for a visit, but a servant should never treat visitors to an estate in such a manner.

The housekeeper came to the door in response to their knock, and when Darcy stated their purpose, she made no comment other than that they should follow her. They were led through a hallway toward a room which was obviously the master's study and led in, where they were greeted with the sight of Pearce, staring at them with anger.

Wishing to make the man wait, if only to see if he would betray some knowledge of why they had come, Darcy looked around the room with interest. Whereas Darcy's study at Pemberley was large and spacious, his shelves stocked with ledgers and books to aid his stewardship of the land, and Mr. Bennet's was filled with bookshelves, all laden with a bounty of his own tastes in literature, Pearce's was almost bare of any adornment, austere and lifeless. It appeared like the man did not read in any great detail, even those books which even the most slothful master of an estate would have ready at hand. It did not speak well of the man at all.

"Have you come to my estate to look over my study, sir?" asked Pearce after Darcy had ignored him for some minutes. "Perhaps you are one who can tell much of a man by his reading material. Or perhaps by how he organizes his possessions. What does my study tell you of me?"

"Very little," was Darcy's reply. "In fact, seeing this room, I would hardly know you own your own estate. There seems to be relatively little to indicate anything of you."

Pearce laughed, a harsh, sardonic sort of sound. "My uncle, whose estate I am to inherit, maintains much of that style of work in his study. When I require something, I simply go there. When he dies and I inherit, that will be my home regardless. It is the ancestral family home, you understand.

"Please state your business. I do not wish to be in company with the thief who made off with the woman I was to marry."

Sensing this was an attempt to rile him, Darcy ignored his claims. Instead, he turned his attention on Pearce and glared at him. "In fact, Elizabeth is why we have come. She has disappeared, and I believe you know something of the matter."

Another laugh escaped the man's lips. "She has gone and left you, has she? Perhaps she found the son of an earl or a duke, who could give her more in life than you can? It would not surprise me."

"If you wish for our meeting to remain amicable, you will refrain from insulting Elizabeth."

"I care not if this meeting is friendly. In fact, I would be happy never to see you again."

"Mr. Pearce," said Darcy, holding onto his temper by a thread, "my fiancée has disappeared. She left the house to walk the estate this morning, and she did not return. I believe you had something to do with this, considering how you have refused to leave her be. I must insist upon your telling me where she is."

"You will insist upon nothing, sir," replied Pearce, sneering at Darcy. "Your *fiancée* is no concern of mine, and I feel myself well rid of her."

"Perhaps you do not understand the situation," said Fitzwilliam stepping forward. "Miss Elizabeth *will* be found, and if you do not acknowledge your complicity in the matter, it will go ill with you."

"And who are you, sir? One of this man's vaunted connections?"

"It matters not who I am. You should know that we know of your connection with Wickham, and we know Miss Elizabeth's disappearance was your doing."

"I know of no one by that name," the man replied shortly. "I have told you that I do not have any information concerning Miss Bennet's whereabouts. Now, you will leave, or I will have you removed from the premises."

"I know you are lying," said Darcy heatedly. He stepped forward and grasped Pearce by the lapels of his coat and pressed him against the wall behind his desk. "I will find Elizabeth, and when I do, I shall know the truth."

"I am not afraid of you or your connections, and your wealth is nothing to me. Leave me or suffer the consequences!"

"Darcy," said Fitzwilliam, as he and Bingley stepped forward to intervene.

Darcy kept his hold on the man's jacket, but though he glared at Darcy, he did not say anything further. Darcy thought he was lying, but he had to own to a grudging respect for the man's ability to stay calm. Releasing him with a bit of a shove, Darcy stepped back and glared at him, Pearce returning his glare and not even bothering to fix his jacket.

"When I find Elizabeth, you had better pray that I do not uncover a link back to you, sir."

Then he turned and strode from the room, with Bingley and Fitzwilliam following closely behind. They were soon mounted on their horses, leaving the estate behind.

When they had gone some distance, Darcy slowed his horse to a walk, and Fitzwilliam and Bingley fell in beside him. "Well, what do you think?"

"The man is guilty," replied Fitzwilliam. "I have no doubt of that. The question is, where does he have her and what is his purpose."

"If he has her, his tenacity can only mean that he means to marry her," said Bingley.

"I shall not allow that to happen!" exclaimed Darcy, a cold fury settling over him. "We should return and search the house and every building on that estate."

"That would accomplish nothing," said Fitzwilliam. "He would not be so foolish as to keep her at his estate where she can be discovered. The servants would know immediately, and servants are known for their gossip."

"We cannot simply allow him to follow through with his plan."

"He will not make a move for some days, Darcy. He knows we will be watching him and expecting him to do something rash. For now we shall have to be patient."

"I am afraid I have little patience at present," growled Darcy.

"I understand that, Cousin. But if you wish to have your betrothed back, we must do this the proper way."

And with that, Darcy was forced to agree. They made their way swiftly back to Longbourn and reported their experience to Mr. Bennet. While it was clear that the man was not happy with what they had to tell him, it was equally clear that he had expected nothing less. They organized for some additional searches to be undertaken that night, and then Bingley, Darcy, and Fitzwilliam joined the family for dinner.

There was little joy to be had, for all felt the absence of their most effervescent member keenly. Even Mrs. Bennet, who could almost always be counted on to fill the dinner conversation with chatter, was subdued that evening. The sisters ate quietly, and Miss Bennet was showing red-rimmed eyes to the company.

After dinner, the gentlemen held a silent vigil in Bennet's study, their company broken occasionally when reports were made by those still searching for Miss Bennet. There was still no sign of her, not that Darcy had expected any. In reality, only his iron control prevented him from returning to Pearce's estate and throttling the man. He was responsible for this. Darcy could feel it.

The night had become quite late when a message arrived for Fitzwilliam. Darcy watched his cousin with interest, noting the way he glanced at the missive, his countenance revealing nothing. What pulled Darcy from his seat was when Fitzwilliam turned back to the man who had brought the missive and instructed his horse to be readied for an immediate departure.

"What news have you received, Fitzwilliam?" asked Darcy.

"Wickham has been discovered returning to London."

Elizabeth had never spent such a miserable time in all her life. The cabin was cold, the wood doing little to keep out the chill of the weather outside, though she found that if she laid out several blankets on the floor and covered herself up in the rest she could maintain enough heat to remain reasonably comfortable. But it was only within this cocoon where she could feel any warmth at all, and she knew that if the weather became much colder she would undoubtedly suffer because of it.

The worst of it all was the monotony. There was no one with whom to converse, no sounds out in the forest beyond at all. Nothing but the sound of her own voice, the sounds of her movements, and the constant thumping of her heart, which she often fancied she could hear becoming louder. She took to singing to herself, if only to have a little noise and prove to herself that she was not losing her mind.

In a desperate bid to affect her own escape, Elizabeth had worked to try to free herself from her prison. The door and the bar which held it closed were quickly abandoned as a hopeless cause. The windows, however, were another matter. It was clear, given the relative ages of the wood, that the boarding up of the windows had been done recently, no doubt in preparation for her to occupy the cabin. As such, the boards had been nailed to the logs which constituted the walls of the cabin with very little finesse. A thorough examination of the nails holding them in place had revealed that one of the nails had been driven in through the edge of the board, not really secured to it. It had taken Elizabeth some time to remove it, and her hands were scraped and sore from the effort, but finally she was successful and held the metal spike in her hands.

What followed was a painstaking scraping of the wood around the other nails. The boards were wide enough that Elizabeth thought that could she remove enough of the wood on one side, she could force the board away and squeeze through the hole left behind. The cold and the numbness of her hands hampered her progress, and the constant fear that *he* would be back and discover what she was doing caused her to jump and scurry back to her makeshift bed every time she thought she imagined some sound.

In fact, her solitude was only broken once, and it was not by the detested Pearce. It was late in the morning the second day she had been imprisoned in the cabin when she thought she heard the sound of someone approaching. She almost did not respond, so accustomed to hearing sounds that did not exist, but at the last moment, as the wood of the bar over the door began to scrape against the door itself, she dove for the blankets and managed to cover up before the door swung open.

The man who poked his head in was likely some years older than Elizabeth was herself, and upon seeing her face peeking out from under her blankets, he grunted and pushed another sack inside, before he closed and barred the door again. Elizabeth listened at the sound of his retreat and then sank down, breathing a sigh of relief; he had never once looked toward the window.

The sack was filled with more of the same food she had already been given, and though Elizabeth was annoyed with her captor all over again, she carried the sack to her blankets again and rose with her tool to once again pick away at the boards.

"Just a little more and I can escape," said Elizabeth to herself, and the sound of her own voice comforted her all over again.

She would not marry Winston Pearce. She would rather any other fate than to be tied to that man for the rest of her life.

Chapter XXVI

With some difficulty, Fitzwilliam managed to convince Darcy to remain in Hertfordshire while he went to London to interrogate Wickham. It was a near thing—Darcy's countenance held that implacable fury with which Fitzwilliam was so familiar, and Fitzwilliam knew that Darcy wished to take Wickham apart piece by piece to find his beloved.

But Fitzwilliam had a very good reason for preferring that his cousin remain behind. The fact of the matter was that Darcy, for all his anger and resentment toward the man they suspected had abducted his betrothed, was still a civilized man. Wickham would certainly know he might be facing the gallows. Consequently, if he *had* kidnapped Miss Bennet, it might be difficult to induce him to talk.

On the other hand, though Fitzwilliam considered himself a civilized man as well, his profession was decidedly *uncivilized,* and Fitzwilliam knew there were some methods he might employ to induce Wickham to talk that his cousin might find distasteful. Furthermore, Wickham had always been afraid of Fitzwilliam, and he intended to use this to his advantage during the interrogation. If Darcy was there, Wickham would undoubtedly focus on his disdain for Darcy rather than his fear of Fitzwilliam.

"Stay here and continue to direct the search for Miss Bennet," said

Fitzwilliam as he attempted to persuade his cousin to stay behind. "You know that we have no proof of Wickham's involvement with the matter."

Darcy directed a disgusted look at his cousin. "Do you really believe that Wickham was not involved?"

"Oh, I expect that he did the deed himself, though I will own that I do not understand his connection with Pearce. But if we should happen to be wrong, it would be better if you were here to take care of any emergencies which might arise. I will be gone immediately and return as soon as possible."

In the end, Darcy acceded, though with little grace. And thus it was early morning when Fitzwilliam departed in the company of a few of his men as an escort. They made good time to London, and as there was little snow that year, there was little difficulty with the roads. They arrived when the first rays of the sun were peaking over the horizon, bathing the city in its cold glow.

Before confronting Wickham, Fitzwilliam refreshed himself, donning a new uniform and making sure that all was well with his appearance. No need for Wickham to know that he had not slept all night—the man would undoubtedly try to use anything he felt might be to his advantage.

When the time came, Fitzwilliam made his way to the room in which Wickham was being held, and saluted to the soldiers who were guarding the door.

"Tell me what our friend Wickham has been doing with himself."

Within moments Fitzwilliam was acquainted with all the salient facts. Wickham had returned to London the previous day and had almost immediately gotten himself to a gaming den where he had proceeded to gamble and drink the night away. Though he had been discovered before he had entered the city, the men assigned to apprehend him had followed him, waiting until he was well in his cups before moving in to make the arrest. He been found with several hundred pounds on his person, damning evidence, considering the man's past.

The expression on Wickham's face when Fitzwilliam entered the room almost caused him to laugh out loud, and he knew in an instant he had been correct to insist Darcy remain behind. It was clear Wickham had some idea of why he was being held, but he attempted to hide it behind a mask of bravado.

"Fitzwilliam!" exclaimed Wickham, as he scrambled to his feet. "Fancy meeting you here."

Smirking at the man he detested above all others, Fitzwilliam contented himself with watching Wickham squirm. The man attempted to put on a brave face and act like Fitzwilliam was not intimidating him, but it was not long before he was no longer able to maintain his composure.

"Here now, Fitzwilliam, what in the devil is going on? After Darcy refused to honor his father's wishes, I had thought your family had no further interest in the doings of one such as myself."

"If it had been my decision," said Fitzwilliam, finally speaking in a low tone, "you would have been shipped off to Marshalsea many years ago, to never again see the light of day."

Pausing, Fitzwilliam watched with pleasure as Wickham blanched, nodding to himself. The man had received the message in his words.

"However, for some strange reason, Darcy's father actually held you in some affection, and as for Darcy himself, he is far too tender hearted to do with you what needs to be done."

Wickham scowled. "Darcy tenderhearted? Do not make me laugh."

"You still have your freedom, do you not? If you had carried on so with any other patron, I do not doubt they would have tired of your antics many years ago.

"Still," mused Fitzwilliam, stroking his chin, "I suppose it was for the best that you behaved as you did. For if you had not, our only lead toward finding Miss Bennet would be Pearce."

"Pearce?" asked Wickham, "who is that? And I have no idea where Miss Bennet is. Likely at her uncle's house, for all I know."

It was a credible act—Fitzwilliam was forced to concede that much. But where Wickham had always possessed the ability to present himself as an upstanding young man before Darcy's father, Darcy and Fitzwilliam, being of an age with Wickham and having the benefit of seeing him in unguarded situations, had always possessed the ability to see through his lies. And Fitzwilliam had no doubt at all the Wickham was lying.

"Still as glib as ever," said Fitzwilliam shaking his head. "I think you had something to do with Miss Bennet's disappearance, and I will make certain you will tell me what you know."

"Even if I did know something, I would not tell you."

"Oh, you will talk, Wickham. One way or another, you will talk."

The two men glared at each other, though Fitzwilliam felt a certain savage glee when Wickham was the first to look away.

"Let us consider the facts, shall we? You have been known to utter threats of revenge upon Darcy, and you have accosted his intended several times."

"I did not *accost* her," cried Wickham.

"Mere semantics, old boy," said Fitzwilliam, waving him off. "Furthermore, you left town two days ago heading north, and you have now returned after her disappearance was discovered, carrying several hundred pounds on your person, when only a matter of weeks ago you were essentially penniless. Of course, I am certain you have already lost some of the amount you were paid to abduct Miss Bennet."

"I had a lucky run at the gaming tables," replied Wickham flatly.

"Oh, I think not," replied Fitzwilliam pleasantly. He stepped forward, his manner falsely companionable, and Wickham, with apprehension clearly showing in his countenance, backed away until his knees impacted with the chair behind him, and he sat. "We have had men looking for you for weeks now, and we certainly would not have been so neglectful as to miss the fact that you frequent gaming halls and houses of ill repute. You have not been seen in one of those locations in all that time."

Wickham scowled, but he did not say anything.

"Furthermore, you should recall that Darcy owns the credit receipts for all your debts in both Lambton and Cambridge, and he has the power to see you in debtors' prison. With the amount you owe, I doubt you would ever see the outside world again."

Though he blanched, Wickham attempted bravado. "I know Darcy would never do something like that. He would wish to honor his father's memory."

"I would not be so certain of that if I were you, Wickham. Not only has your act worn thin, but you are now playing with his happiness and the woman he loves."

"Love!" exclaimed Wickham, a sneer set upon his face. "I doubt Darcy would even begin to define the emotion. He has always been nothing more than a cold fish."

The rasp of Fitzwilliam's cavalry sabre leaving its sheath halted Wickham's laughter, and when the sword was placed by his throat, Wickham's eyes bulged out of his head. Fitzwilliam smiled grimly, thinking that Wickham was about to soil himself.

"Perhaps you should cease to insult my cousin, Wickham. Now, what shall it be? Will you tell me what I need to know, or shall we call in your debts?"

Licking his lips, Wickham's eyes shot down to the sword positioned no more than an inch from his throat, before once again rising to look at Fitzwilliam, no doubt attempting to determine if he was serious.

"You have given me no good reason why I should speak to you, even if I did know anything. Prison would be preferable to the hangman's noose."

"You should have thought of that before you fell in with Pearce," said Fitzwilliam, his voice now devoid of any humor. "And you should think of the practicalities of your statement. I can ensure your stay in Marshalsea is worse than the lowest pits of hell. Within a year, you would be begging for the noose.

"Or maybe I should just run you through right here and save my family the indignity of having to deal with your worthlessness any longer."

"You would not do such a thing!" cried Wickham. "How would you find Miss Bennet if you did?"

"Miss Bennet will be found, Wickham, with your help or without it. But I thank you for clarifying the matter of your involvement. It makes extracting the information all that much easier."

Though his eyes cast about for some way out of his predicament, Wickham quickly realized there was nothing to be found. Fitzwilliam fancied he could see the moment defiance left his eyes, though he still felt he could make bargains.

"Surely you can offer me something other than the choice between execution and debtors' prison."

"As it turns out, I can," said Fitzwilliam, little though he wished to bargain with the wretch. But Miss Bennet's recovery was paramount. "I can have my father use his influence to affect transportation instead of the scaffold."

"That is not exactly an appealing option."

"What did you expect? Did you think we would give you the keys to Darcy's estate for what you have done? The law will deal with you in the manner it deals with all those who act as you have. At least in Van Diemen's Land you will still have your life."

Though Wickham made a show of mulling over his options, there truly was no other choice; his resistance had crumbled. Fitzwilliam smiled in sardonic amusement; Wickham had ever been a coward, always seeking the easiest path in life. The prospect of execution was far too terrifying to the man for him to continue defiance.

"Miss Bennet is in a small cabin on Pearce's estate," said Wickham finally. "The man paid me to abduct her and deposit her there."

"Excellent," said Fitzwilliam, sheathing his sword with a flourish. "You can detail the particulars as we travel."

"Travel?" asked Wickham, clearly not understanding Fitzwilliam's meaning.

"Of course, old boy," replied Fitzwilliam, almost jovially. "You shall accompany me to Hertfordshire where you will show us where this cabin is, for I suspect, with Darcy's suspicions still firmly focused on Pearce, that she is still there.

"But I warn you, Wickham," said Fitzwilliam, stepping near to Wickham and looking him directly in the eye, "do not attempt to escape. Your hands will be bound and your horse tied to mine. My men will have orders to shoot if you so much as lean the wrong way. Even without your worthless carcass slowing us down, we will still find Miss Bennet. Remember that."

It was clear that George Wickham took Fitzwilliam's threat seriously, for his eyes were wide and his skin turned pasty. In the end the man could not do anything but nod his head vigorously.

When it finally happened, Elizabeth almost exclaimed in surprise and relief.

The cold was hampering her ability to wield her tool effectively, necessitating frequent breaks to warm herself and massage her hands until feeling returned to them, and the fact that there was no heat present other than that which her body produced made it all that much worse. At times she railed against fate for bringing her here—fate, and the ill-judged actions of a man without scruple. And when her frustration became so acute, she would beat against the boards with her fists, releasing her impotent fury against the uncaring boards which sealed her within.

It was turning toward late afternoon—or as close as Elizabeth could tell, given the fact that she was able to see little other than light outside—and Elizabeth had once again risen from her cocoon to scrape away as much wood as she could around the nail holes. That she was not making much progress had not escaped her, but she kept at it with dogged persistence. She would not be forced to submit to that vile man!

When her fingers once again became cold and numb, she felt her frustration once again well up within her, and she pounded on the wood, receiving a splinter for her trouble. She was shocked, however, when the wood gave away and sprung free on the side she had been working on. For a moment, Elizabeth could only gape at it with astonishment.

Then, the thought of her freedom galvanized her into action, and Elizabeth pushed the wood away, the groan of metal on wood protesting, until it sat at an angle which left the one side of the window largely free of impediment. Lifting her head up, Elizabeth found that she could fit her head through the opening. She decided at once that if her head would fit through, her body would too.

"Time to leave," Elizabeth said, as she busied herself in preparing for an immediate departure.

Knowing she might have only a limited amount of time—Elizabeth gathered up the blankets and tied them all into one blanket and took it to the window where she dropped her bundle through. She did not even think of trying to cover the window up with blankets and waiting for the man to deliver food again before trying to make her escape; the next one to come might be the detested Pearce. Her handiwork would be obvious in any case.

It was a tight fit, and though Elizabeth could easily push her head through the opening, trying to lift the rest of her body up through the narrow gap was difficult, and she scraped her shoulders and back on the way through. Finally, she managed it, and she fell down in a heap on the ground on the outside of the cottage, unfortunately missing the bundle of blankets. A quick glance around revealed no one in sight, and with the ever-pressing need to escape crowding her mind, forcing out all other thoughts, Elizabeth gathered the bundle and opened it, throwing three blankets around her shoulders to provide extra warmth. Then, leaving the rest of the bundle behind, she began to hurry from the cabin.

It soon became apparent that the woods through which she walked were completely unfamiliar to her. She had never ranged so far north before, contenting herself with going no further than Oakham Mount. However, she knew that the day was moving toward late afternoon, and as the sun was visible in the sky—a reddish, indistinct disk through a light cover of clouds and the brilliant reflection of ice crystals in the air—she was able to gain her bearings and set out in a direction which she thought would lead her back toward home.

The silence of the wood was an even more oppressive on the outside of the cabin than it was on the inside, and though Elizabeth longed to make some sort of sound, if only to remind herself that she was alive and not dreaming, she refrained.

"It would not do to bring Pearce or his loathsome servant on me unaware," muttered Elizabeth. "I must return to Longbourn before they can find me."

In the end, it was not difficult to find the road. The trail by which Wickham had brought her to the cabin began some distance from one of the corners of the small structure, and from there it wound through trees and foliage, over rises and through depressions, leading back to the main path which led toward Longbourn. Elizabeth's plan was simply—she would follow the two paths until she arrived in an area which she recognized, and then strike off on her own. Thus, if Pearce was out looking for her, he would have less chance of finding her along paths with which he was unfamiliar. But she took care to stay off the path in the woods, so she could hide if anyone should come along.

The main path was attained before much time had passed, and quicker than Elizabeth thought possible. Somehow it had seemed to take longer astride with Wickham. She quickly turned and began to hike south, hoping to make it past Oakham Mount into more familiar territory before too much time had passed.

She had not walked along the main path for more than fifteen minutes when the sounds of horses' hooves pounding on the ground alerted her to the presence of some unwelcome company. In a panic, Elizabeth realized they were already almost on her. With abandon, she turned and fled into the trees, one thought resounding through her mind. She would not be caught again!

Like a caged animal, Darcy paced the narrow confines of Bennet's study. This inactivity, was wearing on his nerves, and he wished he could be out doing something. The search for Elizabeth had all but been suspended, as it was no longer deemed possible to find her anywhere nearby. But he longed to be doing something—anything!—to rescue his beloved.

"I should have gone to London with Fitzwilliam," growled he, as he made another turn.

"Actually, I agree with his reasons for not wanting you to go," said Bennet.

Darcy turned and scowled at the man, reminding himself that Bennet would be his father-in-law before long, and he *should not* say any of the words which passed through his mind.

Bennet, not realizing what was going through Darcy's mind—or understanding it perfectly—continued to speak, saying: "You have not the emotional distance necessary to properly interrogate the man your cousin's men apprehended. I am sure he will be able to do so much more effectively than if you were present."

"Listen to Mr. Bennet, Darcy," added Bingley. "Excoriating yourself over this matter does not help. You must be prepared to do what is necessary when we find Miss Bennet."

"I understand that," said Darcy stiffly. "But this idleness is grinding away the last of my nerves."

With a laugh, Bennet said: "Shall I call for my wife's smelling salts? She has been complaining about her nerves for almost all of our twenty years of marriage. Perhaps it would help."

In spite of himself, Darcy was forced to laugh at Bennet's irreverent words. The specter of the situation seemed to lessen slightly, though the gloom was ever present.

For some time as they waited, Darcy was able to sit and converse with the other men, though his mind and heart were not on the subjects they discussed. And there were still reports delivered on occasion, as not all of the search had been given up. Given their suspicions concerning Pearce's involvement, Fitzwilliam had set some men to watch Pearce's estate, and even do some discrete searching on his land. But as yet it had all come to naught. It seemed their only hope was to rely on Wickham's information; Darcy was certain the cur was involved.

It was a few hours after noon when Fitzwilliam finally returned, and he was not alone. The commotion outside the door alerted those within of his arrival, and they spilled out into the hallway and the vestibule, Darcy leading them, to see Fitzwilliam leading a bound and bowed Wickham into the house.

"So, our suspicions were correct?" asked Darcy without preamble.

Wickham looked up at him for a brief moment, but then his gaze settled on the floor again. Wickham had never shown much deference to Darcy, and his manner had always been much more confrontational than conciliatory. He must have realized that he had truly misstepped this time.

"They were indeed," said Fitzwilliam, an entirely inappropriate measure of joviality evident in his manner. "It seems that our good friend Wickham was paid by Miss Bennet's good friend Pearce to arrange a reunion of sorts. Georgy even knows where Miss Bennet was stashed."

"And how were they known to one another?"

"They were not." Fitzwilliam eyed Wickham with some distaste. "It appears that when George accosted Miss Bennet in the park near her uncle's home, Pearce had men watching her, intending to take her then. Though our dear Wickham has not been explicit as to his intentions that day, I can only imagine he planned some mischief, and perhaps much more. Regardless, the presence of Jack Thompson was the only thing that prevented them from taking her. They approached Wickham after he left to discover his purpose, and found they had a common objective—Wickham wished for revenge, while Pearce wanted Miss Bennet. Thus, the abduction scheme was born."

Stewing in his own rage, Darcy walked up to Wickham and put himself right in front of the man. Wickham looked up with surprise, but he shrank back when he recognized the expression of hate etched into Darcy's features.

"I will see you hang for this," spat Darcy.

Wickham cringed and looked to Fitzwilliam in a beseeching manner. Fitzwilliam only laughed.

"It would be no more than you deserve, Wickham. But, yes, I have not forgotten about our little deal. As long as you do not lead us astray, I will see you on a prison hulk bound for Van Diemen's Land. Once the period of your punishment is over, I care not what you do there, as I do not doubt you will never have the funds to return to England."

"Where is she?" asked Darcy coldly, caring not what Fitzwilliam had promised the worm.

At Fitzwilliam's prod, Wickham was induced to mutter: "Locked in a cabin in the woods north of Oakham Mount."

"Locked in a cabin?" growled Darcy. "Is she well? Is she being cared for?"

"I know not what Pearce has done with her since I left her," said Wickham. "I was paid to leave her there."

"He no doubt thinks to wait until the search has ebbed before making off with her," said Fitzwilliam.

"Then we must depart at once."

With agreement all around, the men donned their winter gear and soon departed, a company of Fitzwilliam's soldiers formed up around them as an escort, with Jack Thompson joining the party for good measure. The steady drumming of their passage was a comfort to Darcy, as he knew that every stride brought them closer to rescuing his beloved.

"Darcy!" said Fitzwilliam as they rode. "Have you given any thought about what you will do with Pearce once Miss Bennet is recovered?"

Glaring sourly at his cousin, Darcy said: "It is obvious that we cannot prosecute. Elizabeth's ordeal would be revealed far and wide, and I cannot subject her to that."

"Wickham's testimony would be enough to convict him, I should think."

Darcy glanced back at the man. Wickham was bowed over in his saddle, his hands tied in front of him, while his horse was led by a rope attached to Fitzwilliam's saddle. For perhaps the first time in his life he was understanding that his actions had consequences. This time he would not escape justice, though Darcy would prefer the man was hanged. Removing the possibility of his ever harming anyone Darcy loved again would be enough, Darcy decided.

"It likely would, but I will not harm Elizabeth's reputation. The people in and about Meryton know her, and the response will be mostly sympathetic. I would prefer to keep as much of this affair from the wagging tongues in London as possible. Your father will not appreciate a scandal of this nature in the family."

Fitzwilliam snorted. "The old goat would consider it to be a personal affront. But you are likely correct."

"I will tell you this much," said Darcy. "If Pearce so much as looks at Elizabeth again, I will call him out."

"I would if you did not," replied Fitzwilliam.

They continued on for some time, and Darcy looked up at Oakham Mount as they skirted its lowest reaches, thinking of how he had come here soon after Elizabeth had disappeared. To think that he had been so close to her without realizing it filled him with further fury and contempt toward Pearce. Oh, how he ached to make the man pay.

"How close are we to the path you described?"

Darcy turned in his saddle, noting that Fitzwilliam had dropped back to speak to Wickham, and he listened carefully for the answer.

"It should not be long now," said Wickham, "though I am not sure as I am not truly familiar with the area."

As Darcy turned back to the road ahead, he caught sight of something in the trees, some flash of color. He turned his attention and saw a woman disappearing behind the foliage.

Calling a halt with a cry, Darcy vaulted from his horse and chased up into the woods, seeing the woman flee from before him. Startled by the sound of his voice, the woman turned and revealed herself to be his Elizabeth. She stared at him in shock as he approached at a run, seeming almost dazed at his sudden appearance. And then she was in his arms.

Chapter XXVII

The feeling of being in William's arms was bliss, and Elizabeth, shedding her blankets and leaving them lying forgotten on the ground, melted into his embrace.

"Elizabeth, my love," cried he.

Elizabeth found her face peppered with kisses, and she pressed herself up against him as closely as she could get. The softness of his lips upon her face filled her with pleasure, causing an intense feeling of love and devotion for this quiet man to well up within her. She turned her head up to meet his, and their lips met with almost bruising force, both pouring out their passion for each other in their kiss. Elizabeth wanted nothing more than to be joined together with him forever, and as their tongues continued to dance together, she idly wondered if this episode might be used to speed up the date of their nuptials.

A throat clearing behind them interrupted their reunion, and William and Elizabeth turned as one to see her father approaching them. His countenance was one of joy at seeing her again, though she thought she could detect a hint of wistful melancholy in his manner.

"Perhaps we should return Elizabeth to Longbourn where she may recover from her ordeal."

"Papa!" said Elizabeth, as she flung herself into his arms.

At the same time, William said: "Of course, Mr. Bennet. I believe I might have forgotten myself."

Her father laughed. "I am certain you did, Darcy, and I believe that my daughter was an active participant. But I would have you remember that you are not yet married, though with all that has happened, it might be prudent to bring that to pass sooner rather than later."

"I would have no objection to that," said Elizabeth and Darcy at the same time, and her father laughed heartily in response.

"Come, Daughter, your mother and sisters are waiting for you."

Though dazed at finally being free, Elizabeth had the presence of mind to gather up the blankets she had dropped, certain that a journey back to Longbourn on horseback would no doubt be bitterly cold. They made their way down through the trees to the road, and there Elizabeth was greeted with the sight of a grinning Major Fitzwilliam, a relieved Mr. Bingley, and several soldiers, dressed in their scarlet uniforms.

Greetings were shared all around and congratulations for her escape delivered, and they soon made to depart for Longbourn.

"Thank you for setting aside your lives to search for me," said Elizabeth in a shy voice.

"You are very welcome," replied the major. "It seems that Darcy here requires your presence for his happiness, and I would do anything to ensure his continued wellbeing."

"And your sister has been almost frantic since your disappearance," added Mr. Bingley. "We would not wish to disappoint your mother and your sisters."

With gratitude, Elizabeth allowed herself to be wrapped up in the blankets, and then she found herself lifted onto William's horse, feeling like a babe in arms. William was about to climb up behind her when the sound of approaching horses caught the company's attention. Scowling, William placed himself in front of her as the riders came into view. It was Pearce, leading a small group of men.

The sight of Pearce riding toward them filled Darcy with an implacable resolve, and he stepped forward, Bingley and Fitzwilliam at his side, offering support. Behind them, Mr. Bennet heeled his horse up beside Darcy's, on which Elizabeth still sat, providing protection for his daughter. About them, the men under Fitzwilliam's command, mixed with men from Netherfield and Longbourn, formed up, facing the approaching men.

When he had approached to within a few paces, Pearce dismounted, albeit painfully. Darcy directed a grim smile at the man, noting that he was not accustomed to being in the saddle, being a vain and soft man. It would make Darcy's task all that much easier. It was obvious the man had learned of Elizabeth's escape from one of his lackeys and had ridden out to recover her.

"You have something of mine," said Pearce as he stopped in front of Darcy, two of his men flanking him. He nodded at Elizabeth, continuing: "I will not leave without that which is mine."

"I suggest you come and take her, then," growled Darcy. "Of course, I cannot believe you will attempt to do any such thing, as you are as spineless as you are foolish."

His countenance darkening at the insult, Pearce said: "Surely you do not want a woman as tainted as she."

"Do not cast aspersions on the honor of my betrothed," warned Darcy.

"Why? Is she worth it? Is she worth the degradation your obviously *high position* will suffer? I cannot understand what you see in her. She is not especially pretty, she is impertinent, and she is nothing like a man like you would be expected to seek out."

"I might ask you the same thing. Has she not refused you several times? Are you stupid to have pursued this as far as you have?"

"It matters not," said Pearce. "I have determined I will have her, and I shall, even if I must take her by force."

"Do not be daft, man," said Fitzwilliam. "Can you not see the forces arrayed against you? Not only are you outnumbered, but you are faced by hardened, professional soldiers who have seen battle. If you draw weapons against us, you may not leave with a single man alive."

Pearce's eyes flicked over the scarlet coats and stares of the company, and though his reaction was minimal, Darcy thought he saw his eyes acknowledge what was so evident to everyone else. There was also a rustling among his men, as they also were forced to acknowledge the truth of Fitzwilliam's words. It was clear none of them wished to be sacrificed on the altar of their master's obsession. Darcy wondered how many of them actually knew what Pearce had done. Surely his deeds must have been hidden from all but one or two trusted servants.

"And we have your cohort," said Darcy, gesturing toward where Wickham sat quietly on his horse, watched closely by one of Fitzwilliam's men. "Though I would wish to see you charged for your crimes, I will restrain myself for Elizabeth's sake. If you persist, however, I will ensure you are prosecuted to the fullest extent, if you should have the good fortune to leave these woods alive."

Pearce's eyes darted from Darcy to Wickham, to Fitzwilliam, and he looked over the soldiers arrayed against him. He must have seen something in their obdurate glares which told him that their words were not idle threats. And though he seemed to be inclined to push the matter further, he grudgingly seemed to bow to the inevitable. He was not, however, able to simply walk way without one final parting shot.

"Very well, then, take your little doxy and be gone. I have all the victory I require, knowing that I have plucked her before you had the chance to do so."

Infuriated by the man's words, Darcy reacted without thought, striding forward and swinging his fist upwards, connecting with the surprised man's stomach before he could even think to try to avoid the blow. Gasping, Pearce sunk down to one knee, trying to catch his breath, while out of the corner of his eye, Darcy could see Fitzwilliam and several of his men stepped forward to intercept any of Pearce's men who thought to protect their master.

"It is far less than he deserves," said his cousin, "for abducting Darcy's betrothed, and all the misery he has forced on a fine young woman."

The men must have decided Fitzwilliam was correct—or they were wary of his men—for none of them made any further protest. For his part, Darcy grasped Pearce's shoulders and hauled him up, forcing him to look in Darcy's eyes. Though his anger offset his difficulty breathing, that rage soon turned to fear as Darcy turned his resolute glare on him.

"You will not disparage the honor of my betrothed again. If you do, I shall call you out, and I have no doubt who will be victorious, given the softness of your life. Do not test my patience any further, sir, or you may not live to enjoy the bounty of your second estate."

The man blanched, and he looked upon Darcy's countenance with growing dread. Darcy fancied he could almost see in Pearce's face the moment he realized that Darcy's words were not an idle threat, for he whitened, and he nodded once. He had seen his own death in Darcy's eyes, exactly as Darcy had intended, and it was clear he would finally give up this pointless pursuit.

"Take your master home," commanded Darcy, motioning to a nearby servant. "It would be wise for him if he kept to his home until his bruises heal."

Though the man scowled at Darcy, he nodded shortly and assisted Pearce into the saddle. Within moments, the company had departed. If Darcy never saw Pearce again, it would be too soon.

A night spent in a cold cabin with nothing other than a few blankets for warmth had resulted in a night of little sleep and rendered Elizabeth lethargic on the way back to Longbourn. Though the weather was cold and the wind contained bite, the sensation of being held securely in William's arms drove away all thoughts of being chilled, and the blankets which were once again wrapped securely around her left her feeling quite cozy indeed. Elizabeth thought that had the horse's gait and the constant jolting of the animal's hooves on the hard ground not been present, she might almost have fallen asleep.

"I cannot tell you how happy I am to have you back here with me," said William, his voice piercing through the hazy state into which her mind had settled.

"And I am happy to be back with you, William."

Opening her eyes, Elizabeth looked up into the face of the man she loved, her hand rising almost of its own volition to caress the line of his jaw.

"I think, however, your father might wish that you were riding with him instead of with your suitor."

"I do not know," said Elizabeth, feeling far too languid to expend the effort to look for her father. "Papa is not precisely a gifted horseman, though he is competent enough to see to the needs of his estate. I think it likely that he would rather cede the responsibility to someone who possesses a firmer seat."

William smiled down at her tenderly. "Under normal circumstances you might be correct, but you are not taking any thought for the feelings of a father for a beloved daughter, especially considering that daughter will be leaving his protection for that of another before long."

"Oh, Papa," said Elizabeth with a laugh. "I will make it up to him later. But I am certain once he arrives back at Longbourn and realizes how sore he has become from this excursion, he will be happy he left it to you."

A chuckle escaped William's lips, and he shook his head, though dropping the subject. When he spoke again, it was on matters which were much more serious than the state of her father's ability to ride.

"What happened, Elizabeth? And in what circumstances were you held?"

"Mr. Wickham surprised me on the back grounds of Longbourn," said Elizabeth. "As he was stronger and possessed the element of surprise, he was able to bind me and take me away to Pearce's lodge. Other that there is not much to say."

William grunted. "We pulled that much from Wickham, though he was loath to part with even that much. But he would not describe the cabin, and we did not have time to pursue anything more than the most basic of interrogations."

"Does it matter?" asked Elizabeth, reluctant to respond, as she knew it would make William justifiably angry when he found out the conditions in which she had been kept. She had a healthy respect for his ability to think rationally, but he was also a man and would undoubtedly wish to exact further vengeance against the man for his misdeeds.

"I would not have secrets between us, Elizabeth," said William. "You need not worry that I will pursue any further action with Pearce."

Shifting in his arms, Elizabeth looked more closely at his countenance. The tension of the confrontation with Pearce had been replaced with a greater ease, though she did not doubt that he was still furious with the man. Perhaps it would be best to speak of the matter after all, so that it could finally be put completely into the past where it belonged.

Thus, Elizabeth explained in as concise a manner as possible exactly what had happened during her captivity, leaving nothing out. She could see his wrath spike with the revelation that she had been kept in the small cabin without the benefit of heat, but Elizabeth teased him from his anger, noting that she had managed to escape with relatively little damage to either her health or her good humor.

"You likely already understand this about me," said William once she had finished her recitation, "but I am possessed of what some would call a resentful temper. I have difficulty forgetting slights and offenses against me."

"And yet you readily forgave me of my words after the assembly."

William laughed and kissed the top of her head. "I also consider myself to be a rational man, and your comments, though difficult to hear, were nothing more than the truth. There was nothing to forgive, only improvement to make.

"Regarding my propensity toward resentment, I must own that I am even *less* able to forgive those who offend those I love. Pearce should hope he never crosses our paths again, for it will go ill for him if he does."

"He is nothing but a ridiculous man who could not look past his obsession." Elizabeth directed an arch smile at her betrothed. "You must take my philosophy, Mr. Darcy; think only on the past as it gives you pleasure. In Pearce's case, if we should ever come across him again, laughing at him would be a much greater blow to his vanity than any vengeance you might exact."

"And this is why I love you," said William, leaning forward to brush her lips with his. "You are instantly able to see the humor in any situation, whereas I am far too quick to see the insult."

"This is the *only* reason you love me?"

William laughed again with sheer delight, Elizabeth soon joining in. "Of course not, dearest. But at the present time, it is the virtue which is on my mind the most."

Shortly after this exchange, they rode into the drive of Longbourn, and before long, William had dismounted in front of the estate, before turning back to assist Elizabeth down. The front doors opened, and Elizabeth's family spilled out into the rapidly dwindling light, along with Georgiana and several others.

"Oh, Lizzy!" exclaimed Jane, catching her up in an enthusiastic embrace. "I am so happy they were able to rescue you from that horrid man!"

"Jane!" replied Elizabeth, affecting astonishment. "That is the most unforgiving speech I have ever heard pass from your lips!"

Jane blushed a little, but Elizabeth's comments prompted laughter from the rest of the group. Elizabeth greeted her sisters and mother, expressing her happiness at once again being home. Georgiana flew into her arms at the first opportunity, exclaiming her own delight at Elizabeth's recovery. Then Elizabeth was confronted by a sight she had not expected to see, when Charity approached her, catching her up in her own embrace.

"Charity!" exclaimed Elizabeth when she pulled away. "How did you come to be here?"

"Mr. Spencer and I followed my brother to Hertfordshire when word of your capture arrived." She turned a sly look on the major. "After all, I could not leave it all to him. No doubt he would have botched it had I done so."

Laughter once again rang out, and Major Fitzwilliam laughed the loudest himself. "No doubt. You should have been a soldier, Charity. You would have put us all to shame."

"*Two* children of an earl in my house!" exclaimed Mrs. Bennet. "I did not think I should ever be so favored."

"You have a wonderful home, Mrs. Bennet," said Charity. "You should be proud."

The Bennet matron blushed beet red, and Elizabeth thought she had just experienced the most wonderful moment of her life. And that it was because of her least favorite daughter had to be perplexing to her mother, but Elizabeth decided there was no reason to think on the matter any longer.

She was ushered into the house, and soon she was bathed and dressed in new clothes. The feeling had never seemed so wonderful. Jane and Charity, who had attended her, pressed her to rest for a time, but Elizabeth would not hear of it; she wished for nothing more than to be once again in William's presence.

Thus it was only a few moments later that she found herself in the dining room with the rest of the company. Mrs. Bennet, claiming she had expected her daughter to be recovered, had prepared a special dinner for the company. The conversation flowed freely, and the company was in good spirits, and for once, Elizabeth thought her mother was awed enough by the illustrious company in her dining room, and Mary, Kitty, Lydia, and Georgiana were engrossed in their conversation, that she did not feel embarrassed because of her relations.

"Are you well, Elizabeth?" asked William softly, as they sat quietly, eating their soup.

Elizabeth turned and smiled at him. "How could I not be? I am recovered, the threat of that odious man is gone forever, and I anticipate many such dinners in this lively company in the future."

Elizabeth laughed at his slightly pained look; she knew he did not look down on her family any longer, but as a reticent man, he would not wish for such liveliness all the time.

"Do not worry, my sweet William. I am more than happy to live quietly with you at your estate. I would not wish to always be in such noisy company."

"I will hold you to that, dearest. I believe we shall be very happy together."

"I think we shall."

And there, in the midst of the tumult and noise of good family and friends, other distractions ceased to exist for the happy couple. They had faced the challenges and triumphed, and Elizabeth did not doubt there would be further challenges to overcome in the future.

Epilogue

Covent Garden's lobby was a teeming mass of humanity. It was always thus at the height of the season, though tonight it seemed especially so. The rumble of conversation, at times a jarring cacophony of competing voices and sounds, was somehow comforting, speaking of society and friendship, of happiness and belonging. As the last great event of the season, many of society's leading lights were present, and as such it was a time for prancing and strutting, seeing and being seen, of one last attempt to make an impression before the season ended and high society departed for their summer estates. To Elizabeth, it was exciting.

"I will be happy when we retire to Pemberley," said the man at her side, and Elizabeth looked up and smiled at her husband.

"So you have told me many times, William."

"But I have endured, have I not?"

"You have indeed," said Elizabeth. "In fact, I dare say your behavior has been exemplary. You must simply endure this one last event before the torture will come to an end."

"The torture, my dear," said William, leaning closely, "is being so near to you when you are so tempting and not being able to do a thing about it."

Blushing, Elizabeth looked away to regain her composure. In the noise of the room, it was doubtful anyone could hear him, but her reaction might give away much to the discerning observer. Of course, she was aware that she and William had gained a reputation for being besotted with each other, so perhaps it would not matter anyway. Still, he should not be saying such things in the middle of a crowded room.

"The torture will continue indefinitely if you embarrass me in front of society, sir," said Elizabeth, albeit in a playful tone.

"We cannot have that. I will behave."

It had been ever thus, since the time of their marriage almost four months before. The event of her abduction and subsequent recovery had served to accelerate their marriage, though by the time she had finally met her husband at the altar she was ready to be done with her mother's frenzied preparations anyway. In that regard, she supposed she was forced to thank Pearce for his actions. It had been an immeasurable boon to her sanity to have been able to forgo a further month of her mother's nerves!

Once their marriage had been solemnized, they had repaired to Pemberley and had been ensconced there for two months, only returning to London once the season was in full swing, and then only reluctantly by her husband. Though Elizabeth was a social being herself, she was forced to take her husband's view on the matter more than once, as they eschewed many of the invitations they received, only attending those which were given by family, friends, or other respectable people William knew. Even so, it was still such an exhausting array of parties, balls, dinners, and other such revelries that Elizabeth was quite willing to accede to her husband's wishes and leave it behind. That he had insisted they proceed from London directly to the lakes for some weeks was nothing more than a pleasure, as she had always wished to travel.

They were to be on their own for another month complete. Georgiana, along with Kitty and Lydia, were still at the school they had been sent to after Elizabeth and Darcy's marriage, though they would be returning home in a few days, Kitty and Lydia to Longbourn, and Georgiana to stay with the earl and countess for some weeks before returning to Pemberley. Though reports were still sketchy, to say the least, Elizabeth had heard that her sisters had made great strides in their education.

Mary was staying at present with the Gardiners and was taking advantage of some music masters. Elizabeth had promised her sister that when she came out into society, the Darcys would host her for a season, and though Mary still claimed to have little interest in balls, Elizabeth was certain that she was anticipating her debut eagerly. And as for her dearest sister Jane . . .

"William, when do you think my sister will arrive? Should they not have been here by now?"

"I will confess Bingley has taken to being uncharacteristically late recently," said William. "But if you will look up, I believe you will see them approaching even now."

Following her husband's instructions, Elizabeth had the pleasure of seeing Jane make her way toward them, a beaming smile present on her face. The two sisters greeted each other with an enthusiasm only the closest of siblings could possess and exclaimed at having been separated so long.

"I am so happy you have made it back to town tonight!" said Elizabeth.

"Indeed, we had wondered if you were inclined to come at all," added William.

"Perhaps we were not quite inclined," replied Bingley, displaying his customary grin. "But I could not disappoint my wife and her closest sister."

"You are the best of brothers, Mr. Bingley. It would not have been the same had I not seen my sister once throughout the season."

The four fell into conversation, and Elizabeth watched Jane and her new husband of only a few weeks with a certain smugness. She had known almost from the beginning the Mr. Bingley would be perfect for her dearest sister. As they had married at the height of the season and had honeymooned after, they had not been in London for most of the events. Jane would be introduced to society formally the next year, though Elizabeth knew she did not truly care for such things.

It was a mark of Miss Bingley's understanding of the power of connections that she had made little objection to the match. Since Jane was Elizabeth's sister, a coveted connection to the Darcys of Pemberley—and though a little more distantly, to the Earl of Matlock—was the prize for her swallowing her objections to her brother's marriage to the daughter of a country squire of little fortune. Miss Bingley had had her season, and though she was not yet married or courting, by all accounts there had been several men who had paid attention to her. Elizabeth wondered if the woman was setting her sights too high, but in the end, she thought Miss Bingley would be able to make a good match.

It was not long before the two couples were joined by some others of William's extended family, including the earl and countess, Charity and her husband, Major Fitzwilliam, and a few of Darcy's acquaintances. The earl had been a surprise as, though he had not been happy with Darcy's marriage initially, he had followed the countess's advice and welcomed her. Now, he was known to say that she was a pleasant, intelligent sort of girl, which Elizabeth knew would be the closest thing to a compliment she ever heard from the man.

Charity remained a good friend and confidant, and she had accepted Jane as well, which only completed Elizabeth's happiness. And her sister Rachel, who had often been spoken of as haughty and above her company, had also welcomed Elizabeth, though with much more reserve than her two younger siblings. Only the viscount remained unmoved, and though he was respectful and kind, it was clear he had little desire to know her. That was no great loss, in Elizabeth's opinion, as she considered him to be a supercilious and vain man.

At length the bell rang, indicating the production would soon start, and the company parted, the earl and countess, along with Charity and a few friends to their box, while Mr. and Mrs. Bingley and the colonel were to sit in the Darcy box. The press in the lobby began to thin as they began to move toward the stairs leading up to their seats.

"At least we shall now be able to enjoy what we came for," said William in a low voice. "I have little patience for the preening of feathers and attempts to be noticed by everyone in attendance."

"Are you to tell me now that all of my preparations for the evening were for naught?" asked Elizabeth with feigned disapproval.

"You are well aware that I appreciate your preparations, Mrs. Darcy. But the rest of these peacocks are not worth our time."

Laughing, Elizabeth said: "Patience, my dear. We shall soon be away from London."

When they reached the stairs, they stood aside to allow another couple to pass, and Elizabeth was shocked when she happened to glance up at them and see the man was none other than Winston Pearce. On his arm was a woman about Elizabeth's age, and though a little taller, she was quite thin and willowy.

William became aware of them at the same time as did Elizabeth. For a moment, the three known to one another froze.

"Mr. Pearce?" asked the woman by his side, her voice pitched high and nasally. "Shall you not introduce me to your acquaintances?"

"I am afraid they are not worth your time," replied Pearce shortly, raising his nose in the air with disdain.

All at once a laugh bubbled up in Elizabeth's chest and spilled forth from her mouth, and though William was initially inclined to anger, William soon joined her in marking their contempt for the ridiculous man in accordance with their conversation the night of her recovery. Mr.

Pearce's countenance turned purple in his affront, but Elizabeth simply shook her head, and William stepped forward to precede the other couple up the stairs.

Before she left the man and his companion, however, Elizabeth could not resist the urge to stop and speak in a low voice to the woman.

"I would be wary of this one; he can be quite a handful." Elizabeth smiled at the other woman, who was regarding her, perplexity written across her brow. "Of course, his bark is far worse than his bite."

Then, laughing again, Elizabeth turned her back and made her way up the stairs with her husband, a murmur of conversation swelling up behind her.

"Mrs. Darcy, might I say that you were completely masterful? The way we laughed at him, I do not doubt that it will set tongues wagging all over town."

"Was that not the point?" Her archness inspired an intense look from her husband, which made Elizabeth feel almost breathless.

"I suppose it was. You are wonderful, Mrs. Darcy. And my sagacity in seeking you out was uncommonly clever of me."

"I cannot deny that, sir. It has all worked out for the best indeed."

The End

Please enjoy the following excerpt from the upcoming novel *On Lonely Paths*, book two of the *Earth and Sky* fantasy trilogy.

It was night in the sky realm. And what a night it was.

The sky was clear and the stars as visible as if there was nothing in between the firmament above and the earth below. The wind shifted and swirled about the settlements of the Skychildren, the area at once calm and peaceful, yet giving a hint of a world which, though not flush with youth, was alive and rich with life.

On the ground world below, the night was equally fine—warm, as dictated by the summer season yet calm and gentle, with no hint of the sometimes spectacular storms which plagued the area during the summer.

But the world below was of no concern to the two who lay upon the soft grasses of the sky realm. Here and there, hints of nearby foliage, though certainly not as lush and green as that found on the earth below, could be seen in the darkness. Heathers, brush, and even the occasional stunted trees covered the landscape, bringing life to what would otherwise be a blasted land.

The two people themselves were a study in contrast, and one which, not many months ago, would not have been seen anywhere in the world. The man was tall and slender, possessed of short locks of straight blond hair and cobalt-colored eyes. He was intelligent and kind, but quick to anger and lacking patience, something which his companion would often tease him about, though always with the utmost of affection.

By contrast, the woman was small in stature, though her determination and intelligence more than made up for her short height, and while she did not possess a particularly fiery personality, she was not one to be trifled with. As for her looks, they were the opposite of his, for she sported a mane of long, rich, chestnut hair and had a lovely face with amber-colored eyes.

The fact that their people were the bitterest and oldest of enemies had been all but forgotten by both of them, though their respective peoples were not as quick in embracing one another as the two lovers were. Still, with patience and persistence, they both believed that the change in the relations between their peoples would make their world a better place. This belief and their love for one another drove them to continue their course, no matter what obstacles arose before them. They were determined it would always be thus.

The woman shifted, gazing fondly at the man beside her for a moment before returning her eyes upward once more. She loved the look of peace and contentment upon her fiancé's face; there had been a lot to try their patience lately—much of it involving their impending wedding—yet these stolen moments were theirs to enjoy together in relative solitude. Right now, there was no need to worry about consulting with advisers and family members or handling the variety of problems that had cropped up as they attempted to facilitate peaceful trade relations between their peoples. This time was theirs. It was a period when they could afford to be selfish, if only for a brief time.

"One of the things I love most about the sky realm is how I can see the stars so clearly," Tierra said softly, breaking the comfortable silence between them.

"A Groundbreather who also fancies herself a stargazer? I fear you may soon be disowned by your people for heresy," Skye teased.

She elbowed him gently in the ribs. "I am not the only one demonstrating unusual qualities for one of a certain race. I seem to recall *you* admiring some of the flowers in the castle gardens down in the ground realm, which some of your people up here might view to be just as heretical."

Skye snorted but did not comment; Tierra knew he was well aware of the fact that his opinions of the ground realm had undergone an almost miraculous transformation. Somehow, she had broken through his barriers without even realizing she was doing it. And she was so glad that she had, for his soul had become irrevocably bound to hers in a way that she had never imagined possible.

They were quiet again for a few moments before Tierra asked, "Do you remember my constellation?"

His light chuckle brought a smile to her face. "Of course," he said, pointing. "That crass sword over there has your name written right on its hilt."

"And yours is that primitive old bow over there," Tierra responded in kind, nodding toward a small grouping of stars. "An absolutely useless weapon for a battle."

"I'd say it wasn't that useless when Cirrus used it to save your neck in our battle with the Fenik," Skye countered.

"Mmhmm," Tierra said. She was glad Skye could speak more lightly of the battle and her role in it now—he had admitted to having some nightmares about it after the fact which she suspected centered on losing her—but she was less than pleased that she owed something to Skye's friend.

While the man was all smiles and joviality when it came to Skye, Cirrus's expression always took on a disapproving cast when he focused on her. She had considered asking Skye to talk to his friend, but Skye seemed so glad Cirrus was alive that she did not want to cause his happiness to dim even a whit. So she held her tongue, hoping that Cirrus would eventually come to see that her motives were pure when it came to Skye. In marrying him, she was not seeking to be queen; she was seeking love and companionship. And she knew she would have it in ample measure.

"You know," Skye said, twisting and propping his head up on an elbow while he lazily draped an arm across Tierra's stomach, "I still can't believe you disguised yourself as a soldier so you could participate in a fight with a giant beast."

As he began to draw circles with his fingers on Tierra's side, she had to fight against the urge to shy away from the ticklish sensation. "I had no idea that was what I was going to face." "If you had known, would it have stopped you?"

"No."

Skye laughed, his amusement clearly seeping through their mental bond. "That's my little Groundbreather."

Tierra raised an eyebrow. "*Your* little Groundbreather?"

"That's right," he said, wrapping his arm tightly around her. "*Mine*."

"I ought to imprison you in a ground cage for that one and teach you just what your place is."

"Probably. But then you wouldn't have someone to take you stargazing."

"I would just have to find another Skychild to serve as my personal form of transport. I imagine Mista would not protest."

"You're probably right. But I think her fear of insects and becoming dirty might hamper her willingness to partake in such outdoor activities as reclining on sky soil. And all that's not even taking into account her insipid personality, which I think would be the more important factor when considering whether to use her as your transportation."

"Skye," Tierra chided, "you know she has a good heart."

"I still don't know what you see in that woman," he grumbled, shaking his head.

"As I have told you before, I find her innocence refreshing. But come—you cannot tell me you brought me up here to complain about your stepmother, now, can you?" Her lip quirked. "I am certain you had something more interesting in mind if you were willing to brave my mother's wrath. She is still angry that I snuck away from the castle to help with the battle against the Seneschal. If she knew how often you snuck me away from the castle, she would have both of our hides hung up outside the castle walls for all the world to see what happens to those who bring about her displeasure."

"I think your mother would like my hide regardless. If it weren't for the water connecting us . . ."

"Yes, Terrain's water has indeed brought us great good," Tierra said with a smile, reaching up to touch his lips at the memory of their first kiss. "Because of his gift, our two peoples have been drawn together at last."

For Readers Who Liked Obsession

A Bevy of Suitors
When a chance remark from Mr. Darcy causes Mr. Bingley to rethink which Bennet daughter he wishes to pursue, Elizabeth Bennet finds herself forced to choose from among a bevy of suitors.

An Unlikely Friendship
Elizabeth Bennet has always possessed pride in her powers of discernment. She discovers, however, that first impressions are not always accurate.

Bound by Love
Lost as a young child, Elizabeth Bennet is found by the Darcys and raised by the family as a beloved daughter. Bound by love with the family of her adoption, she has no hint of what awaits her when she and Mr. Darcy join Mr. Bingley in Hertfordshire at his newly leased estate, Netherfield.

Cassandra
The pain of losing a beloved wife threatens to undo Darcy's very sanity, but the introduction of a young woman gives him reason to hope. Through her patient tutelage and love, Darcy learns to put the past behind him and comes to see the precious gift he has been given.

Implacable Resentment
A grudge forces Elizabeth Bennet from Longbourn, necessitating her removal to the Gardiners' home in London. Ten years later, she returns to Hertfordshire at the request of her father and learns that the prejudice has not subsided. Elizabeth must withstand her family's machinations if she is to have any hope of finding her happy ending.

Love and Laughter: A Pride and Prejudice Short Stories Anthology
Those who need a little love and laughter in their lives need look no further than this anthology, which gives a lighthearted look at beloved *Pride and Prejudice* characters in unique situations.

ALSO BY ONE GOOD SONNET PUBLISHING

THE SMOTHERED ROSE TRILOGY

BOOK 1: THORNY

In this retelling of "Beauty and the Beast," a spoiled boy who is forced to watch over a flock of sheep finds himself more interested in catching the eye of a girl with lovely ground-trailing tresses than he is in protecting his charges. But when he cries "wolf" twice, a determined fairy decides to teach him a lesson once and for all.

BOOK 2: UNSOILED

When Elle finds herself practically enslaved by her stepmother, she scarcely has time to even clean the soot off her hands before she collapses in exhaustion. So when Thorny tries to convince her to go on a quest and leave her identity as Cinderbella behind her, she consents. Little does she know that she will face challenges such as a determined huntsman, hungry dwarves, and powerful curses . . . .

BOOK 3: ROSEBLOOD

Both Elle and Thorny are unhappy with the way their lives are going, and the revelations they have had about each other have only served to drive them apart. What is a mother to do? Reunite them, of course. Unfortunately, things are not quite so simple when a magical lettuce called "rapunzel" is involved.

About the Author

Jann Rowland

Jann Rowland is a Canadian. He enjoys reading and sports, and he also dabbles a little in music, taking pleasure in singing and playing the piano.

Though Jann did not start writing until his mid-twenties, writing has grown from a hobby to an all-consuming passion. His interest in Jane Austen stems from his university days when he took a class in which *Pride and Prejudice* was required reading. However, his first love is fantasy fiction, which he hopes to pursue writing in the future.

He now lives in Alberta with his wife of more than twenty years and his three children.

For more information on Jann Rowland, please visit:
http://onegoodsonnet.com.